A Fine Boy for Killing

JAN NEEDLE

A Fine Boy for Killing

HarperCollins*Publishers*

Author's Note

This is the first publication of the full, original,
unabridged text of *A Fine Boy for Killing*.
A substantially different, abridged version of the
story by the same author was published under
the title *A Fine Boy for Killing* in 1979 by
André Deutsch.

HarperCollins*Publishers*
77-85 Fulham Palace Road,
Hammersmith, London W6 8JB

Published by HarperCollins*Publishers* 1996
1 3 5 7 9 8 6 4 2

A catalogue record for this book
is available from the British Library

ISBN 0 00 225349 6

Set in Linotron Janson with Castellar display
at The Spartan Press Ltd,
Lymington, Hants

Printed in Scotland

For Chris and Judy

A Fine Boy for
Killing

One

At about the time that Thomas Fox was pulling on his old dark coat and wondering if the morning mist would clear before he reached the marshiest parts of his road, William Bentley was taking his second glass of green tea with his uncle on board the frigate Welfare. They were only about eight miles apart – eight miles of land and water – and they were destined to meet later that day. Thomas, who was fifteen and the son of a small farmer, was excited. He was to take twelve sheep to the market at Portsmouth, on his own; a full day's work. William, who was fourteen, was not excited; he was business-like, a little worried. Faced with a difficult and responsible task.

'You will find the cutter adequate,' his uncle told him, sipping his glass of tea. 'She can be manned by a small crew, but there is room enough on board of her if you manage anything. But William. Remember this much. You are not entitled to do this work. It is, let us say, not strictly within the bounds of legality. Let the men go unarmed. Dolby and Evans may carry pistols, but let them be out of sight.'

William Bentley smiled at his uncle. He felt very grateful, although nervous. He hoped he could bring the trick off.

'I'll do my best, uncle,' he replied. 'How many men do we need in all?'

Daniel Swift returned the smile grimly.

'Officially, my boy, we are within ten men of our full complement. Officially. But what have we got? Riffraff, gutter scrapings. I tell you, William, if we do not find some seamen soon we will come to grief. We have far to go.'

William would have liked to have known how far, but he could not ask. Far it must certainly be, however, for the provisions and spare gear taken on board the Welfare in the last few days had been prodigious. In his long life at sea he had seen nothing to match it.

He smiled once more, to himself this time. He had been at sea, in fact, merely eleven months. But he had been on the Navy's books since he was seven years old. His sea-time was excellent.

Uncle Daniel tinkled his fingernails against the glass.

'Think you can do it, my boy?' he asked. 'Are you aware just how delicate a situation you find yourself in?'

'Sir,' said William. 'Individual pressing is against the law. We must bow on all occasions to the wishes of those above us. A captain who resorted to the personal press gang, on shore, in England, in these days would be villainous indeed. I would not dream of such a step were I a commanding officer, nor would I expect any in His Majesty's Navy to ask it of his officers or young gentlemen.'

As he spoke, he stared through the square glass windows in the stern. The ship was swinging as the west-going tide along the Solent set in. Portsmouth, shrouded in mist, appeared to bob slowly into sight. Rising above the white carpet was the brownish shape of Portsdown Hill. It had been a warm, dry summer.

'But let me take a good boat's crew, uncle,' he went on, 'and who knows . . . It looks like a good day again. The pleasant weather, my sweet tongue, the thought of the bounty, of prize-money . . . We are not the press, however. I shall not forget it.'

He finished his tea as word was brought that the cutter was ready. His uncle waved him out with a muttered 'Good luck' – then called him back.

'Mr Bentley,' he said. 'Good men we want, but bad will do. The people in this ship are villains and the sons of whores. But we can shape 'em. And William,' he added. 'Livestock too, my boy. We need more. We have far to go. You have the money?'

William nodded and went on deck. He sniffed the air. A keen westerly, with the bite of approaching winter in it. A soldier's wind; to Portsmouth and back to St Helen's Roads with never a tack. He ordered the boat lowered.

Thomas Fox whistled tunefully as he wandered through the mist towards Portsmouth. He was cold and the sheep were a nuisance, but he was happy. Soon the mist would clear completely, which would be a help. Two or three times he'd stepped off the track into the salty marsh, and his right foot was wet. The sheep behaved even more stupidly than usual in the mist, too. He'd led one by a string at

4

first, hoping the others would follow. But now he walked behind them, swishing a stick and occasionally barking savagely and with great effect.

The eastern side of the island, where Thomas lived with his parents and two sisters, was not good land, tending to dampness and desertion. As he walked along the track to more civilised parts, listening to the moaning of the sheep and the mysterious gurglings of the marshland, he dreamed idly of what he would rather do. Portsmouth was the good place to be. It was noisy, and dirty, and full of wild sailormen and their even wilder women. Even Kingston, he thought, as his track joined a bigger path that eventually became the main road through Kingston and on to Portsmouth, even Kingston would be better than the marshy hamlet in the east. It had an air of liveliness, of bustle.

As the mist drifted away, the old bent spire of the Kingston church rose into view over the fields, and Thomas concentrated on keeping the sheep in a bunch on the wider road. The sun burst through, the mist rolled back like a carpet. Beyond the church the fortifications were becoming visible.

From the seaward, William Bentley stared just as hard at the city that seemed to bound towards the cutter. To the east of it the land lay like a board, still sullenly holding a thin layer of white. But Portsmouth had a different whiteness, the whiteness of the stone defences. Between the Square Tower and the Round Tower, outside the actual entrance to the harbour, was the entrance to the city that the man at the tiller was heading for. The Sallyport.

It was good sailing, but William felt a little guilty about enjoying it so much. He was a midshipman, not a pleasure-seeker. He had in his direct command two other mids – one of them at least thirty years his senior – and fourteen seamen. Possibly the only fourteen real seamen on the Welfare, he thought ruefully. He was off on a mission that could not be easy, would probably break the law in several places, and may well be totally unsuccessful.

Watching the short green seas that leapt almost broadside on to the cutter, and huddling deeper into his boat-cloak against the constant spray, William considered the problem of the people. They were indeed a vile and ruffianly lot, pressed scrapings from the bottom of the barrel, two-legged creatures of such awful

5

lowness that they might just as well have been the animals that his uncle called them. He looked at the quiet figures ranged along the windward side of the cutter. Sturdy, steady fellows in neat clothes and pigtails. Good men, good seamen, all. Then he looked at Dolby, the grey-haired mid. Two pistols were outlined beneath his boat-cloak. Without the threat of those, perhaps even these men would run.

Some captains, William knew, found no hardship getting up a complement. A few posters, perhaps a handbill, a little music and the beating of drums. A ship could be filled in days. Prime seamen would plead to join, would be turned away. Not his uncle. Captain Daniel Swift, veteran of several brilliant frigate actions, courageous to the last drop of his or any seaman's blood, had a reputation; but not the kind that filled a ship with volunteers.

The cutter, swooping over the short green seas like a bird, approached the steep-to shingle beach and the black pier a trifle fast. William cleared his mind of sober thoughts and put it to the job in hand.

'Luff her if you please, Dolby,' he said crisply. 'We'll get the canvas off her and drop in under oars, stern first. We've dry work to do ashore, and dry we'll be to start it.'

As the boat headed into the wind and sea and the big seamen moved with uncanny agility to stifle the flapping sails, he forgot his uncle's evil reputation. In five minutes they would be in Portsmouth. It was his job to complete the ship's complement. A job that was still unfinished after nearly four months.

Just before he entered the first scattering of houses on the edge of the city, Thomas Fox stopped for a spell. The sheep, stupid as they were, were good at stopping and nibbling. He climbed onto a hummock, pulled a long stem of dry grass, and sucked happily.

It was well into the forenoon now, and the roads to Portsmouth were fairly busy. There were big ox-wagons, lighter carts, and innumerable foot-passengers, some coming, some going. Most of the traffic was for the hamlets on the island, but some of the vehicles made purposefully northwards, towards Portsbridge, the causeway, and the lonely turnpike that hauled steeply over Portsdown and on towards London. The sun was shining, and the crowds were noisy and generally good-humoured. Thomas was hailed several times, and lifted his bonnet in greeting – not because he knew the hailers, but because he was hailed.

In fact he had little interest in the roads or the edge of the town. He was still far enough to the eastward to see the ocean (as he thought it) stretching from beyond the great common over to the Isle of Wight. On its white-capped surface lay the ships that were Britain's defence. Mostly yellow, they were, and almost unbelievably big and noble. The humble merchant craft that threaded among them, lying to the steady breeze, seemed dingy and contemptible by comparison.

Thomas sometimes thought he would like to go to sea, and in fact his family had connections with it. His cousin Silas, whom Thomas vaguely remembered as a tall, thin, fair man twice his age, was a marine. Probably in one of those ships he could see at anchor, if the truth were known. He hadn't been seen by the family for a long age; there was a war on. It was, after all, he thought, perhaps not the life for him. They barely scratched a living as it was, even with his strong arms to help. And when did seamen ever get their pay? According to his aunt, no money had come to them on Silas's account in memory; and *he* was a marine.

He pulled his eyes away from the sea and spat out the straw. The wind chilled him through his old, threadbare coat. He watched a thin dog creeping on its belly towards one of his flock. Waited until it was near, then lifted a flint and hurled it. It hit the dog's bared teeth with a bang. The dog screeched in pain and limped hurriedly away. Thomas took up his whistling again. Now. Let's get to market.

Although the city sprawled rottenly well outside its walls, he followed the road that led through one of the great turreted gates. Now he was in the main stream of traffic the job got rapidly harder. He tied the lead sheep with string and hobbled a couple of the others. But it took all his skill, plus a lot of cursing, barking and shouting, to keep them half together. He wielded the stick ferociously, as well as his bare feet and the pocketful of stones he'd collected. But progress was slow. Every time a wagon passed, the sheep went blind with panic. Every time they spotted a patch of green they stopped and ate. As often as possible he took to the fields, but as he penetrated farther into the busy town the fields got fewer and the job harder.

* * *

7

The progress made by William Bentley and his boat's crew was even slower. Not that driving fourteen seamen was harder than driving twelve sheep, even in the narrow streets of Spice Island. It was rather that he was at a loose end, searching, looking for something but not being quite sure what. As they wandered off Broad Street into the dark narrow alleys of squalid hovels, the people melted away as if by magic. All the men in all the teeming streets seemed to vanish as the sailors turned the corners. Dirty-faced women, spitting streams of filth past their hands, watched them with open hostility. William felt furious, with these people and with himself. He muttered to Dolby: 'My God, what scum these people are. What filth. To think we need such gutter rats to man the nation's ships!'

But Dolby looked away and said nothing. Dolby was of these people. Evans, the other midshipman, who was nearer William in age and station, seemed embarrassed. His shrill voice filled the gap.

'I agree, Mr Bentley. What scum indeed! Things are at a pretty pass.'

And the fourteen seamen stumped stolidly on in silence.

It came to William after some time that, press gang or no, that is what they were being taken for. He had quartered Spice Island – that part of Portsmouth on the easternmost extremity of the harbour entrance, more truly known as Point – several times and drawn a total blank. Of seamen there were none, or even merely able-bodied men, or youths, or cripples. Only women were abroad today, it appeared; only women were visible. How could he offer the King's bounty to thin air? He was beginning to feel foolish. Uncle Daniel expected a lot of him. Was he to let him down completely? He had Dolby halt the shore party, and gestured Evans to one side.

'Listen, Jack,' he said, 'we've been rumbled in this place. I'm going to shed Dolby and the men and go recruiting on my own account.'

Evans looked aghast.

'But our orders?'

'Orders you need not worry about,' William replied. 'I will take all responsibility. I have a free hand with Captain Swift on this expedition.'

8

He did not have to spell it out. Evans knew well enough what it was like to be a favourite nephew.

'I'm with you then, Will,' he said. 'Have you a plan?'

William grinned.

'Less than half a plan. We'll head for the Cambridge and have a bite and some gin. First – ' he did not drop his voice – 'let's get rid of that old fool Dolby.'

Twenty minutes later, while Dolby and the boat's crew waited cold and disconsolate on the windy side of Sallyport, William Bentley and Jack Evans drank gin and ate hot mutton pies at the Cambridge. They talked gaily enough of the problems to be met with in dealing with the lower orders, but William was feeling less than gay. A coolish, even cold, sensation was growing in the pit of his stomach. He'd found no one or nothing so far. It had been a fool's errand, a wild-goose chase. Could he face his Uncle Daniel Swift if he returned bare-handed? No. Could he think of an alternative? So far, certainly not. He half listened in irritation as Evans told some interminable tale of hanging a poacher he and his brothers had caught setting traps, and stared out of the upstairs window across High Street. The city was all a-bustle. The ship-yards, the crowded mean houses, the clattering traffic moving towards the sea.

And the market.

Down towards the market Thomas Fox drove his ragged band of twelve sheep. But at the entrance to the coach yard of the Cambridge he halted. The sheep halted too. They began to nibble the thin grass beside the gateposts. Thomas Fox patted his pouch. It contained bread and a few pence. Bread and beer. He lifted his stick and beat the sheep into the yard. William Bentley finished his glass of gin.

His laugh interrupted Evans.

'Well well,' he said. 'Lambs to the slaughter.'

Two

'How much is that then?' Thomas asked the pot-boy.

'Nothing. Your friends inside've given.'

Thomas lifted his mouth from the pot and ale trickled down his chin. He looked at the grimy-faced little boy, who was grinning like a monkey.

'What you laughing for then, boy?' he said. 'And what you talking about?'

'Fine friends for a country lad to 'ave I must say though,' said the pot-boy. Before Thomas could reply he bobbed back into the tap-room.

Thomas took another pull at the pot and worried for a moment. He took a deeper pull. If the ale was going to mysteriously vanish, or something of that nature, he planned to get a good fill first. He looked uneasily round the yard. The sheep were standing in a corner, quiet. After a few seconds he gave up worrying. He reached into his deep pouch for the hunk of bread his sister had given him. When he looked up again there were two young Navy officers in front of him. He jumped.

'Good ale, young fellow?' one of them said.

Thomas Fox stood up clumsily and pulled the brim of his bonnet. His bread fell to the ground. He felt his face getting hot. He looked downwards.

'Never mind the bread,' the officer said. 'Have you a fancy for a hot mutton pie?'

'They're very good. Highly recommend 'em,' the other chipped in. His voice was high, almost squeaky. Thomas flushed redder. He looked after his sheep, but they were in their corner, unmoving. He mumbled something, not even he could hear what.

'Hey! Boy! Pot-boy!'

The smiling imp appeared and bobbed like a bird in the doorway.

'Your honour?'

'A hot mutton pie for my friend here. And another jug of your best. And two gins.'

'Aye aye sir, your honour!' The boy went in giggling.

'Sit down, sir,' the first officer said. 'Sit down and drink. We won't bite you, won't Jack and me. We're here in friendship. We need your help.'

Thomas could not sit down in such a pair of presences. He gripped his pot tightly. His mouth was dry. He raised it shyly to his chin, very slowly, almost as if he thought they would not notice him drinking if he moved gently enough. He slowly, slowly tipped the big black mug until his face was covered. He stared dimly at the two officers from under his eye-lids.

He saw two young men in blue. The one who had spoken first was small, and golden-haired, smiling an easy, amused smile. He was smooth, in control. Thomas Fox was afraid of him, although he did not know why. The officer – only a boy, younger, almost certainly, than he – had an air of command, and something else. He seemed happy, exultant. He had bought Thomas beer for a reason. Thomas was afraid.

The one who had spoken next was taller than Thomas, much taller than the fair-haired officer. He had a high voice and was clearly not the leader. Alone he would have worried Thomas; to have been in the presence of such a grandly dressed personage would have unsettled him. But alongside the small one, he was nothing to fear. He looked a jolly type, just young. Like himself only not a farm boy but an officer. He drank slowly on, aware of the gulping noise, the movement of his adam's apple. He wished they would go away.

When the hot mutton pie arrived Thomas stood like a criminal. His eyes were stuck on the fair one's face. He tried to speak but could say nothing. His bread lay in the dirt at the pot-boy's feet. His dirty toes wriggled, as though they were hungry and could smell it.

William Bentley, master of all, watched the scene with relish. Before him stood a great booby, this country simpleton. Older than he, bigger, and trembling quite noticeably, in terror and confusion. A boy, a man almost, with pale cheeks, long black hair. What was he afraid of? The lower orders were truly strange. Just the presence of himself, younger and smaller, and that great bore Jack Evans, and he was like jelly. But the booby had nothing to fear, of course. In law. Nothing.

In law, Thomas Fox knew, he was safe. He was too young for the press, even without allowing for the other reasons he could not be taken. He lowered his pot helplessly.

'Well,' said the pot-boy impatiently. 'Ain't anyone a-going to eat this 'ere pie or drink this drink, eh? Begging your honours' pardons, but I've got work to be a-doing of.'

'Take it, dear fellow,' William told the shepherd boy, indicating the ale. 'Take it and spare me a moment of your time if you please. I have business with you.'

The pot-boy took the mug from Thomas's hand. He pushed the full one into its place. He put the hot pie, dripping grease, into his free hand. William Bentley and Jack Evans attended to their gins. William Bentley gave the pot-boy a coin. The pot-boy bobbed and left.

'Beg pardon, your honour,' Thomas mumbled. The grease from the pie ran down his smock. He licked it off his thumb miserably.

'Come now, sir,' said William heartily. 'Business. Drink your ale, eat your pie and listen. But first, sit you down. Jack! Get those barrels over, eh?'

Evans rolled over three small casks, which he upended. William took Thomas by the shoulder and pushed him down. Thomas sat and gulped his ale. He felt dizzy, for he drank little in the normal way. He wished himself at home, or at market. At market. He had to sell his sheep. There they were, all twelve. They were eating the clumps of grass between the flags, quite content. He gulped more ale.

'Now,' said the fair-haired officer. 'Let me introduce myself. I am William Bentley, of His Majesty's frigate Welfare, at present anchored in St Helen's Roads. This is my friend and colleague Mr Jack Evans. Midshipmen, by the grace of God and His Majesty, sworn to save old England from her enemies. And your name, sir?'

Thomas Fox blinked. The grease from the pie had filled the palm of his hand, congealing as it cooled.

'And your name?' squeaked Jack Evans.

'No matter,' said William. 'Listen, Mr No-Name, the King needs your help.'

Thomas's eyes opened wide. The King? He took another pull of ale. It tasted odd. Then the mug was empty. Needed his help?

William laughed.

'It is true, young man. The King needs your aid. Urgently. Are you a loyal subject?'

Thomas Fox shook his head to clear it.

'I cannot go to sea!' he said. He was surprised at his own sharpness. He spoke again, more gently, like an apology. 'I cannot be impressed, your honour,' he muttered. 'I am too young, and vital to my family's needs. We have a farm . . .'

The two officers laughed. He wondered why, then thought of his sheep and his besmocked, country look. He smiled. And the pot-boy appeared, unbidden. More gin. More ale.

He would have refused, but had he not heard the fair one say he would not be pressed? He blinked. He heard it now, in any case.

'You have us wrong, young sir. Who talks of pressing? No no, for the moment your King needs only your services as a farmer. In short, we want to buy your sheep. All twelve of 'em.'

Jack Evans piped up: 'Our men need sheep, our officers need sheep, our ship needs sheep. Therefore, our King needs sheep. You have sheep, therefore our King needs you. What is your name, you helper of Royalty?'

William Bentley watched with satisfaction as the black pot of ale was raised once more to the now rosy face that was getting ever rosier. Judging from the effect it was having, it was more gin than ale – which was, after all, what he had paid the smiling pot-boy to provide. When the adam's apple stopped moving the shepherd boy wiped his mouth on his sleeve.

'Thomas Fox,' he said thickly. 'Begging your honour's pardon.'

'Good man!' said William. ''Tis a pity you will not come yourself, young Thomas, for you are a fine figure and would take to water like a duck. But no matter. Will you sell your sheep? To help the King?'

The noise outside the inn-yard had become blurred in Thomas Fox's ears. Inside the high wall a mist seemed to have gathered. He stared at his sheep. They wobbled in his eyes. Twelve sheep. To serve the King. Well, he had never heard of such a thing, to sell the sheep and not at the market, but he could not see the harm in it. Why not sell to these fine young officers, when all was said – and serve the King to boot?

'I shall serve my lord the King,' he mumbled.

'Speak up, speak up sir!' cried William Bentley. He turned to Jack and beamed. Jack winked heartily.

'I shall serve!' said Thomas. 'How much do you offer though? I must have my price, or the family will suffer. My family shall not suffer, sir, not even for his honour the King!'

'Fine words!' squeaked Jack Evans, beside himself with excitement. 'Fine words, young Fox, and well spoken!'

'Well well,' said the fair-haired one. 'If you were able, I should offer you a full five pounds!'

'Haha!' roared his friend.

'And if you were merely ordinary,' said the fair one, 'two pounds ten shillings would be your price!'

'Haha!' roared his friend.

'But as you are a man of the land, shall we say... thirty shillings!? How does thirty shillings sound, landman?'

Truly, Thomas Fox could not say. He could not think at all clearly. Thirty shillings for twelve sheep. Was that better or worse than he could expect at the market?

'Landman, I say. Will you accept thirty shillings? To serve the King?'

Thomas blinked as the fair-haired boy in blue stood up off his tub and came towards him.

'Hold out your hand, Thomas Fox. I will pay you in . . . silver.'

'Oh good, Will, oh good,' said the squeaky one. 'Oh very good!'

Thomas, who had a heavy black pot in his right hand, held out his left and opened it. There was a gasp from the officer. He looked downwards at his palm. In it were the remains of the mutton pie; a vile mess of cold grease, black meat and dirty pastry. Thomas wiped his palm on his once-white smock and accepted the thirty shillings of the King's bounty.

Suddenly the high-voiced officer said something harsh and abrupt, which Thomas did not catch. But the fair-haired one waved it aside.

'Thomas,' he said pleasantly. 'You must help us to the Sallyport. We are men of the sea. To a flock of sheep we would be like lambs. *They* would rule *us*. Come now.'

It was not easy, but it was done. Thomas had a headache. His arms and legs, let alone the sheep, were not inclined to do what he wanted of them. The trip down High Street, with its heavy traffic, its crowds of people, was difficult. In fact he blessed himself, over and over again, drunkenly, that he did not have to go to market and drive a bargain. He was thankful to the midshipmen officers too, for they occasionally kicked a sheep back into line for him, and chased off marauding dogs. They were very jolly, treating it as a game; they called it a convoy, and Thomas the flagship. Thomas was glad he'd met them, although he wished they had not bought him so much ale. They were fine fellows. But thirty shillings, thirty shillings; was it enough, he wondered.

They drove the sheep, bawling, through the narrow entrance to the Sallyport, under King Charles's head. The stiff breeze, blowing straight onshore, beat Thomas Fox's smock hard against him, cut through his thin coat. It was suddenly cold. His teeth chattered. He felt very sick. He wished he had eaten the pie.

The sheep were nervous as he drove them along the pier. But now Thomas had many more helpers. A large band of sailormen padded the boards behind him and his officer friends. The sheep kept stopping, bleating, turning. But the wall of grim-faced men pressed them forward. The air was clean and cold and wet, the sea darkening as the sun dropped down the late autumn sky. They passed several moored boats, several bunches of Navy men who stared incuriously and said nothing. Then below him, a flight of green slippery steps to a jetty. There was a boat alongside it, pitching in the swell. A muffled boat-keeper sat hunched on a bollard.

Thomas turned to the midshipmen.

'How to get 'em down them steps, your honour,' he said. 'That's a question I should not like to answer.'

The fair-haired one laughed. He shouted something. Three seamen leaped on one of the sheep. There was a swift struggle, a terrified bleating. Before Thomas saw exactly how it was done, the sheep was scampering around the bottom of the boat. Within a few minutes all were in. Only the two midshipmen, another, older, officer, and four seamen were left on the pier. The boat-keeper, hunched on his bollard, had not moved.

'Well, Thomas Fox,' said William Bentley. He looked at the green-faced youth with contempt. 'Do you have to be carried, or can you crawl?'

Thomas stared.

15

'Begging your pardon,' he said. 'I'm off homealong now. It will be dark one time, and there's still work to be done I suppose.'

'Get in the boat, Thomas Fox.'

'That I shan't, young fellow. It was the sheep you bought, not I.'

He made to walk along the jetty. The gate in the city wall was clearly visible, a hundred yards away. Across his path the four seamen stood.

'Thomas Fox,' said William Bentley. 'Get into that cutter before I drop my hand, or you will be carried.'

'And if you disobey another order,' Jack Evans shrilled, 'you shall be flogged. You took the bounty, Thomas Fox. You are the King's man now.'

'The bounty? I sold my sheep! My lords! I sold my sheep! My father's sheep! I took no bounty!'

A sick void opened in his stomach. He dropped to his knees, burying his face in his hands.

'Mr Dolby,' said William Bentley coldly. 'Have this poltroon carried aboard the cutter if you please. My God,' he said to Evans, 'to think we must man the King's ships with suchlike scum . . .'

Three

At two o'clock the next morning William Bentley sat in the stern-sheets of the cutter once more, huddled in his thick boat-cloak, broodingly watching the dark seas off the easternmost point of the Isle of Wight. The boat rocked gently in the swell, and William was perishing with cold. Beside him sat the third lieutenant of the Welfare, a man of twenty-two called Higgins. William despised him for a fool and was glad their task forbade them to speak. All the officers on board his uncle's ship were fools in one way or another, he reflected savagely. He longed for the day he might bring off something splendid, be made acting lieutenant by the captain. But he did not let his dreaming dull his concentration.

The cutter was silent, except for the occasional creaking of the two stern oars, which were shipped and ready. Every now and again the two seamen at them dipped and pulled quietly, to keep the boat's head across the seas towards where France must be. The other oarsmen sat the wrong way round on their thwarts, staring into the blackness over the bow. William stared too, till the dark glittered and flashed in his eyes. They had been there since midnight, waiting. So far nothing had happened.

William was glad to be on the cutter. He had asked his uncle's permission to join the 'expedition' and had got it because of his successful recruiting drive. Higgins did not like him much, and would rather have brought the boat's crew out alone; but that had meant nothing, of course, once Uncle Daniel had given the word.

He had been waiting on the quarterdeck when William had brought the boat neatly alongside with its chaotic cargo of sick sheep and sicker shepherd. William had nipped up the ladder smartly, leaving the mundane task of unloading everything to Dolby and Evans. There was a fairish sea running in the Roads by now and he watched the lubberly antics of the waisters for a few

17

minutes before his uncle invited him to come below. Before they went Swift spoke to the boatswain about the state of the crew. That illustrious warrant officer took deeply to heart the captain's observations about what would happen if some seamanship was not soon beaten into them.

In his uncle's cabin, seated with the glass that warms in his hand, William described his trip ashore.

'The sight of a blue coat has a truly strange effect, uncle. You could almost hear the scurrying of their feet as the loathsome rats disappeared into their holes. Women and children aplenty. But of able-bodied men not a sign. I beg your pardon.'

Daniel Swift chuckled.

'Do not fish for compliments, my boy,' he replied. 'You know you have done admirably. I expected less. Half a dozen sheep and a shepherd. Excellent.'

'A round dozen, sir. And they cost me no more than a landman's bounty.'

'All legal and above board,' said Swift.

William speculated. Did his uncle wish to know of the illegalities, or was he to keep it dark? He cleared his throat.

'As to that, sir . . .'

'Well?'

William put the tips of his forefingers into his mouth and bit them gently.

'Well, sir. Let us say that Thomas Fox might claim he did not volunteer.'

Swift looked at him under his fierce strong brows.

'But he accepted the bounty?'

'He accepted thirty shillings.'

'And?'

'He might claim it was not so much the King's bounty . . . as . . . Well, sir, he was on his way to market.'

Swift smiled bleakly.

'Surely he would not be so foolish as to have parted with his flock for thirty shillings?'

'He seemed satisfied at the time, sir.'

A short laugh.

'No no, Mr Bentley, I'll not believe it. Thirty shillings is thirty shillings. Whatever the value of a dozen sheep, and I confess I have not an inkling, the sum is too pat; too appropriate. Five pounds for an able seaman, two pounds ten shillings for an ordinary, thirty shillings for a landman.'

'As I told him, sir.'

The man looked into the eyes of the boy.

'As you told him?'

'Yes sir. Evans heard me, if it were ever to be in dispute.'

'Perhaps,' said Captain Swift after a moment's silence, 'perhaps I might see my way to offering him some more money, however. For his beasts. Sheerly out of generosity, as there can be no doubt that he took the bounty with his eyes open. Another thirty shillings, perhaps.'

He motioned with his hand and the servant refilled their glasses.

'Most appropriate, sir,' William said gaily. 'But I am sorry indeed to have provided only sheep and a landman. Perhaps you will allow me to try once more?'

That was not to be, however. Daniel Swift dismissed his servant, then dropped his nephew a hint. It was very apparent, without one word breaking such secret matters, that the frigate Welfare would soon be putting to sea. William felt a surge of excitement. By God, he thought, a little action would be a very fine thing.

'As to the people,' said Uncle Daniel, 'I have another string to my bow. It is a gamble, but one worth taking. Higgins will be out tonight with a strong crew, and I hope to catch a prize.'

He watched William's eyes. William asked the question without a word being spoken.

'Smugglers,' the captain continued. 'I have been watching ever since we anchored in the Roads. And I have spoken to several experienced shore officers in the city. The trade's a flourishing one in these parts. They use the beaches at Southsea and Eastney, the bay here, the creek at Bembridge. Tonight I have high hopes.'

It was too much for William.

'Higgins!' he blurted out.

Captain Swift's pale eyes became cold. He stared at his nephew.

'An officer with great potential,' he said. His voice was smooth and hard. William swallowed. He thought Higgins a toady and dangerously weak. But it was not his place to breathe a word of that.

'I beg pardon, sir,' he said clearly. 'My excitement ran away with

19

me. I merely expressed disappointment at not being named. My natural conceit, sir. Forgive me.'

A smile creased the thin face. William felt another rush of excitement, and warmth. Captain Swift was a hard man, and he wondered sometimes at his choice of officers. But of his affection for William there was no doubt. He knew he was forgiven, and went on.

'Please, Uncle Daniel,' he said impulsively. 'Let me go too. Will there be many of them? Will there be a fight? My God, sir! I'd love a fight!'

It didn't take much persuading. He left the cabin a few minutes later as happy as a lark, and clattered down to the midshipmen's berth, deep in the ship, aft. His friends greeted him with good-natured envy. His fame in recruiting twelve sheep and a 'half-wit boy' had gone before him. He revelled in their admiration, freely given, but refrained from telling them of the hot work to come. That would feed the fires of adulation for the next day, perhaps.

At about the same time, right at the farther end of the ship, Thomas Fox came slowly out of his drunkenness with a mounting panic that approached terror. All around him there was darkness, and heat, and the smell of vomit and animals. He lashed out wildly with his arms and legs, and awakened a chorus of bellowings and bleatings. He felt hot fur, saw the outlines of beasts – and slowly remembered.

He remembered the awful voyage from Sallyport, across Spit-head, to the ship anchored off the tail of the Isle of Wight. He remembered a desperate fight for freedom, heavy repeated blows, a bone-shattering descent from the pier to the jetty to the cutter, a long heaving voyage of spray, tears and sickness.

By the time he had been hauled roughly up the steep side of the frigate he was practically insensible. Exhaustion, misery, rage, drunkenness. They had all taken their toll. And he felt the hopeless-ness well up once more. The hopelessness of trying to get a response from the stony-blank face of the fair-haired young mid-shipman who had cheated him.

Thomas lay in a heap, sprawled in the noisome liquid mixture of beasts' manure and his own vomit, crying weakly into the crook of his elbow. Exactly why it had happened he could not fathom still. But what had happened he knew too well. He had been pressed – or tricked, or kidnapped, the words did not matter – into His Majesty's Navy. He was on board a ship and he would never see his home or family again.

Before his tortured brain lapsed into stupor, Thomas remembered something else. As he had stumbled across the deck, he had seen a vision in scarlet. A small company of marines had stood by one of the masts, with long muskets and cocked hats. They had swayed and swum in his sight, until one round, fair-skinned head had stood out from the rest.

Thomas had stopped, reached out, groaned.

'Silas!' he had shouted.

But the shout had come out as a drunken grunt. And the fair-skinned head had not flinched, had not displayed a flicker of emotion or recognition.

Thomas had been hustled and pushed into the bowels of the ship, into the hot stinking darkness, and into a pen with the sheep. And, oh, they had been sick, both beasts and boy.

In the same afternoon another man from this neck of Hampshire, a man named Jesse Broad, had enjoyed the same soldier's wind that had blown William Bentley's cutter to Portsmouth and back without a tack. It blew a big lugger called Beauregard on a reach straight as an arrow from the coast of France to the eastern end of the Isle of Wight. Out in mid-Channel the stiff westerly produced a good-sized lop, but the two lugsails were reefed not because of any enmity in the weather, but because of its very friendliness. Broad and his friend Hardman had consulted several times with Joel Gauthier, the French skipper of the lugger, and all had agreed that they must slow down if they were not to be too near the English coast too early.

Hardman had ragged Jesse Broad, in any case, about the earliness of the trip. Normally the whole affair would take place under cover of darkness. But this time it was different. This time they were not running a real cargo – just a couple of small barrels for 'personal consumption' – and Broad was determined to be home before dawn, in safety and comfort. Hardman too, really. They were bound not to be late for the christening of young Jem, Broad's first son, and Gauthier had been more than ready to risk the channel in daylight, infested as it was with British men-of-war, for the sake of his friends and partners.

About four miles off the coast of the island, in the pitch blackness of the autumn night, Gauthier hauled his wind while his crew helped Broad and Hardman launch their wherry. She was a light boat, fast and quiet, built to a drawing of Jesse's own. They made her bow fast to a stay with a painter, picked her up bodily, six of them, spun her in the air like a top and heaved. There was a splash and the wherry was bobbing alongside.

Two small barrels went on board, then four oars. Jesse Broad and Hardman shook hands with Gauthier warmly. They reminded each other of their next rendezvous, exchanged greetings to families and friends, shook hands again. A few seconds later the Frenchman put up his helm to get some way on, then went about smartly and took the other leg of his soldier's breeze back to France. Broad and Hardman, guided by the wind on their sides, the set of the waves, the glittering stars, headed for the tail of the island.

William Bentley knew that one day he would make a good, if not even a great, sea officer. He knew, sitting hunched in the stern-sheets of the cutter, cold and stiff, that if anything was spotted tonight he would be the one to spot it. He did not know why, because Higgins, although loathsome, was wide awake and watching, and at least half the boat's crew were good steady men with eyes like hawks. But know it he did.

He sat tensely, as he had sat for hours now, watching the rolling waves and the sparkling sky. Save for the occasional creaking of the stern oars, silence. Outside the boat, the splashing of the creaming seas, the low drone of the wind. Far away astern and to larboard a few small lights of Portsmouth. To starboard, on the island, nothing. Then Higgins, beside him, said quietly, 'Well gone two bells. I doubt we'll not see anything tonight.'

William ground his teeth in fury. What could one do with a man like that? My God, why did he not light a lantern and have done with it! The muscles of his cheeks ached with hatred. Hatred and the effort to reconcentrate his hearing.

But it was no good. He kept on hearing the voice, echoing and echoing. 'Well gone two bells, mutter mutter; doubt anything tonight, mutter mutter.' The night seemed full of muttering.

22

'Pity we could not have invited Joel as well, for that matter,' said Hardman. 'He's a hell of a fellow to have at a shindy.'

'Hell of a drinker,' grunted Jesse Broad as his weather blade bit deeper into a sea than he expected. 'Joel, my friend, is a demon when he has the brandy inside him.'

'Well gone two. Doubt anything tonight . . .'

William Bentley cursed the muttering, cursed Higgins, cursed everything. Then the hairs on the back of his neck began to rise.

'Higgins!' he hissed. 'Give orders, sir! There's a boat out there!'

'His sister too,' said Hardman. 'A fine woman that. Damn the war, I say.'

'The war may save your life then,' Jesse Broad replied. 'For Louise would eat you, friend Hardman. Bones and everything.'

Their laughter drifting over the water convinced Higgins, and probably saved William Bentley an unpleasant reward for his incautious mode of addressing the lieutenant. The seamen whirled on their thwarts, braced their feet, and carefully shipped their oars, already muffled in canvas at the rowlocks. Higgins withdrew his pistols from their oilskin covers and cocked them. William Bentley cleared a heavy cudgel. The boat needed to be rowed silently less than two hundred yards to be directly in the path of the wherry. He marvelled once more at his uncle's brilliance. He had predicted the smugglers' course past the island to exactitude. What was more, the scoundrels were still too far out to even bother to look for trouble.

'A fine French wife like Louise would be the making of me,' Hardman was saying. 'The English maids strike so dull when viewed—'

Apart from a few curses, these were the last words he ever uttered. A bullet pierced his throat when one of Higgins's pistols went off in the heat of the struggle. Jesse Broad was knocked unconscious with the loom of an oar. Until the second the wherry struck it, they had no inkling that the cutter was there. It was neatly done.

As they pulled back to the Welfare, William Bentley fumed. He was almost exploding with suppressed rage. A fine strong smuggling man lost. The primest of prime seamen, and fighters too. All thanks

23

to that fool, that dolt, of a third lieutenant and his stupid pistols. He was enraged.

They cast the wherry adrift as being too light for naval use. In it they left the body of Hardman, tossing gently in his own thick blood. But the barrels of brandy went with them.

Four

Jesse Broad was put in irons when he was brought on board the Welfare. The boatswain, a bull of a man called Allgood, had noted Captain Swift's observations on the state of the crew, and he knew a good addition to it when he saw one. Jesse Broad was powerful, impressive – and a seaman. He could also almost smell his own fireside from where they lay at anchor, and would certainly try to run. Jack Allgood put him in irons.

Four hours later, two of the boatswain's crew – he dubbed them mates, although only one was rated so – unshackled him and led him to a large wooden washtub set up near the foremast. The day was cold and bright, much colder than the day before, the wind having backed to the east of south. It was blowing quite hard and the Welfare snubbed uncomfortably at her great cable in the short lop. Broad looked towards Portsmouth, where he was shortly due to see his only son christened. The muscles in his neck worked. He felt little but anger. Anger at his bad luck, at his folly in being taken, at these men for killing his friend. The city was as clear as a bright model, scoured by the clean wind. It seemed near enough to reach out and touch.

When the boatswain's mates ordered him to strip he did not argue. For several years Broad had avoided the Navy, despite being as prime a target of the press as any man ashore, but he was not ignorant of the service. These boatswain's mates were tough and brutal men. One carried a rope's end of careful fancy-work, ending in a knuckly Turk's-head the size of a chestnut. The other had a rattan cane that would lift the skin like wet paper. Behind them stood a gang of villainous sailors – landmen, rather; waisters and other scum. The washing party.

Jesse Broad was a little surprised by this. He was clearly to get the full treatment, as laid down on His Majesty's receiving ships for pressed men. But as he was not on board a receiving ship, and as they knew he would make a fine seaman, he could only think they meant to humiliate him, to break his spirit. He knew the ship by reputation, of course; what seafarer in these parts had not heard of savage Daniel Swift? Still, it seemed an odd sort of way to win the obedience of a good hand.

Standing naked in the biting wind, staring levelly at the dribbling 'barber' who hacked at his hair with a pair of blunt shears, Broad heard a commotion and saw a sight that explained the situation in part. He was not the only new arrival on board. There was to be a receiving party.

Thomas Fox, still ill, his head splitting from gin and misery, was pushed along the deck at arm's length by a laughing bully with a handspike. If he faltered or stumbled the long wooden bar was jabbed viciously into his smock where his kidneys would be. He yelped like a dog and sobbed like a child. Thomas Fox did not see the coast of Hampshire or the Isle of Wight. He saw nothing. Just a spinning kaleidoscope of bright sky, green sea, strange sea things of deck, mast and cordage, flashes of laughing faces, brown and leering, cruel and taunting. He reached the foremast in a rush, propelled by a sharp thrust from the handspike which brought him bang up against something soft and frightening. He opened his eyes and looked at the strong pulsing throat of a naked man.

All sorts of strange notions flashed through Thomas Fox's agonised brain. He could not be in heaven, surely? This could not be an angel? In hell, perhaps? That was more like it. A naked man standing by a steaming tub, surrounded by wild-eyed devils in aprons. The nearest devil, a gibbering thing with a crooked eye and a grin of unmitigated evil, was making passes over the head of the naked sinner with a pair of wicked-looking scissors.

He stared into the strong brown face of the naked sinner. It was kindly, and did not flinch from his hot gaze or panting breath.

'Are we in hell?' he whispered.

The eyes regarded him for some short time. The eyes crinkled, the lips moved in half a smile.

'That we are, my friend,' said the naked man.

There was a whistle of rattan and the teeth, lips and eyes snapped shut.

'Silence!' roared a boatswain's mate.

Thomas would not, could not, take his clothes off when ordered, but it availed him nothing. They were torn from him and he was hurled naked into the tub. There he was held down while sailors with brooms scrubbed him till his skin bled. His hair was lopped off, his skull roughly shaved. An evil-smelling yellow powder was poured into the water and rubbed into his skin, ears, eyes, mouth.

After the washing and delousing Jesse Broad and Thomas Fox stood once more on deck and watched their clothes flung over the side. The smuggler, silent as the grave, blue with cold, stared straight ahead. Thomas, bleeding from one ear and several scalp wounds, snuffled noisily. He still tried to cover his nakedness.

'Now my bright boys,' said Mr Allgood, appearing before them with a bundle of clothes, 'here we have clothes fitting for a prince or even a king. Slops we call 'em, on account they comes out of the sloproom and you receives 'em by courtesy and consent of His Gracious Majesty. Who will, I might remind you, require payment for 'em in full to be docked out of your pay, you lucky sailormen.'

He sorted out a great grey flannel shirt, which he held up in front of Thomas Fox like a London tailor.

''Ere, you scrawny, ill-favoured, half-starved lubber,' he said. 'This is the smallest article of garmentry on board of the Welfare. It's too big for you, no doubt. Too good for you too, having been took off the corpse of a Spanish nobleman no less. But put it on and shut your gob, before my mates shuts it for you.'

Thomas took the shirt gratefully, and struggled into it. The neck was so wide his shoulders almost came through as well as his head. It reached below his knees. The men, laughing at Allgood's speech-making and Fox's appearance, cleared away the tub. Next he was given trousers, wide-bottomed blue breeches, a short wool jacket, neckcloth, and a belt of rope. He felt better dressed, although the slops were old and worn and much too loose for comfort.

'Now you, my bucko,' cried the boatswain, chucking a striped shirt at Jesse Broad. 'Dress up fine now, for you're off to see the captain very soon, to share a drop of fine French brandy that was delivered last night by a friend! Silk I should have brought for you, damn me, but we ain't none. So good old English flannel must serve!'

Jesse Broad dressed without breaking his silence. The clothes would suit well enough, although he regretted the loss of his own more comfortable ones. At sea in a storm these would provide poor

27

protection. But he did not intend to face a storm at sea in them, or the Welfare.

He looked at the pathetically thin figure beside him. The poor boy was yellow-faced, weeping still. Tufts of black hair stuck from his head at angles. His mother, if he had one, would not have known him. A farmer's boy no doubt. And no doubt illegally pressed.

'Not in hell, boy,' he said abruptly. 'For there is always hope while there is life. Obey orders and keep counsel. You will come through.'

He said no more, for the heavy rope's end banged into his back and made him gasp. The farmer's lad turned a pair of large swimming eyes upon him and stared. Deep inside them, something that looked like hope glimmered for an instant.

Inside the captain's cabin the two stood like cattle at a market. Broad noted the wide polished table, the rich hangings, the heavy darkwood furniture. Only a frigate, but decked out like a flagship. Swift was reputed to be a rich man. Obviously rumour was not dressed in her liar's garb on this occasion.

Nor had rumour lied about the appearance of the man. He was small, but bulky and well-made in his blue coat of the finest and his many-ruffled silk shirt. An air of confidence, elegance, self-satisfaction sat on his shoulders, and he had an easy, arrogant smile on his handsome face. The biggest feature on it was a fine hooked nose, a great sickle of bone that give him the look of an emperor. But the features that captured the gaze were Daniel Swift's eyes. They were pale; of no colour that Jesse Broad could distinguish, but pale. Cold and watchful and pale. They watched him now, unblinking. Broad watched back, but he knew more than to stare into the captain's eyes. He dropped his own as if in deference, while in fact taking in the rest of the man's figure. A cold, dangerous, cruel sort of a fellow, he decided. Rumour had not lied.

To Swift's right sat his first lieutenant, a thin, Irish-looking man of Broad's age – about thirty. He had flaming red hair and wet lips. To the captain's left, the second. A butter-barrel of a fat man, with a face like a suet pudding. He was known to the people, it later turned out, as Plumduff. Eyes like a pig.

28

Behind Swift a corporal of marines, at attention easily on the uneasily pitching deck. At the end of the table, in powdered wig of all things, the captain's clerk, at a ledger. He had a quill and horn of ink ready. Broad looked through the square stern windows. He could see Point Gilkicker, the green scrub stretching away behind it. He wondered at the grandeur of the reception he and the boy were getting, and decided the officers must have gathered for a more important purpose. For a moment there was silence. Except, of course, for the noises of the ship and the sea and the wind.

'You sir,' said Swift, 'I propose to rate as able. You are a smuggler, a rogue, a villain. Doubtless the son of a whore, probably the husband of one. But that is my proposal nevertheless. Have you anything to say?'

The first lieutenant, Hagan, licked his lips. Broad stared over the captain's head, at Gilkicker. A coasting brig hove into view, scampering towards Portsmouth harbour. As she rounded the point braces and tacks were tended. In less than an hour she would be alongside in Dirty Corner.

'Your compatriot, your fellow villain, was killed. I might have wished such a fate to overtake you, but God was not kind. I must make room for you in my ship. I propose to rate you able. What do you say?'

Broad stared. He sensed a movement behind him. Someone preparing to swing, of course. Swift raised his hand in a small negative.

'Answer me, able seaman.'

'Aye aye sir,' said Broad.

Swift smiled a tiny smile.

'Good,' he said. Then: 'You are not the ordinary run of fellow, a fool could see that. You probably know that the manner of your coming on board of my ship was a thought irregular. You probably know that I should, to be within the letter of the law, have you taken to Portsmouth to be tried and hanged. You possibly even know that I cannot, in theory, rate you as able from the start of things. Well?'

'Aye aye sir.'

'What else do you know, I wonder? That I found the brandy excellent? That I need good seamen? That you will run at the very first opportunity?'

29

Broad pondered, but his mind felt stodgy, muddled. He watched the coasting brig, fast disappearing. He had protection, in theory, he and his fellows were immune. But here, now, such influence – always nebulous – counted for nothing. Swift was the law and no protection on the earth need sway him from his purpose. Yes, thought Broad, I *will* run. But what does this blue-coated, fish-eyed man mean by saying it?

'You will not run, able seaman, you will not run,' said Swift. 'For as a smuggler you would hang, and as a deserter you would hang. But as an able seaman, you will be of use. You will not run, able seaman, because you will be watched. Well?'

'Aye aye sir.'

'And, able seaman, bear this in mind. No man *has* run from this ship in some little sojourn in St Helen's Roads. Two have tried and two have died. Mr Scrivenor, sign him on board.'

The bewigged clerk scratched in the ledger. Jesse Broad was pushed forward to sign. He held the quill clumsily and made his mark. At least no one need know he could read and write.

When he had been led out, Thomas Fox was prodded forward. He had listened in awe to the weird conversation. His admiration for the silent, powerful smuggler had kept his tears at bay. Now, alone in the lion's den, his teeth chattered audibly.

'Your name?' said Captain Swift.

'T–T–T–Thomas F–F–Fox, your honour,' he whispered.

Captain Swift curled his lips back over prominent teeth in a smile.

'Welcome aboard His Majesty's frigate Welfare,' he said. 'I am sure you will be happy to serve your King here.'

Thomas fell to his knees and began to cry. Keep your counsel, the smuggler had said. But he could not.

He babbled and wept incoherently about the injustice that had been done. He cried for his family and pleaded to be sent home. No one stopped him, but the silence was profound. After a short time he stopped trying to speak. He stared through his tears over the polished edge of the table. He sniffed and staunched his eyes and nose with his sleeve. Captain Swift was smiling at him.

'Boy,' he said at last. 'Are you telling me you were tricked on board this vessel?'

'Yes, your honour.'

'That you accepted thirty shillings not as the King's bounty but in payment for your flock?'

'Yes, your honour.'

'That you have a mother and father, ailing no doubt, a farm that needs you, two little sisters to cry themselves to sleep?'

Thomas almost felt better. The captain understood! He breathed deeply, the sobs gone, his mouth hanging open. The captain understood!

'Yes, your honour,' he breathed.

The captain smiled. Everyone smiled. The officer on his right licked his red lips with a thick tongue, the rotund officer's little eyes disappeared into rolls of fat. Only the marine did not smile; his eyes were blank.

'Well well,' said the captain. 'Something must be done about this state of affairs. Do you agree?'

'Yes, your honour,' said Thomas.

This time they laughed. Even the clerk, a thin, dry man in a dusty coat and lawyer's wig, uttered a noise like a small croak.

'How about thirty shillings? Thirty shillings more? Thirty shillings on top of the thirty shillings bounty you accepted? Thirty shillings for your fine sheep? Eh?'

'But, your honour. Begging your pardon. Not the bounty, your honour.'

'Do you contradict me, boy? Do you dare kneel there and contradict an officer of the King! Good God boy, are you calling me a liar!'

Captain Swift's voice, his face, his manner, all had changed. The deep red colour mounted in his face till it was dark and furious. His flanking officers sat more upright in their chairs. Thomas Fox raised his hands to his mouth, his eyes wide.

'It is *you*, boy! You are the liar!' shouted Swift. 'You freely accepted the King's bounty in front of witnesses and now you would be forsworn. Hell, boy! You will burn in hell! Do you understand!'

Thomas Fox was lost. He felt himself already in hell, burning in agony. He bit his lips, his gums. He wrung his hands and rolled his eyes as if already mad.

31

'No, your honour,' he moaned. 'Yes, your honour! Oh please, your honour.'

Before his eyes, behind the table, the captain rose like a vengeful being. He reached his full height, a barrel-chested fury.

'In future, boy, when you are addressed by an officer, you will say "aye aye sir". Is that clear?'

'Yes your hon—'

A rattan slash bit into his back. Thomas Fox sprawled forward and was pulled upright to his knees once more.

'Aye aye sir,' he mumbled.

Captain Swift sat down. His face was back to normal. As if nothing had happened.

'Good boy,' he said, almost kindly. 'You are prepared to learn, I see. Good boy. Well, Thomas, that is my proposal. I will offer you another thirty shillings, which is alarmingly generous of me. Will you accept?'

Thomas nodded.

'Aye aye sir,' he mumbled.

'Stoutly done,' said Swift. 'Now, make your mark with Mr Scrivenor there. He will rate you as a landman and put thirty shillings down beside your name. And in addition, two months' pay are due, two months' payment in advance, you will be a prince among the people, a very prince! For all of which largesse, Thomas, I beg you will be so good as to consider your duties from this moment forward as tender of the ship's beasts. We have two cows, some few pigs, a couple of dozen fowls, and some sheep. About twenty in all, I think, counting the flock you so kindly sold us. Too many for the manger in any case, so we have pens as well.'

Thomas was pulled upright and stood facing the captain. He was bewildered by this quick-tempered, hot-cold man. He was dug in the ribs.

'Aye aye sir,' he said.

The captain gave him an almost dazzling smile.

'Good,' he said again. 'But Fox, you must not lie on board one of His Majesty's ships. It is a serious crime.' He looked past Thomas. 'Mr Allgood, as Fox has proved himself a liar, a liar let him be. And now dismiss.'

With this cryptic farewell puzzling him more than ever, Thomas was wheeled by the shoulder and prodded outside.

He had proved himself a liar, so a liar let him be. He shook his aching head, but the mists did not clear. All he knew for sure was that he had made his mark. He was a landman in the British Navy.

Five

When Jesse Broad was led out from the cabin he took one last look around him before he went below to find himself a mess. The breeze was still backing easterly, blowing fresher and yet fresher. The deep green of the Hampshire coast, the dry brown of Portsdown, were sparkling and pristine, the softer green of the Solent and Spithead flecked with big white horses. There were many ships of war anchored in Spithead, many merchant vessels threading among them. A bluff-bowed collier, close-hauled on a course that would bring her past the Welfare, was carrying reefed topsails and sending gouts of spray out from under, making heavy weather of it. He breathed the clean air deeply, speculating. If their mission was to the westward, they would soon be off. The frigate had an unmistakeable air of readiness. As he watched, a large naval launch, cutter rigged, cleared a gaggle of men-of-war in Spithead and smashed into the rolling seas towards them. He guessed, for no real reason, that she was bringing their sailing orders.

He turned to the boatswain's mate who had brought him out.

'I don't know these vessels, if you please. How do I find a berth?'

The boatswain's mate, a friendly enough fellow when he was allowed to be, pointed to a hatchway.

'Below there and follow your nose. The first lieutenant has you marked for a topman in the larboard watch. They are below now. Find a mess that wants you.'

Jesse Broad walked across the deck to the hatchway. All around him tars were working, at scrubbing, overhauling gear, a thousand other tasks. There may have been eighty men visible had he looked about, but there was no sound of voices. They worked in silence, under many watchful eyes. At the foremast, like sore thumbs in their scarlet and pipeclay, stood a detachment of marines, long muskets in hand. Further aft another small band stood. Broad felt like spitting, but stopped himself. He knew no naval laws as yet; but that was bound to be among them.

He let himself down the hatchway onto the gun deck. Once there he stood still, to grow accustomed to the differences above and below.

First, the darkness. Although the gunports were all lashed open, the deckspace was very dark. Ahead there was an area of light spilling through the boat-skids that slatted the main hatchway, but it spread only a few feet to either side. The rest was lost in gloom. It was an area of dim square shapes, low-beamed and hollow-sounding. There was the murmur of voices, and from farther forward a steady grinding, which he took to be the main cable as it led out through the hawse into the waters of St Helen's Roads.

Then, the smell. It was compounded of many things, this smell, but it made up a whole that was new to him, but which he would never forget. After the fresh cold breeze of the Channel it was like being stifled, strangled, having his nose plugged. Broad involuntarily gagged. Oddest of all was that he had not noticed it before, while he had been in irons. One advantage of a blow with a cutter oar then; it dulled more senses than one. The smell was rich and complex. The usual ship things were there, like tar, cordage, thick paint, wood. Then there was the rank odour of bodies, many bodies, far too many for such a confined space. Soot, presumably from the galley forward, and the strong stench of the farmyard. A jumbled animal noise ahead of him let him at least guess where the beasts were penned.

Below everything, faint yet insidious, was a rotten smell, almost masked by all the stronger but less all-pervasive ones. It was the smell of the sewers, a smell which was common in Portsmouth's streets but which Broad, who lived in a hamlet a few miles to the east, did not relish. The bilges. Ye Gods; this was before the cruise started, in home waters, where every cleanlinesss would be observed.

His eyes more accustomed to the gloom, he walked to his left, to the ship's larboard side, to seek a mess. Each one, he knew, was formed by the space between two of the great guns – eighteen-pounders in the Welfare's case. The men ate between each pair, on a table slung from the deck beams overhead, and lived there during their waking hours below. He guessed that in this ship, because of

35

her size, all but the most privileged slung their hammocks on the lower deck, one beneath. That would be the main source of the smell of dirty bodies.

Broad was in no hurry, nor did he intend to make a mistake. He walked aft a short way, to the no-man's-land abaft which the marines lived, a buffer between the messes of the men and the quarters of the officers, which were partitioned off by light, collapsible screens. It did not occur to Broad as strange that he should know these things. Everybody did, every seaman anyway. He wanted to spit again at the thought of the marines, billeted between the sailors and their lords. Scum, who would turn their muskets on men of their own condition to protect officers. He almost risked a spit, but smiled instead. Why court punishment for the mere thought of such vermin?

Turning his back on the area, he walked slowly forwards, scrutinising and being scrutinised by the gaggle of seamen in each mess. They were an assorted lot, with a high proportion of aged and semi-crippled among them. Some of the messes abounded in bandannas and flashes of gold, in mouth and earlobe. Pirates, in appearance; and knowing Swift's evil name, pirates in fact probably. Very few smiled as he walked past, but several scowled; bared blackened teeth, made warning noises. Welcome aboard, he thought sardonically. Ah Christ, if only Mary could see me now. A stab of pain and anger caught his chest. The choice of mess mattered nothing. He would not be here long enough.

At the very next space he stopped. A red-haired boy grinned. Two or three older seamen nodded, one removing his empty pipe from between his gums as a mark of courtesy. Broad spread his hands to show he had no dunnage.

'Mind if I join here, kind friends?' he said. 'I have no gear, no bad habits save wine, women, tobacco and music, sleep like a babe and do not snore. Jesse Broad, formerly a businessman from Langstone way. Now an able seaman in His Gracious Majesty's Navy.'

The red-haired boy laughed.

'A businessman he do say!' he crowed. 'A real live gentleman down on his luck. And look at his fancy suit and well-shaved crown!'

From the position nearest the port a man in his mid-thirties half-lifted himself from the gun carriage. He was dressed in dark blue trousers, a blue woollen, and a neckcloth. He looked like a seaman, with a hard, closed face and big square hands. His eyes were grey, and cool, and bright. He could not stand upright, so tall was he. A great disadvantage for the naval man, as Jesse had noted even in the cabin. One of the boatswain's mates had stood almost doubled, and the first lieutenant would have been hard pressed to have stood upright.

'Your business, they say, was smuggling fine brandy from our enemies the French,' the dark-faced man said quietly. 'Do you consider that a proper business for an Englishman?'

One of the older hands tutted in a faintly disapproving way. Not at him, Jesse Broad thought, but as much as to warn the brooding man off from making statements that could be quarrelsome.

'My business I consider to be private,' Broad replied levelly. 'Suffice it to say I never harmed another Englishman, nor my country, by it. Brought great comfort to some I'll wager – while not for a moment telling one word of what my business is.'

'*Was* though, don't you mean?' said the red-haired boy almost anxiously, as though he half-expected to see Broad produce a bottle of brandy from behind his back.

Broad laughed and two or three of the others joined in.

'*Was* indeed. Now I am a pressed man.'

'Along of all here,' said a greybeard. He glanced at the others. 'Well, messmates, what does you say? I say – it's all right by me if this young businessman joins along with us.'

There was a ready chorus of assent. Only the dark-faced man said nothing.

The greybeard looked at him.

'And you, Mr Matthews? What say you?'

'Oh aye, Thomas Fulman, what's the difference? Let him come in and welcome.'

Thomas Fulman smiled, shaking Broad's hand.

'Mr Matthews is a pressed man too,' he said. 'And a—'

A harsh growl from Matthews. Fulman stopped, shrugged, and offered Broad a place to sit on the gun truck.

It was not long before his new messmates had given him a lot of background. Much of it was wild talk, Dame Rumour in her truthless mantle, but much was interesting. His feeling that the crew were unusually old and villainous had been a correct one, apparently.

37

'They'm gutter rats, a lot of 'em,' said the red-haired boy wonderingly. 'I'm surprised they have the likes of 'em in the Navy.'

This caused a general laugh. Broad soon realised that the boy, Peter, was famous for his simpleness of statement. He was as near to being a volunteer as anyone on board, having been the victim of a trick so obvious that to have fallen for it was rated as being completely his own fault. What's more, he was genuinely happy. He had swopped the drab life of a farrier's overworked apprentice in a rat-infested and noisome stables in the stinking heart of Southampton for the life of an overworked ship's boy in a rat-infested and noisome frigate. But as he pointed out, the food was more regular and not much worse, the liquor allowance was more than adequate and knocked what he'd scrounged on shore into a cocked hat, he was beaten no more often if he was careful – and he preferred the company of men to that of horses.

Thomas Fulman confirmed his view on the men though.

'They are a bad lot, friend Jesse,' he said seriously. 'The scum of every prison hereabouts, winkled out by magistrates and put to sea. There's murderers on this deck, and vagabonds and thieves. But seamen? Oh dear, they're hard to find.'

'Where may we be bound do you think, grandfather?' Broad asked the old man. Peter was ready with a reply, but Fulman raised his hand.

'There's been many a week of westerlies ablowing, many a week. And we've swung to this hook until a move in any direction would raise a cheer. But now the wind's making from the east, I reckon, or soon will be. We'll be under way before much longer.'

'Heading westward then?' said Jesse. 'Any suggestion as to where?'

'It'll be far!' squeaked Peter. 'We've a whole dungyard of farm animals. You should smell 'em when we'm battened down at night!'

'Well,' said Grandfather Fulman slowly, 'I don't know. I don't know as how any man can tell, being as how most of the rest of the world lies out that way. But Mr Matthews do reckon as how we're going south. West and south.'

Broad looked along the length of the black gun-barrel to where the dark man sat slumped on the deck, his chin on his chest. He glanced inquiringly at Fulman, as if to say 'How would he know?'

The old man cleared his throat.

'Mr Matthews,' he began; and stopped.

'Is a sea captain!' piped up Peter. 'He was took off of a homeward-bound ship as he was mate of her, and he was on passage to England to take up as a captain! There!'

Jesse Broad stared at the dark man, who had not moved or sought to stop the boy. Pity stirred in his breast. Small wonder Matthews was so bitter-seeming. Another piece of fine illegality by good Captain Swift. To be impressed as a merchant mate!

'Only three days off of port he was,' said Peter. 'Almost there. And he's rated—'

'Hush boy!' Fulman clapped an old and horned hand on Peter's knee and pressed. Matthews stirred his great lantern head. He looked full into Jesse Broad's face.

'The boy tells part of it, at least, friend businessman,' he said. 'And I am rated ordinary seaman now. For making too much of the misfortune that . . . befell me. Let you be warned.'

'Thank you,' Broad replied. 'And where do you think this ship is heading, if I might ask?'

'You might,' said Matthews. 'This ship and all that's in her is heading west, and south, far south. If I have it right we are out to double Good Hope or the Horn. My guess is the Horn.'

Broad did not know why, but he felt afraid. It was not merely the distance. The Horn had a cold ring of mystery to its name.

'Aye, aye,' said Fulman philosophically. 'Mr Matthews may be right, but I reckon it's the West Indies after all. Why, what is there to take us round the Horn? Eh? Nothing as I knows. And the West Indies is always short of men and ships. Mark well what I say.'

Little Peter plumped for a cruise against the Barbary pirates, and the discussion went merrily up and down for a minute or two. In a lull Broad asked: 'Why the Horn, Mr Matthews?'

Matthews creased his sombre mouth until it could almost have been smiling.

'We have the gear for it, Mr Broad. We have storm gear in plenty. More trysails than I've ever seen. We have more complete suits of winter canvas to bend on than—'

There was a row going on aft, getting louder and nearer. Men were shouting, somebody was crying like a beast in pain. A howl, then a shout of laughter. Another cry. Jesse Broad knew the voice. It was the shepherd lad. He made to rise, but old Fulman motioned him down. His eyes warned him to stay clear. He knew the ship. Broad decided to wait, at least. He strained his eyes into the gloom.

Thomas Fox had already lost practically all his worldly possessions. He had lost his neckcloth, he had lost most of his money, and he had lost the new coat he had not even paid the King for.

His troubles had started when he had been led, bemused, out of the cabin. The world was a hostile, desperately frightening one. The green fields that he knew so well were now white wooden decks, hard and treacherous under his feet. There was green all round, true. But it was the sea, cold and rolling. The noise in his ears was a low musical humming, and the rattling of a thousand ropes against a hundred spars. Like the land boy he was, not the landman he was oddly rated, he did not know which way to turn. He stood on the open deck, wringing his hands. He lurched as the ship lurched, he stumbled and fell. The boatswain's mate gave him a cut with his cane – not a hard one truly, more a friendly tap – and told him to find a mess. In seeking one, Thomas made one. He kicked over a bucket and soaked a midshipman's leather shoe. For this he received a blow in the face that shocked him deeply, coming as it did from a child who could not have been above twelve years old. But he remembered another midshipman, the fair-haired midshipman of yesterday, and turned and ran.

He found a hatchway by accident, too, pitching down it with a scream. His fall was broken by a seaman coming up, who aimed another blow at Thomas's head, which missed. He stumbled farther in the strong-smelling darkness, lost and terrified. He brought up in a mess of cut-throats who grabbed at him like greedy vultures. It was there that his coat was stolen.

Running a staggering gauntlet past the breeches of the guns, Thomas felt hands and breaths assail him. He soon realised his pouch was open, and set up a screaming. A fist gripped his windpipe till he gurgled. Cruel fingers explored secret places. Once there was a rattle of money, a glint of silver. As men dived, grunting, he got away. Only to be caught at the next gun along.

Suddenly a hand seized his neck with such purpose that Thomas knew he was to die. He started to pray, while not giving up altogether without a struggle. His legs thrashed like a crazed horse's, his fists worked like flailing sticks. The hand had come from in front of him, but it went behind his neck. There was a sudden and enormous pull. He burst from the mêlée of bodies like a cork from a bottle. His knees sagged, his eyes opened. He almost smiled. Jesse Broad again.

Broad's new messmates, if they objected to Thomas Fox joining them, did not say so. He asked if the lad might stay, they nodded in silence. He was a sad sight, his clothes torn and open, his face newly bloody. Young Peter produced a piece of wet canvas and wiped away the blood and tears.

'You'll learn, young 'un,' he said tenderly. Thomas Fox could not speak. But he did not think he would stay long enough to learn. He did not think he would survive.

Jesse Broad kept his counsel, although he was filled with pain and hatred and rage. He would not stay, he knew. Cape Horn, the West Indies, the East Indies, the end of the earth, no matter; the Welfare would sail without him. Tonight he would run, let watch him who might.

Six

William Bentley watched the launch as she rounded-to under Welfare's stern and slipped smartly alongside with a loud flapping of canvas. Before the sails had been handed and the lines made fast a young officer had been piped on board and conducted rapidly into the captain's cabin. William, despite his dignity as a midshipman, was thrilled to the bottom of his soul. Not a man-jack on board as did not know what this meant. The launch was bringing orders. Welfare would soon be putting to sea.

The launch was apparently bringing other things, as he saw the boatswain gather a party of seamen to rig a tackle from the main yard. He would dearly have liked to have been below with his uncle, hearing the news fresh from the young lieutenant, but if that was not to be he could at least keep himself busy and the men up to the mark. He walked briskly to the waist, not interfering, but letting his presence be known.

'Carry on, Mr Allgood,' he said, as the boatswain acknowledged him.

'Aye aye sir. You up there!' he boomed to a man who had almost reached the yardarm. 'Look alive or I'll send one of my mates to start you!'

'What is it to be swayed up, if you please?' asked William.

The boatswain looked down at him from his great height.

'Vital necessaries for the captain,' he said. There was a note in his voice that William did not enjoy. Was the brute daring to be sardonic with him?

'Pray be more precise.'

'Well, sir, two items to come first. Puncheons of fiery spirits, sir.' His eyes flicked downwards, then away. 'Vital for the tending of the sick, sir.'

William bristled. The boatswain was an important and powerful man on board, but he was bordering on the insolent.

42

'Mr Allgood,' said William.

The boatswain smiled blandly.

'You there!' he spat to a seaman. 'Catch that whip as it comes down.'

The end of rope dropped from the yardarm barely inches from William's head. He flushed. Allgood had known it was coming, hence the order.

'Mr Allgood,' he repeated.

'Aye aye sir? Ah, the vital supplies. Oh, there be wine, tobacco, sweetmeats, silk shirts, twelve yards of Flemish lace . . .'

William's flush deepened as the slow Devon voice itemised these flimflams. He composed his face to a look of haughtiness verging on anger and bared his teeth to speak. But the boatswain, without apparently looking at him to see this reaction, changed his tack and spiked his guns neatly.

'Drugs to aid the sick and needy, new linen bandages, couple of bushels of onions for the scorbutickers, some bags of potatoes to same effect. Item, a new anvil for Mr Gunner and I believe one new spyglass, or telescope, lately manufactured for the owner by his own personal instrument maker in Lunnon. Sir.'

William decided to let the reference to Captain Swift as 'the owner' go past unchallenged. It was a normal conceit and one which his uncle enjoyed. He watched in silence as Allgood gave the orders and the first barrel was hauled into sight over the bulwarks.

'Oh,' said the boatswain, almost as an afterthought dropped over his shoulder. 'And one blind musician-man.'

He turned to his band of sailors and roared at them in his gigantic bass. He snatched a rattan from the hand of one of his mates and laid about him vigorously. The seamen hauled harder.

William fumed. The boatswain was playing with him. He obviously wanted to know more about the blind musician, but of course could not ask now. He would have to wait and see. The boatswain was deliberately trying to humiliate him, and he was the only seaman in the ship who could get away with it. He turned away and sauntered back towards the quarterdeck, every line of his body expressing lost interest in the unloading of the launch. By God, he savagely told the boatswain – inside his head – Christ help you, mister, when I'm a lieutenant. Or a captain!

43

He had not reached his favoured position for pacing, watching, brooding, on that hallowed deck when word was brought him to kindly attend on Captain Swift in the cabin. William's heart leapt and he forgot the boatswain immediately. This then would be the time for orders. He faced to windward, exultantly filling his lungs with the cold easterly air, then made a quick check on his dress, clamped his hat smartly under his arm, and clattered away after the messenger.

Had it not been for the shape, the low beams, the square windows in the stern, they might almost have been at a smart officer's apartment in town. Swift, resplendent as ever in his expensive blue, the many ruffles of his shirt glittering opulently, stood easily near his great mahogany table with a glass of fine crystal in his hand. The other officers stood or sat, depending on their whim or personal comfort. On the rare occasions that he entertained, the captain liked to make his lieutenants feel at their ease. To have required Mr Hagan to stand would not have induced such ease, on account of his great height and the lowness of the deckhead. When Mr Hagan sat, William had noted before, Plumduff liked to sit too. These men faintly annoyed him with their insistence on their small dignities. The third lieutenant, Higgins, was beneath contempt. He sat merely because he was an idle slug.

Sitting more stiffly in a chair, and far less at his ease, was the young lieutenant from the launch. He seemed slightly startled at the richness of it all – more like a cabin in a ship of the line. William was proud to serve with his uncle, and enjoyed his stylish living. This young man may be a lieutenant, although he looked barely seventeen, but he'd clearly never been in a frigate like the Welfare.

Captain Swift welcomed his nephew with a smile. At a signal, a servant moved forward with glass and decanter. William was introduced to Lieutenant Hall, shook hands and bowed, then sipped a glass of wine. They were given no time to become more intimate.

'Gentlemen,' said Daniel Swift, 'I would ask you to be seated at the table. As you know we shall shortly be about our business and I have a few words to say. Few, but important.'

At his voice everyone had risen. Hagan, unfolding like a snake, skilfully missed a beam by stooping his flaming head to one side. The men took their places round the table, Lieutenant Hall remaining where he was, and sat at a gesture from Swift. At another gesture the servants filled each man's glass, then withdrew. As they opened the door, William's eyes were arrested by the flash of scarlet of the marine guard's coat.

Captain Swift raised his glass and proposed a toast. They stood once more.

'Gentlemen,' he said gravely, 'I give you His Majesty's ship Welfare. May God keep us and save us in the work we are about to undertake.'

When they were seated, Captain Swift introduced them once more to Lieutenant Hall, and offered an explanation for his continued presence at their gathering. It would be still some time, he said, before the launch was ready to return to Portsmouth, and although what he had to say was specifically about the running of the ship, there was no reason why the visiting gentleman should not be privy to it. Lieutenant Hall expressed his honour. Of William's presence, a mere midshipman, Daniel Swift made no explanation. That was entirely a matter for him.

The captain wet his lips with his wine, carefully placed the glass on the table, and began.

'As you all know, gentlemen, we are now in a state of readiness to sail. We are fully manned, fully provisioned, and fully watered. Our ship is sound, our gear is good, and by the grace of God our people will serve.'

The cold pale eyes searched the faces in front of him. William smiled inwardly, although he kept his face like a poker. His uncle was looking for signs, he knew. Signs of disagreement at such blatant falsehoods. To describe the Welfare as fully manned, when she was under complement and had a higher scum element than most ships could stand, was a measure of the man. He was admirable, and so was his method. If the people served, he thought, it would be grace of his uncle, not any other deity.

Seeing no flicker of dissent or questioning, Swift clearly felt able to go on. There was his method revealed. He had given his officers a picture of the state of his vessel which they knew to be false, and also the theoretical opportunity to challenge it. William revelled in such tactics. They distilled the fine paradox by which the Navy was run. Officers were required by law to obey their superiors, while being also required to guard that nothing illegal or untrue was

45

done, even by those same superiors. Now the officers had assented in the fiction that the ship was well-manned. If anything were to go wrong in the future, no finger could be pointed at Swift alone. All were involved and all would therefore make sure that nothing *should* go wrong.

'I cannot, of course, tell you what our orders are,' continued Captain Swift, 'but you will all have gathered that our mission will take us to the far-flung corners of the earth. We sail, God willing and this easterly continuing to blow, before noon tomorrow. We are, of course, heading west, to clear into the Atlantic as soon as may be. Further sailing instructions will be conveyed to all of you, and the master, when necessary. Any questions?'

A mere courtesy; none was expected. The captain wetted his lips again.

'Now, gentlemen. As to the running of this vessel. You all know me and you all know my requirements. But I make no apology for restatement. I want a taut ship, and I want a hard ship. I want iron discipline and I want total and immediate obedience. I want – I require – that, from the top to the bottom. You, gentlemen, are the top.'

He stared at their faces one by one. William did not move a muscle, even when the pale eyes burned into his. Hagan, inevitably, licked his lips. Plumduff quivered almost imperceptibly. Lieutenant Hall did not receive the stare, but reddened nevertheless as Swift's gaze flickered across his face.

'You . . . gentlemen,' the captain repeated with deliberation. 'My officers are gentlemen and will behave as such at all times. Any behaviour that falls below those standards will not go unnoticed.' He turned to William. 'That particularly applies in your berth, Mr Bentley. You will carry the word for me. Any falling off in the behaviour of the *young* gentlemen will likewise not go unnoticed. Nor will it go unpunished.'

He smiled unexpectedly, one of his dazzling open smiles.

'Please drink,' he said. Everybody did, gratefully.

'As to the people,' said Daniel Swift suddenly and with a new, harsh note, 'they are, of course, the scum of the earth. They are blasted, bastard, scum.'

Lieutenant Hall, taken off guard, choked on his fine wine. There was complete silence except for his coughing. His face blazed

46

during the long pause. At last he caught his breath and mumbled apologies, which were waved away.

'The scum of Portsmouth, of Plymouth, of God knows where else. Nay, the scum of the deepest countryside ratholes, for there are damn few seamen among them. They are gutter scrapings, gentlemen, and they must serve us. In short, they must be raised from the level of animals to be fit to work this ship. We have a fine boatswain, as you know, with sturdy mates. He and they know their men and they know their orders. Rope's ends or rattan canes depending on the personal preference of each, but they have been told to start each and every tar who moves slower than his fastest. No man will walk upon this ship, no man will shamble or play the calf. Each order will be offered in a voice of brass and carried out like thunder and lightning. Mr Allgood has that clear. His mates have that clear. Let me be sure that my officers and gentlemen have it clear in their turn.'

No one moved. Swift's face was flushed, his pale eyes strangely bright. His great bony nose moved in the air like a sickle.

'As to more formal punishments,' he went on, 'they will be made full use of. Every punishment allowed by the Articles of War, and by usage, will play its part in raising our people from their present disgraceful level. Each punishment will be logged, but none will be shirked. He who transgresses shall be brought to book. He who deserves the lash shall be lashed till the bones of his back are bare and the breath shrieks in his lungs. Do I make myself clear? Are there questions? Anything?'

His voice had risen, but at the last it fell to a quiet urbanity. No man spoke, but William wished he could have proposed a toast to his uncle. The blood raced through his veins, he was enriched, renewed.

And the method! Revealed this time was why Lieutenant Hall had been asked to remain. He had heard Captain Swift's bitterness at the scum he had as crew; he had heard the determination to raise them to a degree of discipline and competence; he had heard the officers' silent assent at both diagnosis and proposed cure. If anything went wrong, if even a superhuman commander like his Uncle Daniel met with troubles too vague to be defined, there could never be any doubt but that he knew his men and he knew his officers and he had taken the only course possible with their full

47

knowledge and consent. It was masterly, and it had surely been noted.

Captain Swift stood up, as did the whole company.

'Lieutenant Hagan, I will address the people after breakfast tomorrow. Half an hour after that we sail. Pass the necessary orders if you please. And now I must beg your pardons, I have much to address myself to. Lieutenant Higgins, would you be so good as to convey Lieutenant Hall to his launch?'

He bowed briefly at the young man, who was red and rather shaken.

'A pleasure, Lieutenant,' he said. 'I wish you a pleasant sail to Portsmouth. My compliments to your uncle.'

When the others had left the cabin, William, who had remained at a sign, was invited to sit. Swift reached for the decanter and poured them each a full glass.

'Well,' he said, almost gaily. 'Looking forward to it, my boy? This time tomorrow and we will be well down Channel, God willing. To sea at last. It's been a damn long time.'

'Indeed I am, sir,' said William. 'In fact I cannot say how anxious I am to see some action, of any sort, the hotter the better. I have high hopes that once we are at sea—'

Swift raised a hand and William fell silent. His uncle turned the pale eyes full on him and stared sombrely into his.

'I will not beat about the bush, William,' he said queerly. 'I have a task to put to you. It is a secret one, perhaps a dangerous. I think you can well undertake it.'

A flush of pleasure rose in William's cheek, much against his wishes.

'We have a long voyage ahead of us, my boy, and I fear a very hard one. The people as I said are all damned scum, and the officers.' He stopped, took a mouthful of wine and swilled it around his mouth. 'Nay, enough to say this – I trust no one on this ship, my boy, except you and I. One flesh, one blood; and perhaps one brain . . .

'The captain on a ship of war, William, is in a position of great power – and great liability. I can see everything, do anything, in a manner more befitting God than a mere mortal. But in another way I am blind.'

William took his meaning. As captain, Uncle Daniel must live in isolation. Splendid, true, but almost complete.

'Therefore, my boy, hear this. I want you to be my eyes and ears. Among the people, among the young gentlemen, among the officers. You must be secret and you must trust no one. Except me. Do you understand me? Will you agree?'

William felt dizzy with pride. His voice trembled as he gave his assent. The honour was a dazzling one for a boy of fourteen. My God, if only he could tell Jack Evans and the others about this! But he couldn't, and in a way that made it even better. True trust, that – to be the captain's eyes and ears and never to be suspected.

Daniel Swift smiled at him, a queerly crooked smile.

'Thank you, my boy,' he said. 'My sister's child. I knew I could count on you.'

It was a rare moment of emotion for Uncle Daniel. William left the cabin in a glow of warmth and happiness. A pity, he reflected, that the world could not see Swift as he had seen him. Surely a misunderstood man. Strict he might be. But for the common good, only for the common good.

On deck the pile of gear unloaded from the launch was rapidly dwindling as it was transferred and stowed. One last item was being hauled on board, and it must have been an unusual one judging by the string of seamen who crowded the rail to watch.

He strained his eyes in the gathering gloom of the overcast afternoon. Slowly a small, odd-shaped object appeared above the line of heads at the ship's side. A ragged cheer went up and the seamen leaned outwards, trying to catch at something that rose steadily on the tackle.

The odd-shaped object was a bagpipe. As he gaped, an arm came into view below it, holding it on high. Below the arm, as the men on the tackle swayed up again, a pale, thin face. Then an emaciated body, wrapped in a brown cloak or blanket, clinging to the falls with its other arm.

Another cheer and the brown-clad body was seized and hauled over the bulwarks. An order from the boatswain and it dropped gently to the deck.

The blind piper put out his arms and took a step forward. The dark sockets of his eyes seemed to range over all; the deck, the masts, the men.

William Bentley shuddered.

Seven

Rumour travels fast on a ship, and in any case the visit by the launch and Lieutenant Hall, the arrival of fresh vegetables and the blind musician, left little room for doubt. They were to sail, it was obvious to the meanest intelligence. The wind was in the east and blowing fresh and steady, Captain Swift had certainly received his orders, the tension in the air could almost be smelt. On any other ship, as was the custom, they might even have been paid, to clinch the matter. With Swift, though, no man expected that.

As darkness fell many eyes were turned towards the glimmering lights of Portsmouth, that could be seen perhaps for the last time. The last time for months at the very least. The last time for years more than likely. The last time – the very last time – quite possibly. A sombre, quiet mood gripped the ship. Not one man who did not well know the city or another seaport like it. A place of warmth and liquor and friendly doxies who would ease you of ills, miseries, and money.

Not many of them had been ashore in the time that they had lain at anchor within sight. Only a few trusted men, like Bentley's recruiting party, and those discreetly guarded by armed midshipmen or officers. But the very presence of the port and all it represented had a powerful effect on their mood now that they were to lose it. At least it could still be seen, its lights at any rate. Tomorrow it would be gone. It was a bleak time.

Captain Craig, the commanding officer of the marines, had been called in for a conference with Captain Swift, and the guard on all means of escape, which had always been strong, was redoubled for the last night. Red-coated men shivered watchfully at every point. The bulwarks were patrolled regularly. Even the heads – the lavatories right in the eyes of the ship – had their guard. Swift knew his men; he was determined that none should run.

In the mess shared by Jesse Broad and Thomas Fox, the mood of

50

intense brooding prevailed. The gunports were battened down for the night and a lantern cast a flickering, stinking light. Peter, the boy, tried to strike up a conversation with Fox, but the wide, swimming eyes were sightless.

'I do believe he be drunk!' exclaimed Peter, after a while. 'Why Thomas Fox, you be drunk!'

Grandfather Fulman tutted gently.

'Leave him be, Peter lad. If he do be drunk it is surely better for him, but just try to mind the situation he finds himself in.'

Thomas did not know if he were drunk or sober. Truly the amount of beer he had consumed during the afternoon was amazing, much more than he ever drunk on shore. But his mind was racing so fast, his thoughts were so like a rat in a trap, circling, circling, searching hopelessly for a way out, that he had noticed no effect from the liquor. The biscuit he had eaten for supper, with an end of rindy cheese, had likewise gone down his throat unnoticed, despite Peter's attempts to amuse him with the small animals that could be made to 'come out and beg'.

He knew the ship was to sail tomorrow, and his world had grown inwards into his head, smaller and smaller. It was one day only since he had been pressed, but he could not grasp that. The whole of his life was crushed into the tiny, reeking space that he filled on earth. He had been born into the Welfare, born into this misery. Every time his mind stumbled accidentally onto the cottage where he lived it gave him a sharp physical pain. Occasionally a gasp or a small shriek would escape from his lips when this happened. Father, mother, Maggie and Sue. He could not think about them. He sat beside the wheel of a gun, his shoulders hunched so far forward that he found it hard to breathe, staring at the deck in front of him without seeing it. It was an agony of missing that he could not explain, could hardly endure.

The others in the mess must have recognised the signs, for apart from Peter no one tried to offer comfort or give advice. Very few words were spoken, in fact. Grandfather Fulman sucked at his empty pipe, another old shellback called Samuel whittled away at the deformed skin on the end of his thumb with a knife. Matthews, the lantern-jawed merchant sailorman, kept his usual place nearest the port. His eyes were closed, his lips were sealed, his thoughts were secret.

51

Jesse Broad looked at Thomas Fox a lot. He felt desperately sorry for the shepherd boy, and toyed with the idea of taking him with him. But he knew it was crazy. The boy could not swim, for a certainty, despite having been born and raised on the coast. In fact, Broad knew, it was unlikely that half a dozen of the whole ship's company could stay afloat unaided for more than five seconds. Strange fellows, seamen. Maybe they thought it better to drown quickly if they had to than kick about in hope and anguish for hours before sinking just the same.

But Jesse Broad could swim. Ever since a lad he had treated the green waters as his second home. Even Mary could swim, rare indeed for a woman. In years gone by they had swum together, secretly, in the wooded creeks round Langstone. The pleasure of the sport made a thousandfold better by the fear of being caught.

He had a grinding pain of loss run through his belly then. He thought of the christening day. Today, only today! To Broad, too, it was as though he had been years in the Navy. He shook the pain away with a grunt. Why the feeling of loss, when tonight Mary would be in his arms again? And Jem, his tiny boy.

Well, not tonight, but soon. Tonight, with the easterly driving the waves straight onto the Isle of Wight, he would make Priory Bay. An hour or less to walk round the coast to Bembridge, and James Sweet would hide him readily enough. The Welfare would make sail tomorrow – no single deserter would hold her up – he would lie low for a day or two in case Swift got word ashore to the preventive men or the Navy to try and flush him out – then heigh ho back to Portsmouth.

He thought about Swift for a while. What had he said about desertions? Two men had tried and two men had died. That was clearly why he had anchored at St Helen's. There were many ships much farther in towards Portsmouth, in Spithead. But out here the chances of getting ashore were far remoter. The rocks off St Helen's were very dangerous and the tidal currents powerful and treacherous. Broad, thanks to the contraband trade, knew those currents and tidal movements like the back of his hand. With the breeze to help and the set of the waves, he was pretty sure he could make it.

There was a muffled sob and a grey movement as Thomas Fox stood up. He stumbled away from his messmates towards the pens

52

where the beasts were kept. Jesse Broad shook his head. The desperate thin boy; he had never seen so much misery in a human being. And only a child.

What if he found a spar? A barrel, or a plank, to hold them both afloat? Madness. Out of the question. If he was to see Mary again, and his child, he must think of no one but himself. In any case . . . He remembered Hardman, his dear friend Hardman. He would have liked to have revenged him, for the sake of old times and dear times. Dull anger stirred. Where was his body? Where was the wherry? Oh God, he must get to Portsmouth and home before the wherry was found to terrify Mary.

Jesse Broad stood slowly until his head pressed against the rough underside of a deck beam. The pale round of a face followed him. It was Grandfather Fulman.

'Where are you going to, friend Jesse?'

Broad stared at the old man. The face was open, and kind, and strangely sad. It occurred to the younger man that this old salt probably had had a Mary once. A wife, sons, daughters. Was probably wrenched away, to never see them again. He almost spoke his mind. But stopped.

'Heads,' he muttered.

Grandfather Fulman gazed for a long time.

'If you are seen you'll be shot, or flogged, or put in irons,' he said softly.

'For going to the heads?' Broad whispered stubbornly.

'If you like to say so,' answered Fulman. 'You are an animal now, friend Jesse. You have no right to even breathe if someone decides you should not.'

There was a pause. The others in the mess seemed to be unaware of the conversation.

The old man went on: 'Go very gentle, friend Jesse. There's marines on this ship would kill a seaman for sport. The boatswain's mates are murderers to a man, and Captain Swift, they say, is first cousin to the devil. Avoid all lighted parts, remember that there's dark and shadows round the main chains, and if you gets in the water, think on this . . .'

Broad listened, tense, unsmiling.

'Keep your feet, what's white, under the waves, and keep your face, what shines, covered in your jacket, what's dark. That is, don't

53

leave your jacket, although heavy, on account it'll keep you secret. Drop him when you're clear. If they puts a boat out for you, swim across wind and waves for a while. You'll be safe.'

Jesse Broad said nothing still.

'By the by, friend Jesse,' said old Fulman. 'Can you swim?'

'Don't need to swim, grandfather,' Broad replied. 'I am only going to the heads.'

The whispered conversation was over. Jesse Broad set off across the dark and silent deck like a cat, straining every nerve and muscle to see and hear. It was a strange world, of curved hammocks, snores, odd points of flickering light and crouched men. There was a ghostly silence over all, which was in fact no silence at all, more a threatening calm. There was a constant low groaning from the ship, a desolate sighing of wind, a mournful grinding of the main cable. Every so often there was a splashing slap as a sea broke against the side and rose up for a moment before subsiding. Then the shuffling of beasts from the pen, and from among them a thin piping wail, mysterious and horrible, which he knew to be the suffering boy.

For minutes he stood below a hatchway, tense as a bowstring. It was night, but the blackness of the sky, starless and thick with low cloud, was as light compared with the blackness between decks. Strain as he might, he could make out no figures. Were there marine guards waiting in the darkness? If there were they were immobile as statues. He could not wait for ever, either. If he stayed too long he might lose his resolve, or be spotted, or even, God forbid, be called to duty; he had little idea of the system on the ship. Perhaps boatswain's mates or master-at-arms would be along checking on those below, or dowsing glims. He must go.

Broad raised his head through the hatchway in trembling degrees. He blessed his dark skin, and kept his eyes hooded as far as possible so as not to reflect any light they might catch. It was almost two minutes before his eyes were fully on a level with the deck. The wind, which was a low moan below, swept briskly now, blustering and gusty. Loud creaks of spar and cordage. When his eyes had grown used to the different light he cautiously looked all round.

At first he could see no one – marine, officer or seaman. But as he stared at objects they sometimes moved, startlingly, and became people. Mostly they were downwind of fixed points, getting what warmth they could from the shelter. The decks looked terribly bare. Great open spaces stretched ahead and astern, and to both sides of him. If he attempted to reach the bulwarks discovery would be inevitable. Strange that earlier the space had seemed so cluttered, so jammed with gear.

But as he watched and racked his brains, the problem became slightly less daunting. His heart slowed as he considered, the fear crowded out of his mind.

About six feet from him was a set of bitts, surrounded by a fair mass of coiled rope. It was bulky and dark, with angular shapes that could easily conceal a man. And perhaps did? Broad bit his lip. And perhaps did. Then a little beyond the bitts was a jumble of long blacknesses which he guessed must be spare spars. There were thick things, almost tree-trunks, that could be made into new masts if need be. A lot of smaller wood for yards and booms. Sitting just beyond this pile, the ship's boats on their skids. The jolly boat, judging by her length, was on the outer side.

If he could once make the curved bilge of the jolly boat, Broad figured, he could lie in its shade not six feet from the ship's side. What had Fulman said? It was dark at the chains. Well, true; but maybe the marines would have thought of that too, and posted a sentry there. At any rate, the jolly boat was stowed very near the middle of the ship, where the side was not desperately high, and there were the spare spars and other wood. Perhaps he could get a piece overboard with him, to act as a raft or float. It would be a great help that. It might save him. Jesse Broad reckoned he could be in the sea for up to two hours. The cold autumn sea. It would be a help if he could keep his woollen jacket on, but that would be heavy. A spar would make it possible.

As he stared at the bitts, part of them suddenly moved, broke away and turned into a marine. He very nearly plunged back down the hatchway in surprise. He had to struggle to keep his breath quiet. He had been within an ace of crawling straight into the soldier's arms. As he hung there, a feeling of hopelessness swept over him. What if every shadow . . . ?

The dark figure stretched upright and walked round the bitts and away. Without being aware of making a decision Broad moved. He might be observed but that was that. The marine had been at the bitts and would return no doubt. But for the moment he was not there. With a low grunt Broad hauled himself onto the white deck, incredibly exposed, then made a stooping run to the shadow of the bitts. It was the work of perhaps a second, but when he arrived the blood was hammering in his ears and eyes and he was sweating. He tried to control his lungs, which were forcing his breath in and out in juddering gasps. In one of the silences between breaths, he heard the measured tread of booted feet. The marine was returning.

Down below, in the foetid darkness of the animal pen, Thomas Fox lay like one dead. He had wedged himself between three of the sheep he had brought onto the ship the day before. He knew them somehow, by smell, or feel, or familiarity, and they behaved towards him as if they knew him too. He buried his face in the warm, reeking wool, bathing it with his tears, smothering his sobs in the soft pulsing flanks. Although he still could not let his mind dwell on his lost home, it was oddly as if he was back there. The warmth of the sheep-pen by the cottage. The years with these and other animals. His mind wandered, drifted, as though he was dying, or was perhaps already dead.

He allowed a hazy picture of the north-eastern part of Portsea Island to swim in his mind. It was flat, and marshy, and misty, and very blurred. There was a long line of trees in view, that were about a mile from where he lived. His mind's eye moved towards the line of trees, the natural windbreak. But he did not part them, did not go beyond.

Thomas was making a noise, a thin, keening noise, but he did not know it. He was making a high-pitched humming that served to drive certain thoughts from his head. It was so high he could not think. Except vague thoughts; of flat green marshy lands, a line of trees. And death.

He was thinking of death when Peter found him.

The red-haired boy reached the edge of the pens, drawn by the steady, monotonous, high-pitched whine. He pushed and burrowed his way through the animals, looking for the source. When he found Thomas he lay down beside him and put his hand on his cheek. Thomas kept his eyes closed. His mouth was also closed. The high whine came from in his throat.

After stroking his cheek for a while, Peter began to talk. He talked a lot, and fast, but Thomas did not listen. It flowed over him in a tide, gentle, insistent, meaningless. Peter stroked, Thomas whined, the animals moaned and slept. At last Peter moved his hand to Thomas Fox's eyes. He gently took an eyelid and pulled it open.

'Jesse Broad has run,' he said.

He said it simply, not loud, but it cut into Thomas's brain like a knife. His mouth fell open, the strange noise stopped. His eyes, pale and tear-drowned, cleared and focused.

'Jesse Broad?'

'Has run. Has flown. He's gone over the side, has swum to glory or beyond.'

Peter smiled his simple smile. Thomas Fox sat up, gazing into the round, happy face.

'Jesse Broad?' he said again.

'The bird has flown,' said Peter gaily. 'He'll drown, of course!'

'He must take me too,' said Thomas. He stood up. He knocked his head against a deck beam, hard, and staggered. 'He must take me with him.'

'No, no!' laughed Peter softly. 'How can that be? You must stay with me, Thomas Fox, and be my friend! This is a nice ship this is.'

He put out his hand and touched Thomas. But Thomas was bemused.

'I must go,' he said.

Peter looked frightened now.

'No, no, Thomas,' he said imploringly. 'Do not you go too! This is a nice ship this is. Do not you go. You'm drunk is all!'

Indeed, as Thomas ran he might well have been. He banged his head on deck beams, he ran into the yielding shapes of hammocked men, he bruised his toes and barked his shins on ringbolts, stanchions, gun-trucks. He was making a new noise now, a hoarse grunting moan. He was crying aloud his longing to be free.

As the marine reached the forward side of the bitts on deck, Jesse Broad, with a daring born of naked desperation, left the after side. He stooped and tried to move silently, but this was merely done by reflex. If the marine had been looking he must have seen him. A split-second later Broad was full-length among the rough logs and half-shaped spars stowed on the deck. His breath was rasping,

57

sweat blinded him, his limbs were shaking. But he had not been spotted.

There was no time, no purpose anyway, in drawing out each move over a long period. The quicker he got over the side the better. Any shadow on the whole length and breadth of the ship could be a man, every move he made, however cautious, could be seen by bad luck. The marine had failed to spot him by good luck; so let him trust in his star and move.

Broad abandoned the idea of trying to free a log or spar to act as a float. His every nerve screamed to be in the water, to be off the ship. Fast, but still with deadly care, he wormed under the jolly boat, cleared the other side, and gathered his courage for the last few feet of exposed deck.

In a moment when the night's blackness grew magically even blacker, when the noise of the wind and the waves slapping at the frigate's sides reached a sudden crescendo, Jesse Broad rose to his feet, paced evenly across the deck, climbed nimbly over the bulwarks, and dropped neatly into the dark waters of St Helen's Roads.

It was cold, but he had expected that. It was bone-achingly cold, but he had been ready for that. He fought and fought the chest-crushing cold, until he could fill his lungs and think. No shout, no alarm. Filled with an elation, a sense of crazy disbelief, Broad began to pull himself along the side of the frigate, grabbing at the fronds of weed. The waves picked him up and bounced him down, the barnacles and limpets sticking to her belly threatened to tear his flesh. But he wanted to stay in close, to get the shadow, the protection of that dense blackness, as the waves pushed him rapidly towards the stern. Beyond which, in the freezing dark, lay the Isle of Wight.

His exultation was short-lived. Even in the crashing water he heard the banshee wail. As he stared up the ship's steep side, he saw a grey flash, like a dark comet, fly over his head. It was a screaming comet, and it was screaming his name.

When the scream was extinguished in a mighty splash, Jesse Broad did not hesitate.

It was fifteen minutes before the quarter boat picked them up, and by that time Thomas Fox was almost dead.

Eight

Next morning the wind had hauled round so that it blew almost due east. It had strengthened considerably, with tearing low cloud and biting cold. Flurries of rain occasionally tore into the ship. Below decks the fug was already being replaced by a damp chill, mainly from the solid blasts of air that howled through the hawse pipes, sometimes accompanied with gushes of icy water when a bigger sea smashed against the frigate's snubby bow.

William Bentley, taking breakfast tea with his uncle as had become their custom, was exultant. The weather could not be better, nor from a better quarter. They would fly down-Channel like a charging army. Daniel Swift appeared to share his high good humour.

'This wind is excellent, my boy. We shall bear all plain sail and go south-about round the island, of course. By this evening we shall have shaken off the sloth that grips the people for good and all.'

'Will you address them now or when we are cleared away?' asked William. It would be a pity, he thought, to waste even half an hour of this perfect wind. Captain Swift regarded him with his pale, bleak eyes.

'We will sail after punishment,' he said shortly.

William was surprised. Punishment usually took place just before noon.

'But uncle. In four hours with this breeze . . .'

Swift waved his hand to silence the midshipman.

'Punishment will, of course, be brought forward. It is irregular – good. I wish to instil in this rabble a decent sense of the uncertainty of their lives and deaths under my command. They must learn to obey and they must learn that retribution will follow with lightning inevitability. They are used to punishment in the late forenoon. Today they will finish their breakfasts to it.'

Half an hour later all hands were assembled to witness the flogging of Jesse Broad. The red-coated marines stood grim-faced and ready. The master-at-arms had a naked sword in his hand, dripping a mournful dew of cold rain from its ornamental guard. Captain Swift, his officers and young gentlemen, with Captain Craig of the marines, were wrapped in great cloaks, like so many damp vultures. Over all was the sound of the wind, raw and lean, with a deeper musical hum from the rigging.

Jesse Broad stood facing forward while the preparations were made. He wore the clothes he had lain in all night, still wet when he was brought on deck, now soaked. Among the sea of faces in front of him he read many things. Mostly they wore a sort of closed, unmoving look, which was always the safest to assume. Some flashes of pity; many downcast eyes. Some, he knew, were prepared to enjoy his ordeal. He made a strange figure, short and powerful, with dark, secret face and badly cropped and shaven head. He saw smirks of pleasure on a few faces, and these faces he stared at, unblinking. There were many shaved heads there, though none so recent as his own. Men from the receiving hulks moored up-harbour, towards Fareham and Portchester. He studied the company and drew little comfort from them. Old age, degradation, imbecility; all were represented.

The flogging was to take place at the gangway, and a high grating had been lashed there. To this, at an order, Jesse Broad was triced by the wrists and knees. But first his gaily striped shirt was pulled from off his back. It was bitterly cold. His nose began to run. The wind cut deep, he thought sombrely; how would the lash compare?

Captain Swift was in no great hurry. As he had explained to William, a punishment is very little more than wasted effort if it does not achieve a greater purpose than merely crippling a seaman. This one had fallen at an opportune moment. Its timing was almost theatrical. It would give the people a taste of the man and his method, and the lesson would be etched in blood. William had listened and learned. It would never have occurred to him that Broad's attempt at running and the need to flog him for it were anything other than an inconvenience. When his uncle started addressing the people he cleared his mind of all else, determined to go on learning.

'My lads,' said Swift, in an easy, effortless voice that managed, however, to cut through all the many noises and be heard by every man on deck. 'This is a solemn and glorious moment. For me, your captain, for your officers, and for each and every one of you, from the highest warrant to the humblest boy.'

William watched the seamen's faces. They looked confused, shifty. As well they might, for his uncle's words were peculiar enough, truly.

'Yesterday, brave boys, we received our orders. And today we sail. We sail for a far country and for hot work. For each and every man, I say, it is a glorious time.'

The pale eyes glared out over the silent company. William wondered vaguely if he ought to lead a cheer. But those dripping, frozen wretches appeared incapable of taking it up.

'For aeons,' Swift went on, 'we have lain in these damned uncomfortable roads and you have had no opportunity for that exercise which is so necessary to all loyal British tars – seeking, finding and destroying the enemy, Johnny Crapoh. Now my lads, the hunting will commence.'

This time a ragged noise did go up. But not a cheer, by no means a cheer. William sensed the tips of his ears grow pink. Swift went on regardless, in his vibrant, penetrating voice.

'Prize-money too, my lads, prize-money in plenty. You know my luck, you know my reputation. Remember the Bonaventure, remember the Dona Maria, remember the Maitre. Prizes, boys, prizes for the picking.'

The men were warming to him, William thought. The cold grey faces had lightened. And it was true that his uncle had made some notable captures. But how degrading, that this rabble could respond to one thing and one thing only – the thought of plunder.

When he next spoke, Captain Swift had changed his tone.

'A glorious moment for all, I said, lads. But I was wrong. For two of the ship's company, today is a day of villainy, ignominy and retribution. Before you you see one of the shaved-head scum. The other is skulking below.'

A confused sound. Jesse Broad, his teeth chattering, attempted a smile. God help them, he thought, they don't know what to think; whether to be on my side or his.

'This villain, as no doubt you all know, tried to run last night. His

61

chances of survival, had he got clear of the ship, were nil. But as you are all aware, to get clear of this ship is impossible. He was back on board, humbled in the eyes of man and God, within minutes. Now he will be humbled in the eyes of his shipmates.'

Another confused noise. A kind of grumble, perhaps of sympathy, mixed with a few jeers. Broad was too cold to care. He stared out over the tumbling grey seas.

'There is one circumstance that saves this villain from a more proper punishment than a summary whipping,' said Swift. 'And it is this. While in the water, and probably quite by accident, this man saved a miserable youth bent on a far more dastardly act than even the act of desertion from one of His Majesty's ships. That youth was bent on committing the vile and detestable sin of self-destruction. He was prevented, and now lies in the sick-bay close to the death which Providence denied him. When he recovers, lads, rest assured that a suitable punishment will be wrought upon him. Let no man think he can escape the wrath of God. Or of Daniel Swift.'

This blasphemy produced the expected laugh. The captain raised his hand.

'Because of the fortunate, if accidental, circumstance of saving the worthless life of this puling youth, the man you see before you will receive only two dozen. Let not my lenience on this occasion lull you into the dream that all may expect such softness. Witness this punishment, my friends, and think upon it.' He turned slightly. 'Mr Allgood, will you be so good as to direct your men to lay them on? And Mr Allgood,' he added in a voice of chilling penetration. 'If they do not lay on with all their might and main, I would point out that others might like to do so on their own backs.'

Just before Jesse Broad received the first lash, a strange thing happened. A gap in the torn grey cloud appeared and the sun burst through. It was an autumn sun, and the wind remained icy, but it was a hot sun. Within seconds, almost, the decks and all upon them began to steam. A brilliant shaft of light struck Eastney beach. Jesse Broad thought of home.

He rested his cheek against the hard grating and watched the dancing waters of the Solent. Beyond that shingle beach, clean and bright now, with creaming foam breaking ceaselessly along it, lay the creeks, the woods, the hamlet where he had lived out his life. It was a community quite distinct from the life of Portsmouth, although only a few miles distant. They were a tightly knit, self-contained people whose life revolved round the mudflats, marshes, secret creeks and savage tides of Langstone Harbour. They considered themselves a people apart – protected by the difficult waters on one side, and the wild and marshy hinterland on the other.

He stared at the beach, waiting for the first lash, with a great hollow sense of loss growing in his stomach. Only yesterday he was to have attended the christening service at the tiny old church with his wife. He thought of her in something like despair. They had been friends, lovers, for years. Now she was a lifetime away. Six or seven miles, and a lifetime.

'Right then, my boys!' boomed the boatswain. 'You will start, Jefferies, and lay it on hard. Silence among the hands there!'

William watched fascinated as Jefferies, a loose-limbed, shambling man with protruding teeth, left the knot of boatswain's mates. He had seen many floggings, but the sight of the long cat, with its red baize handle and its strangely evil thongs, lumpy and wicked, always made his mouth go dry and his stomach flutter. The boatswain's mate stood a moment, judging his distance, feeling the weight of the cat, getting the balance right. Steam rose in clouds as his hair and shoulders dried. His legs, from the knees downwards, disappeared into the vapour that rose from the deck, as though he were a ghost in a marsh. The whole ship's company, silent, tense, dwindled into the same mist. Only Broad was clear of it, lashed tightly to the vertical grating, shadowed by the main rigging.

Knowing that the first blow was about to fall, Broad relaxed the muscles in his back as far as he could. He made sure his teeth were clear of his tongue, and moved his head a little way off the grating, to avoid banging it. Suddenly he thought of his 'protection', and almost smiled. Ah well, he had to think of something while the punishment took place. He began to concentrate.

The boatswain's mate, grinning with the effort, swung the cat from far behind him in a low, howling arc. It ended in a solid bang, and a gasp from many mouths. William Bentley, biting his own lip, studied the motionless form of Jesse Broad. What he could see of the brown, handsome face was paling visibly before his eyes. It was as though someone was letting the blood flow out

63

of his body. Bentley flicked his eyes to the man's back. Not yet, at any rate. There was a broad red swathe across the white, interspersed with livid patches, but the skin was unbroken.

Jesse Broad opened his eyes and looked at the beach again. The pain had surprised him, but he was not too worried by it. He was strong, and young, and extremely healthy. Two dozen lashes, at this rate, would do him no great damage.

'Mr Allgood,' said Captain Swift, in a queer nasal voice of great menace. 'That man is trifling with me. Do you hear, sir!'

Allgood, the glowering bull, walked up to his mate. He was head and shoulders over him, his huge belly thrusting forward. His eyes glowed.

'Jefferies, you scum,' he spat. 'I told you to lay it on there. Now jump to it!'

A dew of sweat burst out on Jefferies's brow. Depending on Swift's whim he might have the whole two dozen to administer, or maybe as few as six. But each must be delivered with the whole of his strength. His face was impassive as he drew back his arm once more. Just before he took his swing Swift spoke again.

'Let him draw blood with this stroke if you please, Mr Allgood.'

'Aye aye sir.'

The mate's face contorted with effort as he moved his shoulders and trunk round with all his power. The howl as the thongs parted the air was higher and louder. The slapping bang as they bit home was like an axe striking into thick timber. This time there was no gasp from the company.

Jefferies jerked the cat savagely to free the thongs that had stuck to Jesse Broad's back. Three bright strings of blood appeared. They grew rounder, glossier, then trickled like tears towards his belt.

'You have just saved yourself a flogging,' said Swift drily.

After sixteen more lashes the blood had reached the deck and a third boatswain's mate was weakening. At a signal from the boatswain he was relieved by a fourth, who carefully cleared the nine thongs, one at a time, of the thick blood and conglomerated skin and flesh that clogged them. Broad's back was a strange sight now, what could be seen of it through the moving mask of blood. Black at the edges, from blossoming bruises, still streaked in white where the lash had not yet bitten, purple and violet in other parts. Bentley stared at it, fascinated. This man had never been flogged

64

before, he knew. But still, his flesh had flayed far more readily than most. It was perhaps a good job that he was to receive only another half-dozen. For the real reason his punishment was so small, of course, was not because he had saved Fox, but because he was too useful a seaman to be laid up for long. At this rate, he would soon be crippled.

Broad saw Eastney beach only hazily now, through a mist of blood and pain. Somehow, without him knowing it, his lower lip had crept between his teeth and he had bitten it almost through. His eye was cut from the knocking it received against the grating as each lash struck home. It was a lot worse than he had expected. But he tried still to think of other things. Only six more strokes at any rate. He knew of men who had survived three hundred.

Yes, your protection, he thought, as though he was someone else, someone outside his battered, aching body. Well, it served you well enough for a long time. One cannot argue with Fate. And who knows, it might yet serve again.

Broad's protection, like that of so many of his fellows in the hamlets where they lived, was an ironic one. Not just that their skills and knowledge of the secret, dangerous waters more than matched the best endeavours of preventive men, but, in a subtler way, their very trade itself. The country needed—

But the nineteenth lash must have struck a nerve. He felt a pain so excruciating that he thought he could not stand it. His toes smashed into the grating, slippery with blood. His knees twitched and jerked, the flesh splitting against the thin twine that seized him in position. Through the roaring in his head he heard Swift's voice, blurred but penetrating, a clogged saw-blade.

'Good man, Jenkins! That, Mr Allgood, is an example to the lubberly swine you have so far chosen as mates.'

Before this new, sharper pain had died, another replaced it. His bones were being flayed. Tears washed the sweat from his eyes, the foam from his lips. Broad tried hard, so hard, to concentrate his mind once more.

But he could not think clearly. Vague images of brandy-barrels and nights at sea mingled with the next blows and surges of agony. Ah, that was it – the country needed brandy. Yes that was it. Strange as it may seem, when there was a war on, the country needed brandy. He and his fellows, he and his friends, were not expected to answer to anyone. They were the men of Langstone, wild and lawless. Lawless and tough. Protected by people in high places. Because people in high places needed brandy.

Immediately after the twenty-third lash, while the brawny arm of the last boatswain's mate was being drawn round and back, William Bentley saw the livid face of the tortured man move. He watched in fascination as the white lips drew back to reveal the red teeth, stained in blood. There was no doubt of it. Jesse Broad was smiling.

Nine

A few minutes later, the punishment was over. As Broad was cast off from the grating the surgeon stepped forward and gently laid a vinegar-soaked cloth across his back. He shrugged groggily, refusing the help offered to keep him on his feet. He stared for a moment straight into William Bentley's face, but his eyes were not quite focused. Bentley's mouth was dry once more as the bleeding body was ushered below. He looked at his uncle and noted with horror that his face was flecked with blood. Bentley raised a hand to his own. He felt sick. Traces of red slime slid from his cheek to his fingers.

Captain Swift turned to the master.

'Mister Robinson,' he said crisply. 'I want all plain sail and away in the shortest time possible.'

'Aye aye sir.'

To the boatswain Swift said: 'Let your mates set men to clear away this mess, and get the rest stood by.'

'Aye aye sir.'

Within seconds, calls were shrilling, orders were being bellowed, men were running frantically about under whistling blows from rope's-end and rattan. Swift turned to Bentley.

'A most satisfactory beginning, my boy,' he said. 'But my word, did not that blackguard's skin peel easy? We must pray he is not too sorely hit, for he looks a seaman born. Nevertheless, it was a useful thing; discipline may well benefit from such a gory display.'

'There is blood upon your cheek, sir,' said William Bentley.

His uncle laughed heartily.

'And on your own. Come boy, below for a stiffener while all is made ready.'

When word was brought from the master that the capstan was manned, Swift seemed strangely animated.

'Aha,' he said. 'Now here will be a thing to shake the people,

67

William. It is known we have a blind man? Yes. But not a man like this, I'll warrant me.'

On deck the ship had taken on a different air. The capstan bars had been shipped and at each stood tense crews of bare-foot seamen. Some yards were manned and gaggles of waisters waited in readiness. The master stood near the wheel like a lord, as lord he was over the sailing of the frigate, Swift not being a captain who took a great personal interest in what he saw as the mundane side of naval life.

Captain Swift took his place of honour, barely acknowledging the salutes of the lieutenants and midshipmen awaiting him. The boatswain stood expectantly at the after hatchway. He was certainly in on the secret, William could see. Jack Evans made a face at him, as much as to ask 'What goes on?' But William, who did not know, pretended not to notice his friend.

Swift turned from contemplating the sea at last, with a wintry smile.

'My lads,' he said, in the penetrating voice that carried so far, 'when the anchor is weighed and secured, when we are under way, you'll get a double go of grog. How does that strike you?'

It struck them well. This time they were prepared to cheer, the cheer was deafening. Swift raised his hand.

'But before that, my brave boys, I have another thing to please you. I may be a hard man, indeed I am a hard man, and you will do well not to forget it. But I also know what gives pleasure to a tar, and will try to do all in my power to bring it about. Mr Allgood, if you please. Give the word.'

There was a low murmur of expectation. The boatswain growled, but the murmur went on. Seconds later it grew to a positive ripple of sound. Allgood let out a snarl of warning. The babble died away.

All eyes were turned aft. At first William could not see what was happening. He noted his uncle's smile, grim but satisfied. Then he saw the dark musician, one hand held in front of him, the other clutching the bagpipe to his left side, being guided gently forward. He was as thin as a bird, in a strange, long-tailed coat such as no seaman would wear. His shoulders were stooped, his hair long and lank. Beneath the ragged ends of his trousers protruded legs like stripped twigs, feet like pale bunches of bone.

When he reached the capstan he was placed between two of the bars, then turned by the boatswain's mate to face aft. The mate then put his hands beneath the blind man's arms and lifted him with no trace of effort. He sat on the drumhead confused for a moment, then drew his tiny limbs beneath him cross-legged and settled the bagpipes athwart his body.

No man moved. There was no human sound. The piper raised his head and looked aft with the empty sockets of his eyes. They seemed to fasten themselves on the face of William Bentley. He stared in horror at the folded holes. The boatswain turned aft, noted Captain Swift's signal, turned forward.

'Strike up, piper,' he cried. 'And now, my boys – stamp and go!'

As the men drove their chests against the bars and heaved, the eerie noise of the pipes filled the air. First a drone, low and swelling, then a rhythm, slow but getting faster. The music of the pipes, as if by magic, matched the strain and movement of the seamen. It started as a formless growl, an insistent, grunting note to move the bodies as they tried to move the bars to move the capstan. Then a kind of beat, to match the tramping feet as they ground against the deck, scrabbling for a purchase. Then, almost imperceptible, a melody.

It was not a known melody, not a tune any man among them could put a name to. It was slow, and sad, and achingly Irish. It merged into the wind, soared above the whining of the rigging, swallowed up the gasping grunts of the straining men.

As William Bentley looked into the white, emaciated face, it slowly moved away. The empty sockets slid past his shoulder, then the side of the piper's head came into view. This turned, until he saw the lank hair hanging free, unpigtailed, down the skinny back. Then the other side of the head, the line of the jaw, and at last the eyeless eyes. The boatswain's mighty bellow broke the spell.

'One turn, brave boys! Stamp and go!'

For what seemed an age William Bentley stood transfixed as the dark musician revolved in front of him. As the capstan turned faster, so the man on the drumhead turned faster. As if taking his rhythm from this, and the tramping of the sailor's feet, perhaps even their grunting, he piped faster. The mournful, unknown melody became gayer as the great cable began to groan on board fathom by fathom, dripping weed and water from the green depths.

At one stage William was sent below with the other midshipmen to get an idea of how the enormous length of rope was stowed. He returned to the quarterdeck almost reluctantly, distaste and fascination fighting in his breast. The clanking of the pawls had got quicker and quicker. The Welfare snubbed uneasily as she was hauled into wind and sea. And in front of him the strange figure turned on the drumhead.

At last he turned to the captain.

'Where did you get him, uncle?' he asked. 'He is the oddest musician I have ever seen.'

'A fine one, for all that,' replied Swift. 'I was a little uncertain, he was so ragged and sickly. But he makes those lubbers on the bars act almost like seamen.'

It was true. 'Stamp and go' was the boatswain's cry, and the men were at it with a vengeance. Already the cable was growing almost 'a short stay'.

Daniel Swift still did not answer William's question. He glanced at him queerly and said: 'He is mute, you know. Strange, is it not?'

A cry from the foredeck: 'Aft there! Aft there! Cable up and down!'

Within seconds the things had happened that William Bentley still found too mysterious to fully grasp. In his year on board he had had little time at sea, and constant sail drill for the people had left him more confused than competent. But in those seconds the frigate was transformed from a ship at anchor, still and sulky in the passing waves, to a blossoming, vibrating, living thing. As the shouts came from the foredeck – first 'Heaving away', then 'Heaving in sight', at last 'Clear anchor!' – the Welfare, in response to other shouts, grew wings. Teams of men hauled on ropes. Tacks and braces were manned. The headsails clapped like thunder, then quieted, aback, as the ship paid off. Another thunderous roar as they were sheeted to leeward, more orders. And suddenly, to William miraculously, they were under way. With helm up, the ship turned majestically on her heel, farther and farther round until the wind was on her larboard quarter. Not many minutes later all plain sail was set and drawing to the master's satisfaction. The piper had disappeared, the best bower was being stowed, the capstan unrigged by the carpenter and his crew. They were off!

* * *

On the deck below, in the small dark area that served as sick-bay when the Welfare was not at battle stations, Thomas Fox and Jesse Broad sensed, in their different ways, that the voyage had started. Thomas, who had been lying semi-conscious and half-delirious since he had tried to kill himself, was awoken by the many noises of the anchor being weighed. He did not know the noises, but he guessed what they meant. There was the grinding of the capstan spindle in its bearing, the rumbling of the great cable moving slowly along the deck, and vaguer sounds, like distant thunder, as the ship shook off her idleness and felt new strains of wind and sea. His senses were still too dull for him to care that the Welfare was finally moving; that in an hour's time perhaps, or less, the Hampshire coast would be behind the Isle of Wight, to be seen again by him God knew when.

Broad too knew the meaning of the activity by sense and feel rather than by thought. He lay face downwards on the deck with his mind full of physical pain. Time would come later to accept the loss. For the moment his shattered back was enough.

The surgeon, Mr Adamson, swam in and out of his vision. He was a very small man, with bright, bird-like eyes. He knelt over Broad, speaking to him rather as Mary spoke to their child. The words had little meaning, were hardly audible. The voice was soft, cooing. It lulled him as he lay, took the sting out of the dabbing fingers that investigated his back, probing and gently swabbing with cotton and searing vinegar.

After a few minutes Broad attempted a few words.

'Always,' he said. 'From a boy, just a little boy. Soft skin, my mother said, like a maid.'

The surgeon ceased his cooing; dipped his head so that he could see Broad's face. He put on a puzzled look.

'What are you talking about, man?' he said. 'Are you mad? You look like no maid I have ever seen!'

Dab dab went the vinegary cloths. Broad's back ached horribly. He felt apologetic, as if he were causing the surgeon trouble. He felt he ought to get the explanation finished, at whatever cost.

'No, sir,' he said. 'The flesh. Always, even as a boy, sir. I cut easy. A tap, a knock. Bled like a stuck pig, sir.'

Mr Adamson snorted.

'Good God, man, no need to sound so damned humble about it.

71

No shame attached. Why – ' he snorted again, with more of a laugh in it – 'some of the fellows on board here will take the skin off the cat-of-nine-tails! Backs like hide, heads as dense as blue clay. No benefit to man or beast in not feeling pain!'

'Not pain, sir,' Broad grunted. 'Pain no trouble. But cut easy. Cut and bruise. Since a boy.'

'If the pain's no trouble,' Mr Adamson said testily, 'I'm wasting my time, for I'm doing my best to ease it. If you do not feel pain, mister, then you are a damned fool and deserve to die.'

Dab dab dab. Broad said nothing. The vinegar hurt, but soothed too. He explored his bitten lip with his tongue. It stung. A good sign. His back must be recoverable if he could feel a little thing like that.

'Good flesh to heal, sir,' he said, with difficulty. 'Always cut easy, but a quick healer.'

'Oh shut up, man,' said Mr Adamson. 'There is no need to make conversation here.'

'Aye aye sir. It is only—'

'Listen, fellow,' the surgeon said suddenly, as if on a new tack altogether. 'I'll strike a bargain with you. You'll keep your mouth shut for the sake of my tired old brain – and I'll get you a glass of brandy!'

Broad blinked. He could not have heard right. But what to say now? The problem solved itself. The little man with the bright eyes ducked quickly away. Broad lay on his front listening. He heard seas slapping the ship's sides rhythmically. He heard the groans of working timber. He heard the vaguely rasping breath of poor Thomas Fox.

The bird-like form of the surgeon bobbed back into view. A chink, a gurgle, then the impatient, acid, voice: 'Here, man. I suppose you know a fine brandy when it seizes you by the nose. Drink this.'

It was almost too much effort to roll half over onto his side. The searing pain almost cancelled the surprise, the pleasure, of this completely unexpected act. Almost, but not quite. Jesse Broad propped himself on an elbow, took the glass, and tipped the spirit neatly over his torn lip and onto his tongue. The surgeon watched closely.

'Why thank you, sir,' said Broad when he had tasted and swallowed. 'Thank you indeed.'

'Good,' said Adamson. He drank from his own glass. 'And what,' he asked, 'is your opinion? Your professional opinion?'

Broad hesitated. He was unsure what he should say.

'Come on, man,' said Mr Adamson irritably. 'I well know your trade. You are a smuggler and a villain unhung. No matter! Is it not a fine brandy?'

It was. Fine indeed. And Broad told the tiny surgeon so. For this reason, he supposed, he received another glass. Which unfortunately, working with his shocked stomach and torn back, made him feel ill. He made a pillow of his arms, burying his face in it.

'Good,' said the surgeon again, and went away.

Broad wondered what it could all mean, as he lay there fighting nausea. Such unlooked-for kindness. He felt very tired, and hurt, and confused. And he slept.

Ten

For many hours, the wind and weather appeared to have the Welfare, and her Admiralty orders, and everyone on board of her, especially in mind. As William Bentley stood on the quarterdeck he marvelled at his luck, and the ship's.

At first it had seemed as though she had been carrying too much canvas for the weight of the easterly. The master stood at the quarterdeck rail for almost an hour, once they had cleared into the Channel, studying the set of each sail, the tension of each part of the standing rigging. William, ever anxious to learn, had watched closely, listened to orders passed and to opinions shared, and asked for explanations of everything he could not understand. Mr Robinson, who did not seem to approve of the Welfare's young gentlemen, was pleased to instruct if interest was shown. The boatswain appeared to share his eagerness to teach, but William was not so sure of this. The huge West Countryman with the hairy face and sometimes incomprehensible drawl often said things, and in such a way, that made him think a joke was being had at his expense.

'Why is it necessary to keep setting up those backstays, Mr Robinson?' he asked as a party of seamen was put to retensioning shroud lanyards for the third time in as many hours.

'Wind, and newness, and lack of use, Mr Bentley,' Robinson replied. 'All the rigging, running and standing, has been overhauled while we stood at St Helen's. Now, under test, it is stretching and making its way in.'

The boatswain added sardonically: 'Hemp do stretch indeed, Mr Bentley sir. Even under the weight of a man.'

William ignored him.

'Are we carrying too great a press of canvas do you think, Mr Robinson?'

'No sir. For if we were you would feel the ship as it were, staggering, under its burden. You would know it at once.'

William was not at all sure that he would, and neither apparently was Allgood.

'There is another way to tell when the ship is bearing too much, with the young gentleman's permission?' he said politely. He looked serious enough, but William was wary. Nevertheless, he nodded his permission.

The boatswain's eyes twinkled.

'As soon as the master have given the order for sail to be shortened,' he said, his voice almost lost in his whiskers, ''tis a sure sign as the ship was labouring.'

Throughout the day sails and rigging were adjusted as they worked themselves in. Captain Swift, when he came on deck, expressed his satisfaction. The weather was perfect. Enough wind to make sail trimming necessary and keep the people on their toes, enough to bowl the frigate along at about her best speed, not enough to do any damage.

Below in the sick-bay, as the hours wore on, Thomas Fox came fully to his senses and took stock of his situation. He was still far from able to let his mind wander to thoughts of home. For the present he dwelt on his immediate surroundings, and was surprised that they did not seem to be too bad.

For a start, the motion of the ship did not make him feel ill. He had been sure that as soon as they got out of the anchorage he would be sick. He had, after all, been sick on the boat trip from the Sallyport to St Helen's Roads. And sick for hours afterwards. Now here they were at sea, he assumed, and he felt better than he had done for days. Days? He did not know for sure how long he had been away. Certainly he felt better than he had since drinking the first pint offered him by those two young officers. The thought of them made the good feeling seep away. But he had seen nothing of them since that terrible day. Perhaps they would not bother him again.

The sick-bay was unlike any part of the ship he had been in so far. It did not stink, for a start, except for the comforting, friendly smell of the animals, which must be stalled very close by. There was a steady breeze blowing in on them from somewhere ahead, but the dark, cramped room was not cold. Thomas put his hand, not for the first time, to the deck on which his straw palliasse was lying. It was

75

warm. From this, and the fact that men could be heard all around at times when he was given food, he gathered that the kitchens were somewhere close.

Even the food was good, and served in large enough quantities to satisfy his appetite, grown enormous now he felt less like death. There had been salt meat which was tough and rank, but well boiled and vinegared. Not as good as they sometimes had at home, especially when a beast had been slain, but at least meat; and more at one sitting than he ever saw except at Christmastide. Fresh potatoes, which he was very fond of, and onions, and even some cabbage. Thomas lay on his back in the straw, staring at the deck beams not far above him. Well, he was in the Navy now, willy-nilly. If father could only see him! No, let's not think of home. What then? The young officers? The surgeon.

What a strange man that one was. He must be an officer, but he was a fine, jolly, friendly little fellow, as unlike that small fair-haired villain and his squeaky friend as could be imagined. He had treated Thomas well, shown him every kindness, never once chid him for his sinful act in trying to jump overboard. Maybe it was the boys who were villains, then, and the men who were to be trusted?

Thomas recalled the scene in the cabin and shivered. That grand little man with the big nose and the frightful eyes was the captain. *He* was no friend to be relied on. And then, when Thomas had gone below to seek a mess, the people themselves, his fellow-sufferers, his countrymen – they had robbed him and abused him. It was a puzzle.

Jesse Broad, awakening with a groan, made Thomas turn his head. He smiled at the form in the darkness. There was the man he could trust. For Thomas was a simple soul. Although he had tried to end his life, he thanked this smuggler from the bottom of his heart for saving it. Remorse flooded him. In saving him, Broad had forfeited his liberty and been cruelly flogged.

'Mr Broad,' he whispered. 'Are you awake?'

Broad lay face down on the deck and winced as the pain swiftly brought him to life. The bones of his back had a deep ache in them that somehow surprised him. It was as though they had a depth to them which he had never before imagined. Each rib had an individual outline, a bigness, that throbbed. And that after only two dozen!

'Mr Broad. Are you sleeping?'

The whisper was clear enough, but he still did not reply. Jesse Broad was weary, weary to the very marrow. The white-faced boy with the glittering eyes of tragedy was too much for him at the moment. He felt no resentment at the part Fox had played in his downfall, none. But he could not stand the misery, the hopelessness, that welled from him like a tide.

The whisper was insistent.

'Mr Broad! Are we at sea, Mr Broad? Do you feel better, Mr Broad?' A pause. Then: 'I am sorry for the trouble I have caused you, Mr Broad.'

There was something in the voice that made him answer. The shepherd boy no longer sounded hopeless. He lifted his head, placing his cheek onto the straw pillow so that he could see across the sick-bay.

'Do not call me Mister Broad, boy,' he said. 'We are messmates, you and I. My name is Jesse.'

'Oh. Then – I hope you are better, Mr Jesse.'

'Jesse.'

'Yes. Jesse. I am truly sorry, sir, for the pain I have been the cause of. I would not for the world have . . . I . . . Oh sir, your poor back, I have seen it.'

It did not matter to Broad much any more. He thought about it for some moments. No, truly, it did not ache so badly.

'There is a saying, Thomas Fox, used among seafarers. It is a joke of sorts and it is applicable. "Worse things happen at sea." It is so. Think no more of my slight injuries, and I am heartily glad you are better.

'You *are* better?' he added. 'You sound better, lad.'

The boy's voice positively bubbled.

'Indeed I am, Mr Jesse, I—'

'Messmate, among seamen that would be taken as unfriendly.'

'Well then . . . Jesse. I do feel better. I thought to have died, of sickness if nothing else. And I am not even sick!' An anxious note crept into his voice. 'We *are* at sea, are we not? The motion, the sounds . . .'

Broad soaked up the familiar sounds and motions through the front of his body and his ears and senses. They were at sea all right. With the wind dead astern, near as damn it, and carrying just about everything she would hold. His heart sank. God knows the speed they were making, but at this rate they would be clear of the Channel in a twinkling. And this foolish boy, who last night had wished to die, sounding as though it was the very thing he had always wanted! Oh Mary, Mary, he thought, and slowly filled his lungs with air to let it escape in a long sigh.

'Aye, Thomas,' he said. 'We are at sea. And if I am any judge we have a fair wind and a hard one. Does that suit you?'

There was a long silence between them – a sea silence, filled with creaking, rushing water, a constant vibrating drumming given to the wooden hull by the masts and cordage. At last Thomas spoke.

'I cannot tell for certain, Jesse,' he said. 'And I am deeply ashamed for the trouble I have put you to. But . . . well, I have no power with words, but . . .'

'At least you do not feel sick?' suggested Broad with a laugh. Fox returned it; he sounded exhilarated.

'Aye, I do not. I feel . . . I feel very well . . . And . . . and I feel as if . . . As if it were not so bad a thing after all. To be a shepherd lad . . . to live in the marsh of Portsea Island . . . Indeed, my cousin Silas . . . Oh – I feel as if . . . I feel . . .'

The words tumbled, became confused. Broad did not prompt him. He listened in the half-darkness, his own pain forgotten. He even forgot his mental pain as he contemplated the simple soul of Thomas Fox. He did not ask – he did not care to remind – the boy about his parents, his home. He remembered the first time he had joined a lugger's crew, much too young, against his father's strict instructions. The heady wine of sail and sea, the joy when he first heard the strange tongue of the 'colleagues' off the French coast. He understood Thomas Fox perfectly.

He wondered when the boy's punishment would come, and what it would be. The idea was a sombre one. Swift had made some reference to Fox – and his 'crime' – and Swift was not a captain one could expect to let any infringement of the rules, either man's or God's, pass by without punishment. He supposed that the severity of the punishment Fox would receive depended on his importance in the ship. He, Broad, had escaped lightly for reasons too obvious to dwell on. But exactly where did the boy fit into the scheme of things? Firstly, he was no seaman. Bad – for the afterguard, and waisters, and slack hands in general, were bound to be the most numerous of this ship's company. It was skilled men Swift was short of, not landmen. Secondly, he was a boy, and had a strong tang of country humbleness about him. Bad as well – for Swift was known by repute as a man who had an unpredictable regard for those who would stand up to his tongue. Lastly, and the only point in Fox's favour, were the beasts. Broad supposed he had been pressed because Swift required a husbandman. Was it then such a difficult job? He did not know. If it was, maybe the boy would benefit.

Thomas Fox spoke again, suddenly, almost gleefully.

'And did you not know, Jesse, that there is a piper on board? Peter told me when he brought dinner. You were asleep. Is that not fine?'

'A piper? A music-piper?'

'Aye. Peter says he was the finest thing as they hove up the anchor. He was seated on the . . . on the . . .'

'Capstan?'

'Aye, he was seated on the capstan and played a right fine tune, says Peter, as they hove up and sailed away. A bagpipe, says Peter, I would guess an elbow-pipe from the way he told it. And the man is Irish.'

'You understand music then?' Broad was amazed at the liveliness of Fox's voice now. He sounded like a lark.

'Oh yes,' said Thomas. 'I understand little enough 'tis true, friend Jesse, but I know music well. I make whistles by the score, aye and play them right prettily. Or so everyone says, and the sheep don't seem to mind at all!'

'Good,' said Jesse Broad. 'Yes, that's good, Thomas. Music on board a ship is a pleasant thing, pleasant and delightful.'

'Oh, do you think so?' The boy sounded overjoyed.

'Aye, I do. Perhaps you can talk to this piper, if he has the English tongue.'

'Oh.'

A pause.

'Oh?'

'It is sad, but Peter says he has no tongue at all. Nor eyes neither. He is dark, and the poor man is mute and all.'

The conversation tailed off, and presently Thomas Fox slept. Jesse Broad lay and thought. Somehow the ship felt less happy now. She was biting deeper from time to time, and he felt an occasional

79

shock through his belly as her bluff bows hit a steep sea. There were momentary pauses in the vibrating hum, that read to his seaman's mind as if she were shaking herself like a wet dog, or spilling wind from sails she did not want. At times the deck juddered.

A ray of hope entered his head. It was the only hope, or one of only two. If the weather worsened, if a gale ran up behind them, there was at least a chance. At least a stay of execution. If the frigate hit some dirty weather, she might not clear the Channel so damned quick. She had the crew for it! A good blow, some foul South Coast autumn weather, and most of her 'hands' would collapse like pricked bladders. There were precious few seamen on board.

To his surprise Broad caught himself praying. Not only for the stiff easterly to turn stiffer, to become a gale, to blow a bloody tempest, but for the wind to change altogether. Why not a westerly for good measure? Where were they now? Off Portland Bill? Start Point? The Rame Head? A westerly blow, and run for shelter. He could do it. One day, half a day, in any port on the English coast, any bay even, and he'd get ashore, he'd run. Sudden elation swept over Broad then. Rightly or wrongly as it might turn out, Thomas Fox would not be interested in joining him, or his Maker, this time; so no burden. Thomas Fox thought he was happy! But he, Jesse Broad, knew where *his* heart lay. Heart, soul, all!

There was no doubt that the weather was worsening, and even if it refused to change to the west, that was something. Over the next hour the motion grew less steady, the plunging greater. She was beginning to feel it, beginning to feel more than a capful of wind. Hope stirred in Broad's stomach.

The other thing he prayed for, and he was praying without restraint, asking God for a personal favour, was a French ship. He was not, perhaps, asking too much. A full gale in the Channel at the beginning of winter was indeed reasonable, and a westerly or a south-westerly more reasonable still, although the change of direction needed would require a little more effort on Heaven's part. And as for a French ship, well why not? There was a war on, the Channel was narrow. The men-of-war, by policy, tended not to leave harbour without good reason, but one never knew, and there were privateers aplenty. To meet a gallant Frenchman and to lose a spar or two! To lose a mast and put into harbour for repair! Jesse Broad went to the extreme length of rolling onto his raw and aching back to clasp his hands piously upon his chest.

It was not long afterwards that Mr Robinson decided to get the top-gallants off her. He spent some little time explaining why he was going to make the move to William Bentley, who remained interested although he was very cold despite having gone below to take a drink and get into a waterproof coat. Mr Robinson talked of the way the ship was rolling, the difficulty she was beginning to experience in lifting her bows from steep troughs, the feeling that she was unhappy. None of the explanations was in any way specific, which annoyed William vaguely. He knew that things had changed, that the note from the rigging was deeper, that the gouts of spray that flew across the quarterdeck in cold and drenching sheets had become more frequent; but as for 'feeling', as for 'experiencing' – how could *he* tell what the ship knew?

More interesting in one way to William, was the deep sensation of nausea that was growing in his belly. For more than two hours men had been being ill, and at first he had rather enjoyed the spectacle. He had been out in the Channel before, of course. That great grown sailormen should be stricken like boobies had amused him. Now he was not so sure. In fact, by the time hands were piped aloft to hand the upper sails, William watched them with an expression of pained fascination, rather than interest, on his face. What was more, he could not really see them. His eyes were filled with a greenish mist, criss-crossed with cordage and wildly swaying masts and yards, that etched awful patterns against the white and grey clouds racing across the lowering sky.

When his uncle came on deck to speak to the master, William was like an iron man, a dummy, rooted to the spot. Their conversation came into his ears in a drone, as if from a great distance.

'What goes on, Mr Robinson?'

'We are in for a blow, sir, unless I am greatly mistaken,' the master replied. 'And the wind is veering again. We may end up with a westerly yet.'

The first part of Jesse Broad's prayer was apparently being answered.

Eleven

By the middle of the next day the Welfare was making heavy weather of it, and the quality of the people had become a problem that threatened her with real danger. Not all the beating in the world, not all the starting by the boatswain and his men, could turn the scrapings of many a gutter, the scourings of many a jail, into seamen. Already they had lost one man over the side. He had dropped with a long scream from the fore topsail yard as the labouring ship had staggered drunkenly between two big seas. He had bobbed off almost slowly, his face clearly visible between the creaming grey crests, looking imploringly at the struggling frigate. One of the helmsmen had allowed his eyes to stray for a moment to his lost shipmate and a sail had almost been caught aback. Captain Swift, who had been hovering near the wheel, gave a snarl and punched the seaman full in the face while the master and the other helmsman clawed the helm up to get her off the wind once more.

William Bentley, as befitted a young gentleman, was now on the quarterdeck and fighting his sickness manfully. He was not alone. Jack Evans was a vile green colour and Simon Allen, another mid, was as sick as a donkey. The youngest of the young gentlemen, James Finch, had gone below to the berth, which was a very bad move. Bentley was not officially on duty, but to skulk below in a storm, when the crew of scum had to be bullied, cajoled, and given example to, to make them try, at least, to work the ship, might damn him in Swift's eyes forever.

So William stood on the quarterdeck, muffled in his tarpaulin coat, soaked under it to the very skin in freezing water, and suffered in silence. His sickness was awful. He would have welcomed any way out of it. Every now and then, like the others, he vomited, violently, painfully. Then turned his eyes to sails and cordage, wind and sea, once more.

The wind had hauled farther and farther round in the night, as it gained in power. The Welfare was now close-hauled, under double-reefed topsails. Her lee rail was low, and green seas swept the deck every two or three minutes. The process of the gear stretching and working-in that Mr Robinson had explained to him the day before was unfortunately still going on. It was their main problem.

William watched the boatswain with something approaching admiration. For a common man he showed an uncommon determination and endurance. The few really good seamen under his control worked like a team of fine animals, and even the gutter-rats could be made to pull, usually at the correct moment – the gutter-rats that were capable of moving, that is. The boatswain's great strength had stood him in good stead. For he had been on deck for nearly twenty hours, fighting canvas and men. As he sheltered under the weather bulwarks for a moment the midshipman stared at him. His black beard was streaming, his body was like a great sponge – and he was laughing into the teeth of the gale. He did not even wear a tarpaulin jacket, merely a thick flannel shirt that had split almost to his belt. He was a giant.

To windward, the prospect was bleak. The cloud was so low it almost skimmed the wave-tops. These were high, and creaming, and marched in never-ending succession that he found oddly frightening. There was no reason William could see why they should ever stop. Great, grey, cold mountains, that could bear down on the Welfare until she gave up the uneven struggle. He gritted his teeth. It was the sickness merely. That would go; that he would defeat. And his uncle, and Mr Robinson, and that mad boatswain – were they worried? Not a bit of it. Allgood was laughing.

The sickness on deck was confined to the officers, because any man who succumbed in the waist or on the foredeck would have been washed overboard immediately. So the sick among the people were all below, all confined to their living quarters. The gunports were tightly battened down, as were the hatches; under them, in the reeking darkness, conditions were appalling. There was a dim, flickering light at intervals from swaying lanterns, but mostly the men suffered in near-total blindness. The master-at-arms and his corporals patrolled from time to time, but with little purpose, and in fact on his third round one corporal was caught off balance, thrown against a gun-truck, and broke his arm in two places. His screams of agony added a more ghoulish note to the groans of ship and men. The all-pervading smell of sewage that rose from the bilge water being thrown around and stirred up deep below fought a constant and evil battle with the reek of vomit, fresh and stale. Even the livestock was vomiting.

Jesse Broad was not sick, but the battering his body received from the deck he lay on hurt him badly. The sick-bay was up in the eyes of the Welfare, and the cool breeze that had come through the hawse holes the day before was now a dank, chilling blast. Water burst through the holes despite their plugging, and roared back along the deck, bubbling under the light partitions that formed the bay. Broad's palliasse was a sink of dripping straw. Worst was the forward motion. As Welfare's bow lifted over each sea and the wind drove her into the next, she would gather speed until her great flat bow buried itself, and Broad would be inched along, flat on his face, on his straw sledge.

His prayer had been answered, half of it, and that with a vengeance. But so far it had meant only discomfort. There was no sign that the frigate was being much delayed yet, or might run for shelter. With each shock, with each fresh stagger, with each howl of wind through the hawse, he smiled grimly. Blow wind blow, he thought; blow like a bitch. Blow us back to England and to hell with it!

He spent several hours trying to comfort Thomas Fox, whose terror, like his elation the day before, Broad found amazing. The shepherd boy was convinced that the ship was sinking, and he was equally convinced that Broad was lying when he said there was nothing to fear. It had been confirmed for him when the water started coming under the partition and sluicing across the deck. It had been a relief for Broad, although a nuisance because of the mess and stench, when the boy had become too ill to talk. Luckily Thomas Fox was still weak; he spent more time unconscious than most of the sick men on board.

The climax of the storm cost three more lives, and came close to achieving what Broad hoped of it. He knew all about it, too, because sick man that he was meant to be – and Swift knew more than to kill a useful hand by working him too soon after a flogging – he was part of the team that saved the frigate.

The first indication was when the ship's corporal was carried screaming into the sick-bay. He was followed almost immediately by the smell of brandy and the person of the tiny surgeon. Mr Adamson greeted Broad like a friend, with a smile and a nod. The crazy motion of the deck, that had the corporals reeling as they tried to lay their comrade down gently, bothered him not at all. He rode on his skinny legs like a gull, the fat black bottle swinging from his fingers. He raised his eyes to heaven as much as to say 'what a waste' to Broad as he sent two or three huge gulps shooting down the open throat of the screaming man. As the corporal coughed and jerked, Mr Adamson spoke.

'Blowing great guns out there my friend,' he said. 'And about enough seamen on deck to man one of your damned piratical luggers. God help this poor fellow when I try to tie his arm up. She's rolling like a mare in season!'

Seconds later a boatswain's mate fell into the tiny sick-bay. He was streaming water and red in the face with exertion.

'You!' he said to Broad tersely. 'Up. On deck. Aloft, damn you, and make it snappy.'

At that moment the Welfare made a plunge and roll combined that seemed to go on for ever. Broad felt his body turning over, lying down as he was, with the steepness of the angle. The corporal, who had been propped on his side, rolled down the deck like a piece of carpeting. The surgeon grabbed for him, staggered, and repeated a short, sharp oath over and over again. Broad could feel the timbers vibrating. He put up a hand, the boatswain's mate seized it and jerked him upright. He hardly noticed the pain as they scuttled crabwise along the deck.

It was chaos. The frigate was lying over on her ear and a huge jumble of spewing, cursing people had slipped from their places on the high side into a struggling pile on the low. There was shouting, screaming, and the frantic bellowing of animals in pain. Out of the murk boatswain's mates appeared momentarily, thrashing with cane and rope, kicking and swearing. Broad ignored this rabble and crabbed along to a ladder. The Welfare was in trouble, and if this chaos was the response to a call for all hands, then God have mercy on her.

On deck, Broad was appalled by the tiny number of people he saw. More than the crew of a 'damned piratical lugger' by a long way, but not enough, not enough. The short, high grey seas were sweeping across the waist almost without pause. At the hatch he had to wait for nearly a minute before he could claw his way to the windward side in a frantic dash. The boatswain seized his arm at the last and hauled him to shelter.

'Good man!' he shouted.

The noise was dominated by a clapping like a succession of cannons. The fore topsail had blown out and the remaining strips were cracking and creating like wild things. One of the headsails had gone too, which was perhaps a good thing, thought Jesse. The ship was struggling for her life, pressed down by a gust that was doing its immortal best to keep her under while the seas cleared her decks of every object, up to and including the masts. Even the life-lines which the boatswain had rigged so that men could hang above the seas as they moved along the decks were going under from time to time. Aft, the four men now at the wheel were in a bad dream, waistdeep in water, white-faced, fighting.

'Aloft, aloft!' roared the master. 'Hand main topsail! Get him in, boys, get him in!'

It was all a whirl. Broad aloft, flattened against the yard by the enormous pressure of the wind, men on deck in a maelstrom of foam. A scream as a fellow he knew by sight flew over his head, smashed to the deck where he lay like a rag doll for a second, to disappear in a grey welter as the next sea smashed on board and creamed over the lee rail. A weird howling as the fore topgallant mast carried away. Well, that was no loss. The ship would be easier without it. But by God, he thought, this is a blow and a half! Not that he thought coherently. He was weak, and the work was hard, and the old rule of one hand for the ship and one for himself went, as it always did, by the board. He fought hard wet canvas with his hands, his arms, his stomach and legs, his knees and elbows, even his teeth.

They saved her. Gradually the Welfare, canvas stripped, yards braced round to offer least resistance, rose sluggishly from her crippled-shoulder position, put her teeth to the wind, and began to ride them again. The men who had done the work stood in the lee of a shattered cutter and drank wine at the captain's order. One boy stood and cried; his father was one of the lost three. One of the men too old, or too sick, to hang on.

86

The first part of Jesse's prayer ended with the end of the storm's climax. For an hour the frigate lay-to under bare poles with the rain and wind a moving shroud. Then the sky lightened, the wind eased, the rain ceased. Still the seas broke over the battered ship, still the gale tore ceaselessly at her top-hamper. But the worst was over.

With merely a gale blowing, the hands were sent aloft to set canvas. More men were beaten up from below to handle headsail halyards and outhauls. A reef was shaken out of the main topsail. Half an hour later she lay bravely to the seas, belting up great gouts from bow and side as she clawed towards the Atlantic.

During the course of the afternoon the weather moderated, which made the hell below decks worse in some ways for those of the people who had collapsed earlier. The boatswain's mates, freed from their duties on deck, lashed by the tongue of the boatswain who had in turn been lashed by Swift, lashed the moaning bodies below with everything at their disposal. Some discarded rope's-ends and cane for solider battens. Heads were broken and blood flowed. Swift would have had some of them shot, he averred to William, except that not a man-jack of the marines was capable of standing, let alone firing a musket.

William felt superb now that they had lived through the worst. He had worked on the deck almost like one of the people, although he had not, of course, gone so far as to handle a rope. But he – and Jack too, to be fair – had been in the thick of it right the way through. He had been as sick as a dog, had been cut across the face by a wildly lashing sheet when it carried away, but he had kept his end up. He and Jack had even managed to kick a seaman as he stumbled past, for the act of stumbling. He was beginning to be able to tell the lubbers from the seamen, he thought.

He was beside his uncle, who had crossed to the lee side of the quarterdeck to observe some wreckage floating by, when the master approached Swift and coughed deferentially.

'Yes, Mr Robinson? What is in your mind?' said Swift.

'It is in my mind, sir, that she would stand a little more canvas. That it is time, also, to bend a new fore topsail. It is in my mind, sir, that this wind is a thought less powerful. I beg your pardon, sir.'

William looked at the master. He was not an inspiring man to see. Thin, and very ugly, with an attitude to his superiors that bordered on the indifferent. He had helped William, it was true.

But he had to be asked, and passed on his knowledge in ways that were not easy to follow. He talked of ships as though they were thinking, feeling things. But he was a good master, nobody could gainsay it. William looked at the rigid, bellied sails, close-reefed and tiny against the towering, straining masts. He tried to detect a change. *Why* did Robinson think she could now stand more? But the mystery remained.

Captain Swift hardly glanced upwards.

'As you say, Mr Robinson,' he said. 'As you say. Shake 'em out and welcome.'

He turned to William, very unexpectedly.

'Like to go aloft, my boy?' he said in a jovial voice. 'Keep an eye on the scum, eh? Weather's moderating, and it's about time too.'

He turned to Jack Evans, who was lurking a few feet downwind.

'You too, Evans. Aloft the pair of you. See what a breath of wind feels like aloft!'

There was no argument, naturally. The two boys climbed the ratlines with the men, who kept silence, kept their faces clear of expression, slowed down their easy, barefoot pace so as not to show up the clumsy overfed boys in their heavy tarpaulins and leather shoes. They stopped at the top, so as not to get in the way as the men swarmed out along the yards. William was almost overawed at their agility. At the way they swung like monkeys, their feet gripping foot-ropes, their clenched stomachs holding them to the big, swaying yard as their free hands flew at the reef-points and earrings. His sickness, and the sickness of fear, were still with him, but he felt proud also, proud and brave.

Then he saw Jesse Broad. He saw the man he knew as a captured smuggler, the man who had tried to run, the man who had saved the life of that dreadful boy, the man he had seen flogged at the gangway and who had smiled at the last stroke. Through the torn shirt he saw the seaman's back. It was black and blue, swollen like a bolster. The man was doubled across the yard, his face clenched in pain or concentration, his fingers hidden by the sail's belly he was working at.

William Bentley saw blood well through the torn and soaking shirt. The nausea flooded through him anew. His stomach dropped. He raised his eyes past the handsome head, away from the awful, savaged back. He stared out across the wild grey waters.

And he saw the ship. She was close, not above a couple of miles, to his unpractised eye. So close he could not understand why the cry had not gone up. She was close, and she was a ship of war. She was to windward, towards the coast of France. And for a sovereign, for a King's ransom, she was French!

He filled his lungs and roared, his head swimming with excitement.

'Sail ho! On deck there! A sail, a sail!'

The cry rose thinly from the captain's speaking trumpet: 'Where away? Aloft there! Where away?'

'Broad on the larboard bow! Broad on the larboard bow! A ship of war! A ship of war!'

The Welfare took a mighty plunge then, and shook the sea from her foredeck like a dog. The second part of Jesse's prayer had been answered.

Twelve

If the new ship was a Frenchman, there could be only one, inevitable, consequence. Even if the Welfare had been an unarmed merchantman, desperate not to fight, she would have been hard put to escape; the distant ship was well before the frigate's beam, and she was running free. But Welfare was a ship of war, and British, and to every person on board who was not too sick to think, the situation was clear. A ragged cheer went up from the men on the yard, exhausted as they were, and William Bentley found himself cheering with the rest of them. From the deck, a faint hullabaloo arose.

William, who had a good theoretical knowledge of single-ship actions, and who spent many hours working out moves and tactics in the midshipmen's berth, alone and with the others, weighed up the situation. His sickness was waning fast, being replaced by an almost unbearable excitement. He turned his face to Jack Evans, who was clinging to the mast beside him.

'By God, Jack!' he said. 'Now we'll see something!'

Jack's face was flushed where before it had been sallow, almost green.

'Do you not think we ought to get on deck, Will? We must stand to our positions!'

'Orders, Jack, orders.'

'Perhaps your Uncle Daniel has forgot us!'

William turned his eyes to the men on the yards and screamed at them impatiently: 'Move, you lubbers, move! Cannot you see there is action to be had!'

'How will we engage do you think?' Evans asked. His high voice carried well in the howling noise of the rigging, and Bentley had to strain hard to match him.

'Difficult, difficult. She is to windward of us, has the wind abaft the beam, and can lay down the terms. But in this tempest she will

90

be hard put not to merely fly past us. Can you see what she is carrying yet?'

The two boys stared across the heaving waters. The 'enemy' dipped and plunged in the distance, sometimes almost disappearing into the troughs.

'Close-reefed topsails I think,' said Evans doubtfully.

William watched as their own sails grew larger. It seemed an odd tactic, now, to increase the area. In weather like this Welfare would need to be as handy as possible, especially to meet a vessel coming down the wind. Even more so if the fellow didn't want an encounter and had to be chased; and that was always possible with the French, according to everything he had ever heard. The men on the yard were hesitating too, as if expecting the order to take in the reefs once more, or even add to them. It occurred to him that the view from the deck must be considerably less than theirs up here, and on an impulse he cupped his hand to yell at the quarterdeck.

'On deck there! On deck there! She's under close-reefed topsails only, and closing fast.'

There was a short pause, filled by the roaring wind and clapping of canvas. Then the voice of his uncle, distorted by his speaking trumpet. It rose to the heights of the mast as if slowly; an eerie effect.

'Has he made any sign yet? Has he seen us?' A pause. 'Any colours? Any change of course?'

William and Jack Evans strained their eyes. The distance was definitely closing. Had the windward vessel changed course?

'She's coming round, Will, she's coming round! Oh my God, there's going to be a fight!'

William wasn't so sure. The ship looked just the same to him. But he knew Jack's eyes were keener than his.

'Are you sure? Has he altered?'

'Aye, aye!' squeaked Evans. 'Oh, he's changing all right!'

William roared down to the deck as hard as he could. In the middle his voice cracked, but for once he didn't mind this indication of his boyhood. Neither did anyone else, for a bigger cheer yet rose slowly upwards seconds after his words.

'On deck there! On deck there! He's making for us! He's seen us! He's bearing down for us! The devil's on for a tussle!'

His mind was racing, back to tactics once more. With this sea running the gun action would be difficult indeed. The lee ports could certainly not be opened; they were under water half the time. And then the weather ones – well, they were pointing to the sky by the same token. They would either have to go head to wind to get her on an even keel for a minute or two, or be stern to wind at just the moment the Frenchman ranged alongside. But then they'd be completely exposed as they wore, and he had the wind gage in any case. Obviously paper tactics and his sketchy knowledge of seamanship would not suit here; if he was controlling this action, he realised with a thump, he would not know how to begin.

Jack Evans was having the same trouble.

'How will he lay her, Billy?' he asked. 'We cannot rake the dog like this, our shot would be over his trucks. We'd pepper the clouds!'

'Whatever else, Jack,' Bentley shouted, 'we've got to get some canvas off her. He'll run rings round us else. The press is too great.'

The gap was narrowing. Still the seamen on the yards were at sixes and sevens. They must be wondering what to do; when the order would come to close-reef. Maybe Uncle Daniel was planning to clew them up of a sudden when Johnny Crapaud was in range, then shake out and sail her. William could see the master and the captain at the weather rail, heads together. Mr Robinson, that indifferent man, was waving an arm about in animation.

''Tis damn near time to beat to quarters,' Jack said in his ear. His voice was doubtful. William did not reply. With the sea-sickness on board, with the general lubberliness of the people, with the badness of the weather and the closeness of the enemy, he secretly thought it was time and a lot more. The guns were shotted already, but all ports were closed and caulked, all tompions were in, every mess between every pair was full of groaning, useless men. Partitions were up, mess tables were in position. He looked into the wind. Although a very short time had passed since the first sighting, the weather frigate was noticeably closer. He could see what Jack had seen. She was making to intercept them.

'Is she carrying colours yet?'

Evans replied after a long moment.

'Not yet. But hell's teeth, Will, when do you think your unc—'

He broke off. William flushed.

92

'Shut your mouth,' he said viciously. But he said it to himself.

Then the penetratingly thin voice warbled up from below. A sudden stronger gust carried the first part of it away.

'. . . or I'll flog every last son of a whore of you!'

Aha! The word to close-reef. William watched the men. They did nothing. They must not have heard either. He was about to repeat what he guessed was the order when Captain Swift's voice rose once more, full of venom even at that distance.

'Get that canvas set, damn your eyes! Shake out those reefs I say!'

It was unbelievable. William Bentley and Jack Evans exchanged glances. Shake them out! Another order rose from the deck, not directed upwards this time, but still audible.

'Tacks and braces! Tacks and braces there! You sons of dogs! Man the sheets there!'

The master had gone to the helm. The men laid to the spokes with a will. All over the decks others scrambled, to man the topsail halyards, to brace the yards as the frigate altered course. There was a thunderous clapping as the canvas bellied and flapped during a series of sail and helm manoeuvres done at double-quick time. The men on the yard clung on for dear life as they were flung about, then they were all round the two boys, then at other parts of the rigging, then away like lightning towards the deck. Jack Evans was pink around the gills. They felt like a couple of hopeless lubbers. Collapse of the young gentlemen.

'I say,' he shouted miserably. 'Had we better get down off here?'

It was no moment to wait for orders. Captain Swift would have forgotten all about them anyway. No time for worrying about a couple of supernumeraries. William went down the ratlines lost and unhappy. He glanced to windward, which was now over the larboard quarter. The French ship had not altered, as far as he could see. Doubtless her commander was as surprised by the frigate's latest move as were all on board her.

William picked his moment, to avoid the seas that still combed the deck, although less frequently. The knots of seamen standing about had on sullen, closed expressions. An air of depression had replaced the cheeriness. Disbelief too. Not one of them apparently who could believe they were really attempting to run. It must be some ploy on the owner's part. Swift might be a hard man, even a tyrant. But no one had ever caught him playing the coward.

93

As was his duty, William reached the quarterdeck. The first and second lieutenants were there, studiedly looking away to starboard at nothing in particular. Captain Swift was alone, high on the weather side, his lips grim. Mr Robinson looked incuriously at the two midshipmen, then returned his gaze to the masts. At a signal, William approached his uncle.

'On whose instruction have you left your post?'

William Bentley jumped. His uncle's eyes were cold and savage. His voice had a cutting edge that was almost palpable.

'I . . . I am sorry, sir, I—'

'Sorry you *will* be, damn it, and sooner than you think, Mr Bentley. And your friend too. Why sir, did you abandon your post?'

Daniel Swift's face was white. The muscles in his cheeks worked. He seemed to be consumed with rage. It was terrifying.

'I . . . am sorry, sir,' said William. 'I shall return immediately. I . . . misunderstood.'

The captain turned away. There was silence for several seconds. William wondered if he should go aloft. He dared not ask.

'Take that fool Evans with you and keep an eye on the Frenchman. I want to know everything about him. Every move he makes. Understood?'

'Aye aye sir.'

'Then jump, boy, jump!'

William leapt smartly away. He motioned to Jack and they raced along the deck to the main shrouds. The decks were clear of heavy water now, with wind and sea almost astern. The climb was much easier. When they reached the topgallant yard Jack panted: 'What did he say?'

'To shut up and watch,' returned William. 'So get peeping, Jack Evans, or I think we may be flogged like common sailors. Uncle Daniel is not in a happy mood.'

Almost immediately Evans picked out men scrambling aloft in the Frenchman. Within minutes her fore topsail began to blossom as the reefs were shaken out. There was going to be a chase.

Mr Robinson was master of the Welfare, and a master seaman he showed himself to be. Jesse Broad, who above all men wanted the frigate to stand and fight, nevertheless had an eye for a chase, and an inbuilt feeling for the one who was running. He had spent more hours than he could guess escaping from ships – both revenue cutters and the small men-of-war which sometimes thought it would be fine sport to run down a smuggling lugger. He had honed his seamanship on the gentle art of getting clear away, so he could appreciate the finest points of sail-handling and steering. Mr Robinson, quiet and practically motionless, yet had the Welfare in the palm of his hand. He could sense her every response. He kept the sailors busy at tack, sheet and brace, repositioning there, easing or hauling here. The best helmsman on board was handling the wheel, with the second best alongside him to lend weight. Broad felt an urge to have a go himself after they shipped a lump of sea over the quarter; he would have avoided that one.

A stern chase, they say, is always a long chase, and he was interested despite himself to see what would be the outcome. They were heading fairly towards the coast of England, unless he was much mistaken. If they had to come about for fear of getting too close on to the lee shore nothing could save them from an action. He could not see that they would be able to outstrip the Frenchman, who was pretty much of a size, so perhaps the captain was counting on dark to save them. In this weather they would escape in the darkness as easy as winking. Or maybe Swift was putting his money on Robinson's seamanship.

That bold man decided at that moment that Welfare could carry a shade more canvas. Broad did not entirely agree, but that was of little moment. And he granted the master's greater experience of his own ship ungrudgingly. A sudden thought of Mary, and his home, surprised him; but there was nothing he could do but admit to himself that he would do his level best to get the frigate clear. He dearly loved a chase.

After several hours it became clear that Robinson's skill was winning the day. The two frozen boys aloft could see a definite widening of the gap. Shortly after they had reported this to the quarterdeck (after ten minutes' conference on the wisdom of expressing such a dangerously dogmatic opinion) it was confirmed by the Frenchman. She opened up with her bow chasers, which at that range could be little other than a gesture of frustration. The balls fell so far short that their splashes were lost in the creamy caps of the waves. Not long after that, the eagle eyes of Evans saw her fore topsail split. Within seconds his diagnosis was proved to a doubting

William when the sail blew to tatters that flew ahead of the enemy frigate's mast for a half minute then scattered over the waves and disappeared. A short time later, night began rapidly to close in.

Below, after another hour of violent work, shortening sail, bringing the frigate back on the wind, starting the process of clawing off the lee shore that was somewhere in the darkness to the north, Jesse Broad came to realise the furious resentment that most of his shipmates felt. Unlike him, to whom the chase had been absorbing, exciting, the others were filled with outraged shame almost to a man. His whole mess had been on deck throughout, even young Peter. Now, together between the guns that bounded their home, the conversation waxed furious over the tin pannikins of rum and water, that were the only hot thing they were likely to get in their bellies while the dirty weather lasted.

'To run from a damned Frog-eater!' said Grandfather Fulman sadly, shaking his grizzled head. 'I never do recall such a thing. What say you, Samuel?'

The other old fellow had not either. Peter jumped up and down.

'He's a damned coward, and that's the measure of the man,' he said eagerly. 'Why, such goings-on! I'd have stood and fought, aye, and to the death, too!'

There was a shared laugh, but it was not a happy one. Matthews said soberly, from his position nearest the port: 'Keep that talk low, Peter. There is some sort of opinion that must not be voiced, no how. Keep it low.'

Peter spluttered into his grog.

'But by the Lord, Mr Matthews,' he said. ''Tis the unvarnished truth. That captain is a villain and a born—'

The carroty head disappeared under two big, horny hands. Fulman had carefully put down his drink and clapped one over the boy's mouth and the other over his head to stop him moving. The boy struggled, then was still.

'Listen, Peter,' said Fulman. 'Mr Matthews is right. To have run is . . .' He looked around him into the gloom and pitched his voice still lower . . . 'a shameful thing. But say so, and you may yet get a rope collar and a higher position in the world. Listen. We are not alone.'

He stopped speaking. From all around them in the darkness came a fearful noise. Babbling voices, drunken cries, retching men. There was an ugly note to it all, a feeling of anger. The lean, dark figure of Matthews let out a laugh.

'See, Peter, you are not alone in your feelings neither. There will be many a fool here tonight prepared to open his mouth too wide. But remember the master-at-arms. He'll not be absent.'

In his cabin, Captain Swift rode the heaving deck easily and toyed with a wineglass. His eyes, to William, looked still unusual, filled with a dangerous pale fire, but he knew comfortably that the anger was no longer directed at him.

'Damn, damn, damn, damn and double damn it all,' Swift said. He drained his glass, refilled it with a swift movement. The deck bucked heavily and William staggered. But Swift absorbed the motion through bended knees, recommenced swearing quietly. William, dressed in dry clothes, warmer, said nothing. He did not know what to say.

'You know what the people are thinking, no doubt?' Swift snapped suddenly.

William reddened. A good question. Whatever answer he gave would reveal his own position. But apparently Uncle Daniel was not attempting to trap him; he did not wait for a reply.

'They are thinking I am a coward and have turned the ship into a disgrace. Hell!'

William kept his mouth shut. Captain Swift aimed a kick at a cabinet bolted to the deck. It split down the front and his drink spilled.

'Go forward, William, go forward,' said Uncle Daniel. 'If you find one man, if you find one filthy scummy lubber with that word upon his lips . . . Go forward, my boy, and find me a man.'

The boy stood still, uncertain.

'I beg pardon, sir,' he said. 'I am a little . . . I mean, do you desire that . . .'

'Yes, I do desire "that",' said Swift gratingly. 'Are you not aware, nephew, that those filthy scum will now, even *now*, be thinking me a coward? Me, Daniel Swift! Good God, I—' His face contorted and he lashed his boot out at the cabinet a second time. A piece of the rosewood door stove in, then dropped to the deck. He breathed deeply, his cheeks working.

'Eyes and ears, boy, remember? I want you below, now, not with your messmates but among the people. Find me a man, boy, find me a mutinous dog who breathes that filthy word. Understood?'

'Yes sir,' said William, half bemused. 'You think the people will interpret . . . You think that cowardice . . .'

The pale eyes transfixed him.

'William. This ship is a disciplined ship. Those scum, most of whom were too lubberly to get their arses on deck let alone work the ship or fight her, will be forced to know it. Today they saw me run. They will have the infernal insolence to think I ran of my own volition. Me. Who have fought before until my ship was awash with blood, aye, and against odds that would have daunted Beelzebub.' He ran out of breath, choked with rage. 'Well. Well. Well. I shall show them. They cannot know my orders, no one can know my orders. But I will beat into them the respect that is due to me. I will flog the first man to call me coward to within an inch of his life. Now! Forward, sir!'

William felt a flood of joy. He almost laughed with relief. So that was it! Orders. His Uncle Daniel had orders. My God, how could he have doubted? It was so ridiculously obvious. No one could know what those orders were. That was the lonely responsibility of command. But he could guess this much: they involved speed and they involved staying clear of engagements, certainly of the sort of engagement that might cripple them or divert them from the purpose decided by my Lords of the Admiralty. Uncle Daniel was not a coward.

'Get forward, sir!' repeated Swift. 'Find me a man, my boy, and find him quickly.' He drained his glass and refilled it. As William left the cabin he heard him swearing under his breath. And rightly so, thought William. How dare the filthy scum harbour such vile thoughts about his uncle?

In the close, sweet-sickly atmosphere of the main deck, all William's nausea returned. The air was hot and foetid, reeking so strongly of vomit that his stomach tried instantly and violently to climb into his throat. He held on to a ladder, closed his eyes, bit his lip hard. It was more than a minute before he knew he was not going to retch. The deck under his feet was slippery with sick. He would be unable to stay below for long, otherwise he would succumb. He might even join the shadowy forms that lay all around, insensible, indifferent, in their own filth.

The noise was practically unbelievable. A babble of voices, screams, laughs, that merged into a sort of roar, more animal than human. It was deafening. Where would he pick out a man in all that? How could he hope to find a single voice preaching dissent?

It was, in the event, ridiculously easy. William ducked and slipped his way to an area of deep shadow, where he clung to a stanchion to get his bearings. As he listened, the babble of voices gradually sorted itself into those of individuals. There were high voices, low voices, gruff ones and shrill. But one thing struck him most forcibly; many of them were the voices of drunken men.

Even more forcibly, as his ears tuned in to each individual, came the refrain. His uncle had been right; there was a hell's chorus of mutinous talk. Cowardice was the word, and it chimed round the stinking deck as a rhythmic echo.

At the mess directly in front of William there was a lantern hanging from a beam. In its light a huge brute of a man rose unsteadily to his feet, lifted his pannikin to his mouth and drank deeply. William recognised him; a pressed man, and a good enough seaman, named Henry Joyce. He knew the name because he was a dangerous one. An illiterate, violent, drunken dog who obeyed orders in a surly fashion and had an air of brooding menace.

Now, there was nothing at all brooding about him. His long pigtail hung down his back and his thick neck rippled as he threw his head back. His face was dirty, covered in black whiskers, but the whole of the front of his head was bald. His body was bare to the waist. Indeed, he wore only a pair of short canvas drawers. He was built like Mr Allgood, although perhaps a shade less mighty, and all the latent savagery that William sensed in the boatswain was nakedly on view in this drunken animal.

From out of the thrown-back head there came a howl of derision. His messmates banged their pannikins and laughed. The man howled once more, took another drink, coughed.

'Messmates!' he cried. 'The man is a coward, not a doubt in the world of it. A coward!'

He roared the word till it reverberated through the deck, although it did not silence the row from the other messes. His comrades cheered.

'A coward!' he roared again. 'And a craven! And a poltroon! And a damned son of a whore!'

Each epithet was cheered to the echo. William could hardly believe his ears. Where was the master-at-arms to quell this din? And did these men not realise they could be hanged! He did not move, however. The man had, after all, still not named a name.

'"My brave boys", he says, the poltroon, "My brave boys, soon we'll be at sea. And God help the enemy then!" he says.' Joyce laughed until he choked, his messmates banging away with their pots. '"My brave boys", he says, "when we get to sea there'll be prizes galore. Prize-money enough to rot you! Prize-money to have you rolling in gold. Or my name's not Daniel Swift!" he says. Well lads! What the hell is it, eh?'

And as his messmates roared, he answered his own question: 'Captain Lily-liver! That's his name! Captain bloody Coward!'

In a blind fury William took a step towards the mess. That these scum could sink so low! That such mutinous talk could be heard on a ship of His Majesty. In his rage, William Bentley almost walked up to the gang of drunken seamen. But in the last instant, some sense deep within him told him to move no further. Breathing rapidly through his nose he blundered back to the ladder, then worked his way aft to find the master-at-arms.

When Henry Joyce was safe below in irons, after a struggle that had cost dear in corporals' teeth, William went to report to his captain. The little man expelled air through his lips in deep satisfaction.

'Well done, my boy,' he said. 'Well done and quickly done. That is the way of it, you see. We must strike hard and we must strike quickly. That way we shall keep the dogs under.'

Thirteen

Next morning Thomas Fox was hauled out of the sick-bay and set to work. As he felt worse even than he had after his spell in the waters off the Isle of Wight, it came as a surprise. Not that he thought of it as such, because he was unable to think in any clear way.

He was lying on his side when the order came. He was very weak, and when he retched nothing came up except a thin dribble of brown, bitter fluid. From time to time in the long hours that marched backwards to the time he had felt well and even happy, surgeon's mates and Peter had tried to 'tempt' him with food – dry biscuit, cheese and beer – which he had refused even to look at. He had drunk some water, but it had made him sicker, having turned brown and muddy because of the violent motion of the water casks.

Not long before, Mr Adamson had come to check his charges. There were four others in the sick-bay besides Thomas now – the corporal with the broken arm, a seaman who had broken his leg when a sea threw him into the scuppers, another seaman with a knife wound under his arm from a drunken fight the night before, and a marine who seemed to have a disease of the stomach. The fracture cases had given over screaming long before, but uttered sharp, squeaking noises when the ship lurched more violently than usual. The cut sailor lay on his back snoring like a pig, while the marine let out long hollow groans of agony every ten minutes or so. He was doubled up so completely that his chin was below his knees. He still had his scarlet coat on, sadly stained with all manner of stains; he was too contorted for it to be removed.

Mr Adamson had recovered his good humour during the long night, although he can have had very little sleep. He hopped around the sick-bay with a bag in one hand and the inevitable brandy bottle in the other, whistling to himself and tutting occasionally as he looked at his patients. The drunk sailor he did not even waken –

101

merely looked at the knife-wound, dabbed at it with a cloth, and retied the bandage. He caught the sick, bright eyes of Thomas as he pulled the man's shirt back across his chest.

'He'll damn my eyes when he wakes, eh boy?' he chirruped. 'Done up his wound and never offered him a drop!' He winked. 'Only the roughest though,' he confided. 'Not the sort of brandy I'd give to granny!'

Thomas would have smiled had he been able to. The surgeon was so kind. He had treated him like a friend, trying everything he knew to make him comfortable. A long swell of nausea racked him and he puked feebly. Not that the treatment had brought comfort, but how Mr Adamson had tried.

'Still as bad is it, young fellow? Never mind, it's only the seasickness. You'll be over it soon, then we'll have you skipping about like a lamb.' He knelt before Thomas and wiped the vomit from his face. 'It'll moderate soon, the weather, you see if it don't. Then we'll have you skipping.'

The surgeon passed on, to ease bandages, check splints, administer brandy. He obviously used it as a cure-all, thought Thomas, and indeed he looked forward to the moment when he could hold some down. His mother placed *her* reliance on herb teas and other country infusions. He suspected that brandy would do as much good as such medicine, while its other properties were far preferable to some of the things that had been forced down his throat.

When the boatswain's mate swam into his view and told him to get up and follow him, Thomas could make no sense of it. Mr Adamson had said nothing of his being better, or fit to leave the sick-bay, or anything. He tried to focus on the face, which was pressed strangely against the deckhead way above him. His eyes ached and he did not take much in. A shambly sort of fellow, with his yellow teeth sticking out of his lips. Thomas closed his eyes again, hoping the vision would go away.

Instead a searing pain dragged deep into his stomach. The boatswain's mate had kicked him. Thomas retched, but nothing came. He opened panic-stricken eyes to see the big bony foot drawn back once more. He struggled to get to his knees, but fell forward into the kick. He started to cry.

Then another pain and he started to rise. It was a magical pain, excruciating, and his body had to follow it, to rise under it. The man was pulling him upright by a thin tuft of his remaining hair.

Through his tears Thomas Fox looked at the slack-lipped, toothy face. It grinned.

'Charlie Jefferies at your service,' said the boatswain's mate. 'Beg to present the compliments of Captain Swift and Mr Allgood. A small matter of punishment, I believe. On account of you a-trying to do for yourself.'

Again Thomas was too ill to really understand. He was half-pushed, half-carried out of the sick-bay and along the main deck. The stench was alarming, even after the dirty straw he had lain on. Everywhere he sensed guns, vague shapes, and men in the gloom. He stumbled over the main cable once, falling to his hands and knees. The deck was wet and slimy.

Climbing the steep ladder into the open air would have been beyond him if it had not been for Jefferies. He was carrying a stiff cane with which he jabbed the boy frequently and hard. It was like a goad such as Thomas might have used himself on a set of stubborn animals. He was whimpering with pain, and a growing fear of the punishment or torture he was to face.

They emerged from a hatchway in the forward part of the ship and to Thomas Fox it meant a renewal of terror and misery. He could see nothing, for a long while, but greyness; greyness and cold. All around the labouring vessel the sea was like slate. All the greenness and warmth he knew had gone. The sea was a cold, intensely threatening colour, overlaid by a grey-whiteness as the tops of the waves were blown out and forward in front of them. And the waves! In his eyes they were enormous. They rose steeply to the weather of the ship and tore down upon her. Each one must crash straight on board and break away everything in its path, he thought. Enough of them actually did break over the bulwarks and roll fast and solid across the waist to make his fears seem perfectly justified. Sometimes the mainmast grew out of a wilderness of living sea that tried to climb higher and higher up its weather side.

He stood quivering in the strong, icy blast of wind that tore at him, until a stroke from Jefferies's rattan slashed across his back. He scrambled onto the deck, with the boatswain's mate immediately behind him.

'Forrard,' said Jefferies tersely. 'Mr Allgood wishes to see you right in the bows.'

The deck was sloping, and there were many men on it. They were sheltering, for the main part, on the high side. Most of them wore tarpaulin coats or long frocks of canvas. Their faces were muffled deep into their necks, and nearly everyone wore a hat of some sort. Thomas, who no longer even had a jacket, tried to keep his teeth from rattling as he moved slowly from one handhold to the next. Right behind him, all the time, was Jefferies, hurrying him, pushing him, starting him with the stinging cane. It struck Thomas as impossible, this movement from one part of the ship to another; but other men left their sheltered points and scurried about like goats at shouted orders. He was still filled with nausea, but his head was clearer. He managed to duck to avoid the larger lumps of solid water that broke over the bow. But by the time they were clear of the foremast he was wet through.

The chill in his stomach got much worse when he recognised one of the two figures who came towards them. It was small, a lot smaller than himself, wearing a long tarpaulin and a shiny tarpaulin hat. From under it the small clear face looked at Thomas Fox, the eyes bright. A few strands of blond hair were plastered across the bottom of the hat and the forehead. It was the midshipman who had kidnapped him.

Thomas staggered and might have fallen, but Allgood, who was beside William Bentley, put out a hand like a dinnerplate and took him by the shoulder.

'Where are your clothes, my scrawny boy?' he said. 'What sort of gear do you think that is to start your life as a sailor, now?'

'I think the big shirt suits him very well,' said the small midshipman. 'It leaves him plenty of room to manoeuvre.'

The boatswain glanced at him.

'As you say, Mr Bentley, sir,' he replied. 'Plenty of room to move. I was just thinking though – perhaps he'll be too cold to move a muscle soon.'

He still had hold of Thomas. Despite the weather, his enormous hand was warm. It almost struck him as being somehow friendly.

'Then perhaps you had better see to it that he works sufficiently to *keep* warm, Mr Allgood,' the midshipman said. 'I do not have to remind you that this is intended as a punishment.'

104

Mr Allgood thrust his great whiskery face into Thomas Fox's.

'And as such,' he boomed, 'shall be hot work, my fine young lamb. Right, sir,' he said to Bentley. 'You can leave 'un to me and get back to shelter.'

'Thank you, boatswain,' the boy replied icily. 'I shall decide for myself when to return to my duties aft.'

The boatswain moved his shoulders under his coat. It could have been a shrug, or perhaps he was just keeping his balance. But he turned his back on Bentley.

'Listen, my bright spark,' he told Thomas. 'We have a task for you that Captain Swift do think will fit your abilities. On board this vessel, the illustrious Welfare, it is known as being the liar. And if you recall, you did lie when you come on board of her.'

'Please sir, I—'

'Silence!'

Thomas looked from the bland hairy face of the dripping boatswain to the contorted face of the midshipman who had shouted. If only he knew what to make of it all. Surely this boy, this child, was not in control of the mountain of flesh and muscle who was now smiling faintly? But who had himself, in any case, been roaring only seconds before. He wanted to cry out, to tell them that he did not understand, to ask them how he was meant to respond. He kept silent. If nothing else, he had learned that much. He said not a word.

William Bentley spoke. His voice was thin, irascible.

'Captain Swift has been more than generous with you, Thomas Fox. He has decided to neither flog you, nor lock you in irons, nor try you by court martial for your attempted suicide. But for now, starting from the moment Mr Allgood thinks fit to put you to it at last, you are to be the Welfare's liar. That is, you are to clean the heads. And I want them *clean*. They shall be inspected. If you fail in this duty a *real* punishment will quickly follow.

'It has not gone unnoticed, youth, that you have a tendency to slackness, to malingering. If you ever have occasion to return to the sick-bay, it will be because you have been given a more proper reason. Do you understand?'

Thomas goggled. The boatswain shook him.

'Say "Aye aye sir" to the young gentleman,' he said.

'Aye aye sir,' said Thomas.

'Good,' said Allgood. 'Jefferies, get about your business. And now, my lambkin liar. Let's get to the heads.'

Because of his condition, and the condition of the weather, Thomas Fox had forgotten, if he ever knew, what the heads were. No one had used them since the Welfare hit the dirty weather, more especially since it had come round to meet her from the south and west. The bluff bows were constantly burying themselves deep into the short, steep seas, which every so often broke right over the foredeck. Standing right in the eyes of the ship a few moments later, after he had clawed his way along with the boatswain and the midshipman, Thomas looked down beside the bowsprit completely puzzled. Below him, if he ignored the yellow cliff of the bow itself, was nothing but the rigging and gammoning of the huge, groaning spar. And a sort of small gallery. He stared.

'Good God!' shouted the midshipman after a short pause. 'Do you know what I think, Mr Allgood? I think the scoundrel does not recognise 'em at all. He does not know the heads when he sees 'em!'

It was true. All Thomas could see was a gallery, with seats. In the seats, about eighteen inches apart, were cut round holes. Through the holes the boiling sea was visible. On the side of the bow nearest him and below, cut in the bulkhead, was a stout door or hatchway. It was closed and battened.

The boatswain gave his deep, loud laugh. It was whipped away by the wind.

'Them there,' he said, 'is the heads. The jakes. The privies.' Another laugh. 'Although there ain't too much privy about them when all's said, eh!'

'And they are to be cleaned,' said William Bentley. 'It is Captain Swift's orders that men who defile the air with lies must clean the heads. You, Thomas Fox, will clean the heads.'

At that moment, Allgood, whose eyes had never stopped flicking at the marching grey seas the ship was punching into, gave a grunt of warning. His ham-hand gripped Thomas suddenly and he tightened his hold on the bulwarks. The Welfare's nose began to dive with alarming speed. Down and down she went into a trough, as if she were falling. It seemed to Thomas that she could never stop. The midshipman had lost his balance and was scrabbling for a handhold. When the ship hit the bottom, as it were, Bentley fell to his knees at the shock. Thomas looked, fascinated, as the sea, deep green when seen so close, rose in front of them like a wall. The surface of it rushed upwards, up the bow, up the stem, bursting round the gallery. For a split second, weird great gushes of water spouted through the privy holes. Then the gallery was gone and the sea rose higher.

In the roaring before it broke over the foredeck, he heard Allgood yell at him to hang on. He did, with every ounce of his strength. He was saved though, as he well knew, by the fact that the boatswain had spared a hand for him as well as holding the bulwarks.

The sea broke right over them. He thought he would drown before it cleared. He thought his arms would break as the solid water tore at his body. He would have cried out in terror, but his lungs were too busy fighting the cold salt invader that tried to fill them. Time stopped. The fingers of the boatswain bit into his shoulder and back. There was nothing except freezing water, pain, a roaring in his ears.

The deck beneath him began to vibrate. It pushed upwards urgently. The Welfare began to rise, to fight back. Before he fully knew it, the water around his head had become less solid. His lungs sucked in a vast gout of air and spray combined. He coughed and spluttered. Then his shoulders were clear, and rapidly the water rushed past him, across the planking and over the sides. The weed-draped forefoot appeared as the Welfare lifted herself high before beginning the next plunge.

Mr Allgood, streaming like a fountain, smiled at him.

'That was a bitch of a sea, eh my buck!' he said gaily. 'The seventh son of the seventh son!' He laughed at Thomas's blank look, then said to himself, in a lower tone: 'And where's our fine young gent, I wonder?'

William Bentley emerged just then from the lee scuppers. He was white about the face, except for his mouth, where bright blood streamed from a torn lip.

'Ah,' breathed Allgood. There was a strange note in his voice. But the hairy face was as bland as ever.

As Bentley limped up to them the boatswain said stiffly: 'Sorry about your accident, Mr Bentley, sir. I should have sung out earlier.'

The midshipman was shaking; not much, but visibly.

107

'You are wasting time, boatswain,' he said. Despite himself his voice was gaspy. Thomas looked at the deck, at the storm head-sails, anywhere except at his face. He was beginning to work things out.

'Get that dog to his task immediately. I shall have an eye upon you.'

He turned on his heel and walked to the weather rail. Then he began to work his way aft.

It did not occur to Thomas immediately exactly what Bentley's last remark had meant. He took in the scene on the deck where several knots of men were trying to secure everything that had broken free before another big sea swept her. On the quarterdeck stood a few officers, in shiny tarpaulin. Behind them, the wastes of the Channel, bleak and lonely.

He was shivering with cold. He could not be wetter. He had been covered way over his head in water. The keen wind pressed the wet cloth to his thin body. His teeth began to chatter. He turned his eyes to Mr Allgood, fear growing in his stomach. The midshipman had spoken of his task. There was a cold light in Allgood's eyes.

'No,' muttered Thomas. 'Oh no. Sir, I could not.'

Allgood let go of his shoulder.

'You heard the young gentleman,' he said. 'Get about your business before you regret it sorely.'

The heads could not *need* cleaning in this weather, he thought. They were being constantly washed by these waves. And no one could use them.

'No,' he mumbled. 'Please sir. I cannot.'

A new, hard note came into the boatswain's voice.

'Get down there, boy, before I take a cane to you. God damn it, do you dare to defy orders!'

Thomas Fox could not raise his eyes from the deck, although he saw nothing.

'Oh please sir,' he said.

At last, with lifeline and a stiff broom, he found himself in the beakhead gallery. He was not sure how he came to be there. He knew the boatswain had lifted him, had knotted a rope about his waist. His fingers were almost too nerveless to hold the rail, let alone the broom. His head swam. Each time the gallery dipped

108

and the sea rushed up towards him he went rigid with shock. The memory of that monstrous wave that had engulfed him was unbearable.

His bewilderment over Mr Allgood was complete. He was a mighty man, in physique and in power on the ship. He had saved Thomas, and yet he put him to this agony. Even now he stood above him, roaring occasionally when Thomas went numb, and striking out with the free end of the lifeline which he held. Thomas felt nothing except the crashing rise and fall of the bow, saw nothing except the green seas that turned to raging foam as the ship ploughed into them. He moved the broom this way and that as if he was in a dream. The agony was never-ending.

When the boatswain at last told him to come back inboard, Thomas was not able to. His legs were too weak to lift him up the bulkhead and his fingers were too weak to grip it. He looked at the grating beneath his feet, watched the foaming stempost, his head hanging.

'Look at me, boy!' roared Allgood. But he could not raise his head. In the end the boatswain hauled him onto the foredeck as if he had been a parcel. Thomas half walked, half crawled to a hatchway, blindly. If another big sea had raked the deck he would surely have been washed away. He fell through the hatch and lay on the deck below. Peter found him and led him to the mess.

Fourteen

The reason no more big seas came aboard, although Thomas did not know it, was because the weather was moderating. It was also hauling back to the east. When dawn had broken Jesse Broad had been way aloft, sent there with other keen-eyed men to search for signs of the Frenchman. The seas were empty. In every direction there was nothing but rolling water, white-capped and angry, and torn, lowering cloud. They had given her the slip.

Jesse Broad did not have long enough to decide if he regretted it or not. For by the time of full daylight, which came late and was not accompanied in any case by good visibility, another hazard was seen by the highest man on the mainmast. After he had sung out, the other men in the rigging strained their eyes for signs of land. A few minutes later Jesse could see the faint line of breakers away down to leeward.

A great pain seized him. All chances of being weather-bound had gone. The French frigate that he had hoped might force them to make port for repairs had lost them in the night. Now here to leeward were the breakers on the coast of England. He stared until his eyes ached. But he could not tell if he saw land or merely the barriers of cloud that hung over the coastline. The coastline of England. And now the Welfare would claw off and they would be clear; be gone. He wondered if he would ever see it again.

Shortly after the sighting, all the lookouts were called down to normal duties, save the highest. Given the small number of skilful men he had, Captain Swift's way was to make them work on sundry tasks, not necessarily in their normal parts of ship. So Broad, nominally a mainmast topman, was not spared other work as well, even on other masts. It was a killing system. The duty now was to put the ship about, to turn her away from those hungry breakers and steer her out into the Channel. Jesse and the other men raced each other to the deck where the boatswain's mates waited with their rope's ends and rattans, the officers hunched like vultures on the quarterdeck, and the midshipmen strutted like vicious guinea-fowl, ready to pounce and tyrannise for any reason or none.

The Welfare was still carrying the close-reefed topsails and storm headsails she had worn throughout the night. But handling them was even harder if anything, now that another day had broken. More men than ever were down sick, no one had eaten a hot meal since God knew when, and very few had slept. The exhausted sailors stumbled to sheets and braces like donkeys; hands were clumsy and easily torn through long immersion in sea-water. Broad's head was splitting as he did his share of the work. His brain was numb and his limbs seemed all to hurt.

As he crossed from one set of running rigging to another, he staggered against Matthews, head bent into his weather-proofed coat, his face almost hidden in an oiled hat. Matthews gave him a sort of smile.

'Glad you signed to serve the King, Mr Smuggler?' he said sardonically.

Broad smiled back.

'As glad as I guess you are to be handling hemp instead of bawling the orders,' he replied. They passed on to their respective positions.

Huddled under the shelter of the weather bulwarks later, Broad remembered storms at sea when he'd been running cargoes. Many a night he and his friends had battled for hours on end. Joel Gauthier, of the Beauregard, was a great man for working in dirty weather. But this was different. He could not remember ever being so weary, so hungry, so cold. As for the end of it – well, with his old trade, the end was always just over the horizon. As an able seaman in His Majesty's Navy, what end could he ever hope for?

His sombre thoughts were not helped when he saw Thomas Fox being brought on deck by Jefferies. In the times when he was not being kept on his toes by the shouted orders from aft or the manual dexterity of the boatswain's mates, he watched what was going on in the vessel's eyes. Grandfather Fulman, sucking salt-water through his cold and empty clay, told him of Daniel Swift's embracing of the widespread naval custom of appointing a 'liar'. They were usually chosen for a week, he said. The master-at-arms or a corporal would catch someone in a lie – or force someone into one more like – and he would take up the appointment.

'But in weather like this?' said Broad, watching the isolated trio at the bow. 'Hell's teeth, no man on board could *use* the heads, let alone clean them. Are they mad?'

Grandfather Fulman looked around him carefully under his dripping, shaggy eyebrows.

'Mad?' he muttered. 'Ah, friend Jesse. There's many on board of this vessel —'

A shout went up from ahead of them, and the Welfare began the fast, deep plunge into the monster sea that had arisen to weather of her. Broad watched its rise out of the corner of his eye as he reached for a secure handhold.

'Grip hard, lad,' said Fulman.

There was a strange momentary lull before the sea hit them, as the height of it deflected the savage wind above the canvas she was wearing. Then the wall rose in a great black surge over the bow and the weather rail.

In the confusion that followed, with loose timbers careering about the waist and men coughing water from their lungs and stomachs, Broad noticed that the midshipman had gone from the foredeck.

'Grandfather!' he said urgently. 'We've lost that mid!'

The old fellow was a sorry sight himself. He was red with fury and wetter than a drowned cat. He had bitten hard at his pipe to save it, but the weight of water had carried away the bowl. But he turned his face to the foredeck in a flash.

'Damn me, Jesse Broad, I think you're right!' he said excitedly. 'Now there's a cause to rejoice!'

Jesse was shocked at the exultance in his messmate's voice.

'Hold hard, Fulman,' he said. 'It is only a boy!'

Grandfather Fulman spat.

'See that, Broad,' he said viciously. 'I have spat on the deck. My mouth is full of salt and dottle from me pipe. And anyway, I'm an old man, entitled to spitting. Six months ago I spat like that, on a night as black as hell, and over the side, not on the deck, and young master Bentley was a-spying and caught me at it. I wore the spitkid for a week. And was lucky, quoth he, not to be flogged. I shall not mourn the nephew of the uncle.'

112

The ship was wallowing heavily in the aftermath of the sea. There were loose spars to be seized, secured, restowed. The boatswain's mates, as wet as anyone, were venting their fury on any back within reach. Before he jumped to stop a partly adzed yard from rolling overside, Broad saw that Bentley had rejoined Thomas Fox and Allgood. He was relieved, despite what Fulman had said.

After an hour of heavy, wet work, the pair were sheltering once more. The old man was panting painfully, the darkened pipe-stem still gripped in the side of his toothless mouth. Broad said nothing to him, so as not to increase his distress by having to reply. He looked into the eye of the wind, then up at the masts, then at the quarterdeck, where the slight form of Mr Robinson was huddled in a great cloak.

'You'll be needing that breath soon, old fellow,' he told Fulman with a smile. 'We'll be setting more sail before much longer unless I'm not the seaman I used to be. It's falling lighter all the time; aye, and fairer too. I'll wager we'll have back that easterly we lost yesterday. And we'll get it before we get a hot meal!'

After a bit he added: 'What is this of a spitkid, that you were telling me? It cannot be enough to wish the child drowned, whatever.'

Fulman panted for a few minutes longer before answering.

'You have a lot to learn about the Navy,' he said. 'For instance, you probably do not know that on this ship we could incur the wrath of any officer, or snotty little boy even, by merely talking like this. When on deck, on watch, we should be silent. Your eyes are too still, Jesse. You should keep them moving more.'

It was true that Fulman's own hooded eyes never stopped roaming. Even here on the bleak, roaring deck he spoke in whispers and watched like a hawk everyone who moved.

'The spitkid now,' he went on. 'It weighed a great deal for a man of my years, and was full of tobacco juice and spittle and other vilenesses. That young fellow whose miserable hide you value so much had one of Allgood's mates lash it round my neck like the feedbag of a beast. I wore it for six days.'

Jesse Broad shook his head. The punishments on board these ships seemed hardly to be borne.

'And young master Bentley made damned sure that it was kept in use,' said Fulman bitterly. He noted Broad's look. 'Aye, that shakes you, eh? He made sure that any man who wished to spit did it in "Grandfather's spitkid". Now are you so keen on the boy?

'And for another thing,' he said curiously. 'Did he not aid your own taking? Did he not kill your friend? And why do you think young Thomas Fox is suffering under Allgood's lash, the poor simple boy?'

Broad's eyes flinched at the mention of Hardman. The hours of work and hardship had cleared his mind of thoughts of friends, home, wife and family. A vivid picture leapt into his mind. The wherry racing through the waves to the christening; Hardman talking of the French girl, Louise, he'd taken a fancy to. The sudden shock, the sight of sword and pistol, the flash of powder and the blow on his head. But he remembered one thing. It was the oafish third lieutenant, Higgins, who had killed Hardman, not William Bentley.

In many ways it helped, the way each and every conversation, each and every activity, was interrupted on the ship. He hoped he would never have the time to brood, to grow a seed of hatred inside him, if the weather should turn good. He dreaded what might happen if the sea and the wind became kindly and there was too much time to think.

Now the call was to go about, which would be followed for a guinea by the setting of more sail. The wind was backing south and east so fast that on their present tack they would soon be going in the wrong direction. It was still blowing very fresh, but it was easing. He made for his assigned position at the main brace with a sense of relief. He would have to hear more of the old man's tales, he would have to think about the sort of society fate had landed him in; but not now, thank the Lord. Now there was the simple necessity of forcing his weary arms and legs to handle the damp and slippery ropes, to force his aching brain to sort out and interpret the orders which he still found complicated. He was learning to be a deep-sea man. It was enough . . .

In the red-painted fug of the midshipmen's berth, the nephew of the uncle, William Bentley, was stretched across two sea chests, his face twisted, while the surgeon tried to put back his dislocated shoulder. The other midshipmen, both young gentlemen and the older hands whose title and berth they shared, were ranged about

114

the makeshift table trying to give Mr Adamson some assistance, physical and moral.

'Trouble is you see, young Bentley,' the tiny surgeon chirped, 'is that I'm so blessed puny. It is said that a rearing horse frightened me into the world before my time, and I never made up for the lost growth!'

William bared his teeth in his sweat-glistening white face, in what he hoped was a smile. Dolby, the senior midshipman in terms of years if nothing else, tutted as if disapprovingly. Jack Evans laughed obligingly, while the two other young mids, Simon Allen and James Finch, said nothing. Finch, indeed, was prostrate on a large chest. He was only just twelve and had been terribly ill.

'Come on now,' continued the surgeon. 'You, Mr Dolby, sit on his legs, that's the ticket. Now, you, what's your name, Evans. You and him grab that arm you see sticking out to the side.'

William was in agony. He lay on his back, staring at the low deckhead. He was stripped to the waist, with sweat pouring in runnels down his chest and sides. Evans and Simon latched hold of the arm as the surgeon indicated, while he himself moved to the other side of the table. On his way round he bobbed his head close to peer into William's eyes.

'Not looking too good, young chappie,' he said brightly. 'Mouth all cut up too. Drop more brandy, eh?'

William smiled again, but shook his head. The trouble with Mr Adamson was that his surgery sometimes left men dead drunk, if not dead.

'It's a bad sight right enough,' said Adamson. 'Arm stuck out like a semaphore. How did you manage it?'

William wished he would stop talking and get on with it, but he tried to answer to take his mind off the pain.

'A big sea,' he said. 'Perhaps you felt it.'

The surgeon screeched with laughter.

'Oh aye, I felt it, Mr Bentley, I felt it. It kept me very busy for a while in the sick-bay did that.' He paused. 'Else I would have been here sooner.'

'No matter for that, sir,' said William. 'It almost did for me, that sea. I was knocked clear across the foredeck, and fetched up in the chains.'

Jack Evans's high-pitched voice made him turn his head.

115

'And very lucky you were too, Will. I was aft and saw you go. I squeaked so loud I got sent below for my pains.'

William felt a burst of irritation as the colour rose in his friend's cheeks. That was much as one would expect from Jack. It was not the place of a young gentleman to behave in that manner. There was an example to be upheld, always an example.

Evans went on: 'You took it very well too, all upon the quarterdeck could note that. You walked back aft calm as you please, although how you managed it with your arm like that I cannot imagine. Why Will, it sticks out two points to starboard now, but then it was quite flat at your side.'

Well that, thought William, was something. It had cost him a great deal not to let the boatswain know he had been hurt. It was pain enough to have been caught unawares by the sea. One hand for yourself one hand for the ship was one golden rule, and always to keep a weather eye out was another. He had done neither, which was gross stupidity on the foredeck in a gale. Allgood knew it, and William hated the blandness of his face, his remarks that reeked of hidden insolence. His apology for not singing out earlier was a case in point; how could one define the subtlety of the insult?

'I suppose it was the seventh wave,' said old Dolby quietly, from his seat on William's legs. 'They say every seventh wave is a big 'un right enough.'

This only increased his irritation. It was such a typical remark from that old woman.

'Oh for God's sake, Dolby,' he snarled. 'Did we ship every seventh sea like that? In the whole time did we meet a sea like that?'

Dolby's colour deepened.

'That may be, sir,' he said. 'But when you've been at sea as long—'

'Shut up!' snapped William Bentley.

And: 'Hey-up!' chirruped the surgeon, throwing his weight across the table.

The suddenness of it forced a cry from William's lips. A sharp pain across the chest, a definite meaty click, and his shoulder was back. Relief and irritation mingled within him.

'Punishment taken like a man,' sang out Mr Adamson. 'Or a young gentleman, to be sure!'

The boy closed his eyes and muttered his ungracious thanks. Oh hell, he thought, the people on this ship are so low, so near to cowards all. It was vile, always to have to be an example for their better behaviour.

Fifteen

When the larboard watch was piped on deck next morning, Jesse Broad knew at once that all the slim chances he had been praying for had passed. The sky was high and blue, with a few streaks of white wind-cloud. The sea was deep green, with occasional whitecaps, and much longer and easier than it had been. They were in the Atlantic, he reckoned. The wind was on their quarter, and it looked set fair. During the four hours he had been asleep below, Welfare had spread her wings. All plain sail was set and drawing on the main and mizzen masts, and during his watch the task of setting up a new fore topgallant mast, to replace the one that had carried away, was completed. Stunsails were rigged on the lower yards to drive her along at her very best speed. High up in the rigging he stared over the stern towards England. But there was nothing to be seen.

All spare hands were set to clean ship. The hatches were unbattened and a vile reek rose from them, to be blown briskly away over the bow. Thomas Fox was put to tending his beasts, which had suffered miserably during the bad weather. He was glad of the task, for the others had the far worse one of clearing the filth off the decks. Pumps were rigged and manned, buckets ran in chains, water splashed and gurgled everywhere. The portlids were lashed open, making the deck light once more. For an hour Thomas kept his head buried in the smell of the animals, as being sweeter than that from the gun-deck. But gradually the vomit and excrement was sluiced away – much of it into the bilges, true, and the ship became a cleaner, more bearable thing.

After the sluicing came the scrubbing. Thomas had finished mucking out the beasts, so had to join the others with holystone and prayerbook. He needed to give the animals more attention; three hens had already died and others were weak, a pig was looking sick indeed, two poor sheep had injured legs; but he could not bear to say so. The sight of a boatswain's mate, after his ordeal, made his eyes seek the deck. When Jefferies walked by six feet away he began to tremble.

So he knelt with the rest, the heavy sandstone block in front of him, his trousers rolled high, scrubbing for his life.

The work, like all work on the frigate, was meant to be done in silence. But Thomas was beside Peter. Peter talked.

'Every day we do this, young Tommy,' he said. 'Every morning, some afternoons, and not a few night-times.'

Thomas said nothing. The deck beneath him was dark, stained. The boatswain's mates kept yelling 'White – white and glaring till it blinds the eyes out of you!' He had no reason to suppose they did not mean it. He scrubbed harder.

'It is the worst part of all, I suppose,' Peter went on. 'What I hates about it is – on an empty stomach it hurts worse than it need. If they would only wait until *after* breakfast!'

Grandfather Fulman and the other greybeard in the mess sloshed more water from a bucket, followed by two handfuls of sand.

'Then again,' said Peter, 'it do hurt the knees so. But if you keeps your breeches rolled down – why then, soon you has no breeches worth speaking of!'

On they scrubbed. The pain in his arms and knees was getting worse. But the planking was coming up whiter, in one place at least.

A boatswain's mate roared: 'Harder, you lousy scum! Harder! If I can't blind my bleeding eyes on that deck there, I'll see you flayed alive!'

The deck was a mass of men, on their knees, moving rhythmically up and down as if praying to some Eastern god. In front of each knot others walked backwards with buckets. Decrepit old fellows as a rule, or sick men, or cripples.

'Damn his own eyes,' hissed Peter. 'Oh, this be a terrible service to be in Tommy, terrible.

'Why,' he went on, not pausing for a second in his scrubbing although his voice had become quite dreamy, 'why, if I was still on shore now, I'd have had me breakfast inside me, piping hot, and would be sitting like a lord on a bolt of hay, smoking a pipe and supping a can of ale.'

Slosh, went Fulman's bucket, followed by a patter of sand. Peter shook his red hair from his eyes, laughing.

119

'What a fool I am though!' he said. ''Tis all lies, Thomas, all lies. I never came by so much kindness on shore as I do now, and as for hot breakfasts! Well, not long now, my dear messmate, and breakfast will be piped – and piping hot too! Did you ever come by a hot breakfast on shore, Thomas? I'll wager you did not!'

Thomas said nothing. He scrubbed and scrubbed, and thanked God for his strong arms. At least he could make his patch of deck as white as the next boy's, although he doubted he'd ever have a sailor's power; fine muscular men some of them were. He did not answer Peter's question, not even in his own mind. He could not think of breakfast at home, nor yet dinner nor supper. Home was a bright red spot deep in his head, not to be touched on.

When the worst of the stench in the men's quarters was gone, there was still much more scrubbing to be done. Peter explained that this was not usual; but that such sickness and filth was not either. Today, he reckoned, they'd be at scrub and clean until dinner time. But first there were hammocks to stow and breakfast to be had.

In all his time on board Thomas had not yet attempted to sleep in a hammock, far less to lash one ready for stowing. In his time below he had been in the sick-bay, or too tired and ill to know or care where he slept. When the order to lash up came, Grandfather Fulman and Peter took him under their wings. The long unwieldy canvas with its nettles and lines was like a self-willed animal to him. But Peter's dexterity was amazing, and Fulman promised he would teach him more slowly when the occasion arose. Thomas was anxious to learn; to learn anything, because he feared the consequences of making a mistake, however small. Despite Peter's dexterity, despite the bent old man's encouragement, Thomas was afraid he would never get the hang of it. His fingers had always been a countryman's – clumsy and blunt. Only in making and playing musical instruments did they work delicately and well. He was afraid.

At the order 'Up hammocks and stow!' there was a mad dash for the ladders. He was jostled, punched and kicked, although Peter kept close to him and held his arm; a strange bodyguard, more than a foot shorter than his charge. But Peter was a sailor born, of a different breed from Thomas. He would bite, kick, punch with the worst of them if need be. Or wield steel, Thomas guessed. He reminded him of a small ginger stoat, and he was glad to be in his 'family' and not against it.

William Bentley watched the outpouring of men from his position on the quarterdeck. They reminded him of so many cattle, blundering about, jostling each other as they sought their places at the hammock nettings. One big, dark man stopped and looked about him. William shouted to a boatswain's mate.

'Ahoy! Boatswain's mate there! Start that dog, if you please!'

The mate obligingly swung his rope's end, a knobbly affair of Turk's heads and fancy work. The sailor yelped, and jumped towards the nettings. William turned his attention to the others. Stragglers must be punished. Discipline must be instilled. He glanced at the first lieutenant, who had the watch, but Hagan was studying the set of the canvas, not apparently interested in the demeanour of the men, William noted. It irritated him; Hagan was too easy-going. He wondered why his uncle, who was a stickler for discipline, had landed himself with such a weak sort of fellow. At that moment Hagan dropped his eyes from the sails. They met William's, and the first lieutenant smiled. William looked away, although not as abruptly as he would have liked to. The first lieutenant was, after all, still the first lieutenant.

'Set fair at last, Mr Bentley, I should think,' he remarked. 'I think we can perhaps have the people scrub out their hammocks this afternoon.'

'Aye aye sir,' William replied smartly. He made a mental note of it. The first lieutenant was, after all, still the first lieutenant.

Shortly afterwards William was aware that the sentry of marines on ship-time duty had approached him from behind. He knew the time to the minute, but he let the soldier wait for some seconds before he turned. He said nothing, raising his eyebrows in enquiry. Everything must be deliberate; everything must be correct. That way the Welfare would become a taut ship.

The marine, stiff to attention despite the still considerable movement of the ship, told him that it was fifteen minutes past seven a.m. William acknowledged with a nod. As the sentry returned to the hatchway, the midshipman of the watch stepped up to the first lieutenant.

He inclined his head.

'The quarter, sir.'

'Thank you, Mr Bentley.'

William repeated his half-bow and withdrew. The first lieutenant raised his eyebrows at the boatswain. Mr Allgood, also without speaking, passed on the order. The calls shrilled; hands were piped to breakfast.

Thomas went with Peter, who had been designated mess cook that week, to the galley up forward. As they reached it, he realised how hungry he was. As they stood with the crowds of other men, one from each mess, his knees went weak at the smell of the hot oatmeal broth. It occurred to him that he had not eaten for days. He did not know how many, but it had indeed been for days. His hands shook as they carried back the messkid and the burgoo was split up amongst them. He could not wait to fill his mouth with the scalding, soupy food. Whether they had been well enough to eat or not before, his friends behaved much as he did. Within a couple of minutes the platters were licked clean. They sat about for a while, belching noisily, drinking deep draughts of beer. Peter was watching Thomas's face with his button eyes shining.

'Well well, Thomas,' he said. 'Ain't you going to have a sup?'

Thomas was. He had been savouring it, for he liked beer. But when he filled his mouth he almost gagged. The others laughed.

'Not like mother brews 'un, I'll warrant me,' said Grandfather Fulman. 'That's Government ale, young Thomas, and bad already. And it gets worser as we gets further from land!'

Peter looked eagerly at him.

'If you finds him too sour, Tommy,' he said, 'I'll finish him for you. For I've a stomach of iron, and can drink beer that's stood three months or more!'

Everyone laughed again. Thomas closed his eyes and gulped. It was sour and thin. But it was beer.

'Beg pardon, Peter,' he said. 'But I might manage by myself thankee.'

After their half-hour was up, it was hands to scrubbing once more. At the end of another two, even Peter was silenced. Thomas felt as though his arms would drop off, and his knees were both bleeding. Many other men's knees left bloody blotches – you could tell the old hands by the thickness of the calluses on knees and elbows – so the oldsters who walked ahead with the buckets took a turn behind every so often to mop up the new stains. It was deadly work.

* * *

122

Jesse Broad was busy too, but he considered himself luckier than all his messmates, except Matthews, who was at least as useful in some of the finer details of the seaman's craft. They and the other able men were set to overhauling cordage and sails that had strained or carried away. The mizzen topsail had torn along a reef band during the night, so the first main job after the fore topgallant mast was to get it off her and bend a new sail. As before, the normal divisions were ignored. The boatswain and the sailmaker worked in unison, directing the gangs of men to each new task, whether on 'their' mast or not.

Far out along the mizzen topsail yard, Jesse struggled with a feeling that was almost joy. It frightened him that he should feel it, despite the end of all hopes for salvation, but he could not deny it. His ears were filled with a musical, deep-toned thrumming. The ship, under a heavy press of canvas, was flying along, each rope and spar trembling, alive. His eyes were filled with a world of sparkling brilliance, exceeded in beauty only by the Welfare herself. She reminded him of a bird, a great, beautiful, vibrant bird. The cold wind seemed to clear all the degradation and unpleasantness of the past days away from him. His tiredness had vanished. He was a seaman at sea; God help me, he thought ruefully, it is my life!

Down below him the sailors on the bright deck looked small and insignificant. They were scrubbing hammocks and clothes in the afternoon sunshine. What a strange gang, so many old men, so many boys. He tried to crush the feeling that he was better, but in truth he felt it. Whatever the rights and wrongs of it, here was life, up here, in control, in command, of cord and canvas. Aft he could see the man at the wheel; and envied only him.

When his gaze travelled farther aft, and caught the small figure of Daniel Swift, stern and upright in his bright blue coat, a cloud passed over the sun of his happiness. He had spoken to Fulman no more about him yet, but the captain was making his presence and his spirit known quite rapidly enough. His reputation, which Broad had been prepared to water down despite his own treatment, was fast being confirmed by events.

At the turn of the morning, the air of rejoicing that had somehow pervaded the ship had come to an abrupt end. Not, thought Broad, that many had much to rejoice about, himself included. But there it was; rational or not, the end of the storms, the cleaning of the foulness from the quarters, a hot meal, if only of burgoo, had brought a new feeling to the people. A lightness, in some cases almost a jollity.

The cloud had fallen when the marine drummer beat all hands to witness punishment. Matthews and Broad, who had been working together setting up a shroud, had looked at each other, puzzled. Other men too. Because punishment had been forgotten while the weather prevented it, and now the weather had made them feel happy. Punishment was in no one's mind.

They guessed that it was to be Henry Joyce, the man who had been arrested after the episode of running from the Frenchman. The arrest had stilled the wagging tongues instantly, and no one had spoken anything about the matter since. But it bade fair to be a savage punishment, for Swift would hardly take kindly to such talk.

But it had been another man. The man, in fact, Thomas had seen in the sick-bay with the knife wound. When his shirt was stripped off and he was triced to the grating, the wound was clearly visible, closed and healing very well. Ten minutes later it was open, and hidden in a welter of blood from many other slashes. Jesse Broad found the flogging far more sickening than his own, somehow. And when the man had been released, he had stared with black and hate-filled eyes at the unmoving figure of Captain Swift, until he had been beaten below by Allgood's mates. The 'mutineer', Joyce, was said to be still in irons. God knew what Swift had in mind for him.

After the punishment, which the captain prefaced with another of his bitter homilies on discipline, they were served with a good dinner, including fresh vegetables, then the rum ration. Broad had secreted some of his, because he knew he would be working aloft all afternoon and feared a muggy head. But many of the company did get drunk, as how could they not on the great can of fiery spirit, on top of all the beer they had been served? In the course of the next hour, two were arrested and were now below. Perhaps there was to be a flogging every day. Or perhaps Swift might dream up other punishments.

Now below him the waisters worked at scrubbing hammocks, the officers strutted, the purser sold slops.

Another thought came into his mind. That strange man Allgood. He could not make him out. Only yesterday he had terrified poor Thomas Fox half to death on the foredeck, and today he had treated him like a lamb. He had taken him to the purser, Grandfather Fulman had related, and rigged him out in new gear. When the

124

purser had tried to rook him Allgood had intimidated that worthy to such an extent that the boy ended up with shirt, blouse, trousers and tarpaulin at a fairer price than any man on board could boast. The purser had said nothing, but given sour looks; it was, after all, his God-given right to cheat poor sailors. No man would dare rob Thomas again, or take his clothes off his back as they had done, now that Allgood had shown this interest.

But still there remained the day before. True the boatswain had been under orders to make the boy clean the heads, mad as that order was. But he had filled the lad with some sort of terror, that much had been clear. Thomas Fox had become nervous to a degree. He trembled when approached. He cast his eyes always downwards to the deck. Jesse Broad felt an odd protectiveness towards him; he was concerned.

He thought of the purser again. He did not know him, but had seen him and heard his reputation. He was a short, fat, slimy-looking man who rejoiced in the nickname 'Butterbum'. His power on board was equal to Allgood's in his own field; in the field, that is, of robbing seamen or making their lives miserable in many crafty ways. God help Thomas Fox if Mr Purser took it upon himself to seek revenge for the manner in which the boatswain had dealt with him. God help Thomas Fox.

As always, new orders ended coherent thoughts. Seconds later Jesse was racing hand over hand towards the deck, racing to the next task, which was on the fore topgallant yard. As he dodged the rattans on the deck, and darted between outstretched, dripping hammocks, he had only time to envy the men who had the knack of sliding down the stays. It was an art he would have to acquire if he was to be a fast hand.

Sixteen

he good weather continued, much to everyone's surprise and delight, and the Welfare was soon far out into the Atlantic. William Bentley and the other young gentlemen were required to take a noon sight with the master, who also delivered dry lectures on the Trade winds and various other nautical matters – still in his mysterious role as interpreter of the ship's innermost feelings. William found him very vexing, very hard to follow. He sometimes suspected, in fact, that Mr Robinson enjoyed confusing the midshipmen, who were not of his own class and who sometimes showed their resentment at the power the ugly, uncouth little man held over the mysteries of the sun, stars and sea. He dared to mention it to his uncle over tea one morning, but not in any direct fashion. Captain Swift merely laughed and reiterated that Robinson was the best seaman-navigator he had ever encountered.

A man they resented far more was the schoolmaster, Mr Marner. One bad consequence of the reasonable weather was that this old worthy emerged from his hole like a hedgehog in spring and began to torment them. All the boys hated and despised him, but Captain Swift was unapproachable on this score too; his young gentlemen were young gentlemen, and they would behave and be taught as such. When William had tried, in a roundabout way, to get himself excused, the pale eyes had turned on him and grown paler. William wished he had not spoken, for he had certainly angered his uncle. And it was ridiculous, for Marner was a drunk, and a fool, and knew nothing.

Jack Evans had grumbled: 'It is just like being at home, chaps, that's the fact of the matter. I once had a German tutor, a great sausage of a man with an accent like a drain. I soon got rid of him, I can tell you!'

The other mids, lounging about the berth sharing a bottle of rather fine wine Simon Allen had pulled out of his chest, laughed.

126

'How did you do it then, Jack?' asked little James Finch. His eyes were glowing and his face was flushed. Drunk, in fact. He was very young and could not yet control the effect of a few glasses.

Jack Evans twirled the wine round in the light from a lantern before he answered.

'Well,' he said, 'I merely made his life unbearable. I complained to Mama about everything he did, and I absolutely refused to learn to talk the damned language. In the end, I threw a plate of mutton at him during a formal dinner.'

They rolled about, gulping wine and air in equal quantities.

'Did your father whip you?' asked Simon. 'Mine would have thrashed me like a dog.'

'No,' said Jack. 'That's the best of it. My mother wanted to have *him* flogged, for upsetting me! The old father would not allow that, unfortunately, but the fellow was sent packing, of course.'

'I once had a French governess I remember,' James said shyly. 'Some men from the village followed her home one night. They . . . they made . . . suggestions, I believe.'

He blushed deeply as the others roared with laughter.

'They were flogged from the parish,' he ended lamely.

All the boys had memories of various schoolmasters, tutors, governesses, and they flowed fast and free. William Bentley, whose family lived on a large estate near Petersfield, on the London road in Hampshire, had been taught by a succession of men of all types. The earnest young variety had displeased him most, and there had been several of them. They invariably claimed to be from great houses, sadly fallen into decay through no fault of their own. He despised their fawning attitudes, and treated them as they deserved. He had once reduced a young man of about twenty-three to tears in front of his sisters, which had been considered quite a feat for a boy of only nine. The older men in general had more dignity. One fellow, who must have been in his sixties, had packed his bags and disappeared into the night when he could bear the torment no longer. Had not even claimed his wages, so William's father reported to the amazed family circle next lunchtime. A dignified act if a rather foolish one, coming on winter as it had been.

Mr Marner, they all agreed, was incapable of such dignity, and incapable of anything else either. At least some of the earnest young men had known the rudiments of arithmetic, and Evans claimed to have learned some interesting things from a young Frenchwoman once employed on his father's estate. It was Simon Allen who at last suggested they should play a 'stunt' on the Welfare's schoolmaster.

Before they went into the suggestion they made sure the berth was clear of the older midshipmen. Most of them were on deck working, and Dolby, who had been cleaning boots and mending a torn shirt of James Finch's to earn a few pence, was soon sent on a fool's errand. The schoolmaster himself might have been there, for he was officially a midshipman and received the same meagre pay as Finch, the youngest – although unlike James, of course, he did not have a hugely wealthy father back in England. Simon went into the corner where Marner slept and kicked at the pile of blankets, but there was nobody hidden among them.

'What sort of stunt should we play?' Finch asked Bentley. The others looked at him too, and William felt a glow of pleasure, although he expected to be treated as their leader. Jack Evans was bigger and a fair bit older than he, and Simon Allen was older. But his bearing, as well as his position on board, naturally picked him out as the smartest young gentleman.

He yawned behind his hand, affected boredom with the whole affair.

'Are we really sure it's such a good idea?' he replied. 'Is not the thing a little tedious?'

They were having none of it. Allen had brought out more wine and their faces were all flushed. They were enjoying themselves immensely.

'No no!' shouted little James Finch. 'Let us catch the old devil properly. Let's tar and feather him!'

'We could empty his ink bottles over the side,' Evans suggested. 'I have it – let us fill his brandy bottles with ink instead!'

'And drink the brandy ourselves!' said Simon. 'I suppose he drinks reasonable spirit, as he spends all his money on it at least!'

In the end they agreed that a more open stunt was needed. Somehow they had to make Mr Marner look foolish in front of the ship's officers, even the people if possible. William secretly felt it would be better if his uncle were not to get wind of it, but he did not say anything. However, he did try to tone down the idea.

'We must not, of course, do anything that would really hurt the fellow,' he said. 'After all, he has done us no real harm.'

128

They howled him down. How could he say such a thing! The mere presence of the man was harm enough, let alone when he opened his futile damned books. William allowed himself to be persuaded. He doubted if Uncle Daniel would mind a little pranking, as long as it did not actually damage the schoolmaster beyond repair. He considered hard; there must be a suitable scheme somewhere. Drink would be the key to it; for Mr Marner was very old, and drink rendered him quite helpless. He considered hard.

At dinner that day in Broad and Fox's mess, Matthews, as usual, ate in silence. But when he had finished, he announced that he was changing messes.

This came as something of a shock, for although he talked little and did not enter into the normal friendlinesses the others shared, he had seemed quite content. Grandfather Fulman, as the oldest hand, took his cue to ask the questions.

'Have we not been good enough shipmates to you, Mr Matthews? Is it that we have offended in any way?' he asked. His voice was so deep and solemn that Peter looked scared. He hid his face in Thomas Fox's shoulder, as though he was being accused himself of driving the dour man out.

Matthews smiled his slow, long-faced smile.

'My friends,' he said. 'Let me set your minds at ease. There is a man on board that I knew many years ago. An old shipmate. We sailed on the northern routes together many times, and yesterday I met him again by chance. Mr Allgood has obtained leave from the first lieutenant for me to shift, that is all. There is no tension between me and any one of you, and I am grateful to have been allowed to share here.'

This was a very handsome speech, especially from so silent a man. Thomas felt quite proud. The others were pleased as well, he noted. Fulman blew down his unsmoked clay noisily, like another man would perhaps blow his nose, say, to cover a shyness. Jesse Broad was more practical, however.

'What sort of a messmate are we to get in your place, Mr Matthews?' he said evenly. 'Are you displacing any other man? Or are the numbers not made up?'

Matthews looked at him levelly for several seconds.

'I will bring him,' he said at last. 'You can say yea or nay to his face.'

129

As he strode across the deck the others glanced at each other in silence. This was all a little strange. Thomas knew that men were permitted to change messes, but he was not sure whether they themselves had the right to refuse a 'replacement'. He did not like to ask.

A gasp went up as Matthews returned. He was leading someone by the hand. The dark musician.

Matthews stood before them, his hand on the blind man's shoulder. He smiled sardonically.

'May I present Mr Padraig Doyle,' he said. 'Leastways, that is how the boatswain claims he is called. You will find him a quiet messmate, although more than willing to give you a tune should you desire it. Well, what do you say?'

Looking into the piper's face gave Thomas a strange and lonely feeling. The Irishman was thin, as thin a grown man as he had ever seen. His cheeks were sunken and pale, with ridges on them where his teeth showed from inside. His chin was scarred, not carrying the trace of a hair although he must have been thirty at least. His tiny neck disappeared into the loose collar of a crazy old coat, green with age. And the coat still had tails, that eternal mark of the landsman. Padraig Doyle was a long-toggy; yet no skylarking seaman had cut them off. That was the strangest thing of all perhaps.

As the men and boys of the mess watched, the piper smiled. It was a heart-rending thing. Thomas would have looked away, but he could not. The empty sockets of his eyes had a strange movement to them. They seemed to see. They were red and scarry, as though once his eyes had lived in them and since had been ripped out. The dark musician opened his mouth, as if to speak. Then it closed again and the lips curved into the smile. He was mute.

'Well,' said Grandfather Fulman gruffly, with a sort of warm and hopeless look at Matthews, who was watching them closely, 'I have no objection, shipmates. What say you others?'

There was a low murmur. Nobody minded, or nobody cared to say. Peter started to pipe up something, but thought better of it, turned scarlet, subsided.

'Good,' said Matthews. 'Thank you, my friends. Mr Doyle,' he said to the Irishman. 'I leave you in good hands. You will not find better men on board this ship.'

He pushed him forward gently, turned on his heel, and strode off. Jesse Broad stood up to take him by the hand.

'Find a place for Padraig Doyle,' he said to Thomas. 'And take care of him for us, my friend. A musician on board ship is a fine and lucky thing.'

Peter said his piece at last, and the tension left the air.

'One of the great things about the Welfare to my mind, friends,' he said, 'is the fine talking we do enjoy. Lose one messmate who'd chatter the leg off a donkey, and he's immediately taken place of by a man who'd win prizes at it!'

The smile had left Doyle's face, but it showed no hurt at such banter. They soon learned that he did not often smile, and assumed it caused pain to his scarred and crippled face. He was indeed a quiet messmate, and a considerate one who took as much care as he could not to encroach upon the others. He had a knack they found amazing of not getting in the way, not intruding. And without being able to speak, without having the power to smile properly or to see them, he made them aware that he was thanking them, thanking them for the very fact of allowing his existence, of taking care of him in however small a way.

Thomas took his hand and led him to a place. He arranged some shreds of canvas and some wool for him to rest on, he gently took the bagpipe and stilled Doyle's anxiety by describing in detail where it was placed, in a dry spot, well within reach. The Irishman squeezed his hand gently when he was settled, and turned the glaring sockets upon Thomas's eyes. And Thomas could look deep into them, deep into the folds of ruined flesh, and smile.

In the days that followed he became friends with the blind man, in a way that he had never been friends with another human being. It was, in fact, vaguely reminiscent of his feelings for beasts, and the two of them often crawled in among the sheep and sat there for the warmth, the smell, the companionship. He knew that Doyle must have once been a countryman from the manner in which he handled the animals. He helped Thomas with his tasks of husbandry, his hands skilful with the livestock, his fingers deft and sure despite his blindness.

Despite his blindness, despite his being mute, they communicated. For Doyle could talk with his bagpipe in a language that Thomas Fox could understand. Alone, they would sit back-to-back, or half buried in a nest of sheep, and he would play, so quietly that the noise hardly got beyond the pens. Thomas would talk, almost as if to himself, tangled, incoherent sentences about feelings too deep for connected words. And Doyle would answer, in low sighs and throbbing bass notes.

It was well for Thomas, for his life on the ship was a great and increasing terror to him. Every night he cleaned the filthy heads and undertook other dirty, menial tasks. The sight of the stem beneath him, the rushing green waters foaming and gurgling hungrily a few short feet away, made his guts clench. As he scrubbed and picked, he babbled incessant prayers, his eyes often closed, blind to the stares of men who came to lounge or to jeer at him. The sea filled him with a deep and ever-growing dread, although it had been almost gentle for many days. The Welfare, as it happened, had not shipped a green sea since the last night of the storm. But he neither knew nor cared for that. He could not bring himself to look outboard. More and more his eyes remained within the ship, more and more they tended to seek some fixed point on the deck and stick on it.

He could do nothing right. Somehow his very presence seemed to make men mad. Seamen he did not know, whom he had never seen, would appear before him and mock him. Remarks had been made about his new clothes. One boatswain's mate had made some pleasant joke about him being dressed like a gentleman; but when Thomas had smiled, the man had knocked him down. His pleasure in his beasts made him the butt of savage sexual humour and he was often pinched and poked at as he passed the darker corners of the lower decks. His simplicity seemed to infuriate the midshipmen too. At William Bentley's instigation they had got him emptying slops for them. They had simply asked if he would like to slave for them, and he knew no answer but yes. What else could he be expected to reply? They found no pleasure in tormenting him, it was too easy; and that infuriated them worse. He blamed none of these people, nor even tried to find an explanation. The boys were only boys, and high-spirited; he supposed that accounted for them. Why the men misused him, he knew not.

The boatswain, most of all, filled Thomas with nameless fear. He was like a giant in some story, who blew hot and cold. When he saw him coming, Thomas tried to hide. But Allgood had eyes like a hawk and apparently kept a look-out for him. Time and again he would turn a corner and blunder into the great man. Then anything could happen. If he blundered into any other of the mighty superiors on the ship, or even some of the sailors, the result was simply a blow, from fist, cane or rope. But with the boatswain he never knew. It could be a cuff round the head with that huge, terrifying hand; or it could be a smile and a word. More and more Thomas looked to the deck, hunched himself inside himself. Almost pretended to be invisible, and hoped he was.

The midshipmen's prank on Mr Marner came about several days later, and it was a great success.

The lessons were held in the afternoon, after dinner and grog, and after the young gentlemen had completed their morning's duties and their midday seamanship instruction under the master. So Mr Marner, full of food and liquor, was hardly at his most wide awake. The boys had saved a quantity of brandy in a bottle, mixed with a slightly greater quantity of rum, and topped up with some white wine bought from the wardroom servant. This mixture was being held by William, who clenched it between his knees while they sorted out slates and schoolbooks.

Mr Marner was slightly the worse for wear after his ration of rum and water. He was old and tottery, with a ridiculous scruffy wig, wire spectacles that sagged over one cheek, and a dirty, unkempt air. Every man-jack on board was beginning to look a little unclean these days, but the old man managed to appear slightly repulsive rather than merely unwashed. The boys regarded him with loathing, exchanging excited glances as they anticipated his downfall.

'Today, young sirs,' he quavered, 'I hope to give you the rudiments of one of the oldest branches from the tree of knowledge. Would one of you care to hazard a guess as to what it is? I did prepare you yesterday.'

'Please sir,' piped little James boldly, 'is it the property and motion of heavenly bodies? Or am I barking up the wrong tree of knowledge?'

The young gentlemen laughed, but Marner did not quite catch the joke. He blinked at James Finch, called him Simon Allen, and tried to go on. It was hopeless, as it always was, and William once more wondered why his uncle set store by such odd things. After they had ragged him for a time, he decided to put the prank into operation.

'Excuse me, sir,' he said, interrupting the pathetic old man in mid-sentence. 'Do you mind if I take a small drink? It is largely medicinal, and prescribed by Mr Adamson the surgeon.'

The schoolmaster was flummoxed.

'This is highly irregular, Mr Bentley,' he replied. 'Your uncle, I fear . . .' He tailed off, eyeing the bottle hungrily. The pale tip of his tongue ran nervously under his upper lip. William uncorked. The other mids nudged each other in delight.

'May I though, sir?'

'Well, of course . . . if Mr Adamson has recommended . . . What, might I ask, are your symptoms?'

William said calmly: 'I have been having difficulty keeping my feet about the deck of late. A touch of the staggers. Mr Adamson considers that living as we midshipmen must in the . . . ah . . . *bowels* of the ship is the probable cause.'

He took what appeared to be a large mouthful, although only a trickle went down his throat. Jack Evans stood up, his voice shrill with excitement.

'And I too, sir,' he said, reaching for the bottle. 'A very bad attack of the staggers. It might be called the affliction of the midshipman.'

The schoolmaster became more desperate as the bottle went its rounds. It was left to James Finch to spring the trap.

'I am surprised, Mr Marner,' he remarked, 'that you have not manifested such symptoms. Living as you do with the rest of us in the same berth. Well,' he added, jovially, 'here's to medicine!'

Ten minutes later the schoolmaster was well down the bottle, and unsteady on his feet. It was then that part two of the prank began, this time with Simon Allen as leader.

He stood up abruptly, as Marner tried valiantly to struggle through some simple explanation. The old man reeled backwards as Allen let out a loud, strangled gurgle. Then the boy staggered forward clutching his throat, dropped first to his knees then onto his face, twitched violently and lay still.

The other young gentlemen sat rigid, stifling their laughter at this perfect piece of pantomime. But Mr Marner was horrified. His mouth dropped open. He went white. His hands shook.

134

'My God,' he said. 'Allen!' He turned blindly to the class. 'Bentley,' he croaked. 'Fetch the surgeon. I think . . .'

William leapt to his feet, took three paces towards the schoolmaster, let out a shriek and dropped like a stone. Little James Finch ran after him, whooping and twitching, sticking his tongue out the while. Then Jack, not to be outdone, whirled like a top until he was dizzy, staggered about a bit, clutched at the old man's jacket, and collapsed at his feet. As he stared upwards he croaked: 'Poison. Oh Mr Marner! We're all poisoned by that bottle!'

As the drunk old man stumbled towards the deck, clutching at his own throat and pale with shock, the boys clambered up and followed him. They were almost bursting with joy and kept hugging themselves and each other. The prank was superb!

Marner burst onto the upper deck like a thunderbolt. Blinded by the sun and the mixture in the bottle he barged into startled sailors and ran heavily up against the ship's gear. He was uttering a sort of squawking moan as he reached the quarterdeck. Higgins, the third lieutenant, stood blinking at the apparition. Captain Swift, William noted with satisfaction, was not in evidence.

'Poisoned!' croaked Marner. 'Poisoned. All the young gentlemen, sir, all four of 'em! Poisoned! Stark dead!'

Everyone on deck was watching him. Every activity alow and aloft had ceased. The old man fell to his knees.

'I've drunk it too,' he groaned. 'Oh sir, call the surgeon to save the poor young gentlemen!'

Higgins, round-faced and slow-witted, stared from the school-master to the hatchway forward where the four young gentlemen stood, as clear as daylight, as large as life. They were rolling in silent mirth, holding their bellies and shaking with glee. Everyone was transfixed. Only the helmsman, silent and impassive, watched nothing but the sails and compass as he handled the spokes.

'Are you mad, sir!' suddenly roared Higgins. His face blackened.

'Dead, sir,' said Marner pathetically. 'Oh, call the surgeon.'

'Dead drunk! That is it!' shouted the third lieutenant. His eye licked round the deck, spotted a seaman holding a bucket, a nearby boatswain's mate.

'You there!' he cried. 'Boatswain's mate. Fetch that bucket over here. Smartly, man, smartly there!'

The mate seized the bucket, which was full of sea water. He loped across the deck with a smile. The boys were laughing aloud, there was nothing else for it. All around men paused in their work, pleased at the diversion, amused if completely mystified by what was going on.

The boatswain's mate stood four-square in front of the kneeling schoolmaster, who was crying now, and had luckily removed his spectacles. The stream of water knocked him bodily over backwards and he let out a shriek. Laughter rose from the deck in a gale. Even Mr Higgins permitted himself a perfunctory smile before marching off aft. William and his friends were breathless with triumph. What a stunt that had been! That would perhaps teach old Marner in the future, the drunken old sot.

Later, William faced his uncle over the incident, and promised that no such thing would happen again. The captain was not much amused by it, nor even interested, but he made it clear to William that their schooling should not be interrupted. William listened politely, keeping his opinions to himself. He agreed, however, although he made no comment, when Captain Swift suggested they might expend their zeal to better purpose on more recalcitrant cases. A man as old as Marner was if nothing else, easy meat.

Finally he relented a shade, admitting that it had been something of a wheeze. Young gentlemen had to work, true, but all work makes Jack a dull boy.

'There is a place, my lad, for high spirits in a youth,' he said. 'But remember our harsher purpose, William. Do not relax too much.'

Seventeen

The Welfare was in the tail end of the Trade winds before Captain Swift decided it was time to punish Henry Joyce. And although the timing of the event was meant to be a deadly secret, somehow or other the ship's company knew. Which meant that Joyce was so full of rum that had been saved and smuggled to him that it was hoped the ordeal might be bearable.

For Thomas Fox, the anticipation of the event, which would generally have filled him with dread, was overshadowed by a far more terrible possibility – that he himself was shortly to be punished. Whether by accident or the deep design of Swift, there had been a punishment every day since the weather had turned fine. Every forenoon the calls had shrilled, the mates had shouted, and all hands had assembled aft to witness a flogging. Every day the event had been preceded by a speech from the captain, after he had read out the details of the offence and punishment, reviling the lowness of the ship's people and promising that he would flog some common human decency into them. Now Thomas had transgressed.

Usually the cause of punishment was drunkenness, or arose from drunkenness. This upset Thomas terribly, for the men were flogged for an offence it was almost impossible not to commit. Every sailor was given eight pints of beer a day, as well as his rum ration. Although by now the beer was worse than vinegar it was still beer, still capable of making you drunk. Even he, who treated it with care and often poured away his rum ration – a fact known only to Doyle, who did the same – often felt muzzy and unsteady.

Most of the sailors, if for some reason they did not want all their grog, used it as currency. So it was always possible for a man to get not just drunk, but blind, roaring, fighting drunk. Any man on board who could not live without liquor – and there were very many – could always buy it, whether with money, services of various kinds, or even notes of credit. There was one fellow in a nearby mess, a shaking, grey-faced man who looked as if he had not long to live, who had no clothes left other than a long canvas shirt. He needed up to four pints of grog in a day to make him insensible, and he would go to any lengths, however degrading, to get it. He was regularly beaten up by seamen who gave him grog for services he could not render (as they well knew) and who obtained their satisfaction from the thrashing that followed.

So every day the master-at-arms and his corporals had no difficulty in finding tomorrow's victim. Sometimes a man was arrested for being merely drunk, which was a grave enough offence under the Articles of War, but more usually they waited until a fight broke out, when they could take two, or even more, at one swoop. And every day the captain would venomously harangue the people on the evils of drunkenness, and every day the pannikins of fiery spirit and the jugs of sour beer would circulate in a way that many a land-bound drunkard would have found next thing to Paradise itself.

The sin that Thomas had committed, and the way retribution had leapt upon him, had nothing to do with drink. It had nothing to do with sinfulness either, but he was well aware that in terms of shipboard life he had committed a crime, and that punishment was inevitable. He had once seen a peddler hanged on land, pack and all, for allegedly taking a coney, so he did not rail at the injustice of the retribution that would come; that was the way of the world. But it was the form. It could not be flogging though; no, it could not be flogging. Thomas found the spectacle of a man being whipped appalling; the thought that those cruel thongs could tear into his own naked back was unbearable. When his mind touched on it, unbidden, he whimpered; but did not believe.

It was the purser, Butterbum, who had discovered Thomas Fox's crime.

The afternoon before, during the first dog-watch, Thomas had led Padraig Doyle to the foredeck with his pipes. The wind was blowing less steadily than of late, and the sun was beginning to turn some men's faces almost black. Some of them had taken off their shirts and were lying about the deck talking, playing at cards, or snoozing. Thomas enjoyed the dog-watches, when there were no duties to speak of, and music could be played. It was good to be the friend of Doyle, because the piper was in great demand. Some of the friendliness for him rubbed off onto his companion. As he played, his back against the fore-bitts, Thomas sat close and sang. But all the while he was carving away at the pipe he was making. It had taken him a long time to find a suitable piece of wood, but he thought the whistle would be a good one.

Most of the sailors liked singing, and one or two of them made their own songs. They liked songs best that told a sad or heart-rending story, but the tunes had to have a bounce. That bounce, Doyle excelled at giving. The normally mournful note of his pipes could turn wonderfully light. It set the feet a-jigging.

They were well-near through one of Thomas's favourites, a song about a maid who set out to sea in a tiny boat to find her pressed lover, when he saw the purser walking along the deck. He stiffened, although there was nothing to indicate that the man was seeking him, and the words died on his lips.

> *She wrung her hands and she tore her hair*
> *Much like a maiden in deep despair.*
> *Her little boat, 'gainst a rock did run,*
> *How can I live now my William is gone?*

The sonorous voices of the seamen, blending with the rich, sad notes of the elbow-pipe, rolled away in the warm wind. The purser, reminiscent of a suet pudding, his blue coat sticking out over his stern in the way that had helped earn him his nickname, picked his way among them delicately. When the song had ended the conversational murmur from the non-singers had died too. Butterbum was a much-hated man. But one that nobody dared to cross.

The glistening, sweat-streaked face lit up when the purser spotted Thomas. The boy's blood ran cold. Jesse Broad, who had been lounging nearby, got up casually and walked towards his friend. He stopped three feet from Thomas, looking coolly at Butterbum, who stopped at about the same distance.

'Play on, play on!' said the purser, in a transparent attempt at comradeliness. 'It is a fine piper you are, Irishman. Do not let me interrupt!'

Doyle did not move, the pipes lying flaccid in his lap. The

washing of the seas and the mild thrumming of the cordage were the only sounds.

'Well then,' said the purser, in a changed tone. 'You boy, there is a matter of some hens. Come with me.'

Thomas half-stood, glancing helplessly at Jesse once, then at the deck again. Broad said mildly: 'It is the dog-watch, sir.' His tone was neutral; he took care that he could not be accused of insolence or insubordination.

Butterbum looked at him bleakly, his face furtive and mean. At first it looked as if he would turn nasty at Broad's intervention, but a sort of growl arose from the resting men. They were off-duty. They did not like this man upon their deck.

Suddenly the fat purser capitulated.

'See me in half an hour,' he told Thomas. 'The captain wishes to entertain his officers to some fowl. According to my reckoning we have seventeen left. I will inspect them later. Make all ready and perhaps you would do me the great favour of selecting the plumpest. Hm?'

No one responded to the joke. The purser smiled about him nervously. He shrugged and waddled aft again. As he got out of earshot an obscene muttering followed him.

Shortly afterwards the men were singing a gay love song. But Thomas was in despair. Doyle clearly sensed it, for when the song finished he would play no more. Thomas took his hand, leading the blind musician below. Jesse Broad did not interfere. He merely hoped that Butterbum's count of chickens tallied with the number that were there.

It did not, of course. When they were below, in the stifling heat between decks, Thomas flung his arms round Doyle's neck and wept. For he had never told about the three fowl that had died in the storm, nor of another one that had keeled over since from an obscure sickness. He had not had the courage. All four of them had been put through a port in the dark of night, but that was not likely to be believed. The purser stood to make commission on the fowl, as on all the livestock and foodstuffs on board, and kept an exact tally of anything that was killed and eaten. If he said there were seventeen hens left, it was certain that there would be only thirteen.

When the fat man came below after the end of the first

140

dog-watch, he did not make a song and dance at his discovery. He presented Thomas with the figures, and pointed out calmly that the fowl were four short. Thomas could not plead. He stood staring at the deck, the blind man behind him holding his shoulder, and he emitted a low, barely audible moan.

After asking three times for an explanation, the purser smacked his lips with an air of ending the matter.

'Well then, sir,' he said. 'I can only conclude, the conclusion is inescapable, that these hens have been stolen. By you, or by person or persons unknown. Well?'

No reply.

'You are not prepared to claim that they were stolen from your care?'

No reply.

After a pause the purser sighed. In the sound was deep satisfaction, a kind of quiet triumph that sank into Thomas Fox's soul.

'Good,' said Butterbum. 'Then I think I know what I must report to the captain.'

Padraig Doyle made a sound; a horrible, groaning, inarticulate cry. The purser looked at him with deep distaste, turned on his heel and strode towards the ladder.

When Henry Joyce was brought on deck to be punished, he was a bad sight. During the many days of his confinement he had never been released from his iron fetters, for any reason whatever. He was a wild man, huge and violent, of the sort that was common on the sea. On land, Jesse Broad thought, he would not have lasted long. He would have been a thief, or a highway robber, or a hired killer. But whatever he did he would have been marked for death, for the land could not contain such a wild, fierce animal. In the merchant marine, too, he would have been a mad dog, uncontrollable by the officers, a terror to the men. Only in the Navy did he have a chance of life, and that a paradoxical one. A chance that hung always in the balance of his usefulness as a seaman and fighter, and his disruptiveness as a drunken, anarchic, powerful beast.

When Henry Joyce was brought on deck, the beast looked as though it may have been tamed. The sun was shining, the breeze was blowing warm. It was still steady in the north east, but it was losing power daily as they approached the area of the doldrums.

141

Every stitch of light-weather canvas had been bent, all was drawing, but still she threw no great bow-wave. Much of the time, an increasing amount, the water bubbled only gently along her weed-festooned sides. Henry Joyce stood in the sunshine blinking, blinded.

He looked like an animal, but an animal tamed. Still wearing only the canvas drawers he was arrested in, his filthy torso was washed by runnels of sweat. His face was pale, untouched by sun or wind, and it had a sickly, deadly look to it. He had fed on nothing but ship's biscuit and tank water. A weaker man might well have died. Around wrist and ankle Henry Joyce had red, running bands of ulcerated flesh. His drawers were soiled and stinking, his legs beneath them quite black. His hair and beard, wild and long, were matted, stiff with filth.

Only his eyes gave the game away. As Jesse Broad stood silent on the deck, along with the whole ship's company, he looked into Joyce's eyes. The beast was not tamed. Perhaps it was untameable.

The scene was a formal one, that everyone knew and everyone hated. There was an air of brooding violence over all, accentuated by the heat of the day and the feeling that they were witnessing a commonplace, an oft-repeated bloody ritual. Accentuated too, by the smells; the new smell from Joyce, of rank dirtiness and squalor, and the smells of sweat and unwashed bodies which if not new were more obvious now, as the naked sun beat harshly down on the mass of gathered men. The officers, lined across the quarterdeck, were almost clean. But they stank too, in their tight blue coats and high collars.

Hottest and most uncomfortable of all, on the deck abaft the officers, were the marines, in red coats, gaiters, cockaded hats. Unshaded in the violent, violent sun. A glare came off their scarlet coats and shining accoutrements. Their faces were shining also, fixed and shining, covered in veils of sweat that flowed ceaselessly from hat to collar. Broad could almost pity them as they stood like that, in silent, unmoving agony. But each marine had a musket, each marine would shoot a sailor down. Better to save one's pity for a beast like Henry Joyce than for a marine.

As he studied the bald-fronted, pig-tailed head of the man to be flogged, there was a flash of movement among the ranks of soldiers. The movement was brief, but he could tell which one had staggered.

142

There was a white face, a chalk-white face, among them. It was thin with agony.

At a brief sentence of command, Henry Joyce was spun round and triced up to the grating by knees and wrists. He made no attempt to struggle. His back, like his chest, was dirty with slime, blackish with whitish runnels. Captain Swift began to speak.

'My brave boys,' he said, in his quiet, penetrating voice, 'you are to witness today the punishment of the vilest rogue unhung in His Britannic Majesty's Navy. His name is Henry Joyce and the charge against him, which myself and my officers have found proven, is a multiple one. To put it in the language of the people, for I wish to blind no man with fine-sounding words, this rogue is guilty of all that is intolerable in a British tar. He is a liar, a cheat, a coward and a bully. He has spoken mutinous filth, incited his good-hearted messmates to sedition and calumny, and resisted arrest so violently as to cause injury to the ship's corporals in the exercise of their duty.'

Swift's peculiar eyes ranged over the assembled men. His skin was dry, his breathing even. He did not appear to feel the heat, dressed though he was in fine silk and heavy-duty cloth. He started to speak again, and his words were bitter. He held Joyce up as an example of creeping evil that every man should feel with shame and fear as a silent force that could bring them all to ruin.

Thomas Fox had seen the marine stagger too. Unlike Broad, he recognised him, although it took some little time. It was, he was sure, the ill man, the man who had been doubled up in the sick-bay when he had been confined there. But how could it be? For many nights, since his own 'release' from the sick-bay, as he had lain among the snoring seamen, he had heard the muted screams of the soldier; and had had no doubt but that he was dying. Now the man was on the quarterdeck, his face a portrait of agony, a thin line of spittle oozing between his lips. Thomas was fascinated.

There was another man in the marine contingent he thought he knew, although his certainty had diminished as time had gone by. This was the one he had taken for his cousin Silas from the very first. He was a tall, thin man with light hair and a nondescript face, and he was rendered even less easy to be sure about in the uniform red and white he was always seen in. At first there had been no doubt in Thomas's mind, despite the cold lack of recognition in the marine's eyes. But as day followed day it had seemed less likely that

143

this could be his cousin, although a doubt remained, a small and nagging doubt.

Before he had been kidnapped, he had not seen Silas for years, and then he had not known him well. But there is something about relations. He would have probably greeted him as a cousin if they had passed in the street. Now, on board the Welfare, he hardly dared greet his own shadow. In any case the marines were hated by the sailors, he could sense that. In some odd way, although they ate the same food and drank the same drink, they were the enemy, as much as the warrant officers and the gentlemen aft. Indeed, they lived between the two factions and one of their duties was to protect the high from the lowly. Their only duty, some said, for it was a hard thing to have them idling by when seafaring men were hard-pressed at working the ship.

The nondescript, sweating face before him remained a puzzle. He turned his attention to the captain's words.

'Had I not been a merciful man,' Swift was saying, 'I could have – nay would have – had this scum kept in irons and finally court-martialled. As you know, each and every one of you, the result could only have been his inevitable death. Believe me, I would see the life choked out of him at the yardarm with not inconsiderable pleasure. But I am, for my sins, a merciful man.'

He turned to face the boatswain.

'Mr Allgood please. Have your mates do their duty. I need not repeat the usual warning as to the fate of any I consider is not applying himself to the task with all his might.'

'Aye aye sir. May I be permitted to enquire the number of strokes you require, sir?'

There was a long pause. The men were deadly silent.

'That, Mr Allgood, depends largely upon the will of your in-feriors. I require . . . *we* require,' he amended, waving his hand to indicate the officers, 'that this dog be rendered insensible. At least one hundred, however. At least one hundred.'

A low groan went up. The captain smiled his bitter smile.

'Unusual crimes require unusual remedies,' he said. Even Thomas Fox, however, knew that such a number was quite illegal unless under due sentence of court-martial.

It was not long before the brutal rhythm became almost soporific. The whistle of the cat, the thud and cut as it hit into the

144

broad, immensely muscular back, the grunt of effort as the mate in question jerked the thongs back, ran them through his fingers to clear the blood, then swung once more with every sinew cracking. At the end of each dozen Mr Allgood pointed to a fresh mate with his rattan. Brows were wiped, palms rinsed in a bucket of sea water, the rhythm taken up by the new man.

William Bentley, standing not far from his uncle, found the whole affair difficult to keep in his attention. It was distasteful – although he was used to it now – the way his face and uniform kept getting flecked with particles of blood and skin. But he was hot, as hot as Hades, and he feared it would be a long operation. He also had seen the red glare of beastly hatred in Henry Joyce's eyes. The red glare of rum as well. It was apparent that the dogs had fed their friend until he almost overflowed. Please God he would soon pass out, from the alcohol if not the whipping.

The noise behind him, a clattering accompanied by a soft thud, came as a relief. After nearly an hour, Henry Joyce had not yet uttered a cry, not yet closed his tiny, savage eyes in their rings of dirt. He was built like an ox and was as stubborn as one. The boatswain's mate paused in his stroke, his eyes flickering past the officers.

Captain Swift gave a deep-throated cry of rage.

'Lay it on! Lay it on there, God damn you! Keep your eyes on the task, you scum!'

The surgeon slipped away and into the marine contingent like a sparrow. William heard feet behind him. There was a quiet commotion.

Swift's face contorted with fury. He took a step forward and turned to look aft. At a sign from Allgood the mate continued laying it on, impassive, sweating.

'God hang you, Mr Adamson,' said the captain. 'What do you think you are doing? Leave that malingering soldier alone and get back here this instant!'

William dared not look round. The sea of faces in front of him were staring at the quarterdeck. He could guess what had happened though. The marine who had collapsed was on duty at the captain's insistence. He had told Adamson that morning he would tolerate no more shirkers, and to William's amazement the little man had argued back. His action had bordered on the insolent, not to say the

145

insane, given his uncle's low opinion of him, but he had said quite firmly that the marine was ill, not shirking, and that to send him to his post would be an act of folly. At this word William Bentley had actually blushed; he expected some terrible and sudden explosion of retribution. There had been none. But in silence his uncle had glared at the surgeon, and in silence the surgeon had left. The marine was now on duty.

Mr Adamson spoke drily to the captain.

'I beg permission to inform you, sir, that this soldier is desperate ill. I think he is dying.'

There was a ripple of excitement from the ship's company. William Bentley jumped as his uncle rushed past him, screaming in rage.

'Silence! Silence! Silence!' he shouted. Then he seized the up-raised arm of the boatswain's mate and stopped his backward swing. A gout of thick blood ran off the man's hand onto the captain's face and silken collar.

'Cease this punishment!' he shrieked. 'Cease this instant, I say! This man is drunk, drunk as a lord, drunk as a bloody bitch! Allgood, dismiss these scoundrels and rig the pumps. I want this bastard soused until he's stone cold sober, do you hear! Then we'll start again! And this time your men will do the job properly! And there will be no dinner and no grog for any bugger on board until this swine is flogged insensible.'

Watching the closed, angry faces of the people as they obeyed their new orders with a sullenness bordering on insubordination, William Bentley had an uncomfortable feeling arise within him. He could not quite pin it down, but it was unfamiliar and exceedingly disturbing. It was the first vague stirrings of fear.

Two and a half hours later Henry Joyce passed out, although William had the awful suspicion that he was merely shamming, even after the appalling punishment he had received. Forty minutes after that, the marine, who had resumed his monotonous high screaming, vomited blood and expired.

146

Eighteen

At dinner that evening, Captain Daniel Swift was the very picture of gentlemanly urbanity. He had invited all his lieutenants and the four young gentlemen. The captain of marines, brilliant in wig and dress coat, graced the opulent cabin, and behind Swift's chair there stood his servants, domestics from his home estate, stiff, silent, and unseeing, except when passing a decanter or serving from the covered silver bowls. The stern windows were open wide, allowing the musical bubbling of the wake to be heard. It was quiet and soothing, becoming occasionally louder as the rudder was turned to a sharper angle to keep the Welfare on course. Above their heads the tread of Mr Robinson could sometimes be heard, the ever-watchful master.

The food was excellent, although by now the only fresh vegetables left on board were turnips. But there was no shortage of these for captain and officers, and they were splendidly cooked in butter. The first course had been fish, caught half an hour before it was cooked, and accompanied by a good light white wine. Captain Swift sailed always with his own cook, who had both his legs and both his arms, unlike the pensioners who usually served that office in His Majesty's ships. This man had been with Swift's father on his lands ashore, and did office as cellarer also. He had nothing to do with the people's cook, a consumptive old man with a crippled back.

As the red wine went round before the second course was served, Captain Swift turned the conversation from the pointless politenesses they had been mouthing to the matter that was in all their minds.

'I should have hanged that fellow Joyce after all, I think. If he recovers he might still be a fine enough seaman, but I smell trouble. What say you, gentlemen?'

William glanced about. It was not his place to speak, nor the other boys'. By custom, Mr Hagan should have first say. Custom prevailed.

'A stubborn dog for a certainty,' said the tall red-haired man. He paused, twiddling the stem of his glass. 'But after all, Captain Swift, if he proves troublesome, we can surely hang him next time!'

Everyone laughed at this. Hagan licked his lips, pleased with his witticism.

Plumduff added: '*If* he recovers. Mr Adamson says . . .' His voice trailed off. At the mention of the surgeon, Swift's face had darkened visibly. The fat second lieutenant gulped. 'Beg pardon, sir,' he said miserably.

'That damned surgeon has overstepped his duty, in my opinion,' the third lieutenant said ingratiatingly. William Bentley sneered inwardly. Trust Higgins to try the smarmy line. His uncle would soon see through that!

But Swift turned to the man with a faint smile.

'Aye, Mr Higgins,' he said. 'You are damned right.'

Over the mutton, well seasoned as it was the last edible meat of a sheep killed days before, the conversation dwelt on the way Joyce had withstood the lash. It was generously allowed that villain or not, drunk or not, he had shown almost incredible fortitude.

'Like a great beast of burden,' young Jack Evans squeaked. 'Why, on my father's farmlands we have bulls that are smaller than Henry Joyce. Aye, and weaker.'

It was William's right to have a say now.

'I would rather speak of him as a wild beast,' he put in. 'A beast of burden may be strong, but it is also tractable. I consider Henry Joyce to be more a . . . lion . . . or a wolf . . .' He brightened, having found a suitable animal from his limited knowledge of such things. 'No, a bear, a great wild bear. For did you not remark his eyes as he was being flogged? They glowed, yes glowed. They were small and red.' He looked at the attentive faces around him. 'Yes indeed,' he finished. 'He is a wild animal, no beast of burden.'

Later on, over good Cheshire cheese and a dark powerful wine that made William's head sing, the captain dropped a bombshell.

The conversation had drifted from Joyce and others of the people who reminded the assembled company more of animals than men, skated over the conduct of the warrant officers and the peculiar obscenity of the purser's revolting form, and returned by a roundabout route to the surgeon and the dead marine. Swift, more genial now, was prepared to joke about him.

148

'Darting here and there with his little black brandy bottle,' he said. 'I should not be surprised if he had not poisoned that malingerer just to score a point.'

'Like we poisoned poor old Mr Marner,' said James Finch breathlessly. It was the first time he had dared open his mouth in such great company, and he was flushed and excited, as drunk as fun. He was ignored.

'It was an unfortunate episode, however,' put in Captain Craig, the marine officer. 'My men were deeply disturbed by it. It is not a good thing, to have a comrade drop before your eyes like that.'

'Indeed,' replied Swift. 'The lengths to which some people will go are amazing.'

This remark caused an uncomfortable pause. William, whose mind had admittedly grown fuzzy, could not quite make out what it meant. Apparently he was not the only one.

'Well,' continued Craig, clearing his throat. 'Perhaps the funeral will improve their morale. A little drum-beating and the popping of their muskets into the air. That should perk them up.'

'No,' said Captain Swift. His voice was quiet, but it cut like a knife. Everyone was stilled.

'I beg your pardon, sir?' Craig asked at last.

Captain Swift turned those pale, penetrating eyes to him.

'I said "no", Captain Craig. No, sir. No drums. No muskets. No damned funeral at all if I have my way.'

The air in the cabin had become tense. Hagan licked his lips with a small wet sound.

Captain Swift went on: 'That man was a shirker. He had lain in that sick-bay since we left England and refused to move a muscle.' He jerked his head up, the big nose suddenly reminding William of a shark's fin. 'And God knows, Captain Craig, there is little enough for a marine to do in any case.'

The tone was deliberate, the insult unequivocal. William flicked his eyes about, intensely embarrassed. Everyone's hands were resting on the table, unmoving. Jimmy Finch had turned a delicate pale shade of green.

'May one ask, sir,' said Craig levelly, 'what are your intentions?'

Swift blew air noisily through his nostrils, as if to ease the tension.

'You may, sir. I cannot, of course, forbid a funeral. Even scum

149

like that cannot be hurled overboard like carrion. But it will be plain and simple. The plainest and the simplest. He will be slipped over the side with a prayer and a promise. *I* will make the promise: that every damned malingering dog I catch in future will not even get so Christian a burial.'

Every man and boy at the table was looking downwards. They raised their eyes, reluctantly, when Swift gave a short laugh. On his face was one of his strange, dazzling, smiles. It seemed to William most inappropriate.

'Well,' said Swift. 'Have you anything to say, Captain Craig? You may be frank with me.'

'Well sir,' replied Craig. 'Then I will be frank. I do not like it. I do not like it at all.'

'Why?'

'Why? Hmm . . . Because, I think, because . . .'

'Because your *men* will not like it,' said Swift icily. 'That is why, Captain Craig. Because you fear you may have trouble with your men.'

Craig bowed his head as if in deference to the captain's opinion.

'Well, sir,' continued Swift. 'I say this, Captain Craig: Damn your men's opinions, and damn their feelings.' His voice rose: 'This, gentlemen, is what is wrong on board my ship, and this is what I shall stamp out. There is a laxity; there is a softness. These people are scum and they are getting away with what they will. All of you, all you officers, all you silly drunken boys, are playing their game. And you will cease! I want this damned ship tightened up, do you hear? And I want to see *you* do it. Now.'

There was a long silence, broken only by the whistle of air in Captain Swift's thin nose. He had ended his speech loud, very loud. When he spoke it was quietly.

'Now gentlemen, will you be so good as to take a little port with me? And let us converse of happier matters.'

They did, and soon Captain Swift had them all laughing at stories of his boyhood in a ship of the line commanded by a real old character. William's confusion gradually faded away as the port mellowed him and smoothed the rough edges of his drunkenness. Of course Uncle Daniel was right. There *was* only one way to deal with scum, and they *had* been lax. The fine weather, perhaps, lulling them into a false sense of comfort. He

150

determined, fuzzily, that he would mend his ways. And the people's.

In the part of the Welfare where Fulman's mess were taking their dinner, wine was also being drunk. By now the small quantity of beer remaining in the casks had been declared unfit even for seamen to drink. This unprecedented decision had been forced on the reluctant Butterbum by Mr Allgood; probably, it was generally felt, more out of a desire to thwart that character than for the benefit of Jolly Jack. The wine was a thin and highly acid white, but to the people it was paradisial after the vile dregs of ale, which by this time were graced with tiny wiggling creatures that made one cough.

The men's food was also beginning to show signs of life, which most of them bore in good part. But to some, who were laughed at as being too lordly for their own good, eating was becoming a trial. Thomas Fox was one of them. The 'bread', which was as hard as rock and crawling with weevils and maggots, he found particularly repulsive. Peter watched him banging it and picking at it in a vain attempt to separate the livestock from the substance.

'You'm a funny one, Tommy Fox,' he said. 'Why you trying to get rid of them harmless creatures? They gives that bread its taste.'

Thomas did not reply. At home, in those far-off days that were like a dream, bread had been a joy to him.

'Anyone'd think as how you was a proper gent,' continued Peter. 'Them fat white maggots is good to the tongue. They cools you down on days like this.'

Old Fulman butted in.

'Give it a little rest, eh Peter boy? I expect young Tommy do recall a little better grub than you do.'

Peter smiled, chewing heartily at a mouthful of rancid beef, bone-hard biscuit, bitter weevils and slimy, cooling maggots. He swallowed, washing down the rough bits with a long draught of wine.

'Oh aye, very likely, very likely,' he conceded. 'Why, my master gave me nothing at all most days. Well, Tommy, I wager you never did have to feed *after* the house's dogs, did you?'

Thomas, toying with the vile food, flicked his eyes up at the bright, jolly face. It was true, he had not. Oh God, mother, mother! Fresh bread and eggs and cheese and all. Oh God, oh God!

'No, I'll wager. Why some days, Tommy, I fought the very dogs

151

in the street for bones that fell from the slaughterer's cart!' He looked round, as if expecting to be contradicted. 'It is true,' he said.

No one contradicted him. Most were too busy eating. Jesse Broad, who like Thomas found the food almost unbearable, did not bother to say so. He ate doggedly, rather than starve. We all get there in the final reckoning, he thought. Poor little Peter started life eating such filth, I come to it now and must school myself until I stomach it. The maggots did cool the mouth and throat in fact, and the weevils did impart a certain bitterness to the hard, tasteless biscuit. He almost gagged at the thought. The fatness of those maggots!

'I saw yon poor marine sewn in for burial not two hours since,' Peter said brightly, after a pause.

'Hold thy tongue awhile, Peter,' repeated Grandfather Fulman irritably. 'We are at supper. We do not want to hear of dead men.'

'Aye,' said Peter, 'but it was wonderful interesting when all's said. Did you know he did stitch his nose in with him? The sailmaker? He run that great curved needle straight through the poor dead fellow's nose.'

Broad looked at Fulman enquiringly. He could half believe any barbarity on board a Navy ship. Fulman tutted gently.

'My, Peter, how you do chatter on,' he said comfortably. He belched.

'Is it true?' asked Broad. 'About the fellow's nose? I'll skin you, Peter,' he added, mock threateningly.

Grandfather Fulman belched again.

'Oh aye, true enough, friend Jesse.' He indicated a mess of gristly beef on Broad's platter that looked abandoned. 'Ah, by the way . . . if I ain't being forward . . .'

Broad pushed it across with a faint shiver. The old man filled his mouth and chewed solidly. When he had swallowed he went on.

'Ah, well they say it is this way. When a fellow dies on board of a ship and the sailmaker sews him into his last overcoat, as it were, there's always one more chance. Which is, of course, that he's not so much dead as dead drunk.'

Peter squeaked with laughter.

'Nay Peter, you may laugh, but I have seen it more than once. A fellow can go that rigid in rum you'd not credit there could be breath left in him. Gospel.

152

'Any road, friend Jesse, that's the tale. With the last stitch, the sailmaker drives that great needle through the corpse's nose – right through the horny part, there, where it do hurt the worst. And many's the corpse, I suppose, that must have sat right up at that, a-howling blue bloody murder and calling for another dram!'

Peter nodded vigorously.

'I seen it, Jesse,' he said earnestly. Then added with a giggle: 'Tell you what though! That bugger didn't jump up then! Him's as dead as this beef!'

'Aye,' put in the taciturn Samuel. 'And a lot deader than the biscuit.'

There was another silence, a shipboard silence. The noise of the sea, the noise of the rigging, slatting from time to time as the wind fluked. And the louder noise, the strange noise, of Padraig Doyle eating. Broad watched the blind man's mouth as he tried to masticate like other men, wondering dully whatever could have happened to have brought him to such a state. Without a tongue he could hardly eat the hard, stringy naval fare. Awful, dreadful things had happened and were happening in rebel Ireland, Jesse knew. What tales of torture would poor Doyle tell if someone had not ripped his tongue out? Or had he lost it, and his eyes, in an accident? It was not likely, he decided. And decided, also, that his own sufferings since the night of his capture were a minor thing compared with the worlds of misery that were a commonplace on this awful ship.

'They do say, Tommy,' piped up Peter gaily, 'as how you'll be made to run the gantlope for the affair of them four chickens.'

'Hush hush,' said Grandfather Fulman. 'Leave it be, Peter.'

'Well, 'tis only a rumour I dare say,' Peter added, a little chastened. But after a short while he chattered on.

'Old Butterbum will put it to the gentlemen, you see, that by stealing them, you was robbing your shipmates and so must run it. Well that's a fine joke, for when did *we* taste chicken last?'

'Now shut your silly mouth,' said Fulman harshly.

Surprisingly, Thomas spoke. It was the first time he had uttered a word to his messmates for days. He did not look up, however, and his voice was thin with misery.

'What is a gantlope, Peter?' he said. 'And why must I run it?'

Everyone stared at him. Except for Peter, who rattled on in delight.

153

'Oh it is terrible, a terrible thing,' he said, the words tumbling over each other in his excitement. 'You will be carried in a barrel like a king, and all your shipmates will line the decks, all the people in two great rows. Each man shall have a rope's end, I too I suppose, and we must give you great blows on the head as you go along – carried, you will be, in a barrel.'

He paused for breath. No one tried to stop him. No one tried to speak or move.

'We must all beat you hard, Thomas, or else we shall be beat in turn. And the master-at-arms shall walk ahead of you backwards, with his sword at your throat, to make sure you are not drawn through the lines too fast. Oh aye, I forgot – and you shall receive a half-dozen with the cat before you get in your barrel.

'And . . .' his voice was tailing off. He seemed seized with sudden awareness of what the words all meant. 'And afterwards too . . . another half a dozen . . . oh.'

He stared at Thomas with wide, horrified eyes. His mouth hung open. He was spilling his wine.

Thomas Fox was moaning quietly, the Irishman's arm around his shoulder.

Nineteen

As the Welfare slowly approached the Line, as she lost all last vestiges of steady, useful wind and entered the band of hot, light, fluky airs known as the doldrums, Jesse Broad lost all traces of the strange contentment he had intermittently felt at the mere fact of being a seaman at sea.

Whereas before the ship had plunged and sung, filling him with wild joy despite himself by her living, vibrant beauty, she was now a floundering, sluggish thing. The fitful breezes left her alone for hours on end, then took her briefly and cruelly, often aback. The thrum of taut cordage and bellying sails had been replaced by the slap of idle ropes against swinging spars, the flapping of heavy, leaden canvas that hung like dense sheets from the creaking yards. She was becalmed, bewildered, the wild fronds of green weed floating out along her sides to prove how little headway she was making. Usually it was none. And these doldrums went on and on. She lopped interminably in the brazen sea, glowing with heat, the bright cruel sun bubbling the pitch on her deck planks, bleaching even the tarred ropes that swung uneasily aloft.

Below decks it was bad enough. As they had driven down into warmer latitudes the heat in the men's living quarters had risen day by day. At night, at first, it had grown cooler, with damp, salt air blowing softly through the open ports and hatches. But for days the night air had been as hot as that which stirred by day. On the upper deck it was stifling, almost unbreathable. But below it was far worse. Every man lived in a bath of sweat and grime, every article of clothing was stinking and stiff with salt. The drinking water was undrinkable, had been for ages; the beer was condemned; the wine and grog aggravated thirst, not assuaged it.

Then there were the bugs. The bugs, the lice, the cockroaches. The biting, stinging, stinking insects. Not a piece of bedding that did not have its full complement of 'passengers'. Not a shirt or

155

blouse or pair of trousers. The men spent hours every day searching seams, bursting blood-filled bodies, heaving useful items over the side. But the invaders marched on, invincible. The stench of cockroaches, the buzz and tick as they flew about in the dark and bumped into things, was awful. Even on deck, where many men now slept, they nibbled at dirty ears and eyebrows, chewed at calloused skin.

From the bilges, the underlying smell of sewage that Broad had noticed right from the first, had taken on a new power. It overlay everything, and with a vengeance. The foetid shingle, mud and stones that kept the Welfare upright and made her sail so stiff, was warm and rotting. All the filth and slime washed from the decks above over the years was cooking gently, exhaling a charnel-house odour that could all but be felt. The biscuit, stored in porous bags in the bread-room deep in the hold, took on the smell. The weevils and maggots thrived on it; but the most hardened seaman found his staple revolting now it reeked so strong of excrement.

At the instigation of Mr Adamson, the captain allowed – or rather ordered – that the living areas should be scrubbed thoroughly every day with lashings of water, then sprinkled with vinegar. This had the effect of keeping the men busy all the time, so was allowed to be a good thing. It also, however, kept them below decks, kept the living spaces constantly damp and steamy, and kept the bilges in a never-ending turmoil as the pumps removed the cleansing-water that had flowed into them. Daily the smells were revolved, churned, renewed. As to the vinegar – well, maybe it fought the vapours that were said to spread diseases; but the 'wildlife', against all predictions, seemed to like it as well as the dirt it was meant to replace.

The rotting of the food, already well advanced, increased rapidly. Cheese and butter there were in the stores, as well as opened casks of salted pork and beef. The former items went off very rapidly, with a smell so greasy and pervasive from the rancid butter that much of it went over the side, to the purser's eternal misery. The cheese became uneatable unless soaked in wine for days. Broad had never believed the tales of seamen making buttons and model ships from lumps of cheese; but in the doldrums he found it true. As for the pork and beef – well, some of it had already achieved several years of age. But even so, one or two barrels went rotten. He marvelled at the power of a maggot's jaws.

In the sick-bay there were many men. Ulcers were the most common complaint, along with boils and general sores. Jesse Broad spent two days in there after a languidly swinging block had rendered him unconscious for twelve hours and affected his sight. The surgeon, as gay as ever, had treated him like an old friend, plied him with special stocks of brandy instead of the rotgut he doled out to other men. It was apparently his only real answer to the diseases he was faced with. His small stocks of garlic and other beneficial herbs had gone long before, he was no great believer in the effectiveness of bleeding (having seen it, he said, kill more than it had cured) and he had a fixed hatred of quackery. Broad got out as soon as he could see half-straight. He would rather risk death from double-vision and walking overboard than stay among the dirty, groaning men.

Below decks it was bad enough, in the sick-bay it was dreadful. But aloft it was worse. Captain Swift, and his officers, and his young gentlemen, and his warrants, saw to that.

Swift's idea, apparently, was that now there were only light airs, every one of them should be made to work for the ship. What this really meant was that he wanted the men to work. If the devil truly made work for idle hands, Captain Swift was making damned sure there were no idle hands. Dead ones maybe; but not idle ones.

He stood upon the quarterdeck, under an awning, and watched the sea like a hawk. He lifted his great nose at every air, however light, and studied every catspaw, however faint. At each and every one, he gave orders to the master or the boatswain. These were passed to the boatswain's mates, then to the men. Canes whistled and thwacked, tired, aching, sweating men jumped to sheets and braces. Hour after hour the performance went on. The yards were braced this way and that, sheets were eased and hauled in, headsails were backed, filled, and changed. The Welfare lay sluggish in the blazing calm, rarely moving. When Swift was tired of it, he would hand over to Hagan, or Plumduff, or Higgins. Then he would sit under the awning, in his silken shirtsleeves, drinking lemonade.

The yards were so hot, so slippery with sweat, that it was a miracle no one died. Swift ordered almost as many sail changes as he did manoeuvres. New sails were brought up from below, yards were lowered and the canvas replaced with lighter, the yards were swayed up again. Stunsails were repositioned, new methods of

157

sheeting were devised. The topmen, dizzy with heat and fatigue, clenched the slimy, burning spars with their bellies. Some were ruptured, as many, even, as in heavy weather. Then they would be helped below to be fitted with a truss. Mr Adamson, mercifully enough, did not follow the practice of some of his fellow naval surgeons and hang hernia victims by their heels to ease the swelling.

'The bastard will kill us all,' Matthews said to Jesse Broad as they lay across the fore topgallant yard one morning.

'Yes,' said Broad dully. 'Do you know, Matthews, I truly think he will.'

No time for any more, no time for thoughts. They were howled to the next task, slipping carelessly among the rigging with leaden limbs, clumsy fingers. Perhaps he would have welcomed the idea of death, had he been able to think clearly. But he was too tired.

William Bentley and the other midshipmen entered into the spirit of the new regime with great gusto. They had discussed it the morning after the dinner, when the worst of their hangovers had evaporated, and agreed that the captain was right. What the people needed was a bit of grit, a bit of fizz, a bit of bounce.

Jack Evans looked at the faces of his friends carefully as if he were going to say something of great importance.

'Can I trust you lads?' he asked, shiftily. 'I do not want to end up on the fore yardarm in a hemp collar for this!'

James Finch was excited.

'Are you planning a mutiny, Jack?' he said.

'Hush!' said William. Mutiny was an uncomfortable word. A disturbing word. It was a word that only a silly child would utter except in the deepest seriousness. Finch went scarlet.

'You are a foolish baby,' Jack Evans said, in as stern a manner as his shrill voice would allow. 'No but listen, lads, I must admit I thought the owner was going a little far at first.'

'Over the matter of the marine?' asked Simon Allen.

'Aye, that certainly. I thought the fire-eater was coming it very hot. Why, to suggest the fellow was shirking!'

'He looked desperate ill to me,' put in Finch, glancing anxiously at them to make sure he wasn't being silly again. 'And after all, he did die!'

Evans and Allen laughed. But William put in darkly: 'It is amazing, to quote my Uncle Daniel, the lengths to which some people will go.'

'Aye,' said Evans. 'I did not catch his meaning on that at first. But he is right, of course.'

'You mean it is a plot?' asked Finch incredulously. 'How can that be though? A man cannot die deliberately.'

'The matter of the burial will cause trouble enough,' said Simon Allen. 'It could almost be seen as an excuse. A way for the damned dogs to start barking and showing their teeth.'

Jimmy Finch shook his head.

'I still cannot get it,' he confessed. 'Jack, you said the owner went too far. Are you now saying—'

'I said "at first". I said I thought "at first" he went too far. Of course he did not. He has the measure of this scum.'

'But surely . . .'

'Oh stow it, Jimmy,' Jack Evans said. 'You are too much of a child. What you cannot understand for God's sake keep your mouth shut on.'

William had a sneaking sympathy for Finch's position, because he wasn't too sure of it all himself. Could the marine's death really have been such a mystery? Judging by the confusion of the way they were discussing it, the others were as flummoxed as he was. Sometimes he felt they were all useless, stupid, himself as well. Mere snotty boys, as the people thought them. It embarrassed him, shamed him horribly. He went for the broad principle, to make the argument less a fatuous mess.

'What I say,' he told them, 'is that Uncle Daniel is right. He knows his men better than anyone. It is uncanny. He sees right into the minds of these people. And he is right.'

There was a chorus of relief. Whatever the ins and outs of it, the overall position was clear. They nodded eagerly, expecting him to drop more words of wisdom. William obliged.

'What my uncle said, when all's done, is that we have been too soft on them. The sunshine and the pleasant breezes have put us in a holiday mood. We have been failing in our duty.'

'Not just us alone, Will,' added Evans, 'but the lieutenants and the warrants and petty officers too.'

'No excuse, no excuse,' said William. 'Just because others have

159

failed, does not make our failure better. Why, I freely admit my own lapses. I have seen men slacking and let it pass when all I had to do was lift a finger and have a boatswain's mate start them.'

Another chorus, of confessions this time. All the mids had let men off in similar situations. They shook their heads in shame.

'What have we done indeed to aid the discipline on board?' asked William. 'Tormented one old schoolmaster and let the real villains run free. It is very bad in us, very bad.'

A chorus of agreement. Then a long and detailed discussion as to how they could win back their self-respect. They decided that nothing should escape them from now on, not a dropped ropeyarn, not a raised eyebrow. They would show the people that they were young gentlemen, and officers born. They would sweep and scour the ship like a cleansing fire. They would provide the iron in the soul that Captain Swift said was what the Welfare lacked.

After the simple burial of the soldier, each of them provided a list to the master-at-arms of men and marines whose attitudes during the service had conveyed anything that smacked of discontent. There were several floggings on their behalf, and Captain Swift thanked them handsomely for their vigilance. On the decks the four became terrible, ranging and watching for the slightest lapse. And it was William himself who suggested to his uncle some days later a new way of keeping the people busy.

When it was first announced, Jesse Broad, who had been standing in the shade of the foremast awaiting the next unnecessary sail order, could hardly believe it. But it was true. Hands were being told off to the boats. He himself, singled out as an experienced and powerful oarsman, was detailed as stroke in one of the cutters.

It was a long and exhausting business getting the bigger boats cleared away and into the water. Tackles were rigged to get them from their positions on the skids and over the side. In the water they leaked alarmingly from the shrinkage in the planks caused by the sunshine. Extra boys with bailing cans were put on board, then heavy warps were coiled into the sternsheets.

William Bentley stood on the quarterdeck, beside his uncle by special invitation, watching the operation with pride. Daniel Swift smiled, nodding his head in satisfaction.

'By God, my boy,' he said. 'This will keep the scum on their toes. An excellent idea, excellent!'

So now, throughout the hours of daylight, the killing sail-work was supplemented by an even more killing task. At each catspaw, at every tiny zephyr, Swift or one of his officers gave the order to pull. The exhausted seamen, blind with sweat, bent to the great ash oars. Slowly they would turn the Welfare's head, slowly they would drag her great, weedy, yellow-hulled bulk towards the area where a little wind played with the gleaming surface of the sea. By the time they got there, always, the breeze would have gambolled off elsewhere, or just disappeared. If the latter, they would rest wearily on their oars, watching the figures on the quarterdeck with slow-burning hatred. If the former, they would swing the great yellow bow once more to pull stolidly towards the elusive catspaw. And they prayed, they prayed for wind.

Thomas Fox prayed during this time, but not for wind. He prayed for deliverance. At every moment that he was not occupied by his tasks, his mind was filled with the terror of the gantlope. He saw visions of himself in the barrel, with blood running from his ears and mouth as the cruel blows rained on him. He saw the master-at-arms's sword pressed to his throat, felt the sharp pain as it broke the tender skin there. He saw the faces of his shipmates, filled with fear and hatred, as they beat and beat him with the knotted ropes. The only person he told this to was Doyle, in their hours spent among the beasts. The blind man listened, his pipes answering the wild ramblings with an eerie sympathy. To the rest of the ship, even Broad, Thomas Fox said nothing. His question to Peter had been the last words he uttered for many days.

He spoke again because he was forced to. The boatswain, Mr Allgood, came prowling along the gun-deck, stooped under the heavy beams, poking about and asking after the shepherd boy. Thomas clutched Padraig Doyle in desperation, then tried to hide himself among the sheep. It was no good.

'Fox,' said the deep voice of the boatswain. 'You there, Irishman, dig the fellow out of there. I won't eat him.'

Thomas burrowed deeper into the soft dark warmth, but an iron hand gripped his shoulder.

'Think I've come to punish you, eh boy?' roared the boatswain.

'Think I've come to have you flogged, eh chicken-thief? Running the gantlope, that's what the purser wants for you, do you know that?'

He pulled Thomas from among the sheep, then tried to lower him to the deck. But the boy's feet were drawn up to his stomach. He hung peculiarly, curled under the giant arm.

'Put your legs down, boy,' he boomed. 'You're a fine one to be at sea, by Christ you are! Put your legs down, damn you!'

Thomas Fox clenched his legs harder into his stomach. Suddenly the boatswain changed his grip, cradled him in his arms as he might a child. Then he took Thomas's chin in his hand, turned his head, tried to look into the downcast eyes. His voice softened, became curiously gentle.

'Ah boy,' he said. 'You are a poor little bastard and no mistake. Tell me, do you know who stole those hens? Eh? Tell me boy, and I'll see he's punished for it.'

Thomas lay in the great arms, cradled, silent. The boatswain's breath was soft upon his cheek.

'Come now, Thomas Fox,' said Allgood gently. 'I know you did not eat them. Was it friends, or was it enemies?'

The dark musician turned his naked sockets to Allgood's face. He touched the pipes and a low, melodious sigh came from them. In Thomas Fox's head the thoughts raced round, darkly muddled, rats in a trap. The pipes sighed again, a calming, soothing note.

'Old Butterbum,' said the boatswain, 'wants your blood, my bonny lad. He wants you flogged, or chained, or chivvied, or beaten black and blue. But you did not eat them, did you boy?'

Slowly, desperately slowly, Thomas Fox turned his face towards the giant cradling him. Slowly, with an immense effort, he lifted his eyes, made them travel up the broad shirt front, across the great black curly beard, the red full lips, the big flared nose. At last, and for the merest instant, he looked into Allgood's eyes.

'Please sir,' he said. 'They died, sir. They died in the storm, and I put them overboard. I was . . . I was . . .'

His eyes dropped, his voice died away.

'You was afeard to say,' said the boatswain quietly. 'Good. Then Butterbum can go to hell, and welcome Old Nick is to him, to be sure. All right, my bonny boy? All right? You're safe, do you hear? Not a hair on your head will anyone touch, do you hear? Butterbum can go to hell!'

Thomas whispered: 'Thank you, sir.' A great relief grew in him, it washed him through. The boatswain ruffled his hair, laughed, and deposited him gently on the deck beside the Irishman, among the sheep. As he picked his way aft, he chuckled.

Although there were many on board who would have liked to have seen the shepherd boy running the gantlope, there was nothing to be done about it. The feud between the boatswain and the purser was well known, and there was no doubt that Captain Swift would support Allgood in any clash between them, despite the purser's social superiority. To him, as to everyone on board, the purser was an evil they had to bear, a fat and ugly vulture who would be better off in a sailcloth shroud. The boatswain was a useful man, a vital man. If it pleased him to free Fox from a perfectly legitimate punishment, then so be it.

William Bentley was particularly sorry that the boy had escaped unscathed. Of late he had come to almost hate him, so violently did he dislike his way of moving silently and miserably about the ship like some tragic ghost. He railed to the other mids about it later the same afternoon, and they all agreed that it was just the sort of thing that would undermine the general discipline once more, after all their care to build up a tautness among the people.

'I shall keep an eye out for Mr Fox,' William promised. 'We have been too namby-pamby with him of late.'

'He is a damned disgrace to the name of seaman or King's Navy anyway,' Jack Evans added. 'He never looks one in the eye even if you cuff him about the ears to do so. And he never says a word.'

'He's a damned mute, like his eerie friend,' said Finch. 'Now *he*, the Irishman, gives *me* the creeps. Those awful eyes!'

William Bentley saw his chance with Thomas a couple of afternoons later. And he took it with both hands.

There had been an unaccustomed air of jollity on board that day, because the Welfare had picked up a breeze in the middle of the morning which had blown steadily, if not strongly, for several hours. The boats were in, the sails were trimmed, the heat had been made almost pleasant by the wind.

On the foredeck Padraig Doyle had played many tunes, while Thomas Fox had remained below putting the finishing touches to his whistle. He sat alone among the beasts, wielding a sharp knife

163

with extreme care and testing the whistle frequently for the exact pitch he wanted. At last, with a feeling almost of happiness, he blew steadily, played a couple of scales, then tried out, haltingly at first but with increasing confidence, a lilting tune. The pipe was perfect.

He climbed the ladder to the foredeck with a lightness in his tread that had been missing for as long as he could remember. His friend sat in the usual place, back resting against the fore-bitts, the bagpipe tucked under his arm, and Thomas went to him and sat at his feet. He did not speak, but when the tune finished he touched his hand with the whistle. The Irishman felt it, turned his blazing sockets, and smiled. They checked that they were in pitch, then without a stumble took up an air together.

All conversation on the foredeck stopped. The men gathered round and studied this new phenomenon. Thomas kept his eyes on Doyle's fingers but he knew he was surrounded, knew he was being watched. He felt relaxed, confident. The pipe and the bagpipe merged, the air swelled with their pure music.

William Bentley noticed the cluster of men from his position on the quarterdeck. He moved curiously forward until he was on the edge of them. When they became aware of his presence the seamen moved apart, touching their foreheads and mumbling. William looked down, at the man and the boy. A smile played about his lips. By the time the tune came to an end most of the men had melted away to watch from a safe distance.

The whistle ended on a high trill, the bagpipe on a low contrasting chord. As the notes died away, William Bentley spoke.

'By whose permission, Thomas Fox,' he said. 'Do you play that instrument?'

Thomas looked up in shock, then down again. Dread swooped in his stomach, a great gush. The whistle slipped from his fingers and rolled across the deck towards William Bentley's feet.

'By whose permission?' repeated William Bentley. 'The blindman is musician here, and as such is on the books. Who said you might play?'

Not a word came. Thomas stared at the deck with unseeing eyes.

'One time more,' said Bentley. 'By whose permission do you play that pipe?'

After a short pause he lifted his foot as if he would crush the whistle that lay before him. There was a sudden movement and Jesse Broad broke from a knot of seamen. He knelt quickly in front of the midshipman and picked up the whistle. He remained on one knee, gazing into the face of the boy. His lips were parted; he was panting slightly.

William Bentley held out his hand for the whistle, but Broad did not move. They stared at each other for a long time, deep into each other's eyes.

Then, quite suddenly, William Bentley filled his mouth with spittle and jetted it into the seaman's face. As it ran down beside his nose and dribbled over his lips, Broad's face darkened. A muscle worked in his cheek and his face grew darker. It grew darker and darker until he was almost black. Nobody moved.

Then William Bentley turned on his heel and walked steadily back towards the quarterdeck.

Twenty

The breeze that had lifted the Welfare from her sluggish misery blew gentle and steady for long enough to take her across the Line. The boats and the interminable pulling were forgotten, the insanely pointless sail-trimming was replaced by genuine work, which nobody objected to. The ship did not sail fast, particularly, but she was sailing. And even if the heat and mildew below decks were still almost unbearable, even if the bugs and cockroaches continued to drive men almost mad, at least on deck there was a cooling wind to dry the sweat and ease the sores and boils that nearly everyone had round mouth and eyes.

The preparations for the ceremony of crossing the Line caused great excitement on board, not least because Henry Joyce was to be Neptune. When he had finally emerged from the sick-bay, he had been a fascinating sight to all hands. He had lost a great amount of bulk, lying near death as he had for days on end. He had practically lived on the surgeon's brandy for one whole week, and for most of the rest of his time below he had been unable to hold down anything other than pease pudding. But emaciated and pale, Henry Joyce retained some awful signs of power. His great shoulders were unbowed, despite the piled scars that swelled onto his neck under his pigtail, and his shambling walk, though less steady, still had an indefinable air of the beast in it. The eyes were usually cast down. But William Bentley, stalking in the waist on the morning he reappeared, had caught Joyce looking at him, and it caused him a shock of something he did not care to contemplate.

It amused the men that Henry Joyce was to play Neptune, the cruel lord, but it gave no pleasure to the young gentlemen. In this one ceremony they were very much at the mercy of tradition. Tradition had it that they must pay tribute to Neptune, after being prepared for the honour by his barbers. And Neptune could do with them what he would. The other boys on board faced the perils too, as did every man who had never crossed the Line before, but the mids guessed that they would receive the roughest treatment of all.

They did. After being stripped, half shaved and thoroughly beaten and ducked, all four young gentlemen were a sorry sight. James Finch, to his shame, was weeping, but he managed to do it quietly at least. William would have liked to have cried, he ached desperately and great patches of his skin were roughened and sore, but it was something that had to be borne. It was a golden opportunity for the men to try to break the boys. He scorned their clumsy physical attempts; he would have laughed aloud at them had not any opening of the mouth been an invitation for Neptune or one of his roughs to fill it with a stinking mess of pig's lard and tar. They were pathetic in their desire to hurt and he despised them.

Jesse Broad despised them too, as he awaited his turn to face the half-drunk villains of 'barbers'. He watched the men drooling with pleasure as they beat and pinched the boys. It was a chance, admittedly, the only chance. Had he retaliated when Bentley had spat at him, he could have hanged for it. He watched the small naked figure of Finch being hoisted high over the deck by his ankle and felt sorry for the child. This was not the way.

One thing surprised him though. Thomas Fox had got off almost scot free.

Broad had been fearful of the ceremony on the shepherd boy's account. After the incident over the whistle, Fox had collapsed in on himself like a pricked bladder. Broad, almost blinded with anger, had yet been aware that the real victim of the midshipman was the boy. The vile excuse that there was only one musician on the ship's books was nonsense; any man could play, if he wanted, during the dog-watches; Thomas was transgressing no laws. But after the incident the life that had come back into his pale, dead face had gone. Broad could not see his eyes, no one could any more. Fox kept them turned always to the deck. But that brief spark that had been in him as he had walked to the piper with his whistle had gone again. Worse, he appeared to have given up all hope; his shoulders had stooped, his arms and hands were always limp. Broad had tried to tell him that he could play; that Bentley had been merely goading him. But Fox did not even seem to hear.

167

To many of the men, not just officers and warrants, Thomas Fox had been a target. He was considered simple, a fool, and fair game for any treatment, however atrocious. Broad had warned off many, as he knew Matthews had too, in his dour way, and the boatswain's ambiguous behaviour towards him kept Fox safe from many vile excesses. But among the lower of the people – and God knew, thought Broad, most of them were the scrapings of the sewer – he was an object of hatred and contempt. Red-headed Peter, who had crossed the Line before, had been gleefully ghoulish, in his childish unthinking way, about what the men would do to Thomas. Thomas had not listened, apparently; but Broad had felt deep pity for the boy.

But it had not happened that way. Thomas Fox had awaited his turn, docile as a broken lamb. And almost as a lamb he had been treated. At first Broad thought it must be a deep and subtle plan by the men to show to Bentley what they felt of his behaviour; but that was surely quite beyond them. It slowly dawned on him that the pity he felt for Fox had somehow become general; the incident at the fore-bitts had brought about a change in the men, even the most beastly. It must be true, for Neptune and his assistants were certainly among the most beastly dregs of humanity on board. And they treated Thomas with an eerie gentleness. He was pushed around, of course, and one or two sly digs went in. But compared with the treatment everyone else received, he got off light indeed.

The day after the Welfare crossed the Line, she lost her breeze. William, invited to take tea with his uncle in the sultry cabin, expected to find him ready to eat fire. The captain, however, stalking moodily up and down by the stern windows, was more thoughtful than furious.

'I had hoped, my boy, that we would have picked up the Trade after the Line. That damned breeze has played me false. Time is running on, William, time is running on. I have never been in the doldrums so solid and long in all my time at sea.'

William sipped his tea. He had learned enough in his lessons with Mr Robinson to know that the doldrums were unpredictable, but he had no intention of suggesting to his uncle that they might be becalmed almost indefinitely. He waited quietly.

'Damned old Neptune!' laughed Swift. 'I would have thought he might have graced us with some good breezes in return for so many new acolytes presented with all due ceremony. Stubborn old lad.' His smile lingered. 'Bah! Damned superstitious nonsense!'

'Shall we clear the boats for towing, sir?' asked William. 'It had the desired effect last time, that and all the sail-handling.'

Swift sat astride a plush chair and sucked his lower lip into his mouth musingly.

'I think not, William,' he said. 'I think we will try a new tack altogether. I think for the moment I will play the hearty fellow with the scum.'

William looked blank. Whatever plan his uncle had would be interesting, no doubt. And would be revealed in his own good time.

After a minute or so, Captain Swift bounded up restlessly and flashed his wide, bright smile. He smacked the palm of his left hand with his right fist.

'Surprise! That's the thing, my boy! Surprise the men, keep 'em guessing! That's the way to have 'em under command. They think they know which way the dog will jump. But they do not! Not a jot!'

William finished his tea. He looked past the small, powerful form of his uncle at the sullen brazen sea outside. It was like a millpond, flat and unmoving. A glowing, violent heat rose from it. He smiled politely.

'Surprise, sir?'

'Surprise, Mr Bentley. They will be expecting work, work, yet more work. They will be expecting kicks and hapence, or kicks at least! They will look for rowing, sail-handling, drudgery. Instead—'

He stopped. Again the dazzling smile, incongruous in the hard face with its cold pale eyes.

'Instead?'

'Haha! You see, my boy! Keep 'em guessing! Tell me – what would be your guess?'

No guess at all, thought William. His uncle was very excited. He found it somehow vaguely disturbing. No guess at all.

'I am afraid, sir, you have me beaten,' he said.

'Right!' said Swift gaily. 'And so I shall the people. They'll be expecting kicks – and I'll give 'em hapence!'

'May I be permitted to know what form the "hapence" will take, uncle?' William asked.

The captain laughed.

'You may not,' he said. 'Keep 'em guessing is the way. But you may invite Mr Allgood to pipe all hands aft when you have finished your tea. Then you can hear the news with everyone else.'

William stood up and bowed. As he turned to go, Swift said: 'Oh, by the by, William, have we any musicians on board? Excepting Doyle, naturally.'

William half smiled, remembering.

'Yes sir,' he said. 'At least one. Rather a fine whistle-pipe player, I believe.'

'Capital!' said Swift. 'Capital. I shall speak further to you of that after the people have had their dinners. Capital!'

Broad found himself alongside Matthews as the men moved slowly aft. Everyone was sweating heavily again and the mood was not good. Another dose of towing to zephyrs was in everyone's mind, and they did not like it.

'No punishment today,' said Matthews drily. 'And this, I suppose, is the reason for it. He will amuse himself with a different form of torture for once. He plays us like a fiddle, damn him, and cares less for us.'

'Why, I wonder,' replied Broad, 'does he bother to call us aft? Why not just have the orders issued? I think you are right, friend Matthews. He wants to play with us a while.'

A boatswain's mate made a threatening movement with his rattan. They joined the thronged, sullen, company in silence.

Captain Swift stood before them in all his glory. He had on a blue coat, a wig, a broad smile. He surveyed the assembled crew with a gaze that was almost affectionate. Jesse Broad found the powerful figure fascinating. So relaxed, so untroubled, so vicious.

'My jolly lads,' Swift said at last, 'I have called you here today to put the fear of God in you. You know I am a stern man, you know I am a tight one. But until this moment you have seen but nothing. Today I will make you quake. Today I will make you quail. Today I will make you damn your mothers' eyes for bringing you into the world.'

His voice was jolly, full of fun, but the words chilled Jesse Broad. He glanced at Matthews, whose face was set and grim. What in the name of hell could Swift be planning now?

The captain's eyes were twinkling. He surveyed the stolid people, his famous smile wide on his face.

'My boys,' he went on. 'You will note the weather. In vain we shaved and lathered yesterday. In vain we paid old Neptune's tribute, aye twice and thrice over. What wind we had, and it was feeble enough God knows, has been taken away from us. Here we wallow in this bloody calm, like a basket of fish in Portsmouth harbour. What's to be done, aye, that's the question.'

Not a man who didn't know Swift's answer to that one, or so Jesse thought. The heat was like a hammer. It would be dreadful in those boats.

'Your shipmates are falling sick like flies,' said Captain Swift. 'Mr Adamson reports the sick-bay overflowing. He is the surgeon, and exercise is his cure. Well lads, we all know about exercise on this ship, eh?'

A groan went among the seamen, low but tangible. Swift gave a brief laugh, his head thrown back.

'Rowing to the breeze, eh men, is that what you are groaning over? Or perhaps it's the thought of trimming, trimming, trimming! Every hour of every day! Aye aye, I've made you sweat I will allow. But no . . .'

His face lost its smile. He gazed about him with his piercing gaze. Broad waited for the stroke.

'But no,' repeated Swift. 'Today I have a new diversion for you. And you'll curse me for it, oh you'll curse me for it!'

Jesse darted glances at faces nearby. I wonder if he knows, he thought, how great the heap of curses already is that these men have laid upon his head.

'It's dancing!' cried Swift at last. 'It's dancing and music and sport! Oh my boys, I'll have you crying out for mercy so I will!'

There was a rumble of confusion as this sank in. What was the man talking about? Had he gone mad? Or was it an odd sort of joke he was trying to make? Matthews shrugged his shoulders and Broad spread his hands in front of him. Little Peter, who was nearby, squeaked excitedly, taking everything at face value, and got a swish for his pains. But it was not a hard one; the boatswain's mates were equally confused.

Captain Swift was delighted at the ripple he had spread. He laughed aloud. The men quietened gradually. There was a certain tenseness in the air as if they expected the news to be false, or to

171

somehow turn out nasty. Broad, in fact, was certain it would. He was wrong.

'Lads,' said the captain. 'This weather is vile, but we must make the best of it. Exercise we must have, but no more towing, no more killing work aloft, eh? You've done stout service for me and I'll ask no more until we get that south-east Trade that must be just around the corner. So it's dance that'll do it, dance and sport. We'll have a band, and we'll have races up and down the rigging, and we'll have a little milling! What say you, men?'

A cheer went up, a genuine cheer. Broad, taking the cue, joined in, although his was not so much a cheer as a loud noise to take the place of silence. Matthews hardly had his heart in it, either. But for most, apparently, it was a cheering matter, and in truth, thought Jesse, anything was better than what had gone before. But what a strange man, what a very strange man the captain was.

Even stranger was Swift's next announcement.

'To start it all off with a fizz, brave boys, I've just one more thing to say. Every one of you, man and boy, will get a double go of grog today. Now, how is that, eh?'

His last words were drowned in a tumult of delight. Layers of hatred, weeks of anger and misery, dissolved before Broad's eyes. The men around him had gone wild. He found himself looking into the calm, implacable face of Matthews. Again they gestured their bewilderment. Swift played them like a fiddle. And cared less for them . . .

By the time dinner was out, the first details of the events were all round the ship. Bentley, who had thrilled to the brilliance of his uncle's tactics, was put in charge of organisation and rose to the challenge superbly. He drew up lists of those who wanted to wrestle, those who wanted free fist-fights, those who wanted to punch over the sea chest. His uncle had insisted over a glass of wine after his speech that fighting should be the main part of the sports. There was violence in the air, he said, and he would have it out. He would have it out under strict control. The men could beat each other bloody and even win prizes for it. But it would be under control, and once out would soon evaporate. But dancing there would be too, and races. Running races on the decks, cannon leaping, and rigging races. Nothing too strenuous, nothing that smacked of hard work. Dancing in the intervals to the piper, the whistler and anyone else who could be found to play.

Old Fulman's mess, like all the others, was full of the announcement. Peter was so excited he could hardly eat. He reckoned to take many a prize in the rigging, because although he was not so strong as the men he was as nimble as a monkey. They talked merrily, full of rum and water, not really noticing the crushing airless heat any more.

'What will you enter for, Jesse?' Fulman said in one of the pauses while Peter stuffed his mouth with rotting beef and biscuit.

'Nothing, I doubt,' replied Jesse. 'Sporting events were never of much interest to me. And I certainly do not fancy being beaten by Henry Joyce or his ilk just to provide Mr Swift with some pleasure.'

'Coward! Coward!' shrieked Peter. 'Why Jesse, if I was not so busy with running I would enter for a milling with the big booby myself!'

They all laughed at the thought of Peter slugging it out with that giant. Allgood the boatswain was the only man on board who could have given him a contest.

'What is this sea chest fighting though?' asked Jesse Broad. 'It is not something I have heard of.'

'Oh, it is marvellous sport!' said Peter. 'Very bloody in the extreme, Jesse!'

'The rules are perfectly simple,' said Grandfather Fulman. 'You sit astride a sea chest, one at each end, and punch each other's heads. It is a game for strong men only.'

'And brave ones!' said Peter.

'Or fools,' said old Samuel.

'Who wins?'

'Again simple,' Fulman went on. 'The man who stays seated when the other is lying in a pool of gore on the deck! An extremely bloody game, as little Peter told you.'

Later they carried on the conversation on the foredeck, mingling with the other off-duty messes. Many men were tipsy, a few very drunk, but there was an air of jollity, almost of happiness. The fights would come later; and this time there would be prizes!

When he had finished sorting out the details with the help of the other midshipmen, William Bentley went forward to see about the music. A hush fell over the lounging men as he walked among them,

173

but it was a good-natured one. He picked his way across the deck to where Fulman and his friends sat by the fore-bitts. They stood up as he approached.

'Be easy, men,' he said heartily. He could feel the tension in the air. A dampness broke out on his brow. The man he had spat at looked levelly at him, face closed. The two greybeards employed the old sailor's trick of looking at the sea, the sails, anything but his face. Bentley felt his eyes drawn to the empty sockets of the Irishman.

'Be easy, men,' he repeated. 'You may sit if you please.'

Nobody moved.

'Well then,' said William Bentley. 'You, Irishman, we will require your services a good deal. Between each race, between each set of matches, there will be dancing. Shake your head if you understand.'

Padraig Doyle shook his thin grey head briefly. William wetted his lips.

'And you, boy,' he said to Thomas Fox. 'Where is your whistle?'

Thomas Fox was standing beside the dark musician, his head bowed. He started when the midshipman addressed him. He did not reply. There was silence all around them.

'Go below to your berth, Thomas Fox, and get your whistle-pipe. I require you to play it.'

The tension was becoming greater. William willed the shepherd boy to look at him. Nothing happened.

Suddenly Peter produced the whistle from inside his shirt. He blushed crimson.

'Please your honour,' he mumbled, 'Tommy give him to me. I think as he don't want him no more.'

'Do you play, boy?'

'No sir, your honour. But he don't want it I guess, so I took him.'

'Then give him back,' said William coldly. 'Thomas Fox, take up your whistle-pipe and play. I command you.'

For a long moment Thomas did not move. Peter held out the pipe, William felt sweat trickle down his neck into his shirt, the surrounding seamen watched surreptitiously. Then Thomas reached out a hand, took the pipe, and began to raise his head. He raised it until his eyes were level with William Bentley's chin. His face was white and tense, the muscles in his neck and cheeks

174

fluttering. He made a great effort to raise his eyes to the midshipman's, but they stuck at his chin. William's own mouth was dry.

Slowly Thomas Fox raised the pipe in front of him. He brought his left hand up to meet his right. He tried once more to raise his eyes to Bentley's. Failed. Then snapped the whistle in two and dropped the pieces on the deck.

There was a noise like a sigh all round William Bentley. He looked aft at the quarterdeck. His uncle was gazing at the scene, had watched it all. He returned his eyes to Fox, who was staring full at the deck again, his arms limply at his sides.

William felt a peculiar mixture of things. Cold rage, cold but blazing, and hot humiliation. He knew his face was red, knew what an incredible fool he must look. He felt awful hatred for Thomas Fox, mixed with a weird elation. An elation at the opportunity he had been given to get his own back. The punishment came to him in an instant, and he enunciated it clearly, although he could not hide a tremor in his voice.

'I will beat you for that, Thomas Fox,' he said. 'I will beat you until you scream.'

There was another odd sigh from the men on the foredeck.

'But it will be all fair and above board,' William added. 'It will be at the sea chest. Ours will be the first milling, Thomas Fox, and I will beat you until you scream. I will beat you for an insolent animal, sir. And I will beat you until you scream.'

He was white now, and trembling violently. There was dead silence as he left the foredeck to the seamen.

Twenty-One

Not even the bubbling Peter spoke until William Bentley had disappeared. At first it looked as though he would return to the quarterdeck, perhaps even talk – if invited – to the captain. But at the after hatchway he swung to his left and clattered below. There was an abrupt babble among the seamen, loud and incoherent. They clustered about Thomas offering congratulations and encouragement. Thomas did not respond in any way, but Peter swelled with pride and strutted like a small cockerel.

'Good man Thomas!' was the general cry. 'Good man to face that snotty boy; you made him such a fool he'll never hold up his head again.'

Peter piped shrilly: 'He is a miserable cur, but we have brought him down. My brave messmate! Did you see how he broke the whistle-pipe? I had him in my shirt and would have learned to play him soon enough!'

The other members of the mess were silent. Doyle's arm was round Fox's shoulders, while Grandfather Fulman had a look of bitter gloom on his face. The mood of the gathered seamen changed rapidly from exhilaration to commiseration. The shepherd boy's gesture had been a bold one, but where would it lead? To a savage beating, legal and above board. Many allowed that it was mightily unfair. Some grudgingly admitted that the midshipman was sharp. But no one doubted that the affair would end disastrously.

Although it was the men's spare time, the boatswain's mates moved in quickly to break up this unseemly meeting, held solely to discuss the demerits of a young gentleman. Broad saw them coming and warned the others, who melted away to the wider open spaces of the deck. They sat in silence for a while as the mates lounged self-consciously about, their rope's-ends swinging lazily.

Jesse Broad did not like to think how the silent, hopeless figure of his messmate would fare against the confident, energetic young mid. True, Thomas was older, probably a year or two, and true he was bigger, quite a bit bigger. But these advantages were nothing. He was beaten before he began, physically and in his heart. He would lie down and take anything that was dealt out. The fearful thing was, to Jesse's mind, that the boy Bentley would have no mercy. He would deal it out until Fox could take no more, until his humiliation was assuaged. His humiliation was as big as his pride and spirit: enormous.

When the mates were out of earshot, Peter hissed excitedly: 'My, Tommy, this is a fine thing. We will make mincemeat of him. How I wish that I—'

Grandfather Fulman growled 'Hold your tongue, Peter!' with such venom that Peter was crushed.

Before the milling could take place, however, the unpredictable weather of the equatorial zones stepped in with a vengeance. Throughout the late morning and early afternoon the sky had been changing almost imperceptibly. But when the squall arrived it took everyone by surprise.

William Bentley, below in the midshipmen's berth, was still shaking with a mixture of anger and excitement when the call for all hands came. He had refused to be drawn on the subject by Simon Allen, who had been writing in his personal log and missed the whole affair, but in his head he was already planning just how and what he would do to the insolent shepherd boy. He seethed with resentment, not least at what the captain might say about his handling of the matter. Uncle Daniel had, after all, been pretty set on his little dancing band.

Almost as soon as 'All hands' was piped and called, he felt the Welfare give a strange shiver. Every timber began to tremble. The quiet creaking that never ceased, even when she was in a flat calm, turned immediately into a loud grumble. The two boys, halfway to the after hatchway, looked at each other in surprise. Then, stranger still, the light pouring in from above dimmed as rapidly as if someone had turned a lamp down. There was a roar, a very violent shaking, then the ship heeled suddenly over, farther and farther. Bentley and Allen both lost their footing. They went skeetering across the deck, from high to low. Stools, partitions, food pannikins and men went with them. William thought for one amazed moment that he would be thrown headlong through an open port, but at the last moment he seized a gun tackle. There was a great shouting and roaring from the men who had tumbled down with them.

As he clawed his way up the canted deck towards the hatch, the noise from above became enormous. The air was filled with darkness, shouts, the rushing of wind. Amid it all he could hear noises like gunfire, which he guessed must be sails carrying away.

On deck the chaos was complete. Jesse Broad and all the topmen had been sent aloft at the first sign. The wind rushing towards them had at first only darkened the glassy surface of the sea, pushing a small steep ledge of white water before it. Iron-red cloud had appeared out of the dull glaring sky, a hard edge of spite. The cloud had climbed with amazing speed, bringing darkness and violence. Mr Robinson had appeared by the wheel as if by magic, sensing from within his cabin and his afternoon nap that something dire was about to happen. The helm was put hard down, hands were sent scurrying for brails, clew garnets, tacks and sheets in an instant. But the Welfare, a hive of activity, her rigging suddenly filled with panting men, sat sedate and unmoving in a stillness as yet un-touched by the wall of howling air that was bearing down on her.

When the squall reached her Jesse Broad was on the main topgallant yard, moving out along the footropes to the yardarm. The sail beneath him was already partly clewed up, but when the wind caught its sagging belly it carried away almost instantaneously. The greyish canvas flattened itself out in front of the yard like a rigid table, there was a thunderous series of reports as it whipped in its agony, then it blew clean out of its boltropes. Broad, pressed against the yard as if by a great thrusting hand, glimpsed the tattered remains of it whip away forward.

Around and below him other men fought their own desperate battles. But the Welfare had been taken all standing, and many of her people were half drunk. She lay farther and farther over under the press of wind. Some sails were saved but more blew out to leeward. When she slowly righted herself and began to answer her helm, lightened by the canvas furled or torn to pieces, she had lost many of the trappings of the hot still weather she had suffered under. The captain's awning that shaded part of the quarterdeck was gone, the lines of washing rigged by the foremast had flown merrily off, flapping their arms and legs, and even the galley chimney had come adrift and taken the plunge overside. Two men, too, one from the mizzenmast and one from the main. Jesse had watched one of them hurled from a bucking yard. His mouth had been open, but no cry could be heard. He had not known him by name.

Within an hour, the sky was black as pitch, relieved only by flickering jags of lightning. The violent wind drove torrents of rain before it, the strange motion of the ship – she was roaring through a practically flat sea at a great rate under bare poles – becoming less strange as the squall made waves, then coamers, and finally a high, pounding sea. Broad and the other seamen, driven by a ferocious boatswain and his mates, got up heavy weather gear, bent new canvas ready to set, overhauled and renewed damaged running rigging, set up stretched and sagging stays.

In the early evening the squall left them. William Bentley, muffled in a cloak and sick as a dog once more, surveyed the chaos from the quarterdeck, which was pitching on the short, jumbled sea. But his uncle put all the midshipmen under the charge of the master then, and for hours they worked away with teams of seamen clearing, running up new gear, organising the chain and hand pumps to clear the water taken through ports, hatchways and strained seams. By midnight they were in a great and steady wind, roaring them southwestward at a rate of knots under topsails and forecourse. Deck sports and milling were forgotten.

The change in the weather brought relief to the bored, sickened crew. The change from stifling heat below decks to bracing draughts, the change from dry, cracking skin to damp freshness, was more than welcome. The bugs, as if by a miracle, lost their taste for human flesh. The cockroaches, while vile as ever in themselves, were less in evidence, presumably preferring dark and warmth in nooks and crannies to the open decks. There was sickness, of course, but on nothing like the earlier scale. Most men could handle anything now; once they had overcome the taste of rotting food their stomachs had rapidly turned to cast iron. And there was work. Good, hard, regular work which the seamen knew and responded to. The loss of gear may have been an unlooked-for disaster to Mr Robinson, but the men did not mind a jot. Every day they had little to think about but preparing and repairing. New sails were made, ropes were spliced, wormed and parcelled, sprung spars were fished or replaced. It was a hard, satisfying time that made the food taste bearable and the grog like absolute heaven.

Strange then, Jesse Broad considered, that it was at this time that the breath of mutiny that stalked the Welfare like a spectre should have found a voice.

Even odder, and it shook him to the core, was mutiny's mouthpiece. It was not Henry Joyce or any of his tearaway companions, although they remained a brooding presence in the ship, a mute threat. It was not any of the more reasonable men who had been brutally flogged and humiliated in the punishments that had gone monotonously on, week after week. It was not any of the hysterical, almost insane element of which the ship had not a few. It was his former messmate, Matthews.

He had buttonholed Broad on the lower deck and asked if they might speak together in private. This in itself was odd, especially in the cramped and noisy accommodation area. There was some privacy in a crowd, certainly; at least one could be seen talking without it arousing suspicion. But Matthews wanted a different sort of privacy. Broad hesitated. He was on watch and had been sent below to restow some cordage. But the chances of his being missed for a while were not high, he decided. In any case, Matthews had an air of urgency, of tension, which was most unlooked for in the man. Broad nodded. Matthews gave a tight, strained smile and led him forward. They went down a ladder into a pitch-black place that had obviously been noted beforehand. It stank vilely, the bilge water slopping audibly beneath them.

For a few moments Jesse Broad listened to the groaning timbers and the mysterious gurglings. He tried to accustom himself to the darkness, but the darkness was impenetrable. A dim light filtered down through the hatch opening some yards away, but where they sat he could not even see Matthews's outline. He pictured the man's face, usually so grim and secret. Had he been wrong? Or had Matthews been strained, jumpy?

When Matthews spoke it was in a whisper. The note of strain was definite. The words came as a violent shock.

'I can trust you, Jesse Broad. We are ready to bring down the captain.'

Broad heard his own breath quicken. In the stinking blackness the two men sat and panted. He was filled with excitement and terror. Also surprise. Was this Matthews talking? Matthews?

'You are mad, Mr Matthews. This is most unlooked for. You are surely mad.'

A pause. Two panting men.

'Not mad, Jesse, but merely sickened. We have had enough. The captain is inhuman. A tyrant. A villain. If any man is mad on board this ship it is Daniel Swift, not I. It is Daniel Swift.'

Each time one or the other of them stopped speaking there was a long pause. The whispered words faded away into the darkness, as if slowly sinking into the bilge. Broad was getting his breathing back to normal. He agreed with his friend, totally. But even alone as they were – and it was death for certain if somewhere in the hold someone sat and listened – he dared not say so.

Instead he said: 'We? You say "we". Who is this "we"? And who is sickened? It would appear to me, in fact, that since we got this wind the people are more content than for many weeks. Now that the dreadful sun and the fluky calms have been blown away.'

Matthews blew through his nose, a whispered laugh.

'That is true in part. But only in part. Are *you* fooled, Broad? Did *your* heart leap in gratitude when the villain offered us sports and dancing? Did you not take it as a mere ploy, another way of keeping us too busy to be hatching trouble?'

'I did. Of course. And no, I was not fooled. But good God man, most men were, and you cannot deny it! They fell into his hand like rotting medlars. And then the weather. A clincher, a clincher!'

In the silence that followed he detected a change in Matthews's breathing. The pant was faster, harder, his breath being forced through tense nostrils brokenly. There was a sound that could only be grinding teeth. Suddenly Matthews spoke. His voice came loud, harsh and strangled.

'Like rotting medlars! Aye! They fell!'

Jesse felt panic rising in him.

'Hush man! Hush for Christ's sake! You'll have us hanged!'

Matthews did hush. Something like a sob came from his throat. Then he hushed. Jesse had a vision, a flash of insight. He saw the shape of a seaman, in neckerchief and baggy trousers, flying through the air, screaming mutely. They fell.

181

He said gently, circumspectly: 'You lost a messmate.'

Matthews gave a long, shuddering sigh.

'It is no matter,' he said. 'It is not the reason.' He repeated the whispered laugh. 'But it is true; you are astute. My friend was lost.'

Broad sat silent, considering. Good God, one could not blame the *squall* on Captain Swift. To lose a friend was hard, but then . . . He thought briefly of Hardman, his dear friend Hardman. Then of Mary and his home. A deep sadness sank slowly into him. He shuddered.

'I am sorry,' he said.

'Thank you,' Matthews replied.

'But no matter,' he went on. 'Listen, Jesse Broad, you are astute. I am *not* myself. I was smashed by that loss, I will own it. But it was not the only reason. And you are not entirely right about the rest of the people neither. There are many more than you ever dream who will rise up at the word. I promise you.'

'The scum?' asked Broad brutally. 'Henry bloody Joyce and his henchmen? I would rather stay penned with a beast like Daniel Swift than a beast like Henry Joyce. At least his tyranny is certain, not an untouched powder keg.'

Another sigh.

'You are too astute. Yes, many of this crew are scum. To rise up would perhaps be to unleash a monster. But Jesse, believe me, there are others. Good men, true men. Men who have been whipped, men who have been scorned. Good God alive, what of yourself? That scummy boy who spat in your face! Other men will not stand such humiliation with equal fortitude. Did you not want to rise and smite him? Did you not want to break his back across your knee?'

'All right. So if I did,' replied Jesse. 'But Matthews, what are you saying? That boy Bentley has a right, if he so desires, to play the beast. There is no one to stop him, no law to touch him. But if we rise up we die. If we overcome the captain, if we overcome the officers, if we overcome the hell-rotten marines who would shoot us like dogs, still we die. The Navy does not forget. The Navy does not forgive. They would track us down across the oceans. They would follow us to heaven or hell.'

Somehow the tension had eased between them. They breathed gently. The silence was long and thoughtful. Matthews's answer, when it came, was a roundabout one.

182

'Jesse Broad,' he said. 'I am a navigator. I was an officer, as you know, and I have much skill and experience. We are heading for Cape Horn, there is no doubt of that. And by the time we reach it, the season will be far, far advanced. It is, indeed, much later than wisdom dictates to attempt to double the Cape. Swift was presumably held up, whether by lack of crew or lack of Admiralty orders, God only knows. And then the doldrums. We flogged about the Line for longer than has ever been my experience. It will be very late when we reach Cape Horn.'

'And?'

'And, friend Jesse? And this. When we double the Horn – *if* we double the Horn – no one will be able to follow. For months. In the winter season there, the wind blows westerly and it blows like the cannons of hell. Once we are round the Horn no ship will be able to follow. For months. Months.'

Jesse Broad considered. He believed Matthews. Despite the unaccustomed wildness, almost hysteria, that the loss of his friend had wrought in him, he knew that he would not be wrong in such details. For a moment he was tempted. To crush that terrible man. To save the poor boy Thomas from that childish ogre. To avenge himself for the spittle that had revolted his lips and seared his mind. But it was only a moment.

'Mr Matthews,' he said gently. 'I said you were mad, for which I am sorry. But it *is* madness, and you must know it. Both you and I have a legitimate sorrow for being on this ghastly ship. You more than myself. However, there is no redress. Our country is at war, the law is the law, the custom is the custom. If we mutiny we are traitors – no more of that. More pertinent still, if we mutiny we die. Horn or no Horn, winter or no winter, we will be sought out. Is it not so?'

'Do you not believe me? About the Horn at winter?'

'Indeed I do.'

Matthews let out his breath slowly.

'Ah well. Maybe you are right. But I am not convinced mind. We would have many months; and the whole of the Pacific Ocean to choose from.'

His voice was calmer. After a few seconds he added: 'In any case, your guess as to the men who would carry the business is a shrewd one. Many there are who would join the act, and with a vengeance.

183

But many more would not. I suppose in terms of all the ship's people, officers, marines and all, it is only a handful. Perhaps I should thank you, man.'

His voice was old, tired. Jesse hauled himself up, until his skull was brought to by the low sliminess of the deckhead.

'Thank me?' he mused. 'I do not know, Mr Matthews. I do not know.

'Certain it is, though,' he added, 'that if this company ever does rise, it will be a bloody business. Not least of which will be keeping the beast in check.'

'Then God help us all,' said Matthews dully. 'God help us all.'

Twenty-Two

They roared on under reduced canvas for nearly three days. But before a new boredom could set in, the boredom of wet, cold, and hard work in heavy weather, the wind began to moderate. Over a ten-hour period the reefs were shaken out, then more sail was set, progressively, until Welfare flogged along under the glory of a full suit. The bows bit deep into the still heavy seas, white water was everywhere. For hours more she flew, with a great musical roaring from aloft. Until at last she settled down to a good but more sedate pace and the sea gradually lost its wildness. The sun appeared, but tempered by the breeze. They were solidly in the south-east Trade.

Hatches were thrown open, portlids were triced up, washed clothes and hammocks flapped gaily from newly rigged lines. Captain Swift, seizing the moment, had it announced that the sports would now commence.

In his cabin, he spoke to William Bentley about the milling match that was to come. He looked at his nephew keenly, but made no open criticism.

'Why did he break the whistle, my boy?' he asked. 'It seems a senseless act, and one that could only have brought him to some punishment.'

William laughed.

'I think, uncle, that he has some sense of grievance. It is a strange youth. Perhaps he still thinks he should not be on board here, and that I am to blame for that.'

'Still though,' said Swift. 'He is quite a sturdy lad. He is older than you I think.'

William blushed. He found this rather distasteful. Was his uncle suggesting he might not be able to handle such a booby?

'Well sir,' he said stiffly. 'That is true, I imagine. Older and certainly bigger. But . . . well sir, I hope you do not think I cannot

185

give good account of myself? He is a country boy, a boy of the people. I am confident—'

Swift laughed now. He lifted his head, the shark's-fin nose cutting the air. When he looked at William again his eyes were twinkling.

'You are high-spirited, my boy, and I like it. I have every confidence in you, never fear. It is only . . .'

William kept a respectful silence.

'It is only . . . Well, as a form of punishment it is unusual, to say the least. The boy deserves a flogging for such a piece of infernal insolence. I had set my heart on a dancing band. Make a change from that damned lugubrious Irishman and his hateful sockets staring at you, eh?'

William thought of Doyle's face. It was indeed horrible. But to his mind, Fox's was not much better. The weird musicians . . . He felt hatred for the shepherd boy. He wanted to smash that face.

'I suppose, sir,' he said, half seriously, 'you could flog him as well if you feel so strongly. But I beg you – let me have my way with him first of all.'

Later on, in the berth, the other midshipmen took up the subject. They were all excited by the prospect, although James Finch, who was inexperienced in the ways of the lower orders, was a little fearful of Fox's size, weight and origins.

'Well, William,' he said, a shade breathlessly, 'I must say it is rather you than me.'

'Ah,' shrilled Evans, 'but that is because you are but a little worm, Jimmy!'

Finch shook his head vigorously.

'No no, not at all, Jack,' he said. 'I mean, yes, of course I am. But then, even compared with Will here the lout is quite a good size.'

'Shambling monkey,' growled Simon Allen.

'No,' insisted little James, 'but he is a country lad too. Skinny maybe, but bred to handling and working and lifting heavy bales and all. Some of the countrymen I have known have been alarming strong. You would scarce believe it!'

'You are insulting,' said William. He spoke in a jocular manner, but he did in fact feel it to be true. Sometimes James Finch was a pest. Children ought not to be allowed to sea. The boy flushed and stammered.

'I beg pardon, Will, indeed I do. I do not mean to imply . . . But you see – on my father's farms . . . Well, it is only–'

'You are insulting, Jimmy Finch,' William went on, 'because you overlook this: I am fourteen, which may not be a great age, but I have been at sea for long enough. I too work, I too have not been pampered. Are you suggesting that the boys of the lower deck are more manly than we? Can you seriously mean that? Good Lord, child, if you do not feel the equal of any one of them, and not the boys, mark, but the men too; if you do not recognise the superiority conferred on us by nature, then God help you.'

'Amen to that,' said Simon. 'Why hell, James–'

'Yes hell,' said William, not to be interrupted. 'If anything, James, if you are intent upon insulting me, you might take the view which I am sure the people have hit upon. And that is this: They will say, I am sure, that the fight is unfair because of the very superiority I enjoy.'

James Finch looked ashamed and confused. Jack Evans tried to explain the point for his benefit.

'They'll think it not quite manly in Will, you see, James,' he said. 'The country boy is but a country boy; but William is a young gentleman. They will think it a trifle unfair.'

'And you see,' said William triumphantly, 'that's the point exactly. This youth *is* bigger than I. He is a great shambling lout as Simon says. Good God James, you do not think I would fight a poltroon smaller than myself, or even of my own size? This country lump is bigger and older. And so our superiority may be shown. It is necessary that we are respected and obeyed.'

The smallest mid nodded eagerly. His mouth opened and shut, as if he wanted to ask more. The others laughed at him. William leaned over to ruffle his hair.

'I see you still do not understand, Jimmy,' he said. 'But you will, I promise you. This loutish boy is big and strong. That is why a beating from me is necessary. Is that clearer?'

James nodded vigorously, but they could all see he had not followed a word, and they roared with laughter when he answered: 'Oh yes, Will, of course. Thank you for explaining.'

They laughed even louder when he followed this up, a few seconds later, with a diffident question.

'You say then, Will, that I was right? He is a country man, like on father's farms, and may in fact trounce you?'

187

'Aye, aye,' spluttered William, when they had recovered their breath. 'You have it exactly now, James. He may indeed trounce me. He may indeed.'

Among the people, the sports were greeted with varying degrees of interest and enthusiasm. Mostly they were seen as a welcome diversion, with the chance of some extra rum to be won, for it was assumed that the prizes would take the form of extra spirits; what else could they be? Each mess chose their 'champion' from the fittest, the strongest, the lithest, depending on the events they fancied entering for, and offered innumerable words of advice, encouragement and accumulated wisdom. Remarkable how many of the old shellbacks had been noted fighters, or runners, or leapers in their day; and what a pity they were now too old to do anything but talk about it and criticise the youngsters who could not have held a candle to them in their heyday!

The hot, breezy afternoon was alive with cheering, excitement, music and drinking. Captain Swift, who knew how to do things properly, had had a new awning rigged, and under it were placed a large cask of sweet white wine and a smaller puncheon of black rum. The victor of each event was invited on to the quarterdeck to take his pannikin of spirit – unwatered and damn near explosive – and every so often a defeated man or team, depending on luck and the captain's whim, would be given wine as consolation. Very few men or boys who did not drink deep of the cup at some time or other.

The first events were running races, just to get the people warmed up and cheering. Teams of brawny men and slight boys, stripped to the waist and sweating, set off from the mainmast in relays, tagging others at the fore, the extreme bow, the fore again, the main again, and the mizzenmast, which was the finishing point. These were followed by leaping relays, in which all the upper deck twelve-pounders had to be vaulted or jumped over; a dangerous enough sport in which several heads were badly banged and one or two teeth knocked out. The spectators perched mostly in the lower rigging, cheering themselves hoarse and enjoying the best of the breeze.

Little Peter was the only one in Grandfather Fulman's mess who had any enthusiasm for the games, but his was such that it made up for the others' lack of it. He shrieked encouragement or abuse until

188

he was black in the face, and jumped up and down so much that he was in danger of wasting all his energy before the rigging races, for which he had put down his mark. The messmates were all together, on the shaded side of the foredeck, and no one resented his excitement. He, for his part, occasionally tried to temper his maniac whoops of delight when he spotted Broad's sombre looks or the hunched and silent form of Thomas Fox. When it came his turn to race he lived up to his own expectations and more. He beat the fastest topman on board to the main truck, and came down a backstay so fast it looked as though he must hurtle straight through the deck, if not the bottom of the ship. But Peter bounced to his feet, carried back a pannikin of rum in triumph, then joined in and won the stem-to-stern race. Within the space of twenty-five minutes he had amassed nearly a quart of rum – riches beyond his wildest dreams.

As the races drew towards their end Jesse Broad and the other older hands in the mess grew more gloomy. Fox was unapproachable on the subject, showed no sign of being aware of his impending match, but the weight of foreboding was heavy on the rest of them. Before it could come about, though, Captain Swift ordered Padraig Doyle to provide music for the dance.

The blind man was led to the capstan – not by Thomas Fox – and helped to his official position on the drumhead. He seemed thinner and more bowed than ever. Obviously, thought Broad, in no mood to play at all, and perhaps the captain knew it too. All part of the jollifications to him, no doubt. It would not have surprised Jesse if Thomas had been called upon to give a solo dance, to make up for having broken his instrument.

In the mood or not, Doyle soon coaxed tunes lively and gay from his bagpipes. The tipsy company fell to the dancing with a great will and not a little dexterity. As well as solo dances there were formations made and country dances galore. Even those like red-haired Peter, who in his life ashore had never had the chance to learn the simplest step, having had no home to speak of, footed it gaily on the edges of the throng. Under the captain's awning aft the officers stood at a respectful distance from their lord, smiling indulgently as he smiled. William Bentley stood there too, but the gaily swirling people, ridiculous to his eyes in their rolled trousers and dirty, sweaty torsos, did not engage his attention much. He was excited, tense. The time for milling was drawing near.

189

Captain Swift, that manipulator of his men, chose every moment with great care. For this reason he had overruled William's decision that he and Thomas Fox should fight first. He had also somewhat amended the programme to provide a kind of build-up to the main event. Instead of many free-form punching matches, followed by several fights over the chest, he had laid down that the programme should go thus: Half a dozen single-sticks combats, half a dozen wrestling bouts, a mêlée fight, then the contest between William Bentley and the shepherd boy. His justification (not that he need ever voice one, but he knew that an announcement from the quarterdeck would enhance the excitement on this occasion) was that the midshipman was the only gentleman taking part in the sports. It was unusual, to say the least, so should end the day's amusement. A great cheer of approval showed him to have been right.

As only twelve men could fight at single-sticks, in a knock-out to choose a champion, the crew lounged on the deck or hung in the rigging and got down to the serious business of festive drinking. As match followed match the excitement grew. The final bout was one of skill and duration, the participants ducking and striking with almost unbelievable dexterity. Rumour had it that the man who finally won had been a fencing master in happier times ashore, and his handling of the stave was certainly a joy to watch. One spectator, full of wine and hopes that the money he had put on his choice would make him a wealthy man, fell twenty feet from the ratlines onto the deck shrieking 'Foul stroke' when his man got a hard blow to the temple – and scuttled up the rigging again as if nothing had happened.

There were a surprising number of wrestlers in the company, as it turned out. Some of the Welfare's impress men had come from far far inland and the North. One bout between two former Cumbrian farmhands, one reputedly a convicted murderer, amazed the generality. They wrestled in the style called Cumberland and Westmorland, hugging each other like desperate lovers and grunting and hopping about the deck. The winner of the bout was matched with a giant of a man who had never wrestled in his life to any rules, but whose great bulk and quickness made him a formidable opponent. It quickly turned into a comedy turn, with the Cumbrian seeking to smother the flailing arms of the other, who in his turn appeared to be attempting to pull off any limb he could get a grip on. In the end it was called off amid gales of laughter and both received an equal share of the spirit prize.

The mêlée bout was a far less friendly affair, as Swift had clearly intended. Henry Joyce, who had entered for nothing else, but had nevertheless been fed his fair share of alcohol, was led into the corner of a ring that had been rigged in the waist, between the main and fore masts. He reminded Jesse Broad of nothing so much as a bull being led by his keeper. The lowered shoulders, the red, dangerous eyes, the shambling walk. It would not have been out of place had he been fitted with a nose-ring and lanyard. He shook his head in wonder and said to Fulman: 'There is madness in this, Grandfather. There stands the heart of violence, and the terriers will rush to bait it.'

In fact he was not entirely right. At first there were not many in the entire ship's company ready to enter the ring with Joyce. Big men she had in abundance; violent men she had by the score; brave men too, there was no shortage of courage in the Welfare's crew. But Swift had to up the ante to half a pint of rum per man just to go in the ring, win or lose, before he got any takers.

At last there were six. They ranged themselves around three sides of the rope square with Joyce in the fourth corner. The thought came to Broad once more. It was bull-baiting to the life. Despite himself he felt a tug of excitement.

The first move was made by a shock-haired wildman from Wales. He was short, but powerful and fast. He suddenly dashed across the ring and gave Joyce a great clout on the side of the head with his fist, dancing away before the bull had chance to raise a hand. Henry Joyce shook his head as if to shake off a fly. Before he had finished shaking it the small man darted in once more. Another blow landed.

At this, two of the others rushed in. Blows rained down on Joyce's head. He never had time to respond or even react. Each time he raised his great head the biting flies were away. He swung his arms about for a moment or two, but there was no one there. When he stopped four rushed in, punching wildly.

All around the ring the press of seamen went wild, hollering with excitement and swigging at their drink. The lower rigging was black with men. Joyce glowered around him. A cut had been opened on his face but otherwise he seemed untouched. But Broad, quite close, could hear a vague rumbling noise coming from the man. He was getting impatient.

The six men in the ring with him were enjoying themselves immensely now. There was an air of elation. They darted in in relays, prodding and smacking, with fist or open palm. Joyce's pale and dirty face, bald-fronted and hairy, was reddening under the onslaught. The people were half-jeering at him. Was this the mighty Joyce?

It was the bulky Welshman who had started it who was caught first. As he bounced in with a smile, Joyce's hand shot out like a striking snake. The man, who must have weighed twelve stone, rose from the deck two feet, his face a picture of shock. The blow had caught him in the throat, and as he fell he gave a rasping squawk, then lay in a heap, writhing. The others, made wary, were too late. Joyce leapt forward and grabbed two by their necks. The crunch as their heads came together was alarming. He chased the other three round the ring to the howls of the people; now this was *real* sport! Two of them got out, despite all the efforts of the ringsiders to prevent it, but the last was fairly trapped. Luckily for him Joyce was apparently not much interested in the whole affair, coming as it had as an unwelcome interruption to his drinking. He snuffed out the fellow's consciousness with a chop behind the ear, stepped over the rope, and pushed his way aft to collect his can of rum. He was not even panting.

While bumpers were filled and emptied, while wagers were paid or collected, the boatswain's mates supervised the carrying up of a sea chest and the carrying below of the four victims of Henry Joyce. The festive air had reached its peak when William Bentley, resplendent in silk shirt and blue breeches, stepped into the ring. Thomas Fox came at a shamble, led by Jesse Broad. He had spent the last half-hour below, communing with Doyle and the beasts, and he made a pitiful sight. He was wearing a torn and dirty blouse with old duck trousers. His face was filthy, with the clear evidence of tears on each cheek. With his head bowed and his rounded shoulders he was not much taller than Bentley. An odd mood fell on the ship's people. The excitement, the elation, the bloodlust aroused by the last event, became modified. The arrogant smile of the young gentleman somehow incensed them. There was a wave of pity and anger, almost palpable. For Broad's part, he would gladly have killed the blond, dandified midshipman, child though he was.

A passage was cleared from the rope ring to the quarterdeck, so that the officers might see the sport uninterrupted. Captain Swift made the announcement, with characteristic grandeur.

'My brave lads,' he said. 'Here is the event you have been waiting for. Here is the match of the afternoon. In all my years at sea I have seen no such thing. And I dare not reveal how long that is, eh?'

He paused for the laughter, but there was none. Allgood, the boatswain, looked particularly sour. Daniel Swift smiled full at Bentley. A smile which seemed to say: It is you against the people, my boy.

'Well lads,' he continued. 'Here it is. This young gentleman – and the tender of beasts. They will sit astride that sea chest and slug it out in the good old way. I will say no more but this: May the best man win. Now: Set to!'

As William Bentley sat astride the box, pity stirred in him for the first time. The shepherd boy was so hopeless, such a booby, that perhaps it was, after all, not quite manly in him to teach him such a strong lesson. The boy looked incapable of raising his head, let alone his fists. If he did not respond, it would be a hard thing to make a match. How could you strike a man who would not strike back?

At first, that is what happened. Thomas Fox was sat astride, with whispered words of encouragement. In fact, what Jesse Broad had told him was to fall. Put up a pretence for a few minutes, then fall. There would be no shame in it, said Broad, nor would the men think badly of him. He had done nothing to deserve this, and need fear no retribution. He was being used as a dupe, a sop to the other boy's vanity. Let him think he was the victor; let him think he was a fine young blade. But do not let him hurt you, Thomas, for he is not worth it, truly.

So in pity and confusion the fight began. Thomas at last managed to put up his fists to shield his face, so William, with some misgiving, let fly an almost gentle blow. It caught Thomas's hand, which in turn caught his eye. It hurt and the tears sprang to his eyes once more. He thought of God, and his mother, and the quiet farm on Portsea Island. He thought of Padraig Doyle, below among the warm and reeking sheep.

William Bentley jabbed again, in the silence that surrounded him from the men. He felt uncomfortable, bad. The shepherd lad was not responding. But good God! He deserved this match! He had broken the whistle. He had disobeyed an order. This was madness, this was softness. The whole damned people would be in a rabble if such filthy laxness were not punished!

In a fervour of disgust, mostly at himself although he did not know it, Bentley lashed out with his hard right fist. It was him against the people!

Again the blow hit Thomas Fox's hand, again the hand went back into his eye. There was a sharp edge of pain as his nail scratched his eyeball, and he grunted. The captain's voice, echoed as if on a cue by the officers', gave a ragged cheer. From the people followed a lower noise, a noise remarkably like a boo.

William got angry. How dare they? How dare they insult him so? He snarled and lashed out harder. The head in front of him jerked back, then forward again. He threw another punch, drove it home hard, as hard as he could. Another rumble went through the crowd of men, a low, unhappy noise.

Somewhere deep inside Thomas Fox's misery, somewhere in the cave he had built himself to hide in in the last few weeks, a flame flickered and stirred. Another blow banged into his arm, then one broke through and squashed his lip against his teeth. For the first time he lifted his eyes from the knotty surface of the sea chest lid. He saw first another fist race towards him, bang into his face. When he opened his eyes again he looked at William Bentley.

Apart from the glaring, scarry sockets of Padraig Doyle's ruined face, the midshipman's were the first eyes he had looked into for a long time. He saw anger in them and his own eyes slid away. He saw hatred in them and again he averted his gaze. He saw triumph in them, as once again the fist broke through his upraised arm and crushed his lips against his teeth. Thomas Fox spat blood and the flame in his stomach flared so suddenly that he lurched with shock. He threw his head back and he raised his fist. All at once the face before him grew blurred. But in it shone the eyes. And in them there was something new. It was fear.

As Thomas Fox's first blow struck home a roar like thunder rose from all around him. The midshipman rocked back on his buttocks and almost fell. As he rocked forward again Thomas Fox drove two

194

fists into his face one after the other. The fire in his stomach was almost licking off his knuckles. Suddenly the face in front of him cleared in his sight. Fear was blazing in the eyes now, fear and pain. Bentley raised his arms in front of him and waved them like a kitten. Once more Thomas lashed out, first right fist, then left. He felt like screaming, so great was the release. He felt he would smash and smash until the face before him was gone; until the head before him was like a bloody pulp. The tension flowed through his arms, through his fists, in a cataract. The crushing band of iron round his heart melted as he came out of his cave. As William Bentley rocked towards him he screeched, a high, terrifying sound. And aimed another blow like a hammer at the bleeding head.

Jesse Broad watched in fascination. All around him the seamen had gone mad with delight. They were roaring like bulls, stamping their feet and punching each other's backs and shoulders. The midshipman, small and crushed now, dwarfed by the black-haired fury who seemed to tower over him, looked terrible. His silk shirt was drenched with blood, his fine breeches torn from dragging across the edges of the chest. He kept shaking his head, trying to get control so that he could at least defend himself. Wonder was, thought Broad, that he had kept his seat so long. The face of Thomas shocked him. It was bruised and smeared with blood, but transformed. His eyes were rolling, the features tense, the lips drawn back from the teeth. Broad could not be glad, could not be sorry. Was this better than the expected beating, or worse? He was revolted by the cheering animals beside him, revolted by the bloody children on the box. Revolted by the captain and his henchmen, silent and discomfited on the quarterdeck.

Mr Allgood put an end to it, but not in any simple, straight-forward way; as was his wont. He seized a bucket of salt water and held it questioningly above his head, looking at the captain. Swift nodded, and Allgood walked forward to the sea chest, stepping nimbly over the ropes. The roaring died down. The two boys lowered their arms as the massive shape pressed between them. William Bentley was panting, half bemused. Thomas Fox was still transformed, trembling with undischarged energy. He emitted strangled noises, animal-like grunts, and his fists clenched and unclenched themselves. He did not take his eyes off William; seemed, indeed, ready to leap on him and tear him to pieces. A

195

growl of resentment rose from the crowd. Why had Allgood stuck his oar in?

The boatswain put the bucket down beside the boys. He stared round the spectators, alow and in the rigging.

'With the owner's permission, you scum,' he said. 'The lads will have a breather and refresh before they continue.'

Now a mighty roar went up. My God, thought Jesse Broad, this man is dreadful. He'll have the midshipman made capable and the match prolonged. Ah Christ, poor child; but it is his own fault, it is his own fault.

William Bentley, washed, wetted and cooled, eased his aching thighs over the hard box and faced the shepherd boy. His face was smarting, his eyes bruised balls of agony. No hatred now, no contempt, no feeling at all. Just the hope that he would not fall too soon, and the determination to fight his best.

But the fight was over. Thomas Fox, washed, wetted and cooled, looked at the battered face of the midshipman and knew he could not hit it again. When the voice of the boatswain cried 'Commence' he did not even raise a hand. He sat there, breathing slower now, looking at the battered face of the small blond boy.

The people roared and hooted, hooted and roared. When the noise had died away William said, almost plaintively: 'You must fight, Thomas Fox. You must hit me, you know.'

'No,' said Thomas. 'Your poor face, sir. I have hurt you, child, and I am very sorry.'

A silence fell over the ship's company that was appalling. Not a man stirred, hardly a breath was drawn. William Bentley's face, already pale, drained slowly of blood until it was glaring white. His mouth opened, his eyes glittered with rage.

But before he could speak, the spell was broken. A gale, a hurricane, of laughter and contempt exploded from the men. They shrieked themselves hoarse, they screamed and dropped to the deck. Even when he had stumbled below, even when he had buried himself in his blankets in the midshipmen's berth, William Bentley could still hear it. The very timbers of the Welfare were alive with laughter. He buried his face and bit his lips and cursed and swore and raged. And wept. William Bentley wept.

196

Twenty-Three

In the following days the shocking result of the milling match had a profound effect on the Welfare, especially on the lower deck. When William Bentley had disappeared below and the boatswain's mates and ship's corporals had tried to break up the party, something dangerously like chaos ensued. Captain Swift had watched from the quarterdeck after giving Mr Allgood and the master-at-arms the signal. His face was impassive and his eyes like knives. The men ran about in glee, laughing and shrieking. Spirits and wine passed from hand to hand, whole pannikins being tossed through the air and caught when a corporal or mate tried to grab them from a seaman. Very soon the deck was alive with swishing rope's-ends, then knots of fighting men, then a general rough-house. Two boatswain's mates were badly beaten, a corporal was chased into the rigging, and Mr Allgood broke both a sailor's arms. The mob came under control only after the marines fired a volley into the air from the quarterdeck. In the sudden silence Swift told the men in a low, vibrating voice that the next shots would be into them unless the deck was cleared in five seconds.

The next day, as the ship drove towards the south at her best speed, beautiful in the warm sun and sparkling sea, man after man was flogged at the gangway. The punishment seemed never-ending, with Swift, an implacable and avenging fury, standing so close to the grating that he gradually became masked in a fine mist of blood. When he wiped his face with his grand and expensive coat sleeve the effect was awe-inspiring. His pale eyes were white and glaring, in a hideous smear of brown and scarlet. Jesse Broad and Thomas Fox stood side by side among the crew as the miscreants were triced up, flogged, cut down. They had fled below immediately after the milling, with Broad half dragging, half carrying the boy. He had guessed what might happen on deck and was damned sure that they would not be part of it. Little Peter, with no more sense than ever,

197

had stayed on deck, had led, in part, the jeers and shrieks and laughter. They watched in silence as he received his four dozen with the rest of them.

William Bentley stood not far from Swift and watched the scene in horror and anguish. But all his feelings were directed inwards. He felt naked before the ship's company, felt as though every man-jack was laughing at him, scorning him, the humiliated snotty boy. He *felt* like a snotty boy; felt that even little Jimmy Finch must despise him. The hatred and misery inside him churned and rumbled; he caught himself grinding his teeth. It was the only movement in an otherwise rigidly unmoving face and he checked it when he noticed it. But his face itself was sign enough, advertisement and plenty to his humiliation. His mouth was cut and puffy, his eyes blackened, one nostril split. He watched the men being flogged and knew, knew as a certainty, that Daniel Swift would dearly have loved to have had him triced to that grating; aye, and wielded the bloody cat himself into the bargain.

When it was all over, in the days and nights that followed, the subject of the match was the favourite one. The match, the punishments, the way the owner had turned back to iron cruelty to crush the memory and the elation. But all talk was difficult and dangerous now. The corporals were everywhere, stalking silently about, their ears flapping as they tried to catch a whiff of rebellion. The boatswain's mates, too, perhaps even more dangerous with their bare feet and seamanlike skill at finding out the dark and silent places where men occasionally crept to be alone. The daily punishment became an article of faith; the slightest infringement, real or suspected, was jumped on. Men hardly dared look at an officer or midshipman for fear the look was interpreted as insolence. And Daniel Swift's officers, true to form, followed the lead of their superior. The shifty, rangy Hagan, who could look at you through the back of his head; the tub-shaped Plumduff; the slow and malevolent Higgins. All took a delight in following their master's lead. Cane, rope's-end, fist and cat were exercised with something like glee as the Welfare drove south-westward, sun-drenched and beautiful.

At first, below decks, men had been inclined to seek out Thomas Fox to tell him what a fine fellow he was. But it became obvious that to talk to him was regarded with great suspicion by the upholders of the ship's discipline. This fitted Thomas's needs well. In the hours after the match he had crooned out his confusion to the blind musician, and Doyle, as ever, had crooned back with his pipes. He was a strange mixture of elation and depression. The soaring anger that had burst in him returned from time to time, the fantastic relief at feeling the life he had crushed into himself come rushing up from the depths of his gut to explode in Bentley's face. But each time his mind's eye reached the face – the face he had looked at in hatred – he inwardly cringed. He felt ashamed and afraid. Ashamed at tearing into the soft flesh of the small boy, afraid at what the tyrannous young gentleman would do to get his own back. But at suppertime that night, when Broad sought him out in the beast pens, to persuade him to eat with the mess, Thomas looked up briefly, tried to smile, and allowed himself to be led. He held the piper tightly by the hand, but even spoke a few words during the meal. To Broad, it was an advance.

There were no more sports, of course, and no more distractions. They were solidly in the Trades so there was no more sail drill, no more mindless, pointless seamanship exercises. The only break in the drabness of routine repair, upkeep and overhaul was on the odd occasion when a night-time cloud formation gave the cautious Mr Robinson a mind that it might lead to a night-time squall; or in fact, when they even more rarely actually encountered one.

Captain Swift, it was plain to Broad at least, had chosen a new line. Coupled with the instant punishment and cruel discipline was to be the greater cruelty of driving the people to boredom. He said nothing of it to anybody, indeed he rarely spoke to anyone now and spent a lot of time worrying about and longing for his home and family, but he was sure it was a deliberate tactic. In the days of good weather in the North Atlantic, before the violent heat and lethargy of the doldrums, there had been gun drill once a week and musketry drill twice; hard work but useful, although it was obvious that Swift's orders must be to engage no one and make for his destination at all speed. Though the men had grumbled at the heavy work it had been merely grumbling, for anything that broke the day and drove away the monotony was welcome in reality, and, God knew, their gunnery was slack enough. But now, in ideal conditions, the carriage guns remained still. Not once since well before they reached the Line had they been run out, neither had a musket been handled by a sailor. He plans to drive us mad with boredom, thought Jesse; and his mind would wander off and roam the creeks and woods of Langstone with Mary and Jem. He would grind his teeth then; for that was Swift's method, was it not? Inactivity was unmanning him. He thought of his wife and his heart bled. He looked at his filthy, calloused hands. Nothing to do, nothing to do. It was driving him crazy.

There was no more talk of mutiny. In the climate on board the Welfare it would have been too dangerous, impossibly dangerous, for two or more men to meet and breathe any slightest hint of disaffection. Broad saw Matthews occasionally, glanced at the long, lean, secret face. But they never spoke.

Nevertheless, as she roared south and west like a lovely bird, things began to happen. It was more of an atmosphere than anything concrete, more a shared air that all men breathed. No one got together, no one laid dark plans. But things began to happen.

The first incident was in broad daylight, and almost cost Mr Hagan his life. All the morning the master had had an eye cocked on a black ridge of cloud that was climbing threateningly from the horizon, and when the wind began to fluke, with stronger, unexpected gusts, and a darkening sky, he had a word with the captain. Perhaps because it was during their dinner, Swift did not hesitate to call all hands.

The men went aloft grumbling, because any fool could see, they muttered, that the squall would hold off until after dinner, if it ever came at all. And when the yards were fully manned, when the chances of anyone being singled out were infinitesimal, the incident occurred. As the first lieutenant walked towards a knot of men in the waist, a heavy wooden spike came hurtling down from aloft, whether from fore or mainmast it was impossible to tell, and embedded its point deep into a deck seam some two inches from his right shoe. He jumped like a frightened horse, then snapped his eyes aloft. The spike quivered in the deck, anonymous, mocking. Even Captain Swift could not flog every man on two masts. The squall came to nothing.

That night, at dinner in the captain's cabin, the officers, invited for the purpose, discussed what had happened. The midshipmen were there, for Daniel Swift had made it plain that the time had come for a new marking of divisions, a retrenchment. He was clearly stimulated by the mood in the ship. He ate the meal – less sumptuous this one, with fresh vegetables a vague and misty memory – with great relish.

'Well, Mr Hagan,' he said at one point, 'that was a close shave, eh? What would Mrs Hagan have said if we'd brought you home with ten inches of lignum vitae buried in your skull?'

Everyone laughed, including the first lieutenant. Even if the food was not so good Captain Swift's 'cellar' still yielded up an excellent drop. They were all in good spirits.

'I doubt, sir, that the fid would have penetrated, even had it struck me,' replied Hagan. 'I was bred to the Navy, you know, and my skull, like everything else about me, is of seamanlike toughness. Why, I believe I could mumble ship's biscuit even before I grew my first teeth – including the reefer's nut! Many a grown man would have envied me my gums at three months!'

'And what of your nostrils?' asked the captain, when the chuckles had died. 'How is your nose Mr Hagan, eh?'

Hagan looked puzzled. He felt that organ, as if there might be something unpleasant sticking to it.

'Your nose, aye, Mr Hagan,' repeated Swift. He gave a loud, merry laugh, a dazzling smile. 'There is nothing disgusting about it man, do not fear. But what do you smell? On board of my ship? Eh, what do you smell?'

William knew what his uncle meant immediately. He glanced at Swift, seeking permission to speak. The two were somewhat back on terms now, he was slightly easier with the man, although no word of the milling match had ever been uttered between them. He caught the pale, merry eyes. Permission was granted.

'I know, sir, with respect to Mr Hagan,' he said eagerly. 'The smell is . . . is . . . discontent. Disaffection. That, surely, is what the smell is?'

There was a silence among the officers and the giggling boys. They glanced about cautiously, as if worried how the captain might take such talk. But he laughed more loudly still.

'Be not so mealy-mouthed about it, William,' he cried. 'Will no one put another word to it? You sir, you, James Finch! You are a man of the world! What do you smell?'

James Finch blushed but said nothing. The stupid eyes of the third lieutenant goggled a little.

'Mutiny?' he said in a low, astonished voice. 'Good God, sir! Can you mean mutiny?'

There was irritation plain in Swift's reply.

'Yes sir, I can. I can and do. And I would sleep easier o' nights if you could smell it too. Mutiny smells, Mr Higgins, it smells to high heaven. I take it rather bad that the children can get the whiff and my third lieutenant cannot.'

Higgins, to Bentley's satisfaction, collapsed in shame. Captain Craig, the officer of the marines, coughed. He was a kindly man.

'With respect, sir,' he said. 'The sense of grievance among the people is very palpable. The ... er ... accident to Lieutenant Hagan could most easily have been fatal. It seems unlikely that it will be the last.'

Swift banged the table with his knife.

'I'm damned sure it will not, Captain Craig,' he replied. 'As damned sure as I am that it was no accident. A spike like that aloft! You are a soldier, sir. But I assure you, one does not use a fid to trim a topsail!'

Craig shook his head and took a small drink.

'Of course, sir,' he replied politely. 'But again – with respect – should one not perhaps be a little concerned as to where it might all end?'

Another awkward silence fell. Captain Craig had a knack, it appeared, of asking questions that Swift's sea officers would leave unasked. Again, though, the angry response they half expected was not forthcoming. Instead Swift beamed, his hatchet face transformed as if by sunshine.

'Craig,' he said approvingly, 'you are a good man and a sharp officer. Listen, I will tell you my strategy, you will enjoy it. It has become clear to me, it became clear some long time ago, that I am cursed with as vile a gaggle of scum as ever man was cursed with. They are bad, sir, desperate bad. But you will agree, if you've half an eye, that I've played them, sir, played them all the way. And now that there's this smell in the air, this heady smell that excites the dogs, gives them the strange idea that they have control of their destinies, we can make another move. Do you play chess, sir? Of course you do. Well, Captain Craig, they are the pawns; and I have a move in mind for them.'

Craig smiled a small, tight smile.

'I have always found pawns to be peculiarly important in a well-fought game of chess. They have to be moved with great care.'

William Bentley could hardly believe the impudence that could be read into Craig's reply. Or, for that matter, the marine officer's courage in stating a viewpoint. But Swift laughed again, as if in deep enjoyment.

'With care yes, Captain Craig. I see that we must have a match, you and I. My method, on this occasion though, might upset you. For I intend – I hope to have the opportunity and I think I shall – I intend to sacrifice a few of them. My pawns. What do you say to that, eh? As a player, you understand?'

There was silence. Men and boys watched the captain and the soldier. There was an edge to the conversation somehow, it had a dangerous ring. Craig considered, then spoke.

'Sacrificing pawns is usually very perilous, Captain Swift,' he replied. 'Unless, of course, it is part of a greater strategy.'

Swift smiled in delight. He leaned back in his chair, took a deep draught of wine.

'I shall enjoy playing with you, Captain Craig,' he said, 'I certainly shall. So listen. Drink please, gentlemen.'

They did. Then Swift went on.

'I know these men,' he said seriously, 'and I know them to be scum. I have manipulated them by many methods so far, and I have kept them in check. The overall tactic, gentlemen, is to keep 'em guessing. Keep the fellows muddled, keep them on their toes. That is the way, overall.'

He stared around the company. James Finch could not meet his eyes. Plumduff, the second lieutenant, wriggled in his seat. Hagan, inevitably, slipped out a long red tongue and ran it round his lips.

'But the time has come for a new ploy,' went on Swift. 'And I have been building up to it. Slowly but very sure. The end result is this: the smell of mutiny is in the air.'

Again a pause. Everyone was still, waiting.

'Very definite, the smell, very definite indeed,' said Daniel Swift. 'And what I say to that is – good. For believe me, gentlemen, and in particular you, Captain Craig, the time has come to sacrifice a few pawns. I have been leaving the dogs to their own devices, and whipping them when they moved a muscle out of turn. They have had nothing to do but hate. And when the hate spills over – good again. Well, Captain Craig? Do you like my gambit?'

Craig scratched his eye.

'The bloodshed – I presume there will be bloodshed – is part of the plan?'

William jumped. He had been listening very carefully, but this shocked him. He did not fully understand.

'Captain Craig,' replied his uncle, 'we *must* play some chess, you and I. You are very shrewd. Yes. That possibility is always there. As Lieutenant Hagan will vouch for.'

This appeared to be an invitation for Hagan to speak. He said nothing.

'These men,' said Swift, 'take me for a monster. God knows I have done my best by them. I have fed them, housed them, kept them as well as captain can. They have not gone short of food or drink, they have been punished only for crimes, and then purely for the good of their souls. But they take me for a monster. So be it. As I see it there is but one method to bring them back to their senses. I will *play* the monster. I will drive them to distraction with boredom and punish-ment. Then when they break out – I shall break them.'

Hagan spoke at last.

'You think the incident of the spike was merely a beginning, sir?' he said.

'Of course,' replied the captain. 'And cleverly done, although the scum missed, when all's said. But they are breaking out, yes. There will be other incidents.'

A silence. Craig broke it.

'The bloodshed? The sacrificing of the pawns?'

'I know these men, Captain Craig. I grew up with them. I am a sailor born. The only way to keep them down now is to crush them. What I want, why I welcome these "incidents", is this: The next time, they will not be so smart. Or the next, who knows? And then, sir, I can kill a few of them. It's an excuse I'm seeking, that is all. I want to hang a man or two, or shoot them, I care not. They have lost their respect, sir, they have got above themselves. We shall bring them down.'

Hours later, as he walked the waist in the sighing coolness of the night, William Bentley pondered his uncle's strategy. He was right about the mutiny in the air, no doubt of that. It was almost tangible. But the strange thing about the captain was the way his moods changed on all these things. To Hagan, although he jested about it, the incident of the fid must have been a shaker. And Uncle Daniel spoke almost gaily about what would happen next. But he, Bentley, felt far differently. When he thought of the people his gall rose. How dare they be rebellious? How dare they be disrespectful? How dare they contemplate such action against their officers? It was madness. The last stages of the milling rose into his mind's eye and he shivered with remembered shame. That was it, exactly! Lack of respect; contempt. The echoing laughter of the people came to him and he shivered a little more. Curse that silent boy. He was filled with dreadful hatred, for Fox, for all of them. He shivered again. It was suddenly cold.

Suddenly, too, he saw a movement forward. In the dark shadows of the deck he saw shapes flitting about. Then there came a loud crash, and a rumbling, thunderous sound. Then another, a third, a fourth. The thudding roar passed him and he realised what it was. Shot was being rolled. The seamen were hurling cannonballs about.

Before he could move, there was a screaming from the quarterdeck. It was high and pain-filled, as if a pig were being slaughtered. The rumbles faded but the screaming did not.

William did not know what to do. It was Plumduff who had been hit, for certain. Plumduff had the watch, and some of the rolled shot must have caught him. Shouts from aft cleared his mind. If there were people already there to look to Plumduff, he must look to the culprits. Motionless as he had been, thinking and watching the dark and friendly sea, the men up forward had obviously not seen him. Right!

He sprinted forward, with fury in his breast. The scum were rising, were they! It was shot rolling now, to catch and break the legs of unwary officers. Well by God, he would show them, that he would!

William Bentley was unarmed, but that only occurred to him much later. In any case he had no chance. The seamen who had rolled the heavy iron balls were still by the foremast, had more shot ready to roll. But when they heard him coming they were away. As he reached the shrouds, noisy in his leather shoes, the barefoot seamen were already in the lower rigging. They laughed as they climbed, not loudly but with feeling. The note of mockery brought a savage hatred to his breast that made him choke with rage.

He stood at the lee shrouds, staring upwards. The mast and cordage dwindled into blackness, the sails were paler blotches, whispering softly as they held the wind. A last faint sound of laughter came to him, but not even the ghost of a human form was visible.

The screaming on the quarterdeck had stopped. There were shouting men there now. The dim light of swaying lanterns threw weird shadows briefly. William Bentley stared about the dark, deserted deck. He shivered, more violently. It was getting cold.

Twenty-Four

The unfortunate Plumduff, probably because of his size and shape, came off far worse from the shot rolling than he might have done. In fact the first fracture, caused when the eighteen-pound ball hit his right calf, was perfectly simple and would have healed easily. But as he went down his side caught a hatch coaming or a fife-rail, he did not know which, and he was twisted in the fall. His hip came out, which caused the screaming. Later, when Mr Adamson tried to put it back, he found the joint to be badly broken. For many hours the second lieutenant could be kept quiet only by the internal application of a large amount of spirits.

During the last hours of the night the Welfare was in a ferment. The marine detachment was called to arms and Swift issued pistols to his officers, the master, and the young gentlemen, even James Finch. Corporals and boatswain's mates patrolled below decks to still the rumble of conversation in the accommodation, although each time they had passed a given point the whispers resumed. But although there was excitement in the air, both forward and aft, there was no further action.

Just before dawn Captain Swift called the young gentlemen to his cabin to give them a glass of grog and relieve them of their pistols. He said little while they drank, but kept William behind when he dismissed the others to snatch a half-hour of sleep before morning duty. He was calm, almost urbane, as he saw them off, thanking them for the trouble they had been put to. But when he was alone with his nephew, his eyes told a different story.

'The chance to shoot a few of them,' he spat. 'The chance to hang a few of them. That is what I wanted, and what have I got? That damned pudding of a second lieutenant screaming like a woman in labour, and once more, not a soul to blame. You were there, William. You were in the waist. What happened?'

'I am very sorry, sir, but I could catch nobody. They were away like wraiths. I ran, sir, but with shoes on . . . well. They flew aloft. Laughing.'

Swift expelled air noisily through his great beak.

'Laughing. Laughing. Laughing.' He threw his empty glass savagely against the bulkhead. It shattered across a polished chest and onto the deck. 'First they laugh at you, then they laugh at me. I will not have it!'

William swallowed. Please God let Swift not bring the milling match up now. In a way he had started all this, he felt. He said nothing.

'I will not have it, Mr Bentley. My officers are lax, my young gentlemen are . . .' He stopped, turned piercing eyes on Bentley. They were very pale, even paler than usual. He was breathing unsteadily. William Bentley felt his face begin to burn. He was very uncomfortable.

'William, my boy,' said the captain, 'I think I was wrong. I no longer think this is just a normal outburst of discontent. I think there is a plot afoot. It is too organised. Too successful. They miss Hagan, good; but they get the second. Thank God it was not the other way about, but it is a pattern; there is a will behind it. Agreed?'

William swallowed again. He made a vague gesture, opened his mouth to reply; although he had nothing to utter, if the truth were known. Swift, however, carried on.

'That shepherd lad, that Thomas Fox. Well boy, were you not surprised? And the breaking of the whistle-pipe. An act of provocation. Insane, yes? He could have been flogged. He could have been locked in irons and left to rot. And yet, what happens? There is a will, I tell you, a will.'

William Bentley could not quite follow. It was somehow incoherent. He fixed his gaze on a knothole in a deckhead beam. He remembered, inconsequentially, the end of the dinner party the evening before. Captain Swift, after expounding his tactics in his great game of 'chess' with the people, had invited Craig to agree that they were good ones. Craig had not declined, exactly, but his nod had been very brief. 'We must play together, Captain Swift,' he had said in the end. And William had received the sensation, yet again, that the soldier was overstepping the mark.

'You are tongue-tied, my boy,' said Swift. 'Do not be. I know

208

what is troubling you. The beating that that scum handed out. Yes, yes, that is it, no shame now, no shame. It was not what it seemed, I am certain; I am certain it was not what it seemed!'

Maybe, just maybe, Swift's explanation was not so very far-fetched, William Bentley thought. At any rate, he dearly wanted to believe it. The boy's behaviour had been odd in the extreme, true. The silence, the refusal to respond in any way, even to the wildest taunts that Simon Allen and little James threw at him. And God, true it was that his fists had been like bombshells. He had certainly been shamming on *that* score. He *had* been playing meek. So why not on the others too?

His uncle spoke again: 'We have set ourselves up, William, and you are lucky not to have got a knife between your ribs today. Has it occurred to you, yet, that the shot may have been meant for your legs? Or that when you went forward you were to be bludgeoned or knifed?'

It had not. But somehow the idea was not far-fetched. That shepherd boy. Since the fight, what had been the villain's manner? He had been seen abroad. Had he not dropped this pretence, this humble, eyes-glued-down pretence? William was not sure. But by hell, he'd find out soon enough.

He looked at his uncle's face and was startled by the paleness of his eyes. They were almost white, and he was breathing rapidly. All the fury that had not been apparent the night before at dinner was there, although still deeply suppressed.

'Be my eyes, boy!' he said, and his voice was strangled. 'Be my eyes as I commanded you. But take care! Take care! We are in control of these scum and we will defeat them. But take care!'

William wanted to ask his uncle whether he thought the boat-swain was to be trusted. He had wondered at the way the giant warrant officer hung round the shepherd boy. But for the moment, better to say nothing. His uncle's face was working; he appeared deeply moved.

'We will make an example, my boy,' Swift choked out. 'Be my eyes and find me someone. We will make an example. Find me someone.'

It was a weird interview, it had a strange quality, it was disturbing; and how, he wondered almost idly, could they make an example in a crew that had been whipped practically to a man? But over all, he had a wonderful, growing, sense of lightness, of relief. That damned, dissembling snake of a boy. The laughter of the people rang in his ears again. That damned dissembling snake. His uncle was right.

Loudly, on deck above them, the ship's bell rang the half. Daniel Swift gave a great sigh and relaxed. The wide, bright smile flooded across his drawn face, changing it with striking completeness.

'Off with you then, boy,' he said jovially. 'And William – mind how you go. We are targets now, but we will show the scum. Find me a swine, William, find me a swine. And we will lead him to the slaughter house!' He threw back his head and laughed.

William Bentley, as he went about his duties, was not certain, to be honest with himself, if he quite believed in all his uncle had said about the affair. He was tired, and tense, and the night had been long and very strange. But this much he *could* hang on to – he could expunge his shame; he could hold up his head in pride once more. There was something afoot in the ship, and he had been trusted anew to root it out. As he came onto the deck he was checked by the sudden chill. The air was keen and icy. He filled his lungs with pleasure, surveying the clean decks and the foam-flecked sea. The cold he had felt in the night had come in with a vengeance. Good. It was appropriate somehow; it suited the new mood. He would find a victim, sure enough. He would not let his uncle down this time. He breathed again, then shivered. Jesu, it was cold.

As always, the worsening of the weather and the accompanying absorption of the people pushed at least the outward signs of bad feeling out of sight. The wind veered southerly in a steady arc, until the Welfare was close-hauled and battering into seas that became ever steeper and ever colder. The wind got stronger, and to Jesse Broad, handing the main topgallants in the late afternoon, the air felt like razors as it struck through his jacket and trousers. After an hour aloft his feet were bone-white and clumsy, his fingers numb. In the mess, Grandfather Fulman grumbled as he tried to get some feeling back into his bony old shanks.

''Tis too early for this weather, to be sure,' he said. 'We should not be getting it cold like this yet, I reckon. This damned ship is cursed and that's a fact.'

The gunports were all lashed and weather-proofed, and by

nightfall the hatches had had to be battened. But the main and lower decks were as cold as charity, and getting colder. A brisk trade in woollen clothes and waterproof coats began, and some of the more pathetic drunkards, left by now with practically nothing to cover themselves, caused merriment or pity, depending on whom they tried to touch for an old or unwanted garment. The purser began to tout for customers at greatly inflated prices – that even the worst-off had to agree to if he did not want to freeze to death when sent on deck or aloft.

Butterbum chose this moment, too, to make a further inventory check of the beasts in Thomas Fox's care. He could hardly have chosen a worse one.

Throughout the hot and foetid weather of the doldrums, Thomas had been fighting a battle to keep the animals healthy. Most of the chickens had finally gone to the captain's table by then, which was a blessing for they could hardly have survived, and Allgood, without explanation, had one day released him from his heads-cleaning duties, which gave him more time. But the bigger beasts, especially the sheep, were in deadly trouble. The constant heat, the lack of proper feedstuffs, the filthy, insect-infested water from the deep casks in the ship's hold, all combined to make them a weak and sickly flock.

Many and many a time Thomas had wished to tell the purser that the sheep must be killed and eaten. He knew it was his duty to do so, for the husbandman had also to make the decision when the chances of survival got so slim as to outweigh the advantages of fresh meat on the hoof. But how could he do it? He could no more talk to Butterbum than he could fly. So he had worked and worked at saving them. Had coddled and hand-fed. With a pair of shears and Doyle's help had taken most of their wool off to save them from the awful humid heat below, where they had always to be kept, whatever the weather, by captain's edict. And had watched them grow scrawnier, and weaker, and more and more like walking corpses.

Now there before him stood the repulsive fatness of the purser, his face a carefully arranged mixture of shock and pleasure. Thomas knelt among the shivering sheep, their wool only a little regrown. The air between the decks was damp, with great runnels of condensation pouring down the outer walls and drips from the deckhead constantly wetting everything. It was desperately cold.

'I have come to check the sheep, boy,' he said. 'But before God, I think I am too late. What do you call this then? Good husbandry? Why sir, I have seen nothing like it in twenty years at sea!'

Thomas Fox had at that very moment been trying to massage the shaking rib-cage of a ewe. The heart beneath his hand was rattling. He was filled with a deep dread. Half his mind was on the fat purser, wondering what the result of this meeting would be. The other half was on the ewe. She could not live the day, she could not. Doyle was on the other side of the animal, trying to warm her with his body.

'Well, well,' said Butterbum, in a voice of deep satisfaction, 'Captain Swift will be delighted at this state of affairs, I am sure. How many have died?'

He consulted his ledger. Thomas spoke in a whisper.

'None, sir. All are present.'

'Hah. Is that so? Well, indeed you surprise me. Let me count 'em.'

As he moved into the pen to count, Thomas drew to one side. He kept his arm tightly around the dying ewe. Under his hand her heart shook and rattled. His mind was filled with one prayer. That she should live. Please God let her but live until Butterbum went away. For the moment that would be enough.

The purser swiftly checked the sheep. He was disappointed. All were there, no doubt of it.

'They look sick,' he said abruptly. 'I think they are dying. Definitely on their last legs. What do you say?'

Thomas closed his eyes to get the words out.

'No sir. Cold sir. But very hardy.'

'Hhm.'

Butterbum sighed.

'Ah well, the captain wants one killed. See to it boy, see to it. Though God knows, he'll not be pleased with you when I tell him how desperate thin they've grown.'

He gave a short laugh. 'Not been eating their rations, have you? You and your purblind friend there!'

Under Thomas Fox's hand the rattling heart slowly ran down. It twitched once or twice, then caught a beat, steady, but fainter still. As the purser waddled away, he shuddered with released tension.

'Butcher,' he mumbled. 'Padraig, I have to get to the butcher. Before this poor ewe dies. I cannot take you. Wait, friend, and tend the others. Warm them Padraig, warm them!'

212

The dying sheep was not heavy, but the motion of the ship made it difficult to move fast. He cradled it as best he could as he headed to the galley, where he hoped to find the pressed man, rated able, who kept his hand in at his real trade, of a butcher. He was not there. The old crippled cook was not inclined to say where he might be, despite Thomas's obvious desperation, so at last, following directions from half a dozen hands, he climbed onto the foredeck. The butcher had been seen wandering about with two cleavers in his hand, himself seeking the carpenter's mate to sharpen them.

On deck the half-naked sheep began to shiver violently in the wind. Thomas felt the chill too, but it was the least of his worries. He scanned the damp, pitching deck anxiously. There! He could see the butcher with the carpenter's mate, walking forward from the mainmast. As Thomas hurried towards them the great bulk of the boatswain came from behind one of the ship's boats. He was muffled in an all-enveloping surcoat, his beard flying wildly out from above the collar. He gave a booming laugh.

'Haha, my bucko!' he roared. 'Caught you at the game, have I? Sheep-stealing's your lay!'

Thomas tried not to stop, but the boatswain planted himself in front of him. The sheep hung down from his arms, shaking convulsively.

'Hello, what's this then?' cried Mr Allgood. He was in high good humour, enjoying the joke and the bracing weather. A few hands watched incuriously from nearby.

'The butcher, sir,' Thomas muttered. 'I must see the butcher this instant. The captain requires—'

'This instant!' echoed the boatswain. He laughed again. 'By hell, Thomas Fox, we are the bold one now indeed, since we beat the shrimpish boy! To tell the boatswain your business is urgent! Do you not consider that a shade forward? Has it not occurred to you I might trice you to a grating and strip your back to the bone? "This instant"!'

The butcher and the carpenter's mate had approached. Thomas turned his stricken face to them, and saw, over the butcher's shoulders, that Butterbum was also in the offing. The fat purser, an interrogative sneer on his face, was waddling from the quarterdeck. Beside him was the midshipman of the watch, William Bentley.

'Oh please,' whispered Thomas in desperation. 'Oh please, Mr Allgood sir!'

Under his hand the sheep's heart raced anew. Its whole body shook for a few seconds. The heart slowed down. Slower and slower, slower and slower. It faltered, picked up, faltered again. Then stopped. He squeezed the emaciated rib-cage. Nothing. The heart had stopped.

William Bentley approached the group on the foredeck with distaste and a certain nervousness. The purser nauseated him, but he had made a specific complaint, and as if by magic the person involved, along with one of the sheep mentioned, had appeared before him. It was obvious that something peculiar was going on; he had a duty to investigate. There was another reason, of course, which he did not put into words. He had not approached or spoken to the shepherd boy since the fight. With both of them on the deck it was essential that he should speak to the scum. Otherwise the people, in their oafish ignorance, would take it for a sign that he was uncomfortable, even afraid.

At that moment the boatswain's booming laugh rolled to him on the wind, followed by a jumble of words. William did not catch them all, but he picked out 'Butcher it', and 'Dead as mutton', and 'Killed again'. Butterbum almost grabbed his sleeve in his excitement.

'Did you hear, sir?' he said. 'Did you hear! The sheep is dead! I told you so!'

Then the great hairy face of the boatswain turned itself on to William's. They looked at each other across the cold, sloping deck. For several seconds Allgood stared at him. Then he turned back to the small group.

William quickened his pace and the purser positively skipped. The knot of men in front of them had closed up tightly and moved to the lee rail. There was a sudden scream, half human, half animal.

And then, as William broke into a run, the water in the scuppers suddenly turned bright red. A split second, and a gush of sea burst over the rail as the lee bow plunged. The stain spread, pinkened, then ran through the drain ports.

'Ahoy!' he shouted. 'Mr Allgood! What are you about, man!'

Once more the boatswain turned to face William. There was a wide, insolent smile on his full red lips. He held the carcass of the

214

sheep easily in his huge hand, half-naked and sodden, like a drowned child. Its head was hanging by a fold of skin and gristle.

'Teaching the butcher his business, Mr Bentley,' he said mildly. 'And testing the edge that has been put upon his cleavers.'

William stared around the faces. The butcher and the carpenter's mate looked high into the rigging, their expressions blank. The boy was up to his old trick of studying the deck, his shoulders shaking slightly. A black wave of anger swept through the midshipman.

'You,' he snarled. 'You boy. Look at me, damn you, or I'll have you flogged. That sheep was dead was it not? Dead!'

Thomas did not move. The boatswain made a gesture of surprise.

'Dead when we cut its throat, Mr Bentley?' he said, milder still. 'Do you think I would give such trash-meat to the owner? And did you not hear it scream, sir?'

William opened his mouth and gripped his fists together. He drew a shuddering breath. The boatswain smiled a small smile, an encouraging, wickedly insolent smile.

'Bless your heart, sir, of course it wasn't dead. I cut its little throat myself, sir, sweet as you like.'

'Check the other sheep, sir, check the others,' hissed Butterbum. 'They are all in the same state, sir, on death's door. Trust me, sir, they . . .'

He trailed off. William Bentley looked into the boatswain's eyes, spoke as coolly and as calmly as he knew how.

'Mr Allgood,' he said, 'I am seriously displeased at your conduct in this affair. God only knows what is in your mind to do it. At the very least, to slaughter animals upon the upper deck. I shall express my feelings to the captain instantly. I am most displeased.'

The boatswain had cleared his face of all expression.

'Aye aye sir,' he said. 'Thank you, sir.'

The news of this latest clash between Thomas and the midshipman went round the ship like wildfire. It was exhilarating news that set the messes buzzing with amazement and delight. Fox himself, released by the boatswain when the butcher carried the carcass off forward to dress it, went below filled with nothing but horrified anticipation. He found the blind man draping the sheep that were left in any rags he had managed to gather. They checked each animal in turn, the boy's despair mounting at the state of them. They were a half-starved, half-frozen bunch.

Although the men were excited by the incident, no one sought out Fox. A strange circumspection had become apparent over the past days. There was an air of expectation, a thrilling, heady sense of danger. Once more the shepherd lad had been at its centre, besting the dreadful boy; but only his messmates spoke to him.

Broad was the first. Little Peter would have been, but he had not recovered from the flogging which had racked his skinny form, and was more or less immovable, although not in the sick-bay. Broad leaned over the side of the pens and called softly into the gloom. After a few seconds Fox appeared, his face pale and worried.

'Supper, Thomas,' Broad said gently. 'Did you not hear the call?'

'Oh Jesse Broad,' whispered Thomas Fox. 'The beasts are dying. It is too cold. We cannot come.'

'Nay nay,' said Broad. 'Come you to supper, Thomas, you and Padraig Doyle. There is hot Scotch coffee and we have rum still to lace it with. You need the warmth in this weather.'

'How long will it last, friend Jesse? It is too cold, the beasts are in a frightful way. We can do nothing to help them. They have our blankets already. Oh Jesse, friend Jesse, this ship is hell!'

'But Thomas, no,' said Broad urgently. 'No no, 'tis fine now. Hold yourself together, man, do not despair. You are a hero, the people love you. Come you and eat, with Padraig Doyle too. Then we will see to the animals, myself and all. They shall have my blankets, all our blankets if need be.'

Thomas laid his head on the pen railing, the wood distorting his thin cheeks.

'My cousin Silas,' he gasped. 'Silas, Jesse, my cousin. He is a marine on board here and God help me, soon he will be told to blow my brains out. Oh Jesse, this ship is hell.'

Broad watched the shuddering face in pity, although he did not fully understand the shepherd's drift.

'Your cousin? A marine?'

'Aye Jesse; or maybe, no. It does not matter if he is or not. I can speak to no man, no man can speak to me. The beasts are sick and freezing and I have cruelly hurt the boy once more. Everything is at an end and soon the end will come. Oh Jesse, Jesse, the beasts are cold, so cold.'

The seaman spoke low, his voice urgent.

'No,' he said firmly. 'No, no, no, Thomas Fox. Believe me, I am your friend. This weather is wrong, a freak. We should still be in the warmth and sun. It will return, it will. And as to the rest, you have done nothing, I swear it. Nobody hates you, you will come to no harm. You have never hurt that boy neither; it is not your fault.'

He told him more. Of how Grandfather Fulman and other older hands were complaining about the 'cold snap'. That it was an aberration. That soon, tomorrow even, they would be in the sun again. He further said that all in the mess would turn-to that night to keep the animals warm, with blankets and spare clothes if need be. At last the boy was comforted, and allowed himself to be led to supper, leading in turn his friend the blind man by the hand. True to the word, that night the messmates shivered under rags while the sheep rolled sickly in their blankets.

But the weather prophets were sadly out. Between seven o'clock the next morning and three in the afternoon, during which time the temperature was scarcely over freezing, four of the seven sheep died.

Twenty-Five

William Bentley, for all his threat to the boatswain, did not in fact tell Captain Swift about the incident on the foredeck for a long time. There was, of course, no one else to speak to that august personage of such matters. Higgins, who had had the watch, had probably not realised that anything amiss was taking place, but could hardly have approached Swift with it even if he had. Rumour ran a speedy course around the ship, but there were some ears too grand to be touched by it. William himself simply did not know how to present the matter. He had been bested, or slighted, yet again, and the boatswain had been a party to it. First then, hard to tell of his own humiliation, and second, he did not dare impugn Mr Allgood. His uncle had certain views that William knew were rigid and sacrosanct. There was no doubt in his own mind that the boatswain was an insolent, even a mutinous, dog. But he dreaded to imagine what would happen if he said so. So it was, that in the whole ship's company, only the captain did not know immediately about the 'sheep that died twice' as it was called.

When he did hear, it was, almost incredibly, through the purser; and it led William into a nightmare.

All that day, as the Welfare ploughed south under shortened canvas, Jesse Broad worked hard to keep the terrible secret that the other sheep had died. It was a hopeless, pointless exercise, but it was pursued with fanatical care. Broad had seen a collapse in the shepherd boy that horrified him and his fear as to what would happen when the deaths were discovered spurred him on. He had a vague, wild hope that if the weather worsened, if night fell, they could somehow manufacture a stampede, an accident. Perhaps the damned beasts could be washed overboard; anything. Once it was dark, in a storm, he was prepared to go to almost any lengths to get the dead sheep over the side, if it meant being flogged insensible.

He also had a half-formed plan to see Matthews and try to start a riot. To bribe some of the wilder element with rum, however dearly bought, and have them attack the pens and 'slaughter' the miserable corpses. His brain seethed.

Grandfather Fulman and his messmates knew that something had happened, but only that. Peter's inability to move or poke his nose about was a true blessing at last, despite the poor lad's own agony. They got their blankets back and they kept their mouths shut. Thomas Fox and Doyle, as ever, kept to their darkened pen. Jesse Broad watched from a short distance, casually keeping away men who would pass too close. Towards the end of the dog-watches the cloud-filled sky was growing rapidly gloomy. Broad, seeing the light that filtered below decks dwindling, had a rush of hope. He went to the pen and spoke to Thomas.

'Take heart, boy,' he whispered to the huddled form. 'It will soon be night. We will save the situation, Thomas, do not doubt it. Only wait a little longer.'

At about the same moment, the word was passed to William Bentley, who was lying musing unhappily in the berth, that the captain wanted to see him. The other young gentlemen looked at him with smiles he saw as sneers. William disliked them badly at the moment, waiting as they were, he guessed, for the latest step in his downfall. He smiled back awkwardly.

'Oh damn,' he said, in a voice he hoped was languid, 'if I drink much more green tea with Uncle Daniel I will surely burst.'

As he approached the marine sentry outside the cabin, the door clicked open and Butterbum shuffled out backwards. He closed the door, turned, and flushed when he saw William. He gave him a queer, half-smirking look, put on his hat and bustled off forward. William's stomach dropped away from him as he knocked.

Captain Swift, sitting behind his mahogany table, did not move as his nephew slowly approached. He was still, quite still, apart from the fingers of his right hand. They drummed a soft tattoo on the polished surface. His eyes were steadily on his nephew's face. They looked deadly. William realised, with a shock, that he was afraid of this unpredictable man. He stopped, waited, said nothing. But he was afraid.

'You saw the purser, of course,' said Daniel Swift flatly.

219

'Yes sir.'

'He told me a peculiar tale, William Bentley. A most peculiar tale. Is it true?'

William swallowed, but decided not to throw himself to the lions before he saw the actual shape of their fangs.

'What tale, sir? The purser is . . .'

'Yes?'

'The purser is a man I have not found to be entirely trust . . . Entirely without faults of his own, sir.'

Captain Swift smiled. It was a broad smile, disconcerting in its friendliness.

'Yes, William,' he said. 'Mr . . . Butterbum is a vile, fawning rogue.' The smile disappeared. The pale eyes appeared to flash, it was most odd. A ray of cold anger lit them. 'The last sort of scum, William, that I expect to learn things from.'

The boy gave in to the inevitable. He swallowed once more, then spoke out.

'Sir, I promise you I was trying to keep nothing hidden. The incident was so uncertain. I do not know to this moment if I was being made a dupe or no. Mr Allgood assured me the beast was killed by him.'

'Allgood? You believe my boatswain would butcher a sheep? It is impossible!'

'Must I then believe he lied, sir? For he told me so himself. He told me so.'

The man and the boy stared at each other in the swaying lamplight. Outside, the cold wind moaned. Swift's fingers resumed their drumming.

'The shepherd boy again. He was there.'

'Yes sir.'

'And the purser says he had a dead or dying sheep. That he gave *me – me!* – the flesh to eat of a sheep already dead.'

'Yes sir. As I understand it, sir. Although . . . although Mr Allgood says the beast was not yet dead.'

There was another long silence. William wanted to burst out; wanted to convey his fears. Not only Thomas Fox, he wished to say, but Mr Allgood. They were in it together. He sensed danger, deadly danger. Again he was filled with hatred for the lanky boy. But he said nothing.

220

'Between you and me, my boy,' Swift said, 'this damned shepherd lad has got the better of you. You seem to have made a great muff of things. Eh? As a plotter . . . he has left you standing. In stays, sir! Eh?'

It was not fair, and it was awful. He closed his eyes momentarily, made a movement with his hands. It was unfair, it was dreadful, and . . . was it true? Inwardly, he groaned.

Captain Swift went on thoughtfully: 'I'll tell you what though, he is a damned lot of trouble for a boy, that much is all too certain. And whatever the ins and outs of the matter, he is making me mad. William Bentley, you have let me down, sir. But as for that accursed boy . . .'

It was then that the knock came. The captain gave the command to enter – and there was Butterbum once more, his eyes alight with triumph. He stood in front of Swift, his hat in his hand, trembling.

'Well,' said the captain. 'A quick return, Mr Purser. Your findings?'

The purser was so anxious to get it out that the words tumbled forth in a spray of dribble. He was beside himself, gleeful.

'Dead sir! Aye sir! Dead sir! Three or four of them! By God sir! It is true! The villains!'

Swift said coldly: 'Pray control yourself.' But the strange light flickered in his own eye, quite plainly.

'Beg pardon, sir!' said Butterbum. He gulped, two or three times, got his breath. 'They tried to prevent me, sir. That smuggler lout, what's his name, Broad? And then the blind man, putting the damned evil eye on, I swear it. But I got in for an instant, sir, and it was enough. Dead sheep, dead sheep! They manhandled me, sir! It is a hanging matter!'

William jumped as his uncle stood up. The captain strode to a curtained-off compartment and returned a few seconds later with a wooden box and a great blue cloak. He struggled impatiently into the cloak, opened the box, and took out one of the long pistols that lay there. Not a word was spoken as he checked and primed it. He thrust it into a deep narrow pocket in the cloak, flashing William a preoccupied smile. The purser was standing gasping, a fish out of water, his pasty face pastier yet.

'Thank you, Mr Purser,' said Swift. 'Now sir, get to your cubbyhole and shut your mouth. If a word of this leaks you will be flogged. Understand?'

He ushered the fat man out past the marine sentry, who saluted as the captain hurried by. Butterbum disappeared and William strode along beside his uncle, his heart leaping with excitement. He could hardly believe this was happening, it was unprecedented, absolutely amazing. That the captain should go about his own business like this, that no one on the ship should know he was abroad and with what purpose. They sped along the alleyway like lightning. Hagan, meeting them, gave them a startled look then stepped back as the owner swept by. Seconds later they were picking their way forward in the gloom.

Along the length of the deck the captain's passing caused a groundswell of astonishment and unease. The men were at their dinner, wolfing the food from their platters ravenously. But all sounds ceased when any given mess recognised him. Ahead and behind him was a babble, but as he passed each point a silence fell. It was unprecedented.

Long before he reached the animal pens, Jesse Broad knew he was coming. The wave of shocked excitement gathered speed and raced forward mess by mess. When the captain arrived, short and magnificent with his great strong face above the massive cloak, Grandfather Fulman's mess was ranged before the pens in a ragged line. It was an odd formation, vaguely reminiscent of the last tattered remnants of an army that had been defending a fort. There was something defiant in it, something pathetically defiant.

Behind Daniel Swift and his nephew all men had abandoned food and drink. William, glancing over his shoulder, made out a hundred faces, pressing ever closer to them. In the excitement of the moment he felt no fear, although if ever there was a time ripe for mutiny this was surely it. But the captain was truly awe-inspiring now; truly, he inspired awe.

Even Thomas Fox felt it. As the owner stood before the ragged line the boy, so near collapse before, took a small step forward. He raised his dark eyes to the pale ones that glared at him, and spoke.

'I am sorry, sir,' he said. 'Your beasts are dead.'

Silence fell, spreading outwards from the group of men. It did not spread as fast as the excitement had done, but gradually the ship's people, huddled in the darkness, became quiet. The creaking of the Welfare's timbers, the sad howling of the wind, the fainter crashing of the sea; at last these were the only sounds.

222

When Swift spoke, his voice had the effect of a saw. It was unmusical, harsh, and penetrating. It vibrated slightly, as if it were being forced out under great pressure from great depths.

'Who are your fellows, Thomas Fox? Who are your fellows in this hellish business?'

The silence got deeper. Thomas Fox stood in front of Daniel Swift swaying slightly. His face was blank. He did not speak.

Daniel Swift repeated: 'Who? Tell me, damn you, or it will be the worse for you. Who?'

The boy's pale, worn face looked weary. He moved his head from side to side, slowly. As if trying to understand what was being asked of him, thought William Bentley. He was lost, uncomprehending. And still said nothing.

Before the captain spoke again there was a commotion from aft. The close-pressed men were jostled and broke apart. Mr Allgood, a lantern in his hand, pushed forward at the head of a gaggle of mates and corporals. He stopped when he saw the strange group by the beast pens. Captain Swift half turned and regarded him. He gave a bleak smile.

'Ah Mr Allgood,' he said in the harsh, penetrating voice. 'Just the man. In the matter of some sheep, Mr Allgood . . . in the matter of some . . . dead . . . sheep.'

The monstrous bulk of the boatswain, crouched from the shoulders under the low deckhead, gave a sort of shrug.

'Aye sir?' he said. His tone was neutral.

'In the matter of some . . . dead sheep, Mr Allgood. This . . . young man here. This . . . Thomas Fox. I want him punished.'

Still the deadly silence from the ship's people. Again a sort of shrug.

'Aye sir?'

The captain's voice became more penetrating yet. It rose noticeably. The muscles in his cheeks worked as if the pressure were becoming intolerable.

'Aye sir! Aye sir! Aye sir!'

William Bentley saw the shepherd boy give a long shudder. His own mouth was dry. There was fear in the air, it was almost visible.

Captain Swift was breathing fast, the air hissing through his long, bony nostrils. It was an irregular, disturbing sound. It was some time before he spoke.

223

When he did, it was in a brisk, businesslike way, as if he had suddenly relaxed. But the words were in direct contrast. Any tendency in the people to relax with him was swamped by the chilling words. He turned abruptly to the boy again.

'Thomas Fox, get you to the main topmast yard if you please. And stay there. Mr Allgood will have you conducted.'

There were two sounds then. A low, strangled noise from the throat of Padraig Doyle, like a choke, and a harsh note from the throat of Allgood. A grunt; a fierce, angry sound. The captain turned his cold, pale eyes full upon him.

'You have a comment to offer, sir?'

The stooped giant's eyes glittered. William Bentley saw his big red lips open momentarily. Then shut. Then:

'No sir.'

The amazing, dazzling smile. But Swift's voice was like broken ice.

'Good then. Fox shall go to that yard and stay there.' He passed a quick glance among the ship's company within his sight. 'Until I decide upon the form his punishment shall take . . .'

He turned on his heel with a swirl of heavy cloak and strode aft, scarcely giving men time to bundle out of his way. William had almost to run to keep up.

When they reached the cabin the captain called for wine and two glasses. When they were alone he raised a brimming glass and proposed a toast.

'To mutiny!' he said. 'Much good may it do the scum, eh boy?'

William had to drink, of course. But his thoughts were outside, in the cold, howling night. He watched his uncle's handsome, smiling face, but his thoughts were jumbled. In his mind's eye, the yard where the boy must be. My God, the cold! And was the *punishment* still to come! The wine went down the wrong way and set him coughing. His uncle laughed.

'Come boy, put your mind to it!' he cried. 'It is you who should be proposing a toast, William, for it is a fine thing to see an enemy destroyed.' He clapped a hand on his nephew's shoulder. 'Come, I will be magnanimous,' he added. 'Credit give where credit is deserved. It is *you* who have brought the shepherd down, my boy, with a little outside aid. You found him out, and brought him down. Well done!'

* * *

224

For Thomas Fox, the journey to the yard was a slow and dreadful one. It was, in fact, the first time he had ever been aloft, tender of beasts and landman as he was. He was as hampered by the clothing he wore as by his clumsiness; for under the eye of Allgood, strangely tolerant for a boatswain under orders to punish, his messmates had dressed him in every stitch they could gather. He had found it hard to bend his knees and elbows during the long struggle up the ratlines from the deck. Many times he had paused to recover his strength, closing his eyes and sobbing for breath. The swaying, slippery, alien rigging was a puzzle to him, and the manifold noises – sighing, sawing, thrumming and moaning – only served to frighten him more. His progress was abysmally slow, with sweat blinding him and making his grip dangerously haphazard.

He had known when to stop only at a shout from below; and there he sat, astride some heavy ropes near the mast, desperately clutching others. The yard was far wider than he had expected, but it did not make a solid platform. It moved constantly, not much but enough to make relaxation of his hanging-on impossible. It groaned, too, loudly and all the time, like a great beast in pain. For a long time, when he reached it, Thomas Fox groaned also; the noises merging in his mind like a low symphony of misery.

When the first terror died away, however, an odd, unlooked-for feeling came to Thomas Fox. The sky was like a mighty void, and he seemed to be its centre, rushing through it in a cage of wood and ropework. The sensation of movement was quite marvellous, as the wind tore at him from across the weather bow and from round and under the sails and mast. The white water flung outwards far below him reminded him of breathing, flashing and glittering in the roaring darkness. Horse-rider, horse-rider, he kept thinking, just the words, over and over again. Horse-rider, horse-rider. The blast of air in his nostrils was clean, intensely clean. It burst into his lungs, a strange, mesmeric action. Empty and fill, empty and fill, clean and cold, clean and cold.

Whenever he tried to make sense of what had happened, whenever he tried to put a reason to his presence on the yard, his mind slid away after a short while. Something to do with sheep, he knew, and that poor midshipman Bentley. He had killed some sheep, that was it, and this was his punishment. Or was it? Was there something else to come? Then off would go his mind once more, to

225

think, perhaps, of Padraig Doyle; and his frozen lips would try to form a smile.

Padraig Doyle, at about this time, was weeping in the arms of Jesse Broad. He had put a brave face on it as he had hugged his friend farewell, but when the boy had gone onto the deck he had retired to the pens to weep. There, later, Broad had sought him out – as much to get some comfort, he supposed, as to try and give it. For he was filled with a great sense of despair, and loss. He had almost burst with horror and rage as the shepherd boy had been led up the ladder; a helpless feeling that he guessed was in many hearts. The people, after the confrontation with the captain, had not drifted back to their dinners. The hubbub had never reasserted itself. There had been a numbness, an unspoken revulsion.

The huge bulk of Allgood had been part of it. Impassive yet involved, he had watched over the dressing up of Fox like a dumb animal watching some act of dreadful violence to its young; some chained beast, unable to move or to express itself. How ambiguous was his position, Jesse thought; a man so violently hated by so many of the men. A cruel, vicious instrument of work and discipline. Who yet had some unknown streak in him, who yet seemed somehow linked with Thomas Fox. And who still had had to oversee this awful act of sadism by the captain; who had had to see the pale-faced boy safely into the resting place that would probably be his last alive.

After the act the men had been subdued. But there had been this feeling, too, this brooding air of impending doom. Broad hugged the birdlike, crippled body of the blind man, crooned to it as he had heard young Thomas do. He had a vision of despair and violence.

On deck, at midnight, William Bentley came on watch and stared into the gloom above until he made out the hunched black shape at the yard. It was blowing fierce now, with the Welfare constantly being drenched by icy spray. Huddled deep in his thick wool coat, his hands thrust into big patch pockets, he nevertheless shivered from time to time. He had eaten well that night, and drunk of wine, but when he had been on deck only an hour, the warmth was gone. He huddled ever deeper into the high-collared coat, burrowing into the warmth with his mind as well as his body. He was trying, oh so very hard, to keep away from that cold black shape aloft. But mind

226

and eyes and heart returned and returned. The dim shape, immobile as a part of the topmast furniture, throbbed in his head. Occasionally a sort of horror overwhelmed him, a kind of fear. What had he— But he would take his hands from his pockets, bang his sides vigorously, jig up and down. At one moment he tried to engage the master, on deck to smell the weather as so often when it bade fair to be dirty, in some silly conversation. But the thin, ugly Mr Robinson gave him such a withering look that William felt quite hollow with loneliness. Then the master checked the binnacle and went below.

If there had been, if there *was*, a plot (it flashed into his mind at one point) then why had Uncle Daniel done nothing to anyone except the boy? A moment of panic – it was just a mad act, a piece of vicious . . . William found himself biting his lower lip, clenching his fists in the pockets. His breathing was jerky. He brought it to control, thought rationally.

No, Uncle Daniel knew his men, knew them totally. Uncle Daniel was right. No need for extra precautions if he said not. The sending of the boy to the yard was enough. It would stop them in their tracks, petrify them. Good God, the lad would never— He was biting his lips again, uttering, to his astonishment, a thin, small cry. He looked around in horror in case someone may have heard. But no, no one near. He felt a sob begin, deep inside him, and his horror grew. What was happening, what was happening? He cursed the wine he had drunk, viciously, under his breath, cursed and swore and ranted. The boy too: Ah damn him, damn him, why had he brought this on himself?

Just before the watch was changed, Allgood sought and gained permission to check the boy's condition and have him lashed to the spar if need be. William could not bear to hear the report. He went below and buried himself in blankets. While the watch was changing over, Broad and Matthews exchanged a few quick words, during which fear, anger and regret were expressed; also a garbled tale of Fox's cousin, who might or might not be a marine. Then the men were separated. But not a boatswain's mate who used his rattan that night. There was a brooding in the air.

Thomas Fox did not really know it when he was securely lashed to the yard. He was dimly aware that something was going on, but that was all. He was warm again now, after a long period of mortal agony. During that whole time he had known the strange sensation of feeling sensation die. It did not die fast, all at once, it died slowly, and could always be localised. Extremities first, his nose, and lips and eyebrow-flesh. Then he had felt his fingers go; numb to begin with, then racked with wrenching agony, then numb at last once more. His feet had taken longer and cost more pain. His jawbones hurt the most of all, as if someone were squeezing them in a vice. Gradually the warmth was sucked and drained out of him until he could actually chart the creeping advance of the cold, closer and closer to the centre of the ball that was his thickly covered, clenched body. Now he was warm again.

Now he was warm, and his thoughts drifted sunnily over his father's farm. He wandered along the pebbled shores of Portsea Island, watching the green and shining sea as it crashed merrily onto the beach. He played with his sisters endlessly, he filled his gut with cakes and ale. He got great prices at the market for his flocks and watched with pleasure the happy antics of the sailors at Point, enjoying their liberty. He stared at the men-of-war, lordly and majestic as they swung round their cables in Spithead, against the dark luxurious green of the Isle of Wight. Something tried to encroach upon his mind from time to time, but it faded always after a few seconds' thought. Sometimes he opened his eyes and it was dark, which was surprising. But most of the time, the sun shone. How lovely was the sea, how merry were its waves. And how he envied those who had the chance to sail upon it.

Twenty-Six

I t was shortly before the grey daylight broke that Captain Swift had the word sent for Thomas Fox to be brought down. By accident or design, Mr Allgood told off Jesse Broad as one of the men to go aloft – for there was no response of any kind to hails to Thomas from below. Broad shot up the rigging like a monkey and reached the boy seconds before the other seaman did. His heart sank at what he saw, his eyes momentarily closed. His friend was surely dead.

But he was not. As Broad leaned close he saw a steamy wisp of breath from the bone-white nose. He gasped, and whispered 'Thomas'. No response.

It took the two of them several minutes to free the rigid body of the boy. Despite the fat cocoon of clothing, he had seized up almost solid. They had, after unlashing him, to move his limbs like those of a stiff wooden doll. The trunk, clenched and doubled, they could not move; Thomas Fox had to be taken down closed like a knife. His face was a frightening sight, glaring white with dull red and blue patches, hair, eyebrows and lips rimed with ice.

At deck level, many gentle hands reached out to take the boy, but Jesse Broad would let him go to no one. The boatswain stood nearby, his face sombre. When Broad said he was alive a disbelieving smile lit his face. It did not stay for long.

'Get him to the surgeon quick.'

Mr Adamson was waiting, inevitably with his brandy bottle at the ready. He had hot stones, too, and dried blankets that had been roasted before the galley fire. He worked quickly, nimbly, his usually jolly face grim. He slapped away with warm rags, got some of the outer clothing off, tried to force spirit between the rigidly clenched lips. As long as Jesse Broad could afford to stay he hung there on the outskirts, not daring to ask the question he wanted to ask. He felt helpless, foolish. The surgeon, dipping like a bird, worked furiously.

229

After ten minutes from his duty he knew he could stay no longer. He stood on one foot, then the other. He coughed.

Adamson looked up, gave him a brief, humourless smile.

'Hello, Mr Smuggler,' he said. 'What do you want?'

He did not wait for a reply, knowing full well. The frozen face under his hands remained rigid. The eyes had not so much as flickered.

'I'm sorry, friend,' he went on. 'I do not know. He is not dead, that is one thing. And it is a start, eh?

'Oh, to hell with you!' he cried irritably. 'I'm a surgeon, not a wizard. If heat and brandy can pull him round, he'll pull round. If not, he's dead. Now go!'

Later on, Jesse and the others of the crew who wanted to know, who gravitated to the nearest points they could reach to the sick-bay, heard the screams begin. They were terrible, heart-rending. Little Peter, still sick and weak, was in despair at the pain his friend was suffering. But Grandfather Fulman smiled full and gratefully at Jesse Broad.

'If he screams,' he said, 'he will pull through. Mark me, friend Jesse, I have seen frozen men many times. If he screams, he will live.'

The screams went on for a long time, as Mr Adamson applied more and more heat to Thomas Fox's body. At times they filled the forepart of the ship, drowned out even the roaring of wind and sea. At last the surgeon had him carried to the galley, to heat in front of the fire, and for a time the shrieks became unbearable. It was a nerve-jangling sound that made the nervous people yet more nervous. The atmosphere below decks was tense, passionate. Even aft, in the midshipmen's quarters, some of the noise filtered through, and with it the tension. The boys looked at each other from time to time, all their high spirits quelled. James Finch was very white.

Towards the end of the morning, when the screams had died away, Captain Swift ordered that all hands were to be assembled aft to witness punishment.

During the night the wind had moderated a little, but it was still blowing quite strong. The Welfare was butting against the north-rolling swell, throwing heavy sheets of spray the length of her deck every now and then. She was under reduced sail, making a fair speed in no great discomfort. But the bleakness of the scene, coupled with the bleakness of feeling reflected in the faces of so many of her people, affected William Bentley. He watched with a sensation approaching panic as the marine detachment were mustered on the quarterdeck. They had bayonets fixed and their pieces were charged and ready. Their faces appeared grim to him, filled with anticipation of some action. And the people, too, were frightening. Something wolfish in their eyes and jaws. Something hard and cold as they assembled in the cutting wind. At last they faced each other, these two bodies of men; the marines in their glaring red, the seamen in a nondescript variety of slop clothing. Gouts of spray occasionally drenched them. It flew at the necks of the seamen, into the faces of the marines. Neither body flinched at the icy assaults. Eyeball to eyeball they confronted each other, dripping and expectant.

Captain Swift arrived with a great amount of pomp. He was wearing a splendid blue coat, a brilliant white ruffled shirt, and a pair of cream breeches. He was smiling the while, and sniffing the air appreciatively. No surcoat or cloak; he did not acknowledge the coldness of the weather. He regarded the ship's company sunnily, as though this was the merest routine, as if nothing at all had happened. Behind him the man at the helm stolidly worked on, handing the spokes, meeting the seas. His eyes never left his task; flicked from binnacle, to sails, to approaching rollers, to binnacle again.

'Mr Allgood,' said Captain Swift, in a ringing, cheerful, voice. 'Are the people all assembled?'

The boatswain stepped forward.

'Aye aye sir,' he said. 'Every man-jack, sir. Save the sick, the lame, and the surgeon.'

The captain uttered a sort of laugh.

'And the shepherd boy?' he asked gaily.

William Bentley was nauseated. Sickness rose in his stomach. The scene blurred in front of his eyes. He almost staggered.

The boatswain's face was unchanging.

'Aye aye sir,' he said. 'He is ready with the surgeon.'

From below a screaming started. A movement went through the ranks of men, a low rumble. Heads turned to look forward, towards the sick-bay, then aft again, in some confusion. For the screaming was coming from aft. It was not Thomas Fox.

231

William Bentley, who was behind Swift, stepped slightly backwards as the first lieutenant spoke.

'The second, sir. He must be in pain.'

Without asking permission, banking on the hope that Swift might not see him, and in any case would not have time to recall him except by shouting, William stepped back yet farther, paused for a few moments, then almost crept to the hatchway. As he descended the ladder a pain lifted from his heart. He would suffer for this act afterwards, no doubt of it. But whatever the strength of Daniel Swift's rage might be, he could not stand this any more; he had to get below, he could not watch when the boy was brought to book. He went to Plumduff almost gratefully, fussed over the agonised man, mixed and administered his draught, and tried hard not to think.

His uncle, on the quarterdeck, had not lost his air of gaiety. Before the screams had died away he spoke again to the boatswain, pitching his voice a shade more harshly to carry to all the men.

'Ready is he? Good. Then in a few minutes, Mr Allgood, we will have him brought here to face his punishment.'

He regarded the ship's company with a half-smile; ran his eyes over them as if challenging them to show a sign of rebellion. Few men returned the gaze. They looked aft at him, true, but with the blank unseeing stare that said nothing. Jesse Broad allowed his eyes to flick at the captain's for an instant. They were odd, like statue's eyes, so pale, so very pale. Broad tightened his grip on the arm of little Peter, who he was half supporting. The boy gave a low groan of pain.

'Aye my lads,' Swift went on. His voice had taken on its punishment note, but the mocking smile was still upon his lips. 'Punishment is what that boy deserves, and this time I intend the punishment to be a fitting one. Any fool here who thinks a night on a topmast yard is punishment enough, must think I do not know what is going on on board this ship. Must think I do not know the smell of mutiny when it stinks in my nostrils . . . Mr Allgood.'

'Aye aye sir.'

'Send two of your mates, if you please. Now we will have the boy.'

When they were gone, Captain Swift continued.

'Aye, mutiny,' he said. 'Oh yes, brave lads, I know the smell of mutiny. That puling shepherd boy, so mock meek, so mock afraid. I know, as well as any man among you, what goes on in that black heart, behind that knock-kneed milk-and-water whining-pining face. I know.'

The Welfare butted her bow into an extra large sea. A solid sheet of spray rose high, then drove back over her deck. The front edge of the curtain drummed full into Swift's face, which disappeared from view for a second. As the water ran off him he emerged, hook nose first, the iron smile unchanged. He did not even shake his head.

'And I know too,' he continued, 'that Thomas Fox was not alone in this. No ringleader he, although a black plotter enough. When young Thomas deigns to join me aft today, I shall ask him who his fellows were. And he will tell me.'

The water from the drenching was dripping down Jesse Broad's back, but his shiver had little to do with the creeping chill. The captain's behaviour spoke madness to him, as did his eyes and smile and crazy, vibrant words. Before God, thought Jesse, he'll get nothing to satisfy him from Thomas, from poor innocent Thomas. And how will the captain act then?

'Those men before you,' said Captain Swift, with a gesture at the marines. 'You know them, with their leader, Captain Craig. They are part of my grand scheme today, you will see, my jolly boys, you will see. Thomas Fox has spent a night on the chill yardarm; he will tell us things to make some ears ring, eh? Captain Craig, please to draw your sword. I wish it to be held aloft. To serve, in some small way, as a reminder.'

The marine officer, standing to one side of his men impassively as ever, drew his sword. He held it rigidly in front of him, almost touching his face.

'Yes,' said Daniel Swift. 'Good then.'

At a noise from forward, Jesse Broad, along with many other men, turned his head. But the captain, his face contorted, barked an incoherent order and the rattans and rope's-ends flew. So the first view the people got of Thomas Fox was a back one.

He walked, or rather stumbled, between two burly boatswain's mates. Beside them, almost hovering, his shoulders bent anxiously, came the surgeon. He was clearly nervous, upset, his feet never still. He performed a sort of dance on the outskirts, as the frail boy was brought along, hanging, almost, between the men. Thomas Fox's head was down. So far down that from behind him Jesse Broad could see only a bent neck. He seemed shorter, his body bent, and curled in upon itself. When the mates halted, half turning towards the captain, his face was still hidden from Broad. Slumped low on his chest, and lost behind the bulk of his helpers.

Adamson went up to the captain in a helpless, nervous way.

'Sir,' he said. 'I think I have to say . . . This boy, sir—'

'Shut your mouth, Mr Adamson, or I will have you put in irons.'

The tiny surgeon shrugged and took one or two faltering, dance-like steps.

'But sir, I think—'

'Mr Allgood, have that scoundrel silenced!'

'All right, sir,' gasped Adamson. 'All right. Let me but stay on deck in case of . . . I will say nothing, sir. Forgive me.'

A mate looked enquiringly at Allgood, who shook his head. The surgeon stepped back into the ranks of the people, near the ship's side. Swift took a pace or two away from Fox, looked straight at him.

'Can you not look up, my boy?' he asked gently. 'Can you not raise your tired head to listen to your captain? Can you not stand upon your own two feet?'

Thomas Fox did not respond. Not a man in the ship's company or the detachment of marines moved a muscle. Not an officer stirred. Only the helmsman, easing a couple of spokes to meet a sea. From binnacle to luff, from luff to waves, from waves to binnacle. His eyes were never still.

'I wonder if you are even listening, Thomas?' Captain Swift went on. 'I wonder if you can hear me? Or are you just ashamed? Is that it, eh? Shame has made you dumb? Shame has made you hang your head? Oh Thomas, try to look at me.'

Somewhere deep inside his head, Thomas made out the captain's voice. It came from afar, through a cold, soft, woolly void. He tried to open his eyes but nothing happened. He tried to make out the words but could not. He made a superhuman effort to take his weight upon his legs but the pain was sudden and intense.

'You are a fine example, friend Thomas, of a very vicious breed,' Daniel Swift was saying. It was clear to Broad that he was hardly talking to the boy, but was talking to himself, and them all. His voice was gentle, contemplative. 'You are a fine example of the breed that returns love with hatred and trust with treachery. You are a snake in the grass.'

There was still no response from the shepherd boy. But the people were listening intently, almost rapt. Good God, thought Jesse, Swift believes it all. He thinks he's been betrayed!

As if he had plucked the thought from his brain, the captain said: 'You have betrayed me, Thomas, after the kindness I have shown you. And you are a picture of the blackness in the hearts of your fellows. All, all, would betray me, who has only done his best by them. Oh, it is vile.'

To Broad's astonished eyes, Swift looked actually miserable. The fine arrogance of his hawkish profile was blurred somehow. He looked at the boy before him, then at all his men, with an air of sadness. He believes it, thought Jesse Broad. Now God help us all, he believes he has done his best and we have turned against him!

Suddenly, Swift's face changed. It darkened. The muscles in his cheeks bunched. His pale eyes bulged and his breath hissed in his nostrils.

'You there!' he screeched at the startled mates. 'Let him go! He will stand alone, or before God I will strike him dead!'

The mates let go immediately. Thomas Fox, without a sigh, crumpled into a heap between them.

Swift looked as if he must explode. His face became almost black. He rose up onto the points of his toes and remained there, his fists clenched, his breath grinding in his throat.

'Pick him up.' He was choked, could hardly speak. The mates picked the boy up, his head hanging limply. His face was blotched, with dead white patches where the ice had bitten deep. His eyes were closed.

Captain Swift took two quick paces forward and slapped each side of his face hard.

'Fox! Fox! Listen to me. Stand, boy! Stand! Or it will be the worse for you! Do you hear! Do you hear!'

Deep inside, Thomas Fox heard. He put all the life inside him into the effort. He pressed upwards with his legs. The pain was dull but violent. He gasped.

Captain Swift let out a shriek.

'Haha! He understands! Now, leave him go!'

235

This time the mates eased their grip less swiftly. For perhaps two seconds the boy supported himself between them. As he crumpled they made to grab him, but the captain flew at them, screaming with rage.

At the bottom of the ladder, William Bentley heard the noise and his blood ran cold. He had been listening, his horror ever deepening. Now he rested his forehead against the rough wood, closing his eyes. He remembered the pistols in the alcove in his uncle's cabin. He began to pray.

Captain Swift retired to a distance of several feet from Thomas Fox while he was hauled to his feet again. This time, after some seconds, the boy opened his eyes. It was a great effort, and he geared himself to it with all the determination left in his soul. He tried to focus, but there was nothing. A few hazy shapes, a vague roaring noise. That and the captain's voice; it was all he could make out.

'Thomas Fox,' came the voice, and this time, for the first time, he truly heard, his brain knew he was being addressed. 'Thomas Fox, I want their names. Thomas Fox, look at me, boy. I want their names.'

He felt one of the boatswain's mates let go of his arm, and braced himself to try and stand alone. A rattling came from his throat as his breathing quickened with the effort. It was an all-consuming effort, and he could not try to understand the question at the same time, even when it was repeated.

'Their names, Thomas Fox. What are their names?'

The words throbbed in his head. Names? Names? What names? The other boatswain's mate slowly released his fingers and Thomas took the strain. He swayed, was pushed upright again, swayed the other way. The breath groaned in his throat.

Jesse Broad watched the struggle like the other men. They were fascinated. By the display of willpower by the youth, of fanatical single-mindedness by the man. The two were six feet apart, Fox swaying like a drunk, his eyes swimming in his blotched and horrible face, the captain crouched like a fighter waiting to spring. His eyes were pale and bright, his tongue protruding slightly from his lips. When he spoke his voice was high and piercing.

'Thomas Fox, I want their names. All their names. I will have your fellow mutineers from you, my boy, if it is the last thing I ever do. Their names, scum! Their names!'

236

Fox heard all this. It went into his head and lodged there. But it was incomprehensible. It was meaningless. He took a step forward, and he tried to speak. He tried to say something quite simple, to form a simple question, to convey his lack of understanding. But only a strange and ugly sound came out; a liquid, growling, sob-like noise. It was loud, quite loud. And very horrible.

As Thomas took his stumbling step, the Welfare lifted to a big sea which threw her weather side high. The step became a stumble, the stumble a shambling run. Thomas Fox put out his hands and skittered down the sloping deck. His mouth was wide, the sobbing groan an inarticulate roar. His eyes were open, white and rolling, as he bore down on Captain Swift.

The whole ship's company swayed in unison as the big sea rolled under her. Fox, caught on the point of balance, swayed once more and would have run backwards as the deck sloped the other way. He was a foot from Captain Swift now, his eyes open, his stare wild.

But Swift's face was wilder. As the boy had run towards him he had retreated down the deck as if in terror. His face was riveted on Fox's, as though he were looking at something frightful, something black and unknown. The slobbering boy stood before him, the gurgle rattling in his throat. Captain Swift's mouth was open, his eyes were wild, his face was terribly pale.

She rolled heavily. The clutching hands of the boy reached for the throat, the coat, the shoulders of the man. Swift gave his own cry now, loud and strange. He jumped backwards to the bulwarks. He seized an iron belaying pin from the rail. As the boy staggered open-armed towards him he swung the pin from behind his back with all the strength in his body.

He held the belaying pin by its lighter end, and the swing was enormous. The shaped metal of the heavy end landed square across Thomas Fox's face, on the bridge of his nose. The crunching of bone as his forehead and eye-sockets caved in was clearly audible. It was the only sound from Thomas Fox. He folded to the deck instantly, a vivid gush of blood rising into the air then splashing onto the planks.

Swift stood without sound or movement, his face drained, staring downwards. All the men were silent, as Thomas Fox's bright blood pulsed out over the deck. The wind moaned in the rigging, the steep seas slapped and gurgled along the Welfare's sides.

237

At the helm, nothing had changed. Hand a few spokes, down helm to meet it, up helm to sail her. Close-hauled and watch the luff. Luff, water, binnacle; binnacle, water, luff. The Welfare sighed as a stronger gust took her. The helmsman eased a spoke or two through his hands as she tried to head it. She dipped her bow and battered onwards.

Twenty-Seven

The silence went on and on. To Jesse Broad it seemed endless. His eyes were stretched and his mouth was open. He was gripped by a sense of total strangeness, incapable of movement. The spray-washed deck, the red-coated marines in line before him, the cold wind moaning in the sails and cordage. And there by the lee rail, the white-faced captain, still holding the bloody pin. Broad could not see Thomas Fox through the press of men in front of him, but he could see Swift, and he could see the marines, and he could see the marine officer, whose face was tense and horrified.

Broad could also see Mr Allgood, and it was Allgood who broke the spell. After the timeless, awful, pause he lifted his great head to heaven and opened his mouth.

From it came not a shout, not a cry, but a deep, throbbing groan. Then the boatswain raised his huge hand slowly to his face and pressed it to his eyes.

As if in answer to the groan, a groundswell of noise came from the ship's people. It came from many, many throats, not loud in each, but building up to a sighing, pulsing sound. Still nobody moved, but the noise got louder and louder. Beside Jesse Broad, red-haired Peter added a new note of his own, a shrill, piping, monotonous scream. The thin noise was taken up by other boys, and then by men. A sense of hysteria grew. Broad felt himself grow light, and mad, and hollow. The body of men began to sway. The noise took on a baying tone, a lonely howling.

With a sudden, swift movement, the captain pitched the belaying pin over the side and drew his sword.

'Craig!' he yelled. 'Do your duty!'

The captain of marines jumped. He looked at the swaying body of men. He turned abruptly to his soldiers.

'Cover them, cover them!'

239

The marines moved their muskets to their shoulders quickly and efficiently. Jesse Broad saw a line of muzzles, behind the glittering steel of the bayonets. But his mouth was still open, sound was still pouring from it. With the other bodies all round him, the swaying got greater and greater.

Captain Swift had perched himself on a rail at the bulwarks so that he looked down at the men. He screeched to Craig: 'Fire, damn you! Fire! They have gone mad!'

Craig looked bemused. He stared down at the moving, ululating body of seamen. His sword wavered. Gradually, the men started to move forward.

'Fire, damn you! Fire!' screamed Daniel Swift. His face was black with rage, his sword trembled violently in his fist.

The marine officer raised his sword in a decisive sweep.

'At the front rank!' he cried. 'Prepare to fire!'

With an amazing suddenness, the noise ceased. The ship's people, as if at a signal, became deathly quiet. The swaying continued, but only from momentum. It slowly got less until they were still. A bitter curtain of spray drenched men and soldiers as they silently faced each other.

Daniel Swift turned from the people to the officer of marines. His voice was thick.

'Fire, damn you Craig. Fire, I tell you.'

Jesse Broad saw the marine officer swallow. He looked at the captain, then at his red-coated men. The sword wavered. Slowly his mouth opened.

But Swift spoke before him, choking this time on the word.

'*Fire!*'

There was a single bang and a gasp from the ship's company. Broad and many around him uttered small cries of shock. Everyone looked about to see who had been hit, who had fired. A small cloud of blue smoke was torn away aft. It had come from one musket, from one soldier. Broad stared at the man, a tall, ordinary-looking fellow. The other marines were staring too, and exchanging frightened glances. The man looked sick, panicky; but defiant.

And who was shot? Broad tore his eyes off the man who had fired as a ragged shout went up.

Captain Craig's sword dropped with a clang, bounced once, and landed at the feet of Henry Joyce, who was in the front row. The captain of marines, without uttering any sound, crumpled at the knees and fell to the deck. He did not move again.

Jesse Broad's voice joined in the howl that burst from the people. His body joined in the mad lunge towards the quarterdeck. Like those all around him he became blind to reason or thought in the great surge aft. He did not find a weapon, like many of the others; he did not tear at flesh with his bare hands, for which he later thanked God. But he did become a wild man, a screaming, vengeful thing. He was part of the explosion of hate, revenge, and energy that tore through the Welfare.

After the first madness, though, he became lost in the confusion. The marines on the quarterdeck had opened fire, that much he could tell. There was a volley of shots, and the acrid smell of burnt powder. But whether they were firing at the people, or at each other, or both, he did not know. Balls whistled about the crowded decks and he saw two men fall. Peter fell too, not from a wound but from his great weakness after the flogging. Jesse Broad tried hard to reach him, but the lad disappeared under dozens of trampling feet. It was impossible to break through the struggling hordes.

A great roaring, of many many seamen, was split by screams. At one moment, pushed out of the mass as it staggered drunkenly on the rolling deck, Broad saw a dreadful sight. Higgins, the third lieutenant, was caught by a mob at the mizzen shrouds. He was trying to beat them off with an iron belaying pin, yelling the while. As Jesse watched, the pin was jerked from his hand and five or six seamen grabbed him. Within a split second he was upended, taken by feet and hands, and sent spinning over the side into the grey rollers.

A frantic cannonade went up from the canvas shortly after this. Broad saw that the wheel had finally been abandoned. He wondered dully if the man had been killed or had at last been jerked out of the reverie of concentration that had held him for so long. There was another thunderous clapping and the decks shook ominously, stirring his seaman's instincts. Even under short sail, in this wind the Welfare was in deadly danger. Caught by a gust or blown across sea and wind she might roll her masts out or even roll over. He thought of Matthews, wondered where he was. Christ, he had wanted this mutiny, had wanted the decks thick with blood, had he not? Well, thick they were, and slimy, and where was Matthews now?

241

Down below, a separate rampage took place. William Bentley, hidden in the alcove in his uncle's cabin, heard and vaguely saw awful things. He heard the smashing of wood and the breaking of glass as men sought the first liquor they could lay their hands on. He heard the laughter and the screams as the second lieutenant was woken from his drugged sleep and stabbed and beaten to death. He heard the awful pulsing roars from the deck above, and the gunfire.

William Bentley did not blame himself for cowardice. He had heard the beginning of the affair and he had gone to his uncle's cabin in mental agony to seek the pistols. But he had not known on whom they should be turned. What had happened up there? What had brought about that terrifying noise? Had Thomas Fox been shot? Or his uncle? He had stared long at the big horse-pistols, strange and out of place in the hands of a boy at sea. He felt a boy; a lost boy, dreadfully alone. As the mutiny got under way, as the ragged shooting and the roaring of so many men rolled in waves down the hatchways, as dozens of armed seamen burst about the officers' accommodation, he knew that he could do nothing at first but hide. If he could help to fight the mutiny it must be later. To show himself now would just mean instant death.

It was the loss of the helmsman that indirectly brought the fighting to an end. Jesse Broad had made contact with Matthews at last, and the two of them had got behind one of the boats to talk. The struggle was still raging aft, with the opposing sides more clearly defined. A knot of men, with Mr Robinson and Daniel Swift certainly among them, were holding out fiercely around the mizzen mast. They were under heavy attack from a far greater number of seamen and marines, led by Henry Joyce and his cronies. Cutlasses had been broken out and the musketry was far more sporadic. The marines who had stayed on the side of authority were using bayonets.

'We must try to stop it somehow,' said Jesse Broad. 'It is horrible. It is unbearable.'

'Aye,' Matthews replied, shaking his long, sombre head. 'It is a bloodbath. Believe me, Jesse, I had not this sort of villainy in mind.'

'Ah but the villain himself, the villain himself,' said Broad. 'My poor Thomas, that luckless boy.'

There was between them and the quarterdeck a group of men who had left the fighting. They were standing about as if in a daze, gazing about at the littered corpses and wounded. Some held bloody cutlasses drooping in their hands. One or two were weeping. As the Welfare lurched and another thunderous beating of canvas came from aloft, Mr Allgood emerged from the group. His face was covered in blood and one arm hung limp beside him. He stared aloft, then shook his head. Matthews hailed him.

'Ahoy! Mr Allgood! Here by the cutter! Quick man!'

The boatswain shook his bull head again and began to walk towards them. He seemed drawn by the note of authority in Matthews's voice. Jesse Broad himself was startled by it.

'Here man,' said Matthews, when Allgood arrived. 'We have got to get this ship under control. She will beat herself to pieces else.'

The huge warrant officer stared at Matthews unseeingly. He blinked red-rimmed eyes. His face was livid and bloody. He looked beaten, hurt.

'Oh God,' he said at last. 'Oh God, what have I done? Oh God, the shame of it.'

There was a rending explosion from aloft as a topsail split.

'For God's sake, man!' snapped Matthews. 'Pull yourself together!'

But Allgood mumbled on.

'I started it,' he said. 'The boatswain, me, Jack Allgood. To raise a hand against an officer. To start a mutiny in His Majesty's Navy. Oh God.'

Jesse Broad felt a flash of anger.

'You started nothing, Mister,' he said. 'Have you forgot the boy so quick? Have you forgot what Swift did to that poor boy? You are dazed, you have been hit. Remember Thomas, that is all!'

The eyes cleared a little.

'Ah true,' he said. 'Most true. The man is a villain, double-dyed. But to mutiny, Jesse Broad, to raise a hand against an officer of the King . . .'

Matthews spoke now much like an officer. His lean face had hardened. His great jaw jutted with determination.

'Your feelings do you credit, Jack Allgood. But consider this: although the deed is done now, we can yet save something from it. We can save the Welfare for a start. And next we can stop the bloodbath. But Christ, we must be quick!'

As if to prove him right, the ship staggered to a big grey sea. She was falling off fast now, lying almost in the troughs, and the wave

243

broke right over her side and rushed across the waist. The broken bodies of men and boys were lifted and moved along like sodden logs. At the same time there was a splintering crash from aloft as a spar carried away.

Allgood stared at Matthews.

'We will be hanged,' he said. 'It is too late to change sides now, my friend. We will be hanged.'

'For God's sake!' shouted Matthews. 'Just get to work damn you, get to work. You will not be hanged, Jack Allgood, depend on me. Nor will you change sides. But get to work, before you drown yourself and all the lot of us.'

The boatswain made his decision. He turned about, strode to the men in the waist, and began yelling orders at them. At first they seemed disinclined to move, but he laid about him with the flat of a cutlass and suddenly they began to jump. Matthews looked at Broad with half a smile.

'He'll save the ship, all right,' he said. 'Now let us go and save the owner.' He paused, and the smile deepened. 'The ex-owner,' he added, simply.

On their way aft they found muskets that had not been fired in the chaos. Broad went up the lee shrouds of the mizzen a few yards and Matthews up the weather. They positioned themselves firmly in the rigging and trained their weapons on the struggling men below.

Jesse Broad was sickened by the carnage he saw. The captain, startlingly visible in his fine and gaudy clothes, was fighting like a demon, the centre of energy of a fair-sized group of men. All around the edges of this group there was a low wall of dead and wounded. Around that wall again, on the outside, was a ring of mutineers. The centre of *their* energy was the monstrous figure of Henry Joyce. He still held the marine officer's light sword in his left hand, broken off six inches from the point. But in his right was the weapon most suited to him; a great curved cutlass that he wielded like a toy.

They were not making much noise any more; the fight had been a long, exhausting one. Matthews's voice, a voice of brass, caused a dozen heads to lift.

'Ahoy!' he roared. 'Ahoy below! You will put up your weapons this instant. The mutiny is over. We have won!'

The fighting faltered. But Captain Swift was not impressed, nor was Henry Joyce.

The captain shouted: 'To hell with you! Come, my brave lads, fight on!'

And Joyce, like a refrain, roared: 'Kill the bastards, kill the bastards, kill, kill!'

Some of the impetus was gone, however. Men on the fringes backed off. Matthews shouted: 'We have a musket trained upon you, Captain Swift. Surrender with your men or you must surely die. Surrender.'

More and more men drew back. The clash of cutlasses grew less.

'And you, Henry Joyce!' said Matthews. 'We have you covered. Call off your party or we will shoot.'

Henry Joyce turned up his weird bald head in fury.

'Are you traitors, you bastards! For I'll die fighting till I've spilled his murderous blood!'

The sound of clashing steel had almost died. The panting circles looked at each other, and the men aloft.

'Not traitors, Henry, but not butchers neither. And are you? And are all your men? We have won, we have brought the villain low. Shall we now behave like him? Shall we now be as black as that black devil?'

The argument won through to many of the men. The sound of steel on steel had ceased. Henry Joyce's heavy-bearded face looked aloft, then round the outer ring of tired men. Blood from his upraised cutlass coursed backwards, dripping from the guard. He grunted.

Captain Swift, his pale eyes gleaming, seized the chance.

'Good man!' he cried. 'Good man! By God, whatever your name is, and you too, Jesse Broad, you'll not regret this hour's work! I'll shower guineas on you till your pockets groan. When these scum swing you'll stand beside me in full honour. Your fortunes are made, lads, depend on it. I will see you rich men for this hour's work.'

Broad's eyes, sighting down the barrel of his musket at the captain's handsome head, raised themselves in horror to the figure of his companion in the weather shrouds. He was deeply disturbed by the captain's words. Henry Joyce gave an animal roar of anger. Spittle sprayed from his lips as he barked his hatred.

245

'So, you filthy bastard, Matthews! You'd be bribed, would you? You'd sell your shipmates to this demon, would you? Well damn you then, but I'll die fighting anyway!'

'Do not heed him, Matthews!' cried Swift. 'He is a mutineer and murderer. All will swing, all! But you will be a rich man, that I promise you!'

The two camps squared up once more, and Broad still stared at Matthews. Before the factions could come to blows, however, the brazen voice of his companion stilled their arms.

'I do not want your riches, Captain Swift, nor yet your filthy blood. You may offer me all the world but I will see you in hell before I take it. Likewise you, Joyce. You will die by my hand, I promise you, if you scratch but one more fellow's skin. This filthy bloodshed is over. It is over! Now put up, put up! Another word, Swift, and you die!'

For some minutes, below in his alcove, William Bentley had known it was time to move. The uncontrolled, dangerous motion of the Welfare had been arrested. She had fought and lunged and shivered for a great age, her timbers shrieking sometimes with the unaccustomed strains. Now she had settled down. She rolled and swooped, but in a normal, patterned way. The ship was under command and sailing. The noises, too, had died. No more men had plundered and shouted in the captain's cabin or the officers'. Below decks she was bereft of voices, strangely empty of her teeming men.

He did not know what to do, but he knew he must do something. It appeared to him most unlikely that the mutineers had failed, most unlikely that he would find his uncle alive, or indeed any of the officers. He had a damned fair idea of Plumduff's fate, and of his own if he appeared among the glorying crew and was taken. But he knew he had to act.

In the long time of silence behind the heavy curtain, in the long minutes after all frantic noise had ceased, William Bentley had tried hard to make a decision about right and wrong. He had a vision of monstrosity concerning Thomas Fox that almost choked him; he had a distaste for his uncle's excesses of conduct that amounted to physical horror, that made his muscles crack with tension and his flesh crawl. And yet – and yet ... Mutiny. Ah

Christ, no, it was impossible. And gunfire, and Plumduff, and such filthy mindless beasts as Henry Joyce.

He made the climax of revulsion and confusion project him from the alcove. The pistols were ready, heavy and reassuring in his hands. He moved swiftly and quietly to the door of the cabin, which was swinging open, and looked forward along the dark and silent deck. He took a step, then stopped. If he went forward, if he reached the upper deck from that direction, he could only be taken, it was inevitable. He must try for surprise.

As William turned to go back into the captain's cabin, there was a movement in the dimness before him. He froze, his eyes glaring at the dark shadows around the hatchway to the deck below. He pressed himself behind the door, one long pistol hanging ready by his side to be jerked up and fired. He waited.

There was an odd sighing noise as the shadow moved again. A sighing and a shuffling. It was a man, climbing from the lower deck. He was breathing noisily, almost panting, with the queer sighs intermixed. If no one challenges this noisy item, thought William, at least it will prove the place empty. He waited, impatient and afraid.

As the figure crawled into a lighter patch he came near to gasping. The object had on a wig, and a pair of bent-wire spectacles, and was drunk by the look of it, dead drunk. On an impulse he went up to the crouching figure and spoke; it was worth a try.

'Mr Marner,' he hissed. 'Mr Marner it is I, Will Bentley. Pull yourself together man, and quickly. I need your help.'

He supposed that Marner had been skulking below all the time, had missed it all, rolled in his blankets, and had been missed in his turn by the wandering mutineers. He jerked at the old schoolmaster's shoulder none too gently.

'Get up, damn you, and listen. We will find you an arm. This ship has fallen to a mutiny, Mr Marner, and we are the only men left free. Do you hear me, sir, do you hear me? You are a gentleman, God help us, and you will aid me in this. Do you understand?'

The filthy, drunk old man was on his hands and knees. Very slowly he pushed his trunk upwards until only his knuckles were on the deck. His face was pale beneath its sheen of dirt. He was dribbling a little, trying to form a smile.

247

'Mr Bentley,' he mumbled, and his voice was slurred. 'If you care to go below, sir, to our quarters, you will find your little friend. Little Jimmy Finch, sir, little Jimmy Finch, God rest his soul. They stuck him, sir, like a squealing pig, and I will not tell you where. He is dead. Oh very very dead.'

Mr Marner dropped forward on his hands again, and let out a drunken cackle.

'And I hope,' he said, when he had got his breath, 'I hope, oh how I hope, that when they catch you, sir, they'll do the same to you.'

He slowly sank as his elbows gave way. He was old, and stinking, and unsavoury. William Bentley regarded him through tears. He pulled a sleeve roughly across his blinded eyes and dashed aft through the captain's cabin.

On deck, a very strange situation had come about. After the explosion of energy and hatred, an odd, dislocated calm had settled over the ship. Captain Swift, with all the loyal men, had been gathered on the quarterdeck, penned in at musket-point by the marines who had joined the mutiny. They were disarmed, and ragged, and bloody, some lying on the planks still bleeding while their fellows made rough tourniquets and bandages. There was an air of dull expectation, of awaiting their fate. Which could only be putting over the side, in boats, to sink or swim.

The mutineers, if anything, were even more upset. It appeared that Matthews was in command, with Jesse Broad his right-hand man. Henry Joyce, a cutlass through his belt and two pistols in a band across his chest, hovered near them with a dangerous, arrogant air. His cronies, now half drunk, stayed close by, also heavily armed. Mr Allgood, with the ship under way and safe again, had gone to the waist, where he stood grasping the main lee shrouds and gazing morosely across the grey waste of water. He had taken no part in the proceedings, and refused to answer when Matthews had tried to make him speak. Around the mainmast was the largest group; the seamen who were definitely 'in' but were desperately unhappy. They sought work to occupy their minds – had started off by hurling overboard the many corpses of their shipmates – but had a hopeless air of anxiety and distress. Their injured were in front of them, and Mr Adamson was moving around with brandy and bandages. He had not yet attended to the captain's party.

It was this silent, grim scene that met William Bentley's eyes as he looked cautiously over the taffrail after climbing from one of the stern windows of the cabin. He took in the great pools of blood that lay around, and the awful wounds that many carried. He saw the tired greyness of all their faces, the stooped, exhausted look of mutineers and captives. No one was looking aft.

Almost without thinking he hauled himself over the rail and walked to within point-blank range of Matthews, Broad and Joyce. His pistols were cocked, primed, and rock-steady.

'In the name of the King,' he shouted, and his voice nearly broke on it. 'And the powers vested in me by the Articles of War. I place you under arrest. Drop your weapons.'

Twenty-Eight

The voice cut into Jesse Broad's brain like a knife. He recognised it, high and unsteady though it was, and it flashed through his mind that he had not seen the boy since he slipped away before Thomas Fox was murdered. He turned slowly and faced Bentley. The midshipman was still dressed in blue, still unbloodied and unhurt, still unsweaty; unique among the men on board. His face under his blond hair was quivering with strain. His eyes flickered from the three of them, to the captain's party, to the waist of the ship. But the pistols were steady, and close. Broad, who had only a knife in his belt, dropped it to the deck with a clatter.

He watched the faces of Matthews and Joyce. Matthews's gave away nothing. The lantern jaw, the secret eyes, the tight mouth. He dropped his musket and a pistol, gazing at the boy. Henry Joyce was different. His eyes rolled in his wild, hairy, filthy face. His lips twisted with rage and hatred. A thick growling came from his throat. It seemed for a moment as if he would make a lunge.

William Bentley made a vivid gesture with the horse-pistol in his right hand.

'I count to two,' he said. His voice was transformed, steady. There was a note almost of menace in it. 'One . . .'

In all this time, and it seemed an age to Broad, although it was merely seconds, no one else on the quarterdeck had moved. The marines still trained their muskets on Swift and his men, the captain stared with the rest at the form of Bentley. Breathing was suspended as he confronted the bull of a man who defied him. It did not take Joyce long to make his decision. The muzzle of the pistol was only three feet from his bulging stomach. He pulled out the pistols between finger and thumb and dropped them. The cutlass followed.

'Stand by the rail,' said Bentley. The three men moved across.

Still there was quiet. The men in the waist had seen what was happening now. The air of fear and uncertainty grew.

Jesse Broad was in a turmoil. The nightmare was becoming too much to bear. The death of the poor boy, the dreadful bloodbath, the awful fact of what they had done and what they must suffer for it if they were ever brought to justice. But at least it had been over; for a while the business had been half simple: they could only go on, and they had ended the bloodshed. Now here was chaos again. One boy with two pistols, the marines and mutineers with muskets guarding the captain, and in the waist frightened, sickened men, some armed. It would need very little, practically nothing, to make them attempt a counter-mutiny, to change sides in the hope of being pardoned in the courts for their part in the first revolt.

William Bentley was well aware that the time he had was brief. Every nerve in his body was screaming with tension. He looked at the group around his uncle, and he knew he could not disarm them. So he began to speak.

'Men,' he said. 'You must give up this desperate lunacy now. A frightful thing has happened and we must all be blasted in the sight of God. But it is not too late.'

A roar of rage came from Henry Joyce's throat, but William Bentley turned on him in a kind of frenzy.

'Shut up!' he shouted. 'You shall not take these men to death!'

A low moan of wind swept over the decks, followed by an icy sheet of spray. But no man made a sound any more. All eyes were on the small, determined figure. All eyes, except those of the new man to the helm. For the ceaseless task of keeping the Welfare alive in the sea had resumed. He stood straddle-legged at the wheel, handing spokes. It struck Jesse Broad as somehow desolate, somehow fateful. The whole thing was nightmarish; messy and unreal. All this hell breaking loose, and still she battered south, still a man handed spokes and met the seas, impervious.

William Bentley spoke on.

'You men guarding Captain Swift. You must put up your muskets immediately. You must cease this madness immediately. It is hopeless, you can see this now. It is hopeless.' He paused. 'Men, there has been a mutiny. I can offer no hope for those who took part, saving this: When you are brought to justice, you will

251

get a fair trial. And if you cease your folly now it will be taken into account. It will be noted. It will not be overlooked.'

He could feel sweat running down his back and sides. He blinked as sweat poured into his eye-corners from his forehead. It was taking too long. He must make them drop their muskets. It was taking too long.

'There have been faults,' he said. His voice had gone shrill, like Jack Evans's. Good God, where was Evans? He could not see him in the group. 'Yes, faults,' he stumbled on, crushing the thought. 'On this ship, the Welfare, things have happened that should not. Yes.' He was panting suddenly, the sweat coursing down his body. 'Well listen, men, I make my pledge. Put up your arms now, this instant, and I will hide nothing at your trial. No, nothing, not the least small thing. Everything shall be told.'

Many of the men in the waist had moved aft. They were in a ragged line, reminiscent of how they had stood each day, before the holocaust, to witness punishment. Their weapons had been abandoned. There was a weird look on their faces, a look of bemused hope. Jesse Broad noticed Allgood among their number. On his face there was another expression; of supplication. Shame and supplication. The boatswain looked like a whipped dog. Broad had a huge sadness in him, for himself and all of them. He too wanted to believe the boy; indeed he did believe that he would tell the Welfare's dreadful story. But he knew it would not stop them hanging. Anyway, Bentley could not bring it off even now; the odds were impossible.

Before Bentley said another word, however, one of the marines guarding Captain Swift threw down his musket. A half-minute passed. Then a comrade followed suit. A silent minute, then down went another. Then a fourth, a fifth, then several more at once. A jumble of excited noise rose from the deck.

Hope flooded William Bentley. He licked his lips and swallowed. If only, if only. The heavy pistols were making his arms ache badly, the grips were slippery in his sweating palms. Another musket went down, and another. The marines and seamen with muskets still trained were looking shifty, uncomfortable, even terrified.

He said triumphantly: 'You men, do not be left behind! Do not be alone beyond the Pale! Quickly, quickly, put up your arms!'

For a few seconds, for a few short seconds, it looked as though he

252

would bring it off. More muskets were discarded, until only three or four were levelled at the group. Then Daniel Swift spoke, his voice shaking with exultation. He faced the last muskets boldly, his eyes flaying the unhappy mutineers. He was almost bursting with contempt.

'Put them up, you scum!' he cried. 'That's right, you dirty sons of whores, put up those muskets. Oh Christ I'm not afraid of you! Now put them up!'

William Bentley almost closed his eyes in horror. Oh uncle, uncle, he shouted inwardly, leave it be, leave it be!

'Shoot me in cold blood would you, you scum,' yelled Swift. 'Ah no, I know you will not, for you are cowards all! All of you, all! Scum and cowards!'

The men with the muskets wavered. A low rumble rose from the waist and rolled aft. Swift had his head back now, his pale eyes glaring, his hawk nose raking the air. You fool, thought Bentley passionately. Oh God damn you uncle, for a fool!

Jesse Broad watched the scene almost mesmerised. The captain's arrogance, his idiocy, his total lack of imagination, amazed him. It was somehow as though the battle were between *them* now, the boy and his uncle. A movement aft caught his eye. Ah dear God, then that was it. The boy had lost.

The man who had climbed the taffrail from the cabin was one of Joyce's clique. A tall, raw-boned fellow called Madesly. He had a half-drunk leer on his slack lips, but trod the deck delicately as a dancer; he was a fine seaman. In his hand he carried a capstan bar. In his belt he wore a cutlass. As he slipped across the deck Swift's voice changed. A note of alarm. A warning shout.

William Bentley half turned. He had only time to see a form, to throw up his arm in protection. The heavy bar hit his wrist, breaking it. The gun rose into the air, discharging itself harmlessly into the rigging. The wood crashed into his head and he sprawled unconscious.

Henry Joyce gave a roar and sprang for the other horse-pistol. He held it close to William Bentley's bleeding head and pulled the trigger. The gun misfired.

Before anything else could happen, before more violence could break out, Matthews and Broad had armed themselves. Broad, cold with anger, covered Henry Joyce and Madesly.

'Daniel Swift,' said Matthews. 'One move, one word, and you are a dead man. Your hopes are at an end.'

The sense of dislocation and unreality that had followed the first revolt had been dispelled in large measure by Swift's unbending hatred. There was a sense of fury following his latest action, a furious urgency to get him overboard before he could wreak more madness. The men who had dropped their guns rearmed, even many of those in the waist, and at a few orders from Matthews and Broad they began to prepare boats in combined and definite anger and purpose. Henry Joyce curbed his instincts and those of his gang to seize power after Matthews pointed out, in a brief confrontation, that he was the only man who could navigate. But it was not in Matthews's control, nor Broad's, to prevent Joyce and company making off in the direction of the spirits room. It would not be long before drunkenness would be the order of the day.

At first, Jack Allgood took no part in what went on. He still seemed stunned, disgusted, by the whole affair and his part in it. But in the end he organised the work on the boats, if only out of habit. Broad, watching the great sad face, guessed something of what the boatswain must be thinking. A life in the Navy and a life of pride all gone, blown away for ever. He prepared the boats like a labour of love; but all it represented was lost to him.

When Daniel Swift and his men were lined up and counted, the problems for the self-appointed leaders of the mutineers became more difficult. There were hardly enough boats to take all the loyals if the Welfare was to be left with sufficient. In the cold greyness of the afternoon, the desires of some of the guilty to be counted among the innocent also grew. The captain, ever hopeful, tried to work on it.

'You are aware of what will happen when you are caught, I hope,' he told Matthews loudly at one point, after a wrangle about the stores they were to be allowed. 'And you will be caught I promise you. This is one of the vilest acts that ever I have heard of. You may be sure that His Majesty's Navy will avenge this bloody day, if it takes an hundred years.'

He stared around at some of the mutineers. A large number of them were still shifty; restless and unhappy.

'Why do you fall in with it, you fools?' he demanded. 'Why do you listen to this villain? You have guns, rise up now and use them.

Take over this ship again and I will make sure you do not hang. I can guarantee it as my word of honour.'

'Shut your mouth,' Matthews snarled. He turned to the men who hung about. 'He talks of honour and you do not laugh? Good God he is a monster!'

Later, Swift tried another tack. The three boats Broad and Matthews had agreed to let go were laden with provisions. Nearly fifty men were due to be embarked in them.

'You murderers, you bloody murderers,' suddenly yelled the captain. 'Will you put us to drown in this freezing ocean? Is not your deed already black enough? Will you go against the laws of God now, as well as those of man? We cannot live in those three boats!'

The guards and helpers, ever more jumpy as the long slow time wore on, glanced about at each other. The sea was high and lumpy, the wind cold and ominous. Even Jesse Broad was fearful for the safety of the loyal men. He knew small boats, and these would be overloaded and in frightful waters. Matthews, however, was un-moved.

'You are a villain, Daniel Swift,' he said coldly. 'You know as well as I do that you have a chance. This wind will blow you to Good Hope even southerly as it is. And as you know it is a freak in any case. It will turn westerly soon. The gale is almost gone and there is west in it already. It will blow you to Cape Town in a jiffy.'

'A chance! A chance! That is all you allow to fifty souls, is it? A chance, you murderer!'

'Ach shut your mouth,' said Matthews in disgust. 'You are the murderer, captain, and we shall not forget it.' He spoke to Mr Robinson, who stood close by Swift. 'You sir, you are a trusty man. You are not afraid, I suppose, to sail to Cape Town?'

The ugly little master stared for such a long time without a word that Jesse Broad thought he would not speak. But he did.

'I have no fear of anything my God may send,' he said. 'Except some men. To sail to Cape Town? No, I am not afraid. We might even make the port. And if we do, sir – then may the Lord have mercy on you.'

A burst of drunken cheering drifted from the after hatchway. Jesse Broad said sombrely: 'One thing that must be said. In those boats you have a chance at least. On board here . . .' The drunken noise rose once more. He did not finish the thought.

255

The task got more urgent. It was getting late, and there was thuggery in the air. The injured were wrapped up as well as they could be, Swift was allowed navigational equipment, charts and all his secret papers, and the first boat was made ready for hoisting outboard. It was the jolly boat, the smallest one to go. Allgood and Jesse Broad got together what hands they could while Matthews took a position beside the helmsman to heave the Welfare to.

Simon Allen, the midshipman, was to take command of the jolly boat. He got his men on board, cleared away the oars, and they waited. They waited some little time, for the Welfare was proving unwieldy and her hands lubberly. A fair amount of liquor had found its way down many throats and the atmosphere was tense. Jesse Broad was fully armed with pistols now, for although most of the men on guard duty were sober, the situation could get out of hand. The nightmare was not over yet by a long way.

At last the ship was hove-to. Her motion became uncomfortable, lumpish. Big seas broke high up her sides, solid water sometimes pouring across the waist. As Allgood gave the command to haul, a strange thing happened.

From a hatchway forward, Padraig Doyle appeared. His face was gaunt and awful, his hand clutched his bagpipe. As he staggered aft, one arm outstretched, his mouth gaping, the jolly boat rose off the deck and dangled from the mainyard tackle that had been rigged. The Welfare gave a plunge and the top of a wave raced across the deck. It struck the blind man heavily behind the knees, almost knocking him down. He recovered his balance, taking a pace or two forward. The deck lurched more heavily and another wave-top beat at him. Suddenly he was in danger, staggering towards the side. The swinging jolly boat plunged towards him, cracked him up and under in the back, lifted him – and he was gone. Jesse Broad gave a great shout, racing to the bulwarks. The falls dropped from a dozen hands, and the jolly boat crashed to the deck amid howls of fear and pain and the sound of splintering wood.

Over the side the blind man's head appeared high on a grey roller, the bagpipe stretched above him at arm's length. Broad saw the blazing sockets turn towards the ship. The mouth was open in a silent scream. Then head and arm went under. Followed on the instant by the pipes. The grey sea rolled on.

A frenzy of rage gripped the men on deck, and Jesse Broad was part of it. The jolly boat, smashed beyond repair, was cleared from the falls and hurled over the side. The loyal men, white and panicky, made no complaint as they were forced into the two remaining boats. Swift was to command the launch, with Mr Robinson, and Simon Allen joined Hagan in the cutter. The cutter was filled first, overfilled, and swung briskly out. This time there was no mistake. She rose, swooped overside, landed neatly on a rising wave, and was free. She rode dangerously low, but well. Her reefed lugsail was set, and kept her steady as they waited for the captain.

When the launch was far fuller than common sense allowed, there were several fit men and three unconscious ones still on the Welfare's deck. Daniel Swift, from the sternsheets where he sat, shouted to Broad.

'You there! Are you mad, man? We need another boat. We cannot live in this already, and there are more to come! Give us another boat!'

'To hell with you, Captain Swift,' yelled Jesse Broad. 'You'll get no more of our boats, you villain! Stand by to sway her up, you men there!'

Swift stood up in the launch, his face working.

'You cannot do this, damn you! I demand that you give us another boat!'

'Sit down, Captain Swift,' replied Broad thickly, 'or I will have you shot. You have done enough now, you have done enough. We have lost our patience, all of us. Sit down before you catch a ball.'

One of the abandoned loyalists burst into tears. Swift sat down, but he did not stop.

'My nephew, at least,' he said. 'Good God, could you be so cruel as to deny me that? What chance will Bentley have if you make him stay?'

Jesse Broad looked at the prone form of the midshipman with something like hatred.

'None, I doubt!' he screamed. 'None, you bastard, none! And what chance . . . and what chance did . . .'

He stopped, choking. Swift said no more. After a moment's pause the men on the falls started hauling. The launch rose easily, hovered at the rail, dropped prettily into a sea. Ten minutes later

257

the two boats had disappeared into the bleak and lowering gloom. Their last view of Daniel Swift was a characteristic one. He was wrenched round in the stern of the launch, shouting imprecations at them. His fist was clenched and shaking.

Twenty-Nine

By the time William Bentley recovered consciousness, nearly forty-eight hours later, Jesse Broad had saved his life more than once. When he opened his eyes he immediately closed them again, because the light increased the pain sharply. The nausea was seated deep in his stomach; the whole of the left side of his head was singing in agony; his wrist, which he moved as he woke, sent a stab of fire up his arm.

William lay for a long while with closed eyes, trying to piece together what had happened. It came back slowly, and not in sequence. He could not remember why he was in this state. His last memory was of horror at his uncle's wild verbal attack on the last handful of men with muskets. His thirst made it difficult to think. His mouth was dreadful, bone-dry and foul-tasting. He needed to drink.

With an effort, he opened his eyes. The light struck harshly into them. But he persevered. Soon it became bearable. In fact there was not much light at all. A gleam of sunshine from the windows of the cabin. He gave a start. The cabin! What was he doing here? Had the mutiny failed then? He tried to call out, but managed only a croak. It was enough. Jesse Broad swam into his vision, smiling. He had pistols and a sword at his belt, and his face was clean and relaxed. So. Obviously not. The mutineers were in command.

Although it was hard to concentrate, although the sickness in his stomach came and went with violent pulses of pain, William Bentley listened to Broad's tale. But first, he had a glass of wine, his uncle's best. As he sipped it, he had a great longing for a drink of fresh water. The days of fresh water were long long past. Would they ever return, he wondered.

After the launch and the cutter had gone, Broad told him, he had been carried to the crowded sick-bay, where Mr Adamson had done his best by him. Mr Adamson, who had taken no active part in the uprising, had yet refused to go with the loyal party, whatever the consequence of that action. He had claimed that he would rather take his chance in the Welfare than in one of the 'damned cockleshells', but no one was fooled. The strange fellow thought he could save lives on board, and was determined to try it.

'My uncle hated him, I think,' William whispered.

Broad laughed.

'Aye, no doubt. Who did Captain Swift not hate? But Mr Adamson saved your life, nevertheless.'

'Oh.'

'Aye, and not by medical means neither. You had not been below many hours before some of the less-forgiving fellows among us decided they'd like to see you strung up.'

Ill, nauseated, as he already was, William Bentley had a deeper sense of sickness in his stomach.

'Oh,' he muttered.

'Mr Adamson is a little too small to fight such drunkards with his fists, or even with his brandy bottle. But he managed to send a boy aft, while he kept them at bay with his tongue. He has a sharp tongue and a ready wit. He convinced them you'd look better at the end of a rope when you had life enough to kick a little.'

He watched the boy's bruised, drawn face with pity. It had gone very close with him even when he and Matthews had arrived. After a similar incident a couple of hours later Broad had carried him to the cabin.

'What of the others?' Bentley asked after a pause.

'I suppose you mean of your faction?' said Broad. He said it not unkindly, for when his rage had gone, he had known he could not hate the boy despite his hateful ways. He was young, and born to it, and could not help himself. He was ill too, desperate ill, and doubtless terrified. Nevertheless, Jesse Broad was not prepared to make things too soft.

'They got away all right,' he said. 'With Mr Bloody Swift still shouting oaths and threatening us with ropes and chains and torture. They may make out all right; nay, probably will, for the weather has moderated and the wind is fairer, and the Dutchmen at the Cape will look to them, I guess. But they will not catch us, never fear.'

He watched Bentley's racked face.

'They lost no others after you was hit,' he went on. 'Your pistol discharged and that was the last shot fired. So Swift took away with him fifty or so loyal men, plus Hagan and Robinson. Oh aye, and Simon Allen.'

'The others? The officers and . . . and . . . Was it true what they did to little James?'

Broad gave a laugh; more a grunt, without humour.

'Oh aye it's true. A crime exceeding black. And the other one too, that shrill-voiced child, Evans. And Plumduff is butchered, and Higgins overside, and the purser . . . Good God, what did they *not* do to poor old Butterbum? I suppose the bugger deserved it too.'

'And I am saved . . . Oh Christ, how they must want to kill me . . .'

'Aye,' said Broad briefly.

'On our side,' he went on slowly, 'we lost the piper after that. I saw him above the waves.' He paused. 'I wonder what he saw in Ireland that was worse than he got with us, poor chap.'

William Bentley shuddered. His mind cringed. He remembered the moment he had first seen the piper, remembered his first, uncalled for, irrational shock of horror. He had hated the blind man, loathed him, without reason, or shame. Fear. Hatred and fear. His mind cringed.

'Well,' said Jesse. 'I suppose he had lost his only friend. I do not know what he had been doing during the uprising. In the heat of the moment I lost sight of many. No time to wonder after Padraig Doyle. But he appeared at last, alone, and for all I know he's better dead. I lost a lot of friends, young sir, in that day's business.' He stopped for a moment, then said in an acid tone: 'Which is more than you did, I guess. Dolby died, you know, trying to save the lives and honour of Evans and James Finch. And he'll be no loss to you neither I suppose, if you even remember his name.'

William Bentley turned his face away. Poor stolid Dolby, a wretch the younger mids had heaped with insults and with menial tasks. He was ashamed. He screwed his eyes up, clenched his teeth. It was dreadful, all of it. Dreadful.

Broad lapsed into silence and let his mind wander over the events of two days ago. It was easy to vent his spleen on this helpless boy, but he despised himself for having done it. The strain was great, the lack of sleep telling. At present the situation was calmer, it looked as though they might bring it off. But it had been a hard-won thing.

261

Soon after the two small boats had gone and the Welfare had been brought back to her course, a very dangerous situation had arisen. The men were clamouring for wine and rum and the sweets of the captain's table. Joyce, Madesly and contingent had already opened the spirits store and broached a cask of rum, although Joyce, by some quirk of fortunate selfishness, had locked it securely once again and pocketed the key. At least half the remaining people were incapable of work, and the other half were determined to celebrate their new-found freedom by becoming equally inebriated. No fights had broken out, but if they did they could be fatal. For arms were plentiful now, and they were not in the hands of responsible corporals or marines. Matthews and Broad were sitting on a powder keg, and it worried them sick. They had tried to rope Allgood into their discussions, but he was still sunk in deepest despair. Had he not been so aware, he would probably have asked to go with Swift and face his hanging like a man; but he had well known what that hard captain would have told him. Allgood was in his own juice at present; the darkest hell.

Matthews and Broad had met with Henry Joyce to put their proposition. Matthews would be in command, as being a navigator, deep-sea sailor, and used to government, and Broad would be his lieutenant. His qualifications were more nebulous, but easy for anyone to see for all that. He was an experienced seaman and had commanded coastal (and cross-Channel) ships. He knew how to handle men above all, and was educated and well-liked. More important, the two of them firmly believed this: unless they took control, the whole affair would blow up in their faces. Disaster would follow, swift and inevitable. They did not intend to fall from the pan into the fire – even if they had to meet force with force to avoid it.

At first Joyce and his men had been prepared to argue. They wanted freedom, and no damned jumped-up substitutes for Swift and his bunch of toadies. The situation had been tense, his followers armed and numerous. How the bulk of the people would align themselves was a very open question.

As so often had happened to Broad since he had come on board of her, the Welfare and the weather solved the immediate question by making everything save violent action impossible. The wind had been veering westerly for some time, and with full darkness came a local squall. It was short-lived but quite fierce, and Welfare lost some gear. Those of the crew who were capable went aloft or worked on deck and somehow it gave a purpose to many of the men. Those who were not drunkards and wasters by nature sobered up and worked like demons, while those who were disappeared below and drank themselves into oblivion. Next morning the pattern continued as the squall damage was made good. The weather had improved rapidly overnight, with a return to warmth and sunshine. All sail was made and by mid-morning they were thundering along at their best speed. And even those with the worst headaches could share the feeling of elation that lay light upon the ship.

Towards the end of the morning Matthews had mustered all hands aft. Already several of them were worse for drink, and there was much banter about it being just like the old days, and when was the cat to be produced? The big question, thought Broad, was who would wield it now. He had an uncomfortable feeling that there would be no shortage of volunteers if the matter were put to the test.

Matthews had a manner completely unlike that of Swift save for this: he spoke quietly, but with great and penetrating authority. Many men were surprised, not excluding Jesse Broad. He realised for the first time a little of the frustration that must have burned behind the sombre, taciturn exterior of this merchant officer so cruelly – and illegally – torn from his lawful occasions. Soon the jeering and catcalling had died down. They listened intently as he painted a fair but sobering picture of the situation they were in, and weighed up the chances of their survival or success.

He started with the likely fate of the two boats. Given that they had survived the squall last night – and they may well not even have experienced it – he put their chances high. That, he said, was good; for there had been bloodshed and savagery enough, and even if they did make Cape Town, it would not mean disaster for the mutineers. He had been making calculations, working with the charts. With reasonable luck they would get clear away, whatever happened.

There was a stir of excitement. The remnants of the crew, strangely sparse-looking after the muster of only twenty-four hours before that had set off the whole disaster, clung to the words like drowning men to straws. Matthews had them in his palm.

263

'Because of the bumbling of the Admiralty, or because of the weather we met, because of that interminable lollop around the doldrums, because of all this put together maybe, we were approaching the Horn late. Why we were to double him, God only knows – I doubt *we* ever shall. But make no mistake, we were heading for the Horn, and late. The season will be so well on when we reach him that the job of doubling will be a labour of Hercules. A damned hard job. The westerlies will have set in with a vengeance and they will be blowing like the hounds of hell. It will be gale after gale, gale after gale, with a hurricane in between each for a breather! And it will be so cold the rum will freeze. Do you follow?'

They were bemused. First he says they were to get clear way, now this. Henry Joyce began to shout something but he was hushed. Matthews was going on.

'What I mean to tell you is this: this late in the season the Horn is a terror. He is a vile, living, hateful thing. But we can double him. And when we have . . . and when we have, my boys . . . then what? For three months, maybe four, we are safe. No one, not any man in his proper mind, would try to follow us. For the demon winds we shall meet, the cold, hard, ferocious westerlies, are as little breezes to the ones that come in later months. Once we're round, we're safe!'

Jesse Broad remembered the cheering well. As well as he remembered what Matthews had told him later. Unless the better weather they had picked up blew well for them, they would be hard put to reach the Horn in time themselves. And this much they both knew: mad as any man would be to try to follow them in later weeks, if Swift made it to Cape Town and the British Navy had a presence there, or an Indiaman, even a Hollander, could lift him, maybe, to St Helena, they would be followed. All the same, the fact he had told the people remained; if they doubled the Cape soon they would be in a great position to get clean away.

And then? With their clear start and round the Cape? Matthews had let the question hang in the air.

'Then we have a choice,' he told the waiting men. 'Or rather, many choices. Some are merely good. Some are almost wonderful. And some are too magnificent for words!'

First of all, of course, they would sail northwards into warmer waters. On their way, he pointed out, they would find many places. There was Fernandez, where Robinson Crusoe had lived and waxed fat as in the old book, or where Anson, indeed, had laid up and recovered his strength before he took the Spanish treasure ships. They would have time to stop there, even if it was perhaps not far enough upcoast for total safety: they would see. Or farther north there were the fabled lands where Dons grew fat on wine and oranges; or even better, in the end maybe, would be to seek the islands, a million islands there were said to be, flowing with gold and milk and honey. And women.

It was a heady speech, and mention of the islands clinched it. The million islands, yes, the islands and the friendly, dusky maidens. In the warm sun and steady wind Broad could see the sailors gently dreaming. He tried to clear his mind of the other things: the cannibals Anson had spoke about, the diseases and the reefs, the violent tropical storms and tempests. Matthews was not fooled by his own flights of fancy, Broad could see. The lantern-jaw was tense, the eyes watchful.

'Well men,' he said. 'Are you with us? Will you follow me and Jesse Broad out of hell to paradise?'

There was a tumult of cheering. Henry Joyce and some of his men tried to shout against it but were simply drowned. Broad watched them with foreboding.

When it had died away, Matthews went on. His propositions were sombre, his voice ringing. They responded eagerly, again and again. First, he said, the Horn; agreed? Yes, yes, they all agreed. It will be hard, like hell, the westerlies. All right, all right, we will meet them, we will beat them! We will need discipline, tough discipline, Navy discipline. Yes yes, it is true, if you say so. I will be captain and Jesse Broad lieutenant; we are the men to lead. Aye aye! Ye are the men! True watches kept and normal liquor. Food rations as before. Agreed, agreed! Just lead us, Mr Matthews!

'And then, my brave boys.' (Ah God, thought Jesse, shades of Daniel Swift!) 'And then it's freedom! The islands, the women, the liquor! And then the rumpus can start!'

The men were beside themselves with excitement. When it had died down a little, Henry Joyce had had his say. But he was not sober, and his ideas of total freedom were repugnant. The men realised the danger they were in. A full-sized ship and a depleted crew. They would have to work, to work like hell, and their lives were at stake. Matthews cleverly brought it to a vote, to a show of hands. And when Joyce was defeated he asked for another vote, to see if the liquor store key should be returned. The huge, pig-eyed man was voted down again, and looked at first as if he might fight to keep the key. But in the end he did not. He brought it out from deep inside his pocket and flung it on the deck. Matthews, with no loss of dignity, stooped and picked it up. Then, when Broad thought he had surely tried too much at once, he asked for yet another show of hands on the question of weapons. Again a great majority. All muskets, cutlasses and hand-arms were collected from seamen and marines, and locked away right aft, in a store within pistol-shot of the cabin. Joyce's party gave in quietly, which Broad thought ominous. It could only mean they had others hidden away.

Watches were appointed then, and petty officers chosen. Matthews made no approach to Allgood, but he and Broad had decided to do so later, when he had recovered his spirits more. For without Allgood's skill and authority, their task would be a hundredfold harder.

It was during this work that Henry Joyce voiced a thought that all considered legitimate. What of the non-mutineers, he asked. Should they not be made to act as servants? This Matthews would not have. Each man must act the part he was trained to, he said. No able seaman was to wash out quarters or scour the pots. His service was too valuable.

'And the snotty boy?' roared Joyce. 'Is he to walk the quarterdeck, damn it!?'

Jesse Broad brought his mind back to William Bentley, lying before him in his bunk. He smiled a rueful smile, not unmixed with pity.

'Your name was mentioned after the event, Mr Bentley,' he said. 'You are to tend the few surviving beasts. And clean the heads.'

Thirty

Morale remained very high as the Welfare plunged towards the Horn through green and pleasant seas. The sun shone, the living accommodation and men's clothes dried out, they made extremely good speed. The rum ration was no worse than it had been, the amount of food allowed was actually increased, and because of the kindly weather the work was not excessive. When men were not on watch they could do as they liked – no more holystoning the decks until they shone, no more polishing brasswork until the fingernails bled. Above all, no daily punishment. It was a great weight off the minds of the people. In fact, at Broad's suggestion, every cat, every rattan cane, was flung over the side. Minor acts of indiscipline were infrequent; drunkenness was still the only real problem, and flogging had never solved that anyway. In general it was a sunny, pleasant time.

After a few days, Matthews and Broad called Allgood aft and tried to recruit him to their side. He sat in the cabin sipping a glass of wine, a cowed giant. Matthews had agreed that Broad should do the talking.

'Mr Allgood,' said Broad at last. 'It is time for you to come in with us. We need your help.'

The huge head turned towards him. The full lips no longer wore their sensuous smile.

'Why? You have no problems now. She is running well, the people are in good spirits, tractable. For God's sake, leave me be.'

'Look man,' said Broad brutally, 'you must come out of this. I know your feelings and I share them in great part. Mutiny is an awful crime, not just in the punishment but in the act. To you it was a blasphemy, I well know. To many others too, believe me, even of the most degraded. You are not the only man on board with finer feelings than a pig.'

For a moment something like the old light came into Allgood's eyes. He lifted his black head and stared at Jesse Broad.

'Some men went,' he muttered. 'Some men went with Swift. Risked their lives to keep within the . . .'

'Within the law?' asked Broad harshly. 'Come you, Jack Allgood, the law never bothered that brute. And damn well you know, man, he'd have spat in your face if you had asked to go with him.'

The former boatswain gazed at the deck.

'I feel I started it.' His voice was very soft.

'You did not start it, man, it was inevitable. It was inevitable from the time he sent that poor defenceless child to freeze to death.' He paused. 'That child you loved.'

Allgood turned startled eyes on him. Broad stared back.

'I loved him too,' he said. 'And little Peter in my mess. And the blind man, Doyle. He killed them all, my friend. You know it.'

The wide, hairy face remained startled. Allgood was looking inwards, digesting the naked thrust that Broad had offered him. He shook his head.

'I cannot join the mutiny,' he said. 'I am a boatswain. I hold the warrant. I cannot join these scum, it is impossible.'

'Then do not join them. Join us. They hate you anyway, unless their memories are short. For why should anyone among the people care for you, when all is said? Were you not a vicious rogue? Were you not a man of iron who would maim a seaman on a triviality? Ned Rogers had two broken arms off you, and one of them is quite useless now, bent like an anchor fluke.'

'Not vicious, never!' flashed Allgood. 'It was discipline, discipline! The people are like cattle, they need to be firmly led. I never was a cruel man!'

Matthews laughed quietly.

'Mr Allgood,' he said, without a trace of irony, 'I do fully believe it, and so does Jesse Broad. That is why we want you with us. No, let us be frank. We need you, Mr Allgood. The people need you too, if we are to survive. When things get worse again, if they do, when men like Joyce and his louts find the going hard, this ship will not pull through unless we have some iron in its soul.'

'Think about it, please,' said Broad. 'In the eyes of the law you may be a mutineer. But in your eyes, in ours, you are not. You are fully justified. We all were. Let us get away, and find a place of safety, and who knows what might not happen? Think about it.'

Later on that day Allgood sought them out and agreed. He took up an appointment as third in line after Matthews and Jesse Broad, and the announcement was passed around the crew. Old Grandfather Fulman, who had become Broad's ears and eyes in the people, said it had gone down in general pretty well. Many men had hated Allgood in the old regime, but he was always reckoned fair, if dangerous. Most important, he was a mighty seaman and could keep the mad dogs down. The mad dogs, Fulman reported, were not so keen. I would warn Mr Allgood, he said, to keep a weather eye for Henry and his boys, for they will kill him surely if they get the chance. Jesse doubted if the warning needed passing on.

William Bentley had heard the persuasion of the boatswain and it gave him much food for thought. He had never before had to consider such details as whether or not the lower orders on board had feelings, or whether a man like Allgood, whom he was sure scorned him, was in his turn seen by others as an object of fear or hatred. Certainly it had not occurred to him that such a coarse and brutal man could be worried, almost destroyed, by the idea of having taken part in an uprising. A sense of duty in such a great beast? A sense of shame at having betrayed a sacred trust? He cast his mind back to all the times that Allgood had treated him with barely concealed insolence. He remembered the incident of the 'twice-dead sheep'. He had assumed, had been certain, that the boatswain had been an instigator of mutiny, had been the leader of a ring of plotters. So how did this all fit in? And what was he to make of the talk of Thomas Fox? And love?

He had been feverish and ill for several days, lying in a curtained bunk in the captain's cabin, and it was Jesse Broad who tended him. This circumstance also added to his confusion, for each time he saw the gentle, smiling face he summoned up a vivid picture, much against his will, of that same face dripping with his own spittle. It seared him with shame, shame that was almost a physical pain. And filled him with confusion, that this man, this mutineer, this victim of his childish, vicious arrogance on several occasions, should be kind to him, should nurse him, should indeed have saved his life.

Broad made no reference to the past, but after many many hours' thought in his painful bed, William Bentley decided to bring the matter up. When Broad had mopped his face one afternoon, and

269

given him a drink, and made his aching neck and shoulder more comfortable, he spoke.

'Do you remember, Mr Broad,' he said, 'that one day in the dog-watch I spat at you?'

Jesse Broad gave half a smile.

'Hush boy,' he replied. 'You will upset yourself. Settle down and try to sleep or I will hand you over to Mr Adamson and his brandy bottle treatment.'

Bentley smiled back. That had become something of a joke between them. His head ached constantly; the blow had done more damage than could have been imagined. The thought of spirits as an anodyne revolted him.

'No please,' he said. 'I must speak of it. I wish to say I am sorry. And also . . . to ask.'

'Well ask away then,' said Broad. 'Although I am just a common man, so you will not get much sense out of me. But as to the spitting – you are forgiven. It is past, forgotten.'

'Why though? That is what I want to ask. Why is it forgiven? Why do you show me such kindness? Why?'

He watched the face of the calm, sober-looking seaman pucker in thought. For a long time Broad did not speak. His lips half formed words, then rejected them. When he spoke it was to ask a question.

'You ask me why I do not hate you for a little matter. What, after all, is a spit? A faceful of dribble such as my child might give me a dozen times a day. Why not rather talk of Thomas Fox? He is dead, you know.'

The pulsing headache became instantly worse. William Bentley gasped. It was his turn to be silent, his face contorted with mental agony. At last he forced words out.

'All right then. Thomas Fox. Oh Christ, I am not forgiven! Oh Christ, I cannot be!'

There was a long silence, saving always for the creaking timbers, the rushing sea, the low moaning of the wind.

'Yes,' said Jesse Broad. His voice was deep, slightly husky. 'You are forgiven, I suppose. You could not see the harm. You do not know. You are a stupid, blinded child. You could not know. God will forgive you, I suppose.'

'But you?' cried Bentley. Tears flowed down his face. 'Do *you* forgive me, Mr Broad?'

Another pause, a shorter one.

'Aye, I forgive you, boy. Much good that may do you! But go to sleep, you are not well.'

William Bentley smiled with gratitude, through his tears. It was immensely important to him, this man's forgiveness. Much more so than God's. He went to sleep happy.

In later days, feeling fitter but still too weak to stand, he asked Broad a question that had lain in his mind awaiting its moment.

'You said, Jesse, some days ago, that you had a child. I did not know.'

Jesse Broad was seated near the berth sewing a shirt. He paused in his work and his face clouded. He had not thought of home, or wife, or child for a long time except fleetingly. It was the only way, to crush the thoughts as they formed. It was a painful wound, somewhere deep in the blackness of his skull; an area that he avoided, sometimes almost desperately.

'I cannot talk of that,' he said. 'Forgive me, it is impossible. Do not ask.'

Bentley said slowly: 'I never thought, that is all. It never occurred to me.'

Broad spoke harshly and fast.

'I am thirty-odd years old. I live in a village near Portsmouth, next the sea. I am well-to-do and not unhandsome. I have a wife called Mary and a baby boy. I was returning from a night of honest work to see my baby christened when I was taken. By you, William Bentley, by you! Do you forget so blessed easy! And I shall never see them again.'

He ran from the cabin, the grey old shirt left draggled on the deck. The boy closed his eyes, his burden of shame renewed. And yet; and yet . . .

He pondered deeply, he pondered until his brain sang, hour after weary hour. It was all too hard, too complex, too complicated. A country at war against a deadly enemy; the necessity of the press; the need for discipline; the dreadful rabble that served as crew; his uncle's . . . cruelty. And men like Broad. Fine men, good men, somehow noble men. Yet a smuggler. A smuggler! Actually in trade with France while the war raged on!

They spoke of many things in the time before Bentley was fit

271

enough to take up his democratic appointment as cleaner of the heads, and slowly some of his attitudes cleared. He listened to Broad for hours, learned things that made him disbelieve his ears. Learned, for instance, that this man loved the French, and spoke their language fluently, and visited there often. Was, moreover, godfather to four French children and saw his profession of smuggler as a useful and an honourable thing. He prodded, gently, at William's memories on the subject; and yes, true it was that at his father's estate, and those of his relatives, and at all the houses in London he had visited, including several admirals', French brandy was in good supply, and brandy of the finest. Broad talked too of the causes of the mutiny, not in an angry way, or a dogmatic one, but with a sense of inquiry. The character of Daniel Swift was mulled over, and even he was not hated or condemned out of hand. Many of the things that had impressed Bentley most, early on, about his uncle, crumbled under the keen attention that Broad meted them. He laughed, for instance, at the boy's timid mention of how well the captain knew his crew, recognised the latent rebellion, kept them guessing at his every move.

'He was in the dark, you see,' said Broad. 'He was in the dark. At every turn he searched around for something new to fox us with, but it was foolish, the panic moves of a man quite in the dark.'

'But surely, Jesse,' said Bentley, 'the matter of the sports and all? That made them happy did it not?'

'Happy? Well in this respect it did: that for a moment he had ended all that killing work. But do you not understand, young man, he was not keeping *us* in the dark so much as himself. He never knew exactly what would happen. And when it happened wrong – and viz the sports for that, young bucko, or have you forgot that too? – he blundered on with some other great new scheme. And *still* was in the dark.'

Bentley did remember the sports, too well, so said nothing. Broad went on reflectively: 'You see, your Uncle Daniel lacked the art of . . . he could not tell . . . he could not guess the minds of other men. He thought – thinks – that all men's minds are simple, like his own. But of course, the men, the people, were also merely . . . cattle, to be treated rough. Only he did not know how rough to treat us. He dreamed up splendid schemes to keep us up to mark, but could not see how each man would respond. Look at Henry

Joyce now. The man is an animal, a sort of poor innocent wild beast. You cannot break his spirit with a lash, but merely make him obstinate. Swift could not see such things; it was his tragedy.'

Again the acceptance, again the compassion. There was no note of rancour in Broad's voice, no hint of hatred.

'Good God, Jesse Broad,' William burst out. 'Do you even forgive my uncle!? And see some good in Henry Joyce?'

Broad smiled.

'Forgive is the wrong word, do you see? There is nothing to forgive. Much to *regret*, maybe. Yes, certainly much to regret. In both of them. In all of us caught in this sorry ship. You must see the other side as well; Allgood is not alone in hating mutiny. Not a man-jack on this sorry, sorry ship who does not wish it had not happened. It is a vile, degrading thing for a loyal Briton to do, a crime of deepest dye. But it is hard: the life is hard, the food and drink are vile, the conditions degrading, the discipline . . . and back we come to Daniel Swift! A man who did his duty as he saw it.'

The boy said slowly: 'There seems no hope. So much hatred in such a little vessel. There seems no hope. The people, the officers, even the marines – all against each other, all at loggerheads.'

'You are one-sided again. Even marines are human, you know! It was a marine who fired the first shot, that set the whole thing on wheels. He may have been related to Thomas Fox. A cousin.'

'Good God,' said Bentley. He blinked. 'Thomas Fox had a cousin on board here? On the Welfare? A marine?'

'Ah well,' Broad sighed. 'Probably not, it seems unlikely. At any rate we shall never know. The man who fired that shot, who killed Captain Craig, did not live for many minutes more himself.'

And that in itself, mused Bentley, is a crying shame, to have killed the captain of marines. For he sensed at last that Craig had been with the angels. Perhaps had had that vital imagination that his uncle lacked.

By the time he was fit to go on deck, William Bentley knew he would see things through different eyes. His gratitude to Jesse Broad was boundless, and he tentatively hoped that the relationship they had built up might be truly classed as friendship. He called the man by his first name, and had asked him to return the compliment. Broad had merely smiled an ironical, quiet smile, and called him nothing, really; but that, perhaps, was shyness. He obviously had

273

some regard for him, and exhorted him to take care around the deck, to take nothing for granted.

The deck was beautiful in his hungry eyes, and so was the Welfare. The grey-white straining canvas, the bounding, white-capped sea, the bracing wind. He filled his lungs and spread his arms wide in joy. It was wonderful to be about again. Nothing seemed changed, although the decks had taken on a darker hue, lost the gleaming whiteness induced by hours daily with sandstone and water. They were not dirty though. The ship was clean, and well-rigged, with all plain sail set and drawing.

Men lounged around in comfort, taking the sun, and even this no longer struck him as odd. He returned their stares with what he thought of as a cautious smile, and one or two responded. His heart began to sing for what a teacher Jesse Broad had proved. The men were different. They had different faces, different attitudes. They were not sullen apes, they were not hate-filled animals. They were men, human men, and he thought he under-stood them.

Even the filthy task that had been assigned to him William Bentley accepted with something like pleasure. He knew it would be hard, but he was not afraid of hard work. He knew it would lay him open to jeers and abuse from the sailors, but that no longer worried him. His attitude was different; they could not shame him now. He deserved abuse, he would expect no mercy. But he would show them, however long it took, that he was worthy of regard. He had been harsh with many of them in the past, part of a system of repression that he was still sorting out but recognised as having mighty faults. Now, shown the way by his mentor, he would in turn show these sailors that he could play the man, that he was not just a mindless, petty tyrant.

William collected his equipment – mop, pail and safety rope – from the stores, and went smartly forward. Along the length of the deck he received the same stares, returned the same cautious smile. Sometimes he got a sharp stab of intense loneliness at the bitterness reflected in men's eyes. At others he was warmed by a look of genuine friendliness. Of course they did not know how to react, he reasoned. The first time on deck of the infamous boy, who had last been seen, conscious, with a pair of pistols in his hands threatening to blast their mutiny to blazes! What did he

274

expect? But at least there were no cat-calls, at least no one spat. He was confident, truly confident. He understood them.

It was a false dawn. Standing on the lower platform, his shoulder resting against the trembling bulk of the bowsprit, wielding the heavy mop with his weakened arms and fighting nausea at the reek of excrement and urine, he was arrested by a hoarse cry. The beakhead bulkhead door was open and two or three men were blocking it. He looked up, uncertainly, fear flooding his stomach. Inevitably, one was Henry Joyce, but he stood in the background. The two men who came forward were only vaguely familiar, just two of the mass of seamen the Welfare had once had as crew. He could not remember ever having dealt with them, or having had them punished, or anything. Just two of the mass. But there was murder in their eyes.

They came forward quickly. William let out a scream and flung the bucket. It emptied over the first man, checking him in his tracks. William screamed louder, letting his terror rip out of him like a stuck pig. The man came on again, and he held a belaying pin in his fist. William saw the second seaman reach for the safety line with his knife. A third scream ripped the air, bubbling with fear. His eyes closed and all the images of blood, the nightmare memories of the reign of terror, rushed in upon him. Then there was a vicious jerk on the lifeline round his waist, and an exploding crash on the side of his head.

It was a false dawn in other ways too. That afternoon the glass began to fall. It fell like a stone, plummeted until Matthews could hardly trust his eyes. He called Broad and Allgood to look at it and to have a conference.

'By tonight we will be fighting,' he said. 'I had hoped for good weather for a fair bit longer. Once this starts, however, the chances of it stopping are remote. We are closing the Cape. If this is a westerly gale it will be the first of many.'

Allgood grunted.

'She will be ready, sir, never fear. Perhaps it is a blessing in disguise at that. The scum are getting restive, they need some good hard work. Some discipline.'

He turned to Broad.

'Beg pardon, sir. With respect to your sentiments, I crave

permission to use the lash. If it comes on foul I will need to make up a rope's-end, sir. Me and my mates.'

Broad and Matthews exchanged glances.

'We are undermanned, sir,' said Allgood. 'The good hands are spoiled by the bad. We must have rope's-ends at least, my mates and me. It is imperative.'

'Mr Allgood,' said Broad, almost helplessly. 'We are not in the Navy now. It is not our way, it is impossible.'

The great bulk gave its queer, characteristic shrug. Allgood stared through him.

'Beg pardon, sir, but we *are* in the Navy. Once in the Navy, always in the Navy. Is permission refused, sir?'

'Just get her ready to face a storm, Mister,' said Matthews. 'We'll think of other problems later. Get port-lids down and proofed, hatches battened, storm gear bent, everything.'

'Aye aye sir.'

'For God's sake, man!' said Broad. 'For God's sake stop calling us sir!'

'Aye aye sir,' said Allgood, and turned away. He did not appear to realise he had said it.

Broad set about securing everything in the cabin, thinking about Allgood. The man was cracked, for definite. No, no he was not. Broad was pretty sure he knew what was going on in his mind. Allgood had decided that nothing had happened. He had sunk his shame in a return to the old routine. He was boatswain of the Welfare, sailing round the Horn. With lousy weather ahead and a crew of idle scum. He would pull her through if it were humanly possible. He would serve his officers to the best of his ability. He would show the men no mercy except when they deserved it, give them no praise they had not earned. Well, thought Jesse, it could not save him from the rope if they were ever caught, but it might, just possibly, stop that ever happening.

The storm was a solid Cape Horn westerly. It blew for hour after hour with a ferocity that a near-water man like Broad could scarcely believe possible, and the temperature started a slow dive that went on over the next few days. The Welfare fought and fought, her crew becoming gradually exhausted as they worked four hours on, four hours off, with not-infrequent calls for all hands. When the gale blew itself out a new greyness had stamped itself on all their features. They had hardly time to dry themselves and to eat a proper hot meal, however, before the next westerly began to blow. They were truly in the latitudes of the Horn.

Jesse Broad thought he had seen the worst, but Matthews had no such illusions. As they approached the Cape the weather deteriorated and deteriorated and deteriorated. The galley fire went out and could not be relighted, the living accommodation became thick with mildew that later turned to slimy ice, the men in the sick-bay began to take turns for the worse. In the middle of the fourth successive storm Mr Marner, the drunken old schoolmaster, died on a mouthful of brandy, to be joined over the next seven days by six other men. They left their comrades, wounded on the day of the uprising, praying that they would follow them soon, and God was in the mood, apparently, to answer their prayers. At first the dead were given travesties of a decent burial, slipped through the storm-broken bulwarks into the icy wastes of torn and maddened water, but this ceased after one of the corpses was thrown inboard again by a foaming sea and washed about in the waist. From then on the dead were left to lie until there was a lull, however small, when they were heaved overside without ceremony.

Rheumatism became as great an enemy as the sea. Every man on board periodically lost the use of one or both his hands, while the older men were confined to their hammocks for days on end, with some never emerging alive. Bronchitis took its toll, so did pneumonia. William Bentley, when he recovered from the glancing blow he had received in the bows before Allgood had pulled him to the foredeck by his line, became bronchitic. His chest collapsed, his shoulders hunched, and he lay wheezing and puking in the cabin, alone for twenty hours a day. Once he asked Broad, in a rare moment of conversation, why the attack in the heads had happened, despite all Broad's explanations of the minds of the people, and his own forgiveness. The sailor stared in disbelief.

'Oh you foolish boy, you foolish boy. Can you not accept the fact of hatred?' he said. 'Men hate, Mr Bentley, men hate. I told you to take care.'

Mr Allgood, now fully the boatswain again, complete with blue coat and rope's-end, fought both tempests and his people like a demon. He straddled the deck, a colossus; lent enormous strength to every task, inspired men to move and climb and haul when they were almost too exhausted to breathe. When the battered Welfare began to take in heavy water through her straining seams he kept the pumps working by some sort of miracle. It was as if all his mighty energy, all the immense physical and mental power of the man, was flowing out to ship and crew. He was brutal and inspiring, a terror and a hope. Without him she could not have gone on. But there was something inhuman in the way he achieved it.

By the end of the third week of storms the finish was in sight. Men were so weak that few could climb aloft to man the yards. The level of water in the holds was increasing, slowly but surely, and clearly beating the pumps. On the twenty-third day Mr Adamson the surgeon died, which had an oddly terrible effect on men's spirits. Morale was zero. The ship was beaten. The fight was almost over.

They buried Mr Adamson with pomp, as the Welfare laboured uncomfortably, hove-to. Many men wept openly, and a gun was fired. Then a small cask of brandy was broached in his memory. The men were mustered aft to drink, and as they stood on the windswept deck, shrouded by the ice-encrusted rigging, Matthews made a short speech.

'Men,' he said. 'Today we have lost a good comrade and a noble man. I fear we have lost more. Through no fault of yours, of all of you who have fought so fierce and hard, the old Horn has beaten us. I thought to have beaten him, to have sailed to safety, but we could not bring it off. We are too few to work so great a ship in such a run of weather.

'And so – we must turn about. We must sail eastwards, and stand into danger of a different kind. If we do not turn, we shall surely die.'

He stared at the huddled groups of frozen, sodden men. Most of them were looking at the deck.

'All is not lost, believe me,' he said. 'Many things may happen, and there are many places, friendly places, where we may go. We will talk of that later, we will plan out the alternatives. I still have hope, and so, I trust, will you. But first; we must turn. That is inevitable. May God be with us all.'

Thirty-One

This time there were no cheers after Matthews had said his piece. The brandy was quickly finished, the cask tossed overboard, and the weary seamen manned the gear to wear the ship. Once they had got wind and sea behind her the motion eased, but even under minimal canvas she tore along like a racehorse still, in the grip of an enormous power. Despite this lessening of the strain on men and tackle, the cold remained appalling, and although they had longer spells of uninterrupted sleep, they turned in in soaking, freezing blankets that crackled with the rimed ice in warp and weft.

The greatest and most pressing problem was the state of the vessel. She was making water fast, despite a twenty-four-hour pumping watch. The carpenter and his best mate had gone with Swift, and the men left were not particularly skilled. One was a weak fellow too, and took to drink when the going got hard. Jesse Broad, who had built many boats in his day, turned-to with a caulking gang, but they did not beat the worst. Some seams near the keelson were gushing through the filthy bilge-muck at great pressure. It could be slowed but not defeated.

On the second morning after they had turned and run, the mizzen topmast carried away in a squall, springing the mizzenmast itself in the event. The mighty strain put on the sprung timber by the canvas made its lifespan most uncertain, but without the mizzen the Welfare would be desperate hard to manage. It was a sail that in normal circumstances she would have done without on the leg she was making, but the leaking seams, her bad trim, and the damage to other sails and yards, made it a necessity, even to keep her on a course.

Despite Matthews's brave speech to the crew, he and Jesse knew their chances of escape were infinitesimal. They talked about their course of action long and feverishly, poring over charts in the swaying lamplight of the dark and gloomy cabin.

'Well, friend Jesse, what is it to be? We can go northward or head east. If this leaking tub does not decide to direct us straight another way – to the bottom.'

'What is there northward, though?' asked Jesse doubtfully. 'A few unknown islands and an unknown, unfriendly coast. Or do you think to make it to the Caribbean?'

Matthews fingered his long chin and sighed.

'Ah, in times gone by that would have been the place, no question. A thousand islands and ten thousand friends. Gold, lawlessness and The Account. We would have lived as pirates even if we did no plundering.'

'And now?' asked Jesse. 'I suppose those days are long gone?'

'Oh aye, long gone. The only thing that's left there now from the old days is the disease. No pirates, no lawlessness, just the Yellow Jack, the Bloody Flux and His Majesty's Navy by the hundred. Well, not completely true, there are still safe havens for a buccaneer. But the odds are long I think, very long.'

'So it's east then? East past Africa?'

'What else? We cannot double the Horn, we cannot hide in the Carib. We have this chance only: if we pass Good Hope in safety we can blow into the Pacific east-about. If the ship does not sink under us and we do not starve.'

There was no lightness in face or voice. Broad probed on.

'Could that happen? We are sailing easy now at least, despite the weather is cruel strong. Is it very far? Will the wind and sea stay wild and cold and vicious?'

Matthews smiled briefly.

'Is it long? Aye, long enough. First Good Hope, and that is weeks away. Then Van Diemen's Land, and that may well be months. Then upwards and onwards into seas practically uncharted. These gales, in this season, may take us all the way. Sink, or shake to pieces, or lose our mizzen complete. Jesse Broad, you did not know what you bargained for when you went deep-sea sailing. You should have stayed at home!

'And then again,' he went on. 'There is the food and drink. Not only repairs require that we make a landfall, there is victuals too. If we go straight past Good Hope and sail for the torrid zones we'll likely starve to death. St Mary's, we could try, or Madagascar or

Mauritius, they are nearer, but I do not know the waters, we have no charts, and we might find Frenchmen there, or even British Navy.'

Jesse Broad drummed his fingers on the table where Swift once used to drum his.

'You cannot be serious, though? You do not suggest we head for Cape Town? What if the owner and his boats have made a landfall there?'

'No, we cannot make for Cape Town. We must sail on and hope. There should be islands on the way I guess, if we can find 'em! But there is another point, of course. You talk of Swift, and Cape Town.'

Broad puckered his brow. He looked at the lean, unhappy face before him, the plumes of steaming breath from Matthews's nostrils.

'And?'

'If Captain Bloody Swift made a landfall at the Cape, what will *he* be doing? Recovering? Taking a cure? Writing home to wife and family?'

Broad blew out his breath between his teeth.

'Exactly,' said Matthews. 'He will be buying a Dutch ship, or conferring with a Navy captain, or laying off a course to hit Cape Horn. He might be plugging westward as we talk. And here are we, my friend, blowing eastwards at a rate of knots.'

'Good God,' said Jesse Broad.

'Good God? If God is good to us, my friend, that bastard Swift will be an hundred fathom deep by now, his bones picked clean. That is my prayer.'

There was a long pause.

'Is there no other way?' said Broad at last.

'Do not stop thinking,' replied Matthews. 'Nor shall I. The alternatives are not of the most numerous. But do not stop thinking.'

He gave a sudden laugh, almost a jolly sound.

'Hey Jesse Broad, do not despair! Things may go hard with us, but while there's breath there's hope! We may yet bring it off, you know. It is far far *far* from being an impossibility. Work on the men, my friend, work on the men!'

As Broad stood on the quarterdeck a few days later that advice of Matthews's echoed round his head. The decks ahead of him were clear of human life, except for the muffled figure at the wheel. The sea was a grey, empty waste, wild, unfriendly, alien. Welfare

281

staggered along under close-reefed fore and main topsails, burying her head often in the steep backs of seas that had swept under her. The wind was very strong, moaning in the ice-encrusted cordage, and very very cold. It bit into him through his great cloak, made the bones of his skull ache.

Below decks, he knew, the aspects were even more desolate, although wind and sea were hidden. The interior of the ship had become like a mortuary, with the smell of death heavy in it, mixed with the smell of mildew, and wet, rotting things. She was cold, cold as the tomb, and the stoves that they tried to keep alight in galley and lower deck made little difference; appeared, if anything, to accentuate the creeping, seeping misery.

There was another smell down there as well, and it was this that exercised his mind. It was the smell of disaffection, the smell of incipient revolt. The smell of mutiny.

At first it had been confined to small groups of the people. Fights had broken out at more and more frequent intervals. Knives had been used. One man had lost two fingers, another had been deeply slashed right across his ribs. Rum had been at the root of it and rum was flowing freer now. The cold made it inevitable, necessary. Without large issues, Broad and Matthews knew, one of two things would happen: either men would start to die of cold and misery, or the rum room would be plundered. They could not keep it guarded at all times; manpower was too precious.

But there was more to it than drunkenness, however much the two of them tried to wish it away. The mood among the crew was getting hopeless. With the hopelessness came anger. And the anger was beginning to find a direction. The old ringleaders were behind it, and they were spreading terror to the other men. There was a growing mood of hatred and despair, coupled with another growing mood of violence and wild danger. The society was crumbling.

So Jesse Broad watched and waited. He and Matthews had spoken to some men, not just those who were helping to run the ship, and had realised their great desire to be loyal. But they were afraid of Henry Joyce and company, lived in fear of cold steel in the watches of the night. Joyce and Madesly and their friends were swaggering, openly stealing rum and rations from the weaker men. The marines, unofficered, lost, unarmed, could not be counted on. In the day-to-day details of this struggle, in the working of the ship,

Allgood stood alone as a fount of the old discipline. He was, in truth, a mighty figure.

William Bentley, although not deadly ill, could not be let to leave his bed these times, nor would Broad have let him quit the cabin had he been mobile. As the Welfare laboured through the vicious waters towards the eastward, her little world hung in the balance. Outside her, in the southern oceans, all was chaos. Inside, chaos waited.

To the boy, it was a slow, profound revelation. At first, racked by bronchitis, he had been unable to take in the hours of talk, of worry and consideration, that the two men went through. But when the ship was running headlong before wind and sea, when the motion was easier and his illness not so strong, he propped himself on an elbow, sipping a little rum, and took a silent part in their deliberations.

They were not always sober, despite the dangers that they hourly faced, and both rambled about life in England and about their work. William, like Broad before him, began to see the crime that had been committed against Matthews. Taciturn and modest as he was, it transpired over many talks that he was a sailing merchant with great prospects. Not only were these all lost to him, but there were losses to the nation to be considered. He and two cousins had fitted up a ship for a voyage to the East that would probably have made a fortune – a fortune plucked from the enemy's holdings more than likely. He had also done great services as a navigator and cartographer and hoped to make a survey of the little-known waters he planned to trade in. Broad, of course, Bentley knew more about, but the filling in of the background of his trade, his view that a transitory war between governments did not make two races monsters but merely good men badly led, filled the boy with uncomfortable thought. One night Broad spoke a quiet monologue about his wife and child, about a Hampshire village, about boatbuilding and fishing. He spoke about a man called Hardman, whom he had loved. He painted such a picture of this fine and jolly seaman that William would have given his right arm to have met him. When he asked what he might be doing now, however, Broad gave a start, not realising he had been listening. Then told him he was dead, with a small, sad smile.

Broad even had compassion for Joyce. For Joyce, and Madesly and all the others.

'But surely, Jesse,' said William Bentley, 'they are scum? No, with the best will in the world, they are merely scum?'

'From the quarterdeck most seamen look like scum,' he replied. 'And yes, of course, Mr Bentley, they are. Henry Joyce is scarcely human, I know that, nor Madesly neither. But for Christ's sake man, how are we treated? Not just him, them, but everyone? We are all scum in the officers' eyes, all scum. Degraded, humiliated, starved, beaten, made drunken animals. I wonder they bother to pay us off when war is over. We could be salted down to feed the next generation.'

Matthews laughed loudly. William smiled a sly smile.

'But you are officers now, Jesse. You and Mr Matthews. Do you still feel so much for them?'

'I feel nothing for them,' said Jesse Broad, 'but pity. They are more sinned against than sinning and that is truth.'

'One does not have to do anything *very* wrong,' added Matthews sombrely, 'to find oneself in the Navy. Here is Jesse Broad. And here am I. Our lives, young man, are finished.'

William Bentley found himself with nothing more to say. They seemed more sad than angry with their fate. But also to accept it. As they accepted the dirt, and lice, and cold, and sores.

Neither Broad nor Matthews was on deck when the fabric began to rend. Matthews was in the tiller flat checking on the damage caused to the steering gear by a sea that had almost pooped the ship, and Broad was in the cabin snatching a meal of cold pease pudding and biscuit. There had been no sound from outside to suggest abnormality, when the door burst open and Grandfather Fulman hurried in.

The old man, crippled with rheumatism, bent almost double, was gasping with effort.

'Jesse!' he panted. 'Come out, for Christ's sake. Bring pistols, quick. It's Allgood, it's Allgood.'

Broad dropped his knife, knocked over his platter, dragged the pistol from his belt. He checked the priming carefully, as constant damp played havoc with the powder. Fulman leaned against the door, his breath wheezing.

'Quick, Jesse. It's Joyce's gang. They've got him cornered, oh quick!'

Broad reached the deck in seconds, but he was too late. Allgood had been brought to bay near the fore shrouds and the odds were overwhelming. It was like a bear-baiting; and the two principals were indeed as big as bears. Broad moved forward fast, the pistol cocked. But before he reached the foremast he was stopped. Three of Joyce's men, armed with pistols, lounged against the fife-rail. They levelled the weapons at him, with odd, nervous smiles.

'Go no further, Jesse,' one of them said. 'We will not hurt you, man. Just go no further.'

Broad weighed up the chances. Thought of slipping aft and getting reinforcements, moving forward between decks and taking them unawares. All nonsense. Even if he turned now he would die. He uncocked the pistol, slid it into his belt, advanced. The men let him to within a few feet, still smiling nervously. One cackled, a high, unpleasant sound.

Allgood, his blue coat torn, his nose bleeding, stood with his back to the shrouds, crouched in a fighting stance. Facing him was Henry Joyce, similarly crouching, but with only shirt and breeches. Also, he carried a long, curved knife. Broad noticed the boatswain's fists then. They were clenched, but blood was dribbling from between the fingers. Joyce's idea of fighting fair. Just to make sure there was no chance of a surprise ending, Madesly and two other big fellows stood in readiness on Allgood's flanks. Madesly had a knife, the others iron bars.

The courage of Jack Allgood had never been in question. With a sudden ferocious roar he threw himself on Joyce with a force that was frightening. The two men were almost equally matched in size and weight, both enormous, strong, hard. Joyce's sideways move to avoid the charge was lightning quick, stunning for so vast a bulk. But not fast enough. The plate-like hand of Allgood seized his arm in passing and spun him like a top. The two men fell with a crash and struggled on the deck. The three flankers moved in anxiously, looking for a way to protect and help their champion.

Then an arm rose above the struggling mass. The knife plunged, once, twice, three times. A heave, a roll, and they parted. Jack Allgood scrambled to his feet, stood swaying, blinded with blood. The flesh on one side of his face was stripped, the white of his cheekbone glaring through.

Henry Joyce took longer to get up. His face was congested as though he was half-strangled. His breath gasped and rattled. The flesh round one eye was torn, gouged by Allgood's thumbnail.

The boatswain dragged an arm across his face, clearing his eyes momentarily. He made another spring, uttering only a grunt as he did so. This time Joyce did not clear himself. He went down under the charge, with a sharp hiss as the breath was knocked from his body. Worse, his knife went flying. It landed six feet away, then slid into the scuppers with a corkscrew motion of the Welfare in the following sea.

If it had not been for the reinforcements, Allgood might have pulled it off, wounded as he was. For long moments the two men rolled and fought, silently, viciously, first one on top, then the other, too fast to be sorted out. But when he emerged clearly, straddled over Joyce's chest, his lacerated hands clamped around the other man's windpipe, the flankers moved in for the kill. At a word from Madesly the two men swung at Allgood's head with the bars. It took several blows before he released his grip. Joyce gave a heave and the boatswain rolled to one side, blood pouring from him in streams.

When Joyce was upright he stood gasping, fighting for his breath. Jesse Broad, who had moved back several yards while his armed guard had been engrossed in the killing match, shouted to him.

'You murdering bastard, Henry Joyce. What is your game now? You cannot hope to bring it off, you know.'

The odd, bald-domed face turned towards him. The pig-eyes were congested. It was several seconds before he could speak.

'Never . . . fear . . . Jesse Broad,' he gasped. 'We do not want . . . to bring you . . . down. Only . . . Mr . . . traitor . . . Allgood. You sail us on . . . you sail us on.' He tried a breathy laugh. 'To hell . . . eh? To hell.'

With an intense effort, the boatswain was pushing himself upright. He got to his knees, gasping, breathing blood. He got, at last, to his feet. He swayed, staggering as the Welfare staggered. Madesly turned a wicked smile on Henry Joyce, a gay smile, an awful smile.

'I think Mr Allgood wants a little stroll,' he said.

Prodded with the knife, guided by the iron bars, the bleeding, dazed hulk of the boatswain went to the side of the ship as docile as a lamb. Broad did not wait to see him tipped overboard through the broken bulwark. He took his chance and hurried aft. Within seconds he had checked the weapons-room. It was still locked, with mighty locks, and near enough the cabin to be defendable, if need be. So they had had guns hidden, as he had guessed. Within minutes he had checked the charges and priming of the weapons they held in the cabin. Bentley watched him anxiously as he bustled about, but Broad was in no mood for talking.

When Matthews returned they had a swift discussion as to what to do. Both agreed that a general rearmament would not work. Morale was low, fear and hatred rampant. To issue guns to all the men, or even those who were acting almost as officers in the running of the ship, would just accelerate the time when factional warfare would break out. Henry Joyce and his band were not numerous, and they were well hated. If they had not many arms, they might not attempt a coup.

'In any case,' said Broad. 'They may indeed have no great quarrel with us. Allgood they truly hated, and now the man is dead, God help him. They cannot run the ship themselves, that much is certain. And if they do rise up, they must know some of them will die whatever happens.'

Matthews sucked his teeth.

'I think we must gather a band and arm them, Jesse, all the same. Men we can trust, even down to Fulman and old Samuel, although I doubt they can pull a trigger in this damned cold. A couple in my old mess still survive. I'd put my trust in them.'

'And for this night?'

'I think we hope to God. To make a sudden move would only spark them up. They have the smell of blood in their nostrils. Let's stay quiet, keep good guard, let the steering watches run as normal. And hope to God.'

There was a small noise from the alcove. William Bentley's face looked out, pale and troubled.

'One other soul on board they hate like Allgood,' he said slowly. 'I am willing to go forward and face it if it would help you, friends. I am.'

Broad and Matthews did not speak for long moments.

'Even if there is a bloodbath, young fellow,' said Jesse Broad. 'You will not be the first to go, I promise you.'

He smiled, without much humour.

'But you will be third, I guess, when me and Mr Matthews are both dead.'

Thirty-Two

The end, when it came, had nothing to do with Henry Joyce, or the long night of aching vigilance. In fact men's minds and gazes were directed so firmly inwards that it made the end almost inevitable, when it could probably have been avoided.

The system of watches and helmsmen, along with seamen who could be trusted to stand their turn on the quarterdeck and call out Broad or Matthews in case of any violent change in weather or failure of gear, had meant that the two of them had not had to alternate deck duty, four hours on, four off, except in the worst of the weather the Horn had thrown upon them. But throughout this night one of them was always on the quarterdeck, armed with pistols and cutlass, looking for any move or hint of action that might presage a coup.

In the cabin, too, the vigilance did not cease. William Bentley was armed with a long pistol of the type his uncle favoured, and the elder man who happened to be with him at any moment dozed in a chair facing forward, with a musket cradled handy. The idea was that they should not sleep, but William had not the heart to waken them. In any case, he himself was totally sleepless; they were unlikely to be surprised.

He pondered the situation during the long dragging hours, with a sentiment that was at times amazed. Here he was, a midshipman in His Majesty's Navy, well connected, with impeccable 'interest', not yet fifteen years old. Detained against his will by mutineers, in deadly danger from a gang of cut-throats spoiling for a new uprising, and sharing a cabin with two men, rebels both, whom he was prepared to swear would defend him with . . . He arrested the thought, examined it minutely. With their lives, had he been going to mentally say? Why should they? His mind drifted back over the events of the voyage. Good God, he thought, and it really

288

did amaze him this: I'm not yet fifteen, I am a midshipman, a gentleman. All this is mad, impossible. How could it all have come about?

He looked at Jesse Broad, short, powerful and exhausted, slumped in his uncle's chair, snoring with his grey face hanging on his shoulder. A seaman. A smuggler. Taken by the press, and not illegally. During the preceding months he had reviled this man, humiliated him, scorned him. Worse, had hardly noticed he was doing it. Had scarcely thought of him as human. Jesse Broad not human? It was ghastly. Jesse Broad had done more for him than any other human he had known.

With a sudden flash, like a picture in his mind, he remembered the scene on the quarterdeck before he had been clubbed down. I made a pledge, he thought. I was drenched with terror. I made a pledge. The words half came back to him. 'There have been faults . . . there have been faults here. And I will tell.' Yes, that was it, he had pledged himself to tell. If they would put up their guns. And sworn they would be fairly tried. In his little alcove, damp with condensation as it was, he felt a different dampness on his face, warm at first but quickly chill. He let the tears roll down, tears of utter desolation, that blurred Broad's face in the swaying lamplight. Well, would it ever come to that? Another picture formed, of Broad and Matthews hanging from a yardarm by their necks while he looked on. He tried to make it go away, he shook his head and tightly closed his eyes. He cried in desolation.

The attack never came. In the cold grey light of morning the Welfare was just the same, battering eastward and a trifle north under topsails only, plus jibs and mizzen. Broad and Matthews stood upon the quarterdeck, tired but relieved, to decide if they should issue arms or let it ride. Their feeling was, without a lot of deliberation, that if Joyce meant to take the ship he would have done so fast. He needed them, of course; that much was well known.

'I doubt the scum would even have a ship without us,' muttered Matthews. 'Look at that mizzen, Jesse. I must go up and check the break; it seems a little worse from here. I wish to God we did not need that canvas on the cranky bitch.'

He swung himself into the weather shrouds and climbed as

heartily as if he'd had a good night's sleep in bed. From forty feet above the deck his quiet cry struck ice into Jesse's heart.

'Good God,' he said, and a quirk of wind made the spoken words as loud as if he'd shouted them in Jesse's ears. 'A sail. Ah Christ, a sail.'

Jesse Broad looked up, then followed Matthews's pointing arm. He stared into the bleak morning, almost dead ahead, but saw nothing. There was no one else on deck except the helmsman, who was intent on sailing. Broad leaped into the rigging and hurried up beside Matthews.

The Welfare carried no lookouts, had not done for ages. But the vessel beating up towards them surely did. Dawn had broken half an hour before. They must have been seen. The two men hung on the ratlines in silence, staring out across the miles of ocean. The ship approaching was quite small, reefed down, and making heavy weather of it.

'I do not believe in providence, Jesse Broad,' said Matthews at last. 'She is a British frigate for a thousand pound. Or a sloop maybe, she's not the size that we are.'

They were mesmerised, dazed with shock. For long moments nothing more was said. No plan presented itself. They merely watched.

'Well,' said Jesse Broad. 'Is it possible? Could Swift have made his landfall and set out in pursuit? It is so short a time.'

'Picked up more like,' Matthews replied. 'My guess is that they were found by a cruiser, or someone doing escort round the Cape. And persuaded, or ordered them maybe, that they come after us.'

'Must it be like that?' said Jesse. 'Are we so very sure that the ship is British, and a warship, and in search of us?'

The question was half rhetorical, the answers obvious. Matthews voiced them almost absently.

'I cannot see her too well yet, but I'll swear she's British. And where would she be going if not after us? There is no call to head towards Cape Horn in winter, Jesse. Only desperate men would do it, or determined. Dan Swift would sail a sieve against a hurricane to come up with us, you know it. She is heading for the Horn. She is heading after us.'

They hung in the bitter wind for minutes longer. The Welfare rushed on, closing the miles between them. Broad shook his head, still dazed, unable to react.

'Can we escape?'

There was a pause.

'Do we want to?' said Matthews sombrely.

Jesse stared at him.

'Can we escape?' he said again, his mind shying away from all the other implications. 'We have the wind gage. They may not have seen us even.'

Matthews laughed.

'Our mizzen's sprung, our gear is ruined, we are leaking like a basket. If we tried to run they would intercept us, whatever way we jumped. As to not seeing us! Well . . . I am right glad, my friend, that you have it in your heart to joke! It heartens me.'

'How long? Half an hour? Shall we call all hands?'

The thought occurred to both of them at the same time. If they kept their mouths shut, if they did not reveal the frigate's presence, it might save bloodshed, or cut it down. For what would the people do? How would they face their fate when it was laughing in their faces?

But before they had reached the deck the cry was out. A seaman had come up, seen them in the rigging, and looked ahead. The other ship was clearly visible, gunports too. She was British, a light frigate, and clearing for action.

Within minutes all hands who were able were on deck. They ran around like headless chickens, most of them, not knowing what to do for the best. One man whinnied, time and time again, a demented horse, while others shouted orders, supplications. The panic lasted several minutes. While the two ships inexorably closed.

After a short time the general movement became a surge towards the quarterdeck, with only the most panic-stricken staying forward, staring ahead, mewing with fear and misery. Matthews and Broad stood abaft the mizzen, their hands on pistol-butts, waiting for a silence, a rationality, to come about.

Joyce, Madesly and four or five assorted thugs shouldered forward. They were armed with pistols, cutlasses and dirks. Joyce's face was pale under the shining dome. He seemed mad with anger.

'You have planned this, Matthews!' he yelled when the noise died down. 'This is no accident! This is not luck! It is impossible in such a waste of ocean!'

291

There was a rumble from the men all round him. Broad almost smiled. The suggestion was preposterous, crazy. But had he thought about it, he might have guessed its coming. The men would seize it, sure. Matthews tried to stamp it out immediately.

'You are mad, Henry Joyce,' he roared. 'Do you imagine I would rendezvous with my own death? That vessel's come to kill us, every one, by steel, or ball, or hanging. Stop your madness and get down to tacks.'

Joyce almost spat with rage.

'Bad luck! Bad luck! Do you believe him, lads? Between the Horn and Africa there's a million miles of sea-room. And we meet a British frigate! These men are traitors! Kill them!'

It might have happened. The men, even the most loyal, the most sensible, were sick with fear. They looked at Broad and Matthews, glanced at each other. Joyce and his company had pistols in their fists, were whipping up a general rage. It was contagious.

'Half an hour either way and we would have missed them,' shouted Joyce. 'Half an hour into darkness or a mile or two more room and we would have passed! And this is accident?!'

Matthews used his voice of cutting power. It was chill, like ice. He started with a laugh, devoid of humour.

'Half an hour either way. But here we are. Thank you, Henry, for your congratulations. I must indeed be the finest navigator of all history. And I could not even take a noon sight yesterday for the cloud-rack. As all on deck at the time will tell you.'

There was a moment's silence. Jesse Broad stepped in.

'Half an hour,' he said. 'We now have less. Look, damn you, look. There is a frigate beating up to us. Forget damned Henry Joyce, my friends, forget him. What are we to do? *That* is the question.'

It swung the matter. Joyce shouted more, but others cried him down. They stood before the mizzen, looking to their leaders. Jesse Broad was filled with sadness suddenly. These poor lost fellows with their eager, hopeful faces. Expecting him and Matthews to find a way of escape.

Not so Madesly. He only leered. He was a noted seaman who had probably commanded coasting trade in his time. He touched the pistol he had stuck back in his belt and stepped out of the ruck.

'Just what do you suggest then, Broad? That we down helm and try to claw off upwind? That we set everything she'll take and show that bastard our heels? It is true, lads,' he added with a laugh, 'that we're the bigger, faster ship. So let's get to it! Let's break the canvas out!

'You there!' he shouted to the helmsman, who was a bare few feet from him. 'Down helm and quick about it! Bring her on the wind! We're going to make a run for it!'

The helmsman kept his eyes ahead, watching the sails, sensing the rolling seas that piled up astern of him. The men were confused, not knowing, most of them, if it were good advice or no.

'Well?' shouted Madesly, laughing. 'Come on, Mr Matthews. Do we make a run or not?'

'You know we cannot do it, Arthur Madesly,' Matthews replied. 'Our mizzenmast is sprung, our gear is ruined. We have not enough men to get the canvas on her, even if much of it was bent. And if we come on the wind that mast will give for certain. As you very well know.'

Madesly laughed still more. The men said nothing, digesting the information. So – they could not run.

A voice said from the back: 'But if we cannot run, sir? Then what can we do?'

'Surrender,' said Matthews brutally. 'We cannot run, there is no point. Our gear is wrecked, we are a sinking hulk. We must surrender.'

Jesse, looking at the faces, knew the men would have taken this in silence. They would have thought it out, followed all the paths until they reached the deadlock. Not so Joyce and Madesly. The idea maddened them. Clearly, he guessed, they had drawn the same conclusion. But without acceptance. Why indeed should they, anyway? Mad dogs they may be, mad dogs they were, but why lie down and die without a fight? He was almost on their side.

'Surrender!' Joyce forced out at last. It was a hoot, a shriek, filled with bitter laughter and derision. Then he shouted: 'And what then, you pair of turncoats? Will your bloody little bugger Bentley see us free? Have you got it all arranged in the captain's bedroom?'

Matthews's stony face did not flicker at the insults. When Joyce had finished he spoke as evenly as ever.

'If we surrender I suppose that we shall hang. You shall, certainly, Henry Joyce; and I, and Jesse Broad and your friend Madesly. But there are many men who will not. Those who did not join, and others too. They will not hang the lot of us I doubt; there is too many. An example must be made but that is easy, with the villains we have on board us here.'

He ranged his eyes sombrely over the assembled men.

'My friends, I beg you to listen carefully, and think. If we should not surrender it can only make things worse. If we do there will be retribution, sure. Not a few of us will die at the yardarm in Portsmouth or Spithead. But I tell you truly, we cannot get away. The Welfare is not able, despite her greater size.'

The ship to leeward was very clear by now. She was smallish, probably a twenty-four. She was yellow-painted and trim, what sail she carried very white. There were not many minutes left before they would be on each other.

The matter was decided by Henry Joyce. He was no longer wild with rage, but he had clearly made his decision. He jerked out his pistol and levelled it at Broad. Madesly followed suit, covering Matthews. The others of their party cocked their pieces. Nobody made a move to stop them, nobody made a sound.

'There is another way,' said Joyce thickly. 'And it is the way we take. We stand and fight, and blast them to the bottom of the sea. It is a sloop almost, she cannot match our weight of metal. One good broadside and she's on her way to hell. I say we stand and fight!'

'Good Christ!' cried Jesse Broad – and jumped in shock as a ball buzzed past his ear. His hand half reached towards his belt but stopped; a half a dozen muzzles stared him in the face. One of Henry Joyce's guns was pouring smoke; he changed it for a fresh one with a grin.

'Just shut your mouth up, friend, and get the keys out to the musket room,' he said. Then he turned to face the people.

'Lads,' he cried. 'What do you say? You've listened to the arguments from all sides. We either give in or we turn and run, but there's not much luck in any of those plans, eh? If we surrender like a little flock of puling lambs we end up dangling. If we turn and run it's even worse. For according to Mr Matthews here, a most trustworthy man he does assure you, our mizzenmast will just give up the ghost and totter overside. Well listen, God damn it. We have nothing to lose by making a fight of it. For he's a coward and a damned liar, and if you think we will not all be hanged you're living

294

in a paradise for fools. You know the Navy, you know the worth they put on the life of poor Jack Tar. They'll hang the lot of us, from the highest to the lowest, including you poor innocents that us filthy rebels kept on board that luckless day! There's only one man-jack on here that will not be stretched, and he's that little bastard bugger boy. And I say this: when we've sunk that tin-pot sloop down yonder, let's hang him first! Let's hang Billy Bentley, then his chums! Let's string up Matthews and Jesse Broad to keep him company! But first – let's fight! Or are we dirty, frightened animals!'

Jesse Broad was detached from it all, somehow. How many more orations was he to endure on this ship? How many more times see the heads go up, the mouths fly open wide? He turned his eyes to the leeward ship, tried to count her ports. He could see men, in the rigging and about the decks. He wondered if they could hear the ragged cheer that tore downwind from the Welfare.

It was a ragged cheer, but not so ragged that the issue was in doubt. Henry Joyce had been convincing, no question. Broad tried to size it up. Would they arm the men, take the keys from him and Matthews? Or would that strike them as too dangerous? If all the men were armed, what would break out? For the idea of firing on another Navy ship was a wild idea, a desperate idea. His mind reeled from under it. To open fire on a Navy ship! It was sheerly mad! It was lunacy!

But Henry Joyce was in full cry now.

'All right, my lads, all right! God love you, we'll take them on! And never fear, we'll send her to the bottom! We'll arm, we'll arm, we'll each have sword and musket if the fight gets close! But first, to the guns! Gun captains at the ready, rouse out what you need. Go now, go, make ready! And listen—' His voice became harsh, it cut through the jumbled noise. 'Me and Madesly and our friends will lead you now. And any damned coward who will not fight will feel cold steel, mark; or the bullet! Are you with us?'

There was another ragged cheer, and men began to run about once more. Some ran with purpose, some were clearly lost, frenzied, terrified. Madesly stayed by Henry Joyce, but the rest of their gang hurried here and there, cajoling, threatening, organising gun crews at pistol point. It was chaotic, ridiculous. And clear across the cold grey waves was the man-of-war. As near as Broad could judge, she was almost within range. It was a matter of minutes.

Joyce and Madesly had their pistols in their hands, Matthews and Broad did not. But there were feet of deck, the wheel, the mizzenmast between them. As the two new leaders approached, the two deposed ones drew their weapons. They faced each other in the moaning gale.

'I want the keys, Matthews. We will fight this out like British sailors, not like yellow men. If that bastard closes we will fight them hand to hand.'

'Henry, you are mad. We cannot win it, man. Have we not done enough? Leave it, Henry, leave it.'

'You fool,' said Henry Joyce. 'Does nothing ever touch your sort? Would you let them hang you, just like that?'

His face was pale, his eyes were bright, his tone twisted with bitterness. Broad was speechless, racked with pity. Along the deck he saw men running, aimless, lost. Again he thought of chickens, and nearly smiled; we'll all be headless soon, I guess.

'Come on,' repeated Joyce. 'Give me the keys. If you have not the courage to fight give *us* a chance. You will hang whatever, both of you. If you will not die fighting, for the love of God let me!'

There was a distant bang, flat and torn. All four of them looked to the leeward ship. A trail of smoke blew off downwind of her from a bow-chaser. A couple of hundred yards ahead of them a plume of water rose in the grey sea, collapsed and disappeared. She had fired across the Welfare's bow.

'If you intend to clear for action,' said Matthews quietly, 'I suggest you look to your guns.'

Joyce's small pig-eyes were full of hate.

'And you?'

Broad spoke. His voice was trembling.

'We will not interfere. Of that you have our word.'

Joyce and Madesly looked at each other. Madesly turned.

'Then damn you for filthy cowards,' said Henry Joyce. 'I only hope I live to kill you both.'

It looked as if he might spit on the deck at their feet. He cleared his throat noisily. Then he shrugged and followed Madesly forward.

Thirty-Three

J esse Broad and Matthews took no part in the action, although
they could not find it in their hearts or minds to move. They
stood on the quarterdeck as though paralysed, watching the
strange, slow scene unfold. They saw the downwind frigate snug
down to fighting rig, they saw the officers grouped near her stern,
they saw the well-drilled sailors run out the guns. Now that the ships
were so close the unreality was even greater. For the vengeful frigate
was more or less hove-to, lying in the jumbled, leaden sea waiting,
while the Welfare, sluggish and short-canvased, covered the last
distance that would bring her to her fate straight as an arrow, but oh
so very slowly.

On the deck before them, and on the deck below for all they knew,
the frenzied process of making ready the guns for firing went on. But
it was laughable, horribly pathetic. Half the gun crews were of men
who had no knowledge of the weapons. Half the men on board had
given up all hope. Joyce and his henchmen rushed about like furies,
but little groups, small knots of seamen, could no longer be moved.
They swayed as they were harangued, made half-motions to man a
gun; and then subsided, staring at the rigging or the deck when the
jostler went away.

Firing the long naval guns was an art, or at least a skill that needed
training and application. Broad wondered, standing there, why it was
that Swift had so neglected it. There had been a period, long ago, he
could not quite remember when, that they had done gun-drill, but
even then it had not been intense, and the mood had not affected the
captain long. Since the Line or earlier not a gun had been run out.
Something to do with his orders, perhaps. The mission that would
never now be done, or even be known to Jesse Broad, the reason they
had not stood to fight that time, the reason they had battered south
without a stop. Or was it just another quirk of the owner's character?
Had he merely forgot that they must train?

297

Whichever way it was, Jesse Broad could see that chaos was afoot. The guns were heavy, they were dangerous. In the awkward corkscrew motion of the quartering sea, the upper-deck guns, as they were released from their heavy-weather lashings, began to roll back and forth on their carriages, to be brought up short by their breech ropes. Men manned the tackles, tried to run them out, but with not such marked success. One slewed sideways and a man went down with a cry. Jesse winced for him as the thick truck barely missed his foot. If one of those monsters carried away... The upper-deck twelve-pounders must weigh well above a ton at his guess. He could imagine it careering round the rolling, pitching deck. It would be a juggernaut.

'This is madness, Jesse.' Matthews spoke quietly, his voice reflecting the sadness that Broad felt. 'Cannot they see it? They will not have a dozen guns cleared.'

Broad did not reply. He thought again of trying to end it now, of trying to retake the men by arms or switch of mood. But it was too late. Several were armed, and half a hundred, maybe more, were working with the guns. They were determined, or desperate, or mad, or anything. He half believed them right in any case. Almost anything was better than be bested by the dreadful Daniel Swift at last. To be hanged was a bearable idea; at least inevitable. But that Daniel Swift should end the day triumphant. It was terrible.

'Half the guns won't fire anyway,' Matthews went on. 'I am no expert in this, but consider the conditions. Our cabin, even, is wet and stinking with the damp and condensation, and that's the best accommodation. When we had a proper crew on board the gunner and his mate and yeoman kept up a constant conversation with their powder. Maybe it's gone like porridge; it cannot be dry, surely. Or does it not feel the damp like we do, I do not know? And what about the balls? Some of them below are rusted up to hell. They've gone like chair-cushions some of them. Oh Jesse Broad. It is sheerly madness.'

The downwind ship was nearly ready now. The captain had jockeyed her so that when the Welfare was well in range he could up helm and rake her from stem to stern with his starboard broadside. Even had the Welfare got a broadside manned only the fore portion of it could be brought to bear. She plunged along with the wind over her larboard quarter into the jaws of that battery with chaos still unconfined. Her decks were covered with men in every state, from readiness to panic to demoralised inactivity.

'Will Madesly put himself on the wheel to try and bring her round to bear, I wonder,' Matthews mused. Broad wondered too; and caught himself wondering.

'Good God, Matthews,' he said quietly. 'This is queer, you know. Here we are talking tactics like a pair of armchair admirals, and any minute now the action starts. We are cold fish, you know.'

'I do not think it – Ah!' Matthews's voice changed. 'Yes, Madesly will take the wheel, I thought he might.' He looked aloft. 'You know, Jesse, if he shoves her round we'll likely lose the mizzen. Best watch out.'

Madesly hurried aft and gestured the helmsman to stand down. They were in range, even Jesse could tell that plainly. The downwind ship nudged the head sea, her luffs shaking as she spilled the wind, almost stationary, almost across their path and over to the larboard side. Madesly took the wheel, but did not alter course. He and Henry Joyce had clearly decided to wait as long as the nerves of their fellows could stand it.

The officers on board the adversary were clustered on the quarterdeck, and more were ranged in their gun control positions. They too were playing the waiting game. When the balls started to fly they would not have far to travel. Jesse Broad was helpless, but tensely excited. Henry Joyce must change his mind, must strike the colours before it was too late. At this short range the net result was carnage, on either side or both. The colours! Even now, even with the gap between them closing at a suddenly accelerated rate, it struck him anew as strange, unreal, fantastic; they both carried colours, both the same. Two British men-of-war about to open fire at each other.

All the slowness of the last twenty minutes, all the odd sensation of the two vessels closing imperceptibly, had changed. The Welfare appeared to be charging now, tearing across the last gap of grey-white water as if in a frenzy. Broad's mouth was dry, his fists were clenched. His eyes flicked from the Welfare's decks to the tight little waiting frigate, to the long lanky back of Arthur Madesly. There seemed to be about a half a dozen upper-deck guns manned, the twelve-pounders. Below on the gundeck presumably some eighteen-pounders were out. All those men who had not joined in were standing aimlessly. No one had taken cover, no one had manned sheets or braces in case of an altered course. And yet again the last few seconds changed the way that time was running. It almost stopped for Jesse Broad. The ships were in a limbo for an age. Nothing could happen. Everything was fixed.

With amazing suddenness Henry Joyce thrust his bald-domed, pig-tailed head out of a forward hatchway.

'Put up the helm!' he shouted. 'We're going to blast her now!'

Arthur Madesly did not reply. He began to heave at the spokes. After a few seconds the Welfare started to respond. Her stern swung slowly to larboard, towards the waiting frigate. Farther and farther round it came, until more guns were brought to bear. No one moved to trim the sails.

Matthews was staring at the mizzen, out to starboard.

'It's starting to lift,' he said to Broad. 'She'll be by the lee if he doesn't watch her. He'll gybe the bugger, then we're done, there's no preventer rigged.'

Broad was staring at the adversary. This aggressive manoeuvre by the Welfare had moved them not at all. The sight of the bigger ship's ports swinging round to face them seemed to signify nothing to the man in command or to his people. She hung in the wind, luffs shaking, waiting for the Welfare's guns to speak.

The gap was madly small. 'Almost spitting distance', went through Jesse's mind. Henry Joyce gave a great roar to the men on deck, then dropped out of sight, doubtless to repeat it below.

'Fire!'

Time hung in the balance once again. Broad clearly saw the men apply their linstocks, then spring back. He clearly saw two flashes at the breech, then another slightly afterwards. Then there was a pause, of unbelievable duration.

As the guns went off, Arthur Madesly began to spin the wheel, to get the wind back on her quarter, to lessen the target she presented to the foe. He was too late.

The Welfare's roar was not particularly loud. The forepart of the ship disappeared momentarily in a cloud of smoke. The deck trembled. As it did so, it also gave a lurch. With the flat explosions ringing in his ears, Broad heard Matthews shout: 'Get down! He's gybed her!'

Arthur Madesly was too late. The Welfare's mizzen had already been caught by the lee. The freezing wind, its strength apparent once again now it was no longer merely pushing from astern, got underneath the sail and tore it from its vangs.

It was a huge piece of canvas, on a massive, iron-bound wooden yard. With the full weight of the wind in its wrong side it swung across the quarterdeck with irresistible force, at a speed that was horrible. Broad and Matthews, crouched, heard the roar as it shot above their heads. Even had the mizzenmast not been sprung it could hardly have survived the shock.

But it was sprung. As the flying yard smashed over to larboard the deck beneath them bucked as though alive. There was a crunching, splintering crack, then a prolonged roar. As mast, shrouds, stays, everything came down, they were enveloped in clammy, icy canvas which was beaten from above by other falling gear. By the time they had clawed their way out the end was very near.

Welfare's mizzenmast had gone by the board. It was hanging overside, still firmly attached to her by the rigging. It had taken the mainyard and main topsail with it, so the ship was miraculously back on something like her old course, being dragged slowly downwind by her reefed fore topsail, her headsails flapping uselessly.

There was no one at the wheel and the scene on deck was very much as it had been before. Broad studied it.

Judging by the fact that three of the guns were still run out, only the three he had noted could have fired. Judging further by the amount of noise there had been, he reckoned only three or four of the eighteen-pounders below could have gone off. So. He looked at the adversary, terrifyingly close-to. There was not a mark upon her. Not a yarn of rope had been damaged, not a speck of paint scratched. He licked his lips, looked interrogatively at Matthews. Six or seven guns at point-blank range. And not a hit.

Henry Joyce had come on deck. He and Madesly were shouting at the gun-crews, trying to make them reload and run out. Joyce was cutting the air with a cutlass, dancing in a kind of frenzy. The gun-crews stared back stupidly. One man played idly with a swab, throwing it from one hand to the other. Nobody made so much as a gesture towards a gun.

All the others on the deck were looking at the frigate, only yards ahead now. If she opened fire at this range she would tear the life out of the Welfare. She was still athwart their course, still heading the wind. Broad saw an officer in blue move towards the helm. An order was clearly passed.

As the Welfare drew level with the ship, it became obvious what the order was. The helm was up. The ship was moving off the wind, turning on her heel to bring herself parallel with the cripple. Parallel, and close enough to throw a line. Broad wondered if that was their intention, to throw a line. Not in this sea, surely? It would be too dangerous to lie alongside. They would grind each other badly.

Their intention became clear very quickly. As the ships ranged side by side, gunport to gunport, the captains of the visible guns took up their stances to fire.

Henry Joyce was still dancing, the idler was still playing with his swab, the bulk of the people stood about in their ugly, stolid daze. The crippled Welfare wallowed on, downwind, dragging her mizzenmast clumsily. Broad breathed evenly, unmoved despite the awful cruelty of it all, the terrible, desperate cruelty.

The point at which she fired was lost. An incredible bang, a searing flash, a biting, filthy, burning smell. The Welfare staggered, trembled, shook. Everything disappeared, completely, in a choking mass of smoke. For seconds, minutes, a time that could have been an age, Jesse Broad was lost. Deaf, blind and agonised, neither alive nor dead.

When the smoke cleared away, when he could hear and see again, the Welfare was a wreck. The foremast was a fifteen-foot stump, the larboard main shrouds had gone, and debris from above was piled about the decks as in a dockyard. It was difficult to take it in. The expanse of clear deck had gone. Everywhere broken spars, and blackened canvas, piles of twisted cordage. And smoke. Smoke hanging about in mounds, twirling and melting, blowing from one ragged heap to the next.

For a little while all seemed silent, save for the rhythmic ringing in his ears. Silent and still. He could not see a man, except for Matthews, knelt beside him. Then a moaning started, the moaning of the wind. Then another moaning, of men. Then slowly, building slowly up, came screams, of fear and agony and horror. From the littered deck shapes rose up. Some were bloody, some were not.

302

Some were blackened, some were ghastly pale. Some had arms and legs, some were missing limbs, or bits of torso. As they stood there, more climbed up hatchways from the gundeck, some hardly able to crawl; it was not only the Welfare's upper deck that had been shattered.

The triumphant ship had dropped astern, to sit proudly, spilling wind, to wait and see. To see if the Welfare wanted any more. Broad looked at her. As she dropped into a trough he saw men making for the boats, clearing them for lowering. There was not any doubt, when it came to it. The Welfare had had enough.

'She will not come alongside,' said Matthews quietly. 'Thank God we prevented the issuing of arms. There are some blessings in this sorry world.'

'Will she sink, the Welfare? Will she go down after all this punishment?'

'That, my friend, is no longer our concern.' He laughed. 'I doubt it though, Jesse. She's a fine powerful boat. They'll jury rig her and put on a crew. They'll get her safe to Cape Town.'

'Thank God I won't be on board her,' said Jesse Broad. 'Hang I will, if hang I must. But dear God, my friend, I think I could die happy so long I'm off this ship.'

The Welfare was wallowing. Wallowing in the cold southern ocean, her decks littered with gear and men. Confused men, weeping men, injured men, dead and dying men. The first boat from the frigate was neatly launched. The other boarding parties were drawn up, quiet and well armed. The first boat slipped her falls and began to struggle through the cold and lumpy sea. From behind a pile of jumbled debris near the mainmast, Henry Joyce and Arthur Madesly came into view. With them were two other men. They picked their way towards the stern. They carried cutlasses.

It did not occur to Broad and Matthews for some time what was up. Kneeling in the clutter, they watched the four come aft. The faces, dirty and blackened, one badly cut, were intent. Despite the chaos, they moved fast. Their eyes were firmly fixed; they had a purpose. Broad grabbed Matthews by the arm, horrified.

'The boy,' he said.

Matthews cottoned on immediately. He gave a grunt and they rose to their feet as one. Joyce, seeing them, stopped.

303

'So,' he shouted. 'Hiding like bugs in the woodwork. Stand, you bastards, stand, or we cut you down.'

Broad and Matthews did not wait to argue. They set out at a stumbling run. Joyce snarled with fury and his party started running too. It was laughable in a way, the six men stumbling, panting, racing for the after hatchway.

Matthews got there first, with Broad a pace or two behind. Madesly hauled out a pistol, which misfired. Another of them tried with his. It ignited, and a ball clipped Matthews on the shoulder, making him lose his grip. He half fell down the ladder, but looked up to see if Jesse was all right. Madesly, frustrated, threw his pistol at Broad. It struck him on the temple, but only a glancing blow. As he tumbled down the steps the attackers were on his heels, snorting like pigs with rage and exertion.

The two ran into the cabin pell-mell. Broad tried to slam the door, ram home the bolt, but it was too late. As it swung to, the four dashed themselves against it. Jesse, taken on one foot, was knocked backwards. He banged his hip against the table, lost his pistol far across the deck, fell heavily and nearly broke his wrist. By the time he had got himself half upright, the cabin was full of men. Matthews was to the right, his pistol and cutlass raised. As Jesse watched, the hammer of the pistol fell. A flash around the action, but no bang. He hurled it down, disgusted.

Joyce's pistol was now ready. He aimed it at Matthews and pulled the trigger. But this misfired too. The last of the four looked almost comical as he raised his; he really had no hope of it.

There was a bang, however. The man, instead of wearing triumph on his face, showed horror, and a look of pained surprise. A wound beneath his arm began to gush blood, then he fell. William Bentley, who had fired the shot, was half slumped across a chair, exhausted by his efforts to get out of bed and dressed during the last ten minutes. The musket-kick banged painfully against his ribs. He was gasping, feeling giddy and sick. He had not known his lungs had grown so weak.

The three assassins were bemused for a moment. Matthews gave a loud, glad cry and lunged himself towards them. He led with the point of his cutlass, which was his downfall. It ran easily into the body of Arthur Madesly, who screeched, coughed blood across the deck, then fell. But the weight of him was on the blade. It bent, but

304

did not break. As Matthews, frantic, white with knowledge, hauled on it to get it free, Henry Joyce aimed an enormous swing at him with his own cutlass. There was a bang as it hit the bone, a crunch as it broke through it, and his left arm was ruined. His blade freed itself from Madesly then, and Matthews staggered back. He still had speed and strength enough to parry Joyce's second blow.

Broad was on his feet and moving to the unengaged man. Bentley, gasping in his chair, a cutlass beside him that he could barely lift, watched the bloody fight. In the confined space it was ghastly; the deckhead much too low for high-raised blades, the mess of blood from Madesly's punctured stomach making the deck untenable. The four men slipped and slid, grunted and spat. As he watched it, Matthews's face grew pale, only a mighty determination enabling him to ward off Joyce's swinging, violent blows for a dwindling while.

Bentley wished he could have stopped it somehow, this final loss of blood. But even if he'd cut his throat, as Joyce had come to do, it would have passed unnoticed. He was forced to sit and watch, wheezing painfully, a prematurely aged young man. They had come to make a sacrifice, they had come to drive out some demon with his blood. And he would gladly have spilt it, gladly. But there he sat, helpless, to watch his friends protect him.

Matthews died next, as much of exhaustion, it seemed, as anything else. He raised his cutlass wearily to aim another stroke, and Joyce drove swiftly into him underneath his guard. Before he could clear his blade, as Matthews slipped silently across it, his companion, fighting Jesse Broad, was run through the stomach, and fell gurgling.

There was a strange pause. It would have been a silence if that had been possible. It sounded like a silence to William Bentley. The two surviving men faced each other, panting, their shoulders heaving, black and soaked with blood. There was blood everywhere, they were framed in it, shrouded in it, wallowing in it. They faced each other, the half-mad giant and the small, strong man. They faced each other.

Then slowly, trembling with fatigue, they both drew back their arms.

'And now I'll kill you, Jesse Broad,' said Joyce.

It was then that Daniel Swift arrived. He appeared in the

doorway, behind and to one side of them; slightly to one side. Bentley saw him, and his mouth dropped open. He could not say a word. His uncle looked ill. Gaunt, ill and terrible, with a long pistol in his hand. He looked desperate ill.

For a long moment everything was still. The tired men, their rasping breath awful in the silence, prepared to fight to death. Bentley watched his uncle, his mouth gaping helplessly. His uncle watched the men, who had not seen him there.

He was stooped, his powerful frame oddly less powerful. His face was hollow-cheeked and ulcerated, his eyes a shining pale. Only the great beak was the same, and he lifted it like a scythe.

As Joyce and Broad pulled back their cutlasses, Swift spoke. The two men jumped, the voice was such a shock. It was low, and penetrating, and terrifyingly vibrant. It was throbbing with hate.

'Put down your cutlasses, bastards, or I shoot you where you stand.'

Henry Joyce's face changed in front of Jesse's eyes. He saw the look of shock, of horror, of incomprehension. The pig-like eyes flickered, dropped, moved sideways over his shoulder. A bubbling noise came from Joyce's throat; he swallowed.

As he swallowed, as he turned to look at Daniel Swift, he lowered his cutlass. His adam's apple bobbed in his great, knotted, muscular throat. The bubbling noise came once more.

A veil of red fell over Jesse's eyes. A black, horrific, nauseated violence burst in his stomach, deep inside his guts. His arm knotted, struck out with a force that almost made him lose his balance. As his cutlass bit deep, deep into Henry Joyce's neck, he raised his head and howled, a deep, throbbing, aching roar.

As he stood trembling over Henry Joyce's body, the cutlass dangling in his hand, Daniel Swift levelled the pistol and shot him in the chest. Broad fell, without another sound.

Thirty-Four

The last thing William Bentley remembered of the scene, the last picture that lived on in his head, was of the few seconds after Broad had fallen. His uncle was framed in the doorway, his head emerging from a cloud of smoke. His face was sick but triumphant, the ulcerated features twisted in a smile. Already William felt a numbness sweeping over him.

His uncle made a gesture with the gun, a meaningless movement of his arm, and stepped into the cabin, placing his feet carefully among the pools of blood.

'Ah William,' he said. 'Thank God I've saved you, my boy. Thank God.'

He became unconscious then, or thought he did. Afterwards it occurred to William that perhaps he had not. But some sort of blackness came. He blotted out all thought, he closed his eyes to make his uncle disappear. Yes, in the event he must have lost consciousness, for it was many hours before he was aware again. Many many hours.

For days afterwards he stayed in this blissful state. Whenever he awoke, and thoughts came flooding back to him, the curtain followed close upon their heels. Perhaps he was drugged, perhaps had had a relapse. But he lay in a well-appointed cabin in the frigate Wentworth for a long long time, hardly eating, hardly drinking, acknowledging nobody in his periods awake. All he wanted to do was to remain unaware. The surgeon made a lot of him, did his very best, and William was grateful; for the Wentworth's man was no Mr Adamson. Bleeding, not brandy, was his cure-all, so the boy got progressively weaker and nearer death. Arrived at Cape Town he was feverish, emaciated, and able to spend twenty hours a day or more in limbo. From the way they treated him on shore, he knew he was not expected to live. Which suited him exactly.

The turning point, ironically, came some weeks later, when a

307

Navy ship homeward bound for England – the Wentworth having sailed on belatedly to India – embarked the prisoners and the remnants of the Welfare's crew. It was not considered, at first, that William was fit enough to undertake the voyage. His uncle saw him in a lucid moment, and tested out the idea of his staying. The way he put it, of course, was that the boy should make his recovery in the pleasant climate here among the kindly Dutch, and travel later, when he was fit again. William listened without opening his eyes. He still had the memory burning on them. He could not bear to look on Daniel Swift.

'In any case, my boy,' the man said gently, 'it will be an uncomfortable voyage enough. The ship is not so large, and we must run her as a prison in the main. I doubt you want to spend your sickness cooped up with such scum as Jesse Broad.'

The voice, made hearty for the jest, caused a great lurch inside his stomach. A dizziness descended in his head, coupled with a sick excitement. William Bentley spoke a sentence for the first time in days.

'Broad? Is Jesse Broad alive?'

Daniel Swift laughed with pleasure.

'He speaks! Ah, that's much better, my boy, much better! By God, you'll pull through yet, I must inform the doctors.'

Bentley was panting, impatient.

'Is he? Is Jesse Broad . . . ?'

'Bless your heart, yes,' said Swift. 'But never fear, boy, not for long.' He spoke more soberly. 'I hope he can survive the journey. It is in doubt, he is so very sick.' He brightened. 'Well, live in hope eh? God willing he'll live to be strung up.'

'There will . . . there will be a trial? In Portsmouth, I suppose?'

'Aye, once we have sorted out the innocent from the guilty. You would be of great assistance there, of course, as you were forced to stay on board the Welfare. But there is no doubt in that man's case, at all.'

William was too tired to talk on; knew, in any case, there was no point in trying to contradict. His uncle left him, and he lapsed into a musing dream. Jesse Broad alive. It had simply not occurred to him. He felt elation, felt new energy running in his blood. It was the turning point. There was no doubt any more; he must go back, he must recover. Not just to see Broad, but to save him. He day-

308

dreamed, half delirious. He had made a pledge and he would keep it. He had a vision of Broad set free, a vindicated man. He saw them smile together.

It was three days before they were embarked, during which time he made enough progress to surprise the doctors. They still shook their heads at the idea of him going, but it was no longer in question. Everyone was going back, except for some few able-bodied mutineers who had escaped into the hinterland to risk their fates among the Hottentots, and he was not going to be left. During this time, too, he learnt a little of the background to the rescue. He allowed his uncle to sit with him and talk, reluctant as he was to see the man. He always kept his eyes closed, and responded in grunts. But he wanted to hear.

The story was simple, and Swift did not embellish it. The voyage in the boats was hellish, several men had died. When they had been picked up the illness rate was getting serious, the weather worsening, the chances of survival slim. It had not taken him long to persuade the captain of the Wentworth what their course should be. A combination of bitter rage, invincible courage, and connections with the highest echelons of the service carried the matter. He had not expected to be so quickly lucky, but he had never had a doubt as to the final outcome; he would have followed the Welfare three times to hell and back. It had also been largely his battle when they came on her. Again his great connections alone would save him from the consequences of the decision to fire that point-blank broadside into one of His Majesty's expensive and much-needed ships; for the Welfare had been so badly damaged that she had had to be beached. In Table Bay, in this season, whatever decision might be made in London as to her future, her fate in ultimate was likely sealed already.

Throughout the long voyage to Britain William Bentley maintained the status quo. He was recovering, but the rate was very slow. He found it hard to breathe, he ate and drank very little, he was never strong enough to stand for many minutes. Every time they hit cold weather his lungs reacted badly, things got worse. During the fine spells, when the sun was strong and hot, when the winds were soft and gentle, he would be carried to the quarterdeck and left to his devices. For he conveyed it pretty quickly to the quality on board that he was not to be approached. The young gentlemen

309

tried to make friends, but not for long. He behaved rather like an old and ill-tempered cripple, snarling weakly at any who addressed him. Swift lost patience very early on; stopped talking heartily of how many villains they would hang. William Bentley never contradicted him on this, never betrayed a hint as to what he thought. He just sat quietly, pale face hunched on sunken chest, and grunted with a total lack of interest. He observed the length of the decks morosely, thinking one day to see Jesse Broad. But the prisoners never came on deck, none of them. They were shackled far below, on the orlop deck, where for exercise they shook their manacles. The others of the Welfare's people, the loyal men, were put to work. They would not have dared acknowledge him, in any case.

Jesse Broad was ill as well. Several of the injured mutineers were left below, in chains, and several died. It did not suit that Broad should die, however – Daniel Swift would not have it so. He was placed in the sick-bay under the surgeon's tender care. No guard was needed, for he could not move. He received the best of nursing and a complicated operation to remove the ball. His left shoulder and several of his ribs were badly smashed, and for weeks on end his life hung in the balance. He too dreamed in delirium, but not of Bentley. The nightmare of the past few months was mingled with his earlier life. Sometimes he thought he was back in Langstone, a free man once more and happy. At others, bloody shades rose up before him and he would awaken, racked by screams or sobs. He dreamed often of Thomas Fox.

As they neared England, and his lucid periods got longer, Jesse Broad harboured no happy thoughts. He pondered longest on whether he should get in contact with his wife before he died, or whether it was better just to leave it. That way she might never know, he thought, for the evidence was minimal. If the wherry he and Hardman had been caught in had ever been found, it would have been assumed they had been overwhelmed, or met some other sea-accident, he supposed. Even if it had ever been guessed that the press had had a hand in it, he could have gone to any of a dozen ships. Nothing strange at all if he were never heard of any more. By now Mary might have grown accustomed to her loss; heartless, stupid, cruel to let her know he lived – for the few short weeks before they hanged him. The day it dawned on him that she was bound to know was one of his worst. A black despair settled on him

310

and he writhed in mental torment on his palliasse. For he was a ringleader, of course; the only ringleader left alive, at that. The Welfare mutiny would be noised throughout the land. He would be pilloried, his name would be a household word. Not only would his poor wife come to know, she would share the final agony of his trial and hanging. It was intolerable. He jerked and fumbled, with some idea of reopening his wounds, unknitting the knitting bone, until the pain was appalling. He succeeded only in passing out.

Later on, Broad tried to kill himself. He had crawled six feet across the sick-bay, towards a box he hoped might contain some sharp instruments, before a surgeon's boy discovered him. He cried weakly as they carried him back, tears of sheer frustration. The surgeon, a shrewd man, guessed their meaning, and from that moment on he was tied to his berth.

It never entered Broad's head that William Bentley would plead for him, or tell the truth of the affair. It never entered William Bentley's head that he would not. At one end of the ship the sick boy lay, making his careful plans, at the other lay the sailor, his mind a cauldron of desperate thoughts. Both of them were sleeping uneasily when the anchor plunged into the bright green depths of Spithead early on a sparkling summer morning.

When the full extent of William's revolt became apparent, some days later, it caused a storm that bade fair to swamp him. He was at home, in the big house near Petersfield, some twenty miles from Portsmouth. He was in his own room, in his own bed, and the medical man who had tended him since a child visited daily and had declared him on the road to recovery. Much of the day he spent in thought, sunk deep in bunched-up pillows, breathing the clean warm country air that blew in at the window. He had greeted his father and his older brother with a certain coldness that he could not hide. It troubled him, but the coldness would not go away. His mother, too, even his sisters, were somehow like strangers, he had seen their faces with indifference, tolerated tears of joy with vague distaste. Uncle Daniel had stayed in the house for a time, explained presumably that William was in some kind of state; so fortunately the matter had not been dwelt upon at first.

When it was, he stated his position with great care. Firstly he told his father all about the mutiny, starting so far back that he snorted with impatience. But William insisted. It cost him a lot in energy, holding back his desire to launch into a tirade, as well as resisting the temptation to succumb to his father's tendency to bluster, to try to make him retract, when he said something even mildly critical of Uncle Daniel. However hard he tried to point up his own faults, he was just pooh-poohed. At the end of an afternoon he was exhausted, and the visiting physician was appalled by the worsening of his condition. Next afternoon he tried once more; he had not even reached the incidents in the doldrums.

His father was not a stupid man, and his blustering, hearty approach soon gave way to a much more grave and serious one. He sat in a high, winged chair, his back to the window, his face in shadow. He said so little, contradicting not at all, that William began to believe he understood, condoned. He talked with passion of the acts of Broad and Matthews, painted the scene of Fox's death in tones that shook with horror. Or was it hatred, he wondered in a pause? Self-hatred or for Daniel Swift? Or both?

Finally, stumbling over his slow-picked words, William made his statement on the subject of the court-martial. His Uncle Daniel Swift should stand arraigned, he said, and if need be, he himself. The voyage had been carnage, a slow-unfolding massacre. He could not stand by and see the man who had been its author preside over the murder of any more unfortunates. For *all* the mutineers who had survived, not only Jesse Broad, deserved a better fate. There must be no more killings.

His father had left the room in silence. William had lain in the dwindling light drained of energy but not unhappy. It was later, when Daniel Swift had been told and said his piece, when the family had closed ranks, that the storm broke, that the nightmare began. William, already weak, became yet weaker. He even suspected that his weakness was being used against him, to break down his resistance. But he fought on, despite all threats and cajoling, despite all pleas to think of family honour, despite all hints of faults within himself. It became a fixed point, an anchor for his being, it kept him going. The truth must be told.

In the end, he was very ill again. Much too ill, it was certificated, to give evidence to a court-martial, although he was the only gentleman-witness to the continued atrocities of the mutineers who had seized the Welfare and cast off captain, officers and loyal men to almost certain death. A pity, but he was too ill. Mr William Bentley's evidence will not be heard . . . In fact, it was not until after the trial that they told him it had taken place. And that seven men were to hang. Among them Jesse Broad.

The agony, for Jesse Broad, had not been, as it happened, deciding whether or not to tell his wife and friends, but wondering whether they knew. After the ship had anchored in Spithead, he and the other prisoners had been moved within two days. They had not been blindfolded, and the sight of Portsdown Hill, the yellow beaches, the green waters and the walls of Portsmouth, had been too much. Many wept, all were speechless. Broad was lowered to the waiting boat in an arrangement of planks. He looked at the whitish, dirty faces of his fellows, but no smiles were passed. Less than three hours later they were on board another ship, a dank, foul-smelling hulk at the mouth of Fareham creek; a prison hulk, with a filthy sick-bay with no windows into which Broad was put. There they stayed, with no visitors, no letters in or out, no contact with the outside world. His thoughts of Mary were jumbled now, a touch of madness hovered always near. He let his health sink downwards, it did not bother him. He realised he would die without seeing her, and probably without knowing if she knew. It was, finally, the best way.

The trial was held on board another ship, to which the prisoners were rowed every day. The evidence was long, but all one-sided. Broad did not listen very hard, just lay on his pallet staring at the deckhead. It did not surprise him much that William Bentley was not there, although his name was mentioned very often. Apparently he was deadly ill, having borne the brunt of the last stages of the mutiny. Broad did not blame him for not being there, there was no blame to be attached; easier to keep away, poor lad. He had suffered very much.

Many of the accused men made impassioned speeches, but these did not interest him much either. The accusations of ill-treatment and brutality sounded wrong in the plush, airy great-cabin of the line-of-battle ship where the trial was held. The captain of the Welfare, quiet and restrained in splendid silk and blue, would look down modestly, breathe on his nails and polish them, as wild-faced, inarticulate men spluttered out their hate-filled 'evidence', or told crazy-sounding stories of how he was a monster. It was those who

313

kept their mouths shut, in the main, who pleaded madness and confusion, the heat of the moment, who avoided the rope. They could not hang them all, indeed; but prisons there were in plenty. Jesse Broad, the ringleader, the villain, the scoundrel, declined to speak at all. He smiled wanly when they said he had to die.

The day of the executions was fixed, by accident no doubt, on William Bentley's fifteenth birthday. This time there was no escape. He was much fitter, his father had made the position very clear as to the financial future, and my Lords of the Admiralty required it with equal insistence. If William Bentley did not present himself on board the Duchess in Portsmouth harbour on that bright morning, he would stand alone in the world. All right, he had said at first, then alone in the world I shall stand. As he was rowed across the waters of the harbour, the harbour at its most freshly beautiful, his eyes were blank. He tried to keep them so throughout.

The officers were mustered on the quarterdeck, and the affair was very formal and correct. He did not see the ceremony, did not hear the last words, did not hear the guns, most of all did not watch the bodies as they swung suddenly from deck to yardarm, throttling as they rose. Until it came the time for Jesse Broad, the biggest villain, the last to hang.

Jesse Broad could not go to his death unaided, try as he might. He stood between two seamen, his legs like dolls' legs, his crippled shoulder hunched. He fought desperately to stay upright on his own, but he could not. He had to be held. Even his head had to be lifted up so that the noose could be slipped over it. It was then his eyes met William Bentley's.

They stared at each other for what appeared to be eternity. As if there was no one else on board, as if they were utterly alone. They stared and stared, their faces clenched and rigid. It was like an age.

Then Jesse Broad's feet swung out and upwards with a jerk. His eyes met Bentley's just once more, and they were bulging, filled with pressured blood. Then away, high up in the air he flew, twitching on his rope. The sightless eyes, bulging out obscenely, passed across the island as he turned, then seemed to scan Spithead. Then the Gosport shore, the hill, and then he spun round back again.

William Bentley could look no more. His eyes had seen enough.